BLIND SEARCH

ALSO BY PAULA MUNIER

A BORROWING OF BONES

BLIND
SEARCH

A MERCY *AND* ELVIS
MYSTERY

PAULA MUNIER

MINOTAUR BOOKS
NEW YORK

First published in the United States by Minotaur Books, an imprint of St. Martin's Publishing Group

BLIND SEARCH. Copyright © 2019 by Paula Munier. All rights reserved. Printed in the United States of America. For information, address St. Martin's Publishing Group, 120 Broadway, New York, NY 10271.

www.minotaurbooks.com

The Library of Congress Cataloging-in-Publication Data is available upon request.

ISBN 978-1-250-15305-0 (hardcover)
ISBN 978-1-250-15306-7 (ebook)

Our books may be purchased in bulk for promotional, educational, or business use. Please contact your local bookseller or the Macmillan Corporate and Premium Sales Department at 1-800-221-7945, extension 5442, or by email at MacmillanSpecialMarkets@macmillan.com.

First Edition: November 2019

10 9 8 7 6 5 4 3 2 1

For my mother,
who put the "mama"
in *mama bear*

And if you're lost enough to find yourself . . .

—ROBERT FROST

BLIND SEARCH

OPENING DAY

Bow and Arrow Deer Hunting: Two-deer limit, only one of which may be a legal buck.
　　　　　　—VERMONT FISH AND WILDLIFE REGULATIONS

HENRY JENKINS WAS LOST. He got lost a lot, not because he was nine years old and not because he didn't know where he was going—although his mother always pointed out that that was often the case—but because when he found a good path, he liked to follow it. Until it ended. But sometimes it ended far away from 521 West 23rd Street, Apt 3C, New York, New York, 10011.

An okay address. If you added up the numbers, you got nineteen, a prime number. Henry loved prime numbers.

He also liked the woods better than the city. The city was noisy, crowded, loud with color. But the woods were cool and green, the color of the number two, his favorite number. He liked green.

Most people in Vermont liked autumn the best. His nana said people came from all over the world to see the reds and yellows and oranges.

Henry wasn't like most people. All those brightly colored leaves made his head hurt—although he liked watching them spiral to the ground when the wind picked up.

That's what it was doing now, and leaves were falling all around him. Henry was not wearing his coat or his shoes. He preferred his Batman pajamas and his Batman slippers, which he'd worn whenever he could since his mother gave them to him on his ninth birthday, thirty-three days before she left for California. He was counting the days—127—until he would turn ten.

He knew his mother would come home. His father told him not to get his hopes up, that she was off finding herself, but that made no sense. All you had to do to find yourself was look at your feet. And there you were, like a tree with roots. The kind he had to watch not to trip over here in the forest.

Henry knew his mother would never miss his birthday. She was proud that she gave birth to him on March Fourteenth. Pi Day. She said it was why Henry was so good at math.

He looked up into whorls of color. Thinking about his mother upset him. He started walking again. Walking and counting trees. Counting calmed him down.

Henry focused on the bark of the trunks. The bark was gray and patterned and felt rough against his fingers. He spotted three pine cones and five acorns and six beechnuts, stuffing them into his pajama pants pockets, which were now bulging.

Hunters loved fall, too, because they could hunt deer and bear and moose. His nana said hunting was fine as long as you followed the rules and ate what you shot. He wasn't so sure. In Henry's Game—like Dungeons & Dragons only better, since he'd made it up himself—wild animals could attack you, and you had to fight back, kill or be killed.

But that was just a game.

This was real life, and real life confused him.

He kept walking and counting. He didn't stay on the trail; he went where nature called him. The bright *flash flash flash* of a blue jay. The beating *drum drum drum* of a woodpecker. The quick *skitter skitter skitter* of a red squirrel.

Henry heard human voices in the distance, a reminder that he wasn't alone with the trees and animals. His father was out here somewhere with his boss. This was Mr. Feinberg's woods, and he was having a hunting party. Henry was supposed to stay with the housekeeper at the estate while the grown-ups were out hunting. But she tried to make him eat disgusting runny eggs, so he snuck out when she wasn't looking. His father wouldn't be happy if he found out Henry had gone into the woods. He wasn't allowed to leave the house without an adult.

He changed course, away from the voices. He walked faster, counted more quickly. He heard a fluttering, looked up. Dozens of black crows swooped above, streaking ahead of him before he could count them all. He ran after them but slipped and fell, landing on cold ground smack on his butt. He stumbled back onto his feet, brushing dirt and leaves from his Batman pajamas. He shouldn't have run. He was no good at running.

He sensed movement to his left—or right, he wasn't sure—and turned to see what it was.

Through the trees he spotted a tall woman on the trail. She was wearing pants and boots and a hat with feathers over her long blond hair. A longbow and a quiver of arrows slung across her back. She looked like a fighter from his game. *Monster slayer,* he thought.

She moved quickly and quietly, like his nana's cat, disappearing behind a curtain of golden leaves.

Henry couldn't help but follow.

He'd seen her before, the monster slayer, with his father. He called her Alice. She liked him, he could tell. And his dad liked her. The kissing kind of like. Which made no sense, because he was married to his mother, and she would be coming back. By his birthday.

The woman stayed on the trail. She had long legs and walked fast, like his dad. She was probably going to join the hunting party. If he tracked her quietly, like a Ranger, then he might be able to watch. He'd never seen hunting in real life before.

Henry walked faster, shadowing her about twenty feet from the trail. Off-trail was hard going, and the faster he walked the harder it got. He tripped over a big rock hidden in the fallen leaves and fell down. He cried out as he struck the ground, knees first, right in front of a fallen log. He sat back on his butt and rubbed his shins. His pajamas were torn, and his scraped knees stung. But he did not cry.

The leaves had scattered. The log was a good hiding place. Henry liked hiding places. He scooted over to take a better look. Stuck his head inside the opening and saw a black lump sitting in the middle of the tunnel of old bark. Maybe a raccoon or a baby bear. He crawled in farther, looked closer. Nothing as cool as a raccoon or baby bear. Just a backpack. Still, it could be full of secret treasure. He unzipped the big pocket and peered inside.

Guns.

Lots of them.

He heard a crashing through the woods. He needed to hide for real now. He pushed the backpack deeper into the log and squeezed himself in, too, as far as he could. He wrapped his arms around his legs, trying to make himself as small as possible.

"Henry! What are you doing here?"

He looked up and there she was. The monster slayer.

"You're hurt." She swept her longbow and quiver of arrows off her back and stood them against a tree. She dropped to the ground and sat on her heels, removing her hat, the one with the cream and gray-blue feathers.

"Hat."

"It's pretty, isn't it? Why don't you hold it for me while I check you out." She handed it to him, and he studied it while she stretched the torn fabric away from his bloodied knees. The yellow cap reminded him of Robin Hood. The feathers were attached to the hat with a silver pin in the shape of a flower. He traced the image with his finger.

"That's an Alpine rose, Henry. A wildflower from the mountains where I grew up." She straightened up. "I think you'll live, Henry. But we should get you back to the house so we can clean up those boo-boos properly."

Henry scowled. He hated baby talk.

"Can you walk, or should I carry you?"

He scrambled to his feet before she picked him up and rocked him like a baby.

"What's that?" She pointed behind him, to the backpack. "Is that yours?" She grabbed one of the straps and jerked the pack out of the log. One of the guns fell out.

"Oh my God." She stared at Henry. "Where did you find this?"

A zoom of black to his left. Or his right. Again, he wasn't sure.

A gloved hand reached for the bow and the quiver standing against the tree, where the monster slayer had left it.

Henry tried to speak, but no words came out. He stared at the thing with the gloved hand. There was a tree where its head should be. A tree monster.

"What's wrong?"

"Dark tree," he said, pointing at the tree monster.

"Run, Henry!" she whispered.

Henry ran.

And he didn't look back.

CHAPTER ONE

Of what use, then, are the bow and the arrow and the target?
—*ZEN IN THE ART OF ARCHERY*

R EADY YOUR BOW.
Mercy Carr raised the sleek longbow in a silent salute to her grandfather. He'd designed and built this bow himself, hand carving the black bears on its riser out of red maple with the help of his own grandfather while he was still a young man himself. Before he was killed in the line of duty in an arrest gone wrong.

Grandpa Red bestowed the bow to her upon his death, but she'd never had the heart to use it. When she came home to Vermont from Afghanistan and bought the old cabin, she retrieved her grandfather's bow from storage and hung it in a place of honor over her flagstone fireplace. On the mantelpiece below stood a Kenyon Cox sketch of Diana, goddess of the hunt, her bow in one hand and a staff and a quiver of arrows in the other. A thank-you gift from her billionaire neighbor, for catching the thieves who tried to make off with his art collection a couple of months ago.

The memory of Martinez hung there, too, along with the bow and the picture. Her fiancé had been a champion archer—one of the many ways in which he reminded her of her grandfather—and they would hang out in his hooch with his bomb-sniffing dog Elvis between battles with the Taliban playing archers in *Final Fantasy*.

Before she got shot and Martinez got killed and Elvis got PTSD.
Nock.

Mercy pulled a thin blue arrow from her quiver and brought it over the bow. Just playing target practice now, safe at home in her own backyard on a crisp and clear Saturday morning in October. Aiming not for terrorists or for deer but for a twenty-four-inch poster mounted on a bale of hay and emblazoned with the Olympic pattern of bright concentric circles. White, black, blue, red, and finally, the yellow bull's-eye.

She could feel her cheering section watching her. Amy Walker at her side, an eager Katniss Everdeen in the making. Her grandmother Patience with Amy's baby, Helena, up on the deck behind them. Brodie McDougal, Amy's latest male admirer, who spent more time at Mercy's cabin these days than she did. Muse, the adorable Munchkin kitty they'd rescued over the summer, hiding under her grandmother's chair. And Elvis, the handsomest Belgian shepherd in the world, in his classic Sphinx pose at Patience's feet.

Draw.

She drew the string back with her gloved fingers to kiss the corner of her mouth. She wasn't used to having an audience. When she came home from the war, she'd escaped into a solitude broken only by Elvis and her grandmother. But then she and Elvis discovered the baby in the woods, and before she knew it Amy and Helena were living with her. Mother and child had drawn Mercy right back into the flow of humanity. Like it or not.

Mark.

She eyed the bull's-eye a mere thirty meters away, aiming right for yellow innermost circle of victory. She'd hit every other circle on the target but this one, and now that she was warmed up, she meant to nail it this time.

Loose.

This was the most critical part. The inhaling and the exhaling. The honing in and the letting go.

Mercy let loose the string. The arrow flew. Seven pairs of eyes traced the arc of its flight.

The arrow hurtled toward the hay bale, the autumn sun glinting on the steel field point. Pierced the yellow center of the bull's-eye with a solid *whop*.

"Perfect!" Amy studied Mercy. "You are such a good shot."

"Even better with a gun," said Patience. "Best in her graduating class at Fort Leonard Wood."

"She was a soldier." Brodie shrugged. "Of course, she's a good shot."

"My turn." Amy reached out for Grandpa Red's bow.

Mercy handed it to her. Corrected the girl's stance, eased her gloved fingers closer to her lips as she pulled back the string, told her to breathe.

"Grip it and rip it," said Brodie.

"Let her concentrate," said Mercy. "Take your time. Focus."

Amy squinted her eyes at the target. Breathed heavily. Took her shot.

Missed by a yard.

Elvis raced after the wayward arrow. The Belgian shepherd loved this game. Especially when Amy had the bow, because she missed as often as not. For him, this was a variation of find-and-fetch. Whether he was sniffing out bombs on the battlefield or playing this bow-and-arrow game, he was busy. Busy was happy for Elvis.

Amy's bolt had landed at the foot of a burning bush, ablaze in autumnal glory. The dog scooped it up dead center with his mouth, turning to show off his prize. His dark muzzle marked the midpoint of the arrow's shaft, with the point on one side of his nose and the fletching on the other.

As if his elegant head were the heart shot through by Cupid's arrow itself.

"Here," said Mercy, but he ignored her command. Apparently, there was little joy returning the fancy feathered stick to her when a worthier recipient was close at hand.

Elvis bound across the lawn and up to the deck that stretched behind the length of the cabin. There in a white Adirondack chair sat Patience, holding Helena on her lap. Amy's baby was nine months old, and she'd recently mastered the art of clapping. She blinked her big slate-blue eyes at the dog, slapping chubby little hands together in congratulations.

The shepherd gallantly dropped the arrow at her grandmother's feet, and the baby squealed with delight, all smiles and cheeks and dimples.

"Good boy," said Patience in that soothing singsong veterinarian's voice that endeared her to all her patients.

Elvis raised his head, as if to accept her praise as his rightful due, then sat back on his haunches. Wagging his curlicue tail, he cocked his large triangular ears at little Helena. The baby reached forward to pat his nose.

Mercy watched. Elvis was having more fun than she was. He could enjoy this picture-perfect day—the kind of day that proved all the tourist brochures right and brought out the peepers in force. He was not thinking about hunting season, which began in earnest today with the opening of bow-and-arrow deer hunting. A season she had once enjoyed, but now felt deeply ambivalent about. She'd seen enough of death. And once you'd seen it, there was no unseeing it. No forgetting it. All you could do was acknowledge its terrible dominion. And keep on living.

"I don't get it." Amy stood with her hands on her narrow hips, a frown creasing her heart-shaped face. "I should be better at this by now."

"It takes practice," said Mercy. "You'll get it. You're just trying too hard."

Amy was determined to learn archery. She'd joined the archery club at Bennington College, where she and Brodie were both freshmen. He'd signed up with her. They said that archery helped balance the time they spent at the computer. But Mercy suspected it was more a by-product of their love for all things *Hunger Games* and *Game of Thrones*.

So here she was, heirloom bow in hand, trying to teach them the finer points of the sport. Wherever Grandpa Red was now, he was laughing.

"Let me try again," said Amy.

"You can do it." Mercy grinned at her. "Be the arrow."

"I don't know what that means."

"Yes, you do. Think of it as yoga with a bow and arrow."

"I don't see how."

"It's, like, Zen," added Brodie.

"Martinez used to tell a story about two groups of student archers," said Mercy. "Each group had its own master teacher. One group bragged, 'Our teacher can even hit the bull's-eye blindfolded.' And the other group answered, 'Our teacher is better. He can even miss the bull's-eye with his eyes open.'"

They all laughed.

"Be the arrow," repeated Mercy, and handed Amy the quiver full of arrows. "Keep practicing."

She sat down in the Adirondack chair next to Patience and the baby. Brodie hovered nearby. They all watched as Amy shot arrow after arrow at the target—and missed every time. Elvis ran back and forth, fetching them for Helena with grace and good humor.

"Maybe Amy would be better at stump shooting," said Brodie after Amy missed yet again. "She's not a soldier, but she's a good hiker."

Stump shooting was target practice in the woods—using stumps and logs as targets.

"That's a good idea," said Mercy. "It may be easier for her to relax out in nature."

"She can read the woods just like you do," said Brodie.

"I can hear you, you know." Amy put down the longbow and gathered up the arrows at Helena's feet and put them back in the quiver.

"Your game warden must be a good archer, too," said Amy. "He can read the woods, too."

"He's not my game warden," Mercy said.

Amy and Patience exchanged a look.

Amy was referring to Vermont Game Warden Troy Warner. He and his search-and-rescue dog Susie Bear had helped Mercy and Elvis solve a murder over the past summer.

"Troy's like a Ranger," said Brodie.

"D and D," translated Amy.

"Right."

Brodie's other passion, besides Amy and archery, was Dungeons & Dragons. Most of his conversation revolved around these three obsessions. Mercy didn't understand half of it; it was as if he were speaking in Orc.

"Why don't we try it again, together this time," said Mercy, eager to move the conversation away from her and Troy and what may or may not develop between them and back to archery.

"Okay."

Mercy handed Amy the bow and stood behind her, shadowing her movements as she settled once more into the proper position. Feet shoulder-width apart. Limbs relaxed. Left arm outstretched, holding the bow. Eye on the target. Right arm drawing back the string. The kiss at the corner of her mouth.

"Inhale," she whispered as she gently steadied Amy's stance.

Let it go.

Be the arrow.

Om.

"Exhale." She's got it this time, thought Mercy.

"I heard Madeline Warner's back in town," said Brodie.

Mercy flinched, jostling Amy's elbow just as she released the string. The arrow flew straight over the target, past the lawn's edge, and right into the forest. Elvis sprinted after the blasted bolt, disappearing into a blaze of sugar maples.

Well, in that hit you miss: she'll not be hit with Cupid's arrow. . . . Forget Zen, thought Mercy. Shakespeare nailed it every time.

"Brodie!" Amy rolled her eyes at him. "Way to go."

"What?"

"Her mother is having knee-replacement surgery," Patience told Mercy.

Whatever, she thought. The subject of Madeline Warner would have to wait. "Elvis shouldn't be in there." She whistled—a sharp, penetrating trill that would grab the ear of any New York cabdriver, designed to order Elvis back, pronto. She and Amy collected their equipment and joined Brodie and Patience and the baby. They all waited for the shepherd to streak back into the yard and up to the porch and bring the lost arrow to Helena.

"He's not wearing his hunter orange." Patience rose from her chair, baby in her arms.

"He knows better than that." Mercy whistled again, and waited. No response. She held her breath. It was hunting season. No dog or human should be venturing into the woods without the protection hunter orange could provide.

"Maybe he's having a hard time finding the arrow," said Brodie.

"Impossible," said Patience.

"Maybe he's chasing turkeys," said Amy.

Wild turkeys often roamed the front yard, and Elvis loved playing with them. The Belgian shepherd protected the property from most two- and four-legged creatures with a fierce aggression, but he liked the turkeys. The big birds visited most days, gobbling along, headed for the crab-apple trees fronting the forest line, while Elvis ran around them in circles. It was like herding cats. The wild turkeys would ramble on, pecking at insects and nuts on their way to the apples. Elvis would escort them to the edge of the forest—but he'd stop there. Eventually, the turkeys would go into the woods.

Where the hunters were.

Elvis would not follow them; he knew his job was to guard the perimeter unless and until Mercy said otherwise. She'd posted No Trespassing and No Hunting signs on her acreage, but in the forest beyond her property, hunters were looking to bag their Thanksgiving dinners.

The Malinois was not doing his job now.

"This is taking too long." Mercy shook her head. Something was wrong. This wasn't like Elvis.

Her grandmother shot her a look. "It's open season on bear and deer and turkey. All kinds of hunters with all kinds of weapons will be out in force."

As if to confirm that, they heard a couple of faint booms coming from the forest. Gunshots. Hunters.

"I'm going after him." She couldn't let anything happen to Elvis.

"Change your clothes and your shoes first," said Patience.

"No time."

"At least take your pack and the vests." Patience handed the baby to Amy, and then turned to Mercy. "I'll get the pack. You get the vests."

She jogged back into the cabin, her grandmother on her heels. Hurrying through the living room to the hallway at the front door, she grabbed her orange Orvis puffer vest from the hall tree, along with Elvis's hunter-orange vest. She slipped the puffer vest over her long-sleeved T-shirt. On her way back out of the house, Patience handed her the pack and an orange Field & Stream baseball cap.

She stuffed Elvis's vest into the pack, tossing it over her shoulder.

"Wear that hat," said Patience.

"Okay." Knowing her grandmother was still watching, she slapped it on over the red tangle of curls her mother called The Mess as she raced out on the deck and onto the lawn toward the forest.

"Be careful," Amy called after her as she huffed into the woods.

More gunfire.

Mercy hoped it wasn't aimed at Elvis. She hoped it wasn't one of the turkeys. She hoped she wasn't too late.

CHAPTER TWO

Early Bear Hunting Season: Hounds are allowed, provided the person in charge of the dogs has a bear-dog permit, no more than six dogs are used, and no commercial guiding occurs.

—VERMONT FISH AND WILDLIFE REGULATIONS

MERCY TRACKED THE BELGIAN SHEPHERD by the broken twigs, shuffled leaves, and paw prints left in his wake as he barreled through the forest. The Malinois didn't bother with the trail; he was traveling as the crow flies, toward a target he could smell— and she couldn't. She knew he'd eventually come back to her, if only to lead her to whatever he'd found, just as he always did. But that was little comfort. He was out during hunting season, a mammal roughly the same size and color of a doe, with no blaze-orange protection. She plowed on, listening hard as she scrambled through brush and scrub and over downed tree limbs.

She'd heard no more gunshots since she'd entered the forest. That was good. Elvis had reacted badly to gunfire when they first came home from the war, but in time he'd gotten over that, enough to help catch a murderer a few months ago. But that didn't mean he could outrun a bullet.

She heard faint baying of hounds. She ran toward the riotous bawl- ing, which grew louder and more frenetic with every yard.

Most likely bear dogs.

Likely cornering a bear.

And quite likely accompanied by a billionaire.

Daniel Feinberg—known to the world simply as Feinberg—owned most of the forest around here. They were friends and neighbors, operating on a first-name basis now, but in truth she still thought of him as Feinberg, just like everyone else.

His groundskeeper Gunnar Moe had recently acquired a pack of Norwegian elkhounds, with the aim of helping Troy Warner and his fellow game wardens deal with nuisance bears. Ever since the state of Vermont had established regulations to help restore the population of black bears, more bears were wandering out of the wilderness and onto private property looking for food. These nuisance bears often ended up dead.

Elkhounds offered an alternative. These dogs, originally bred by Vikings, were arguably the fiercest bear-hunting dogs in the world. Not to mention wild boar and the elk that graced their name—known here on this continent as moose. These days, they were used as often to scare nuisance bears back to the forest as they were to hunt them.

Gunnar had bragged as much to Mercy when he introduced her and Elvis to the sturdy, lively silver-gray dogs he'd named after his native Norse gods and goddesses. Elvis treated the elkhounds with respect; they were somewhat smaller than he was but just as tough and determined. They worked hard and played hard. Just like he did.

She'd find Elvis with them, but now they wouldn't be playing. They'd be confronting bears.

Elvis had searched for missing persons, sniffed out explosives, and taken down armed intruders, but he had never faced off with a bear before. Mercy quickened her pace, racing toward the racket. She barreled through a thick copse of young birch trees, through a stand of red-yellow beech trees, and into a clearing rounded by golden oaks.

Half a dozen excited elkhounds encircled the tallest and thickest oak tree. These were Gunnar's dogs. She recognized the leader of the pack, Thor; the smallest of the bunch, Modi; the brothers Balder and Odin, and the females, Saga and Freya. All six hounds were jumping and yelping, dark noses pointing up. Mercy followed their snouts up to a black bear perching some twenty feet above them in the crook of two massive branches of the oak. Elvis danced around the howling hounds, and they greeted him enthusiastically, even as they kept their eyes on their quarry.

Mercy estimated the bear was at least four hundred pounds. A healthy beast, with shiny blue-black fur and huge paws and those long lethal claws curling around the limbs of the tree. At six feet long, maybe more, by Vermont standards this was a big bear. And he didn't seem particularly worried about the elkhounds. So much for scaring bears back up to higher ground.

She found herself rooting for the bear. It was, after all, his tree. Many claw marks scarring the oak's trunk—old and fresh—told her that. He was just hanging out in his tree, waiting out the noisy hounds below.

The bear needed to go higher up the mountain to avoid hunters who would be thrilled to take home a prize like this one. He was a real beauty—a win for any hunter.

Mercy didn't see the sport in shooting any animal cornered up a tree. To her mind, it wasn't much different than baiting a bear with doughnuts, then harvesting the beast as it licked up the sugary treats. The latter was illegal, but she wasn't sure about the former. She'd have to ask Troy.

First, she needed to get away from the bear. Black bears rarely attacked humans, unless you were unfortunate enough to get between a mama bear and her cubs. The size of this guy meant he was a male. Although there were cases of predatory males, they were the exception. Mercy was probably safe enough from the bear. Especially as he was surrounded by the stalwart elkhounds.

But she was not necessarily safe from hunters, who couldn't be far behind these dogs. Thor, the pack leader, had an antenna attached to his collar, a telltale sign that Gunnar was using an expensive GPS dog-tracking system, allowing him to easily trail his dogs.

Mercy didn't want to be caught between some rich gung-ho weekend warrior and the big-game trophy he wanted to take home. She was glad of her hunter-orange vest and hat, but she wouldn't bet her life on any color to save her. And Elvis didn't even have that much.

She snapped her fingers and Elvis trotted over, reluctant but obedient. She secured the hunter-orange vest around the dog, and together they retreated downwind.

They didn't have to wait long. She heard a rustling to her left, and spotted Gunnar leading a large hunting party toward the dogs. They were trying to move quietly, but there were too many of them—Mercy did a quick count of six people plus Daniel Feinberg, Gunnar, and Joey Darosa, Gunnar's assistant. Not that any noise they made mattered, given the bellowing of the elkhounds.

The group were carrying longbows for deer hunting, but Gunnar obviously couldn't pass up the opportunity to show them a black bear.

Mercy watched as they spread out around the edge of the clearing. Two couples. The first, a slim and silver-haired couple with tanned faces and sunglasses, he dressed more for a day on the slopes and she more for a horse show than a day in the woods. The second, a florid-faced middle-aged man and a much younger woman with a long ponytail, both dressed head to toe in spanking new L.L. Bean.

Standing somewhat apart from the couples was a petite brunette with a professional grade camera, her face obscured as she snapped away. Behind her, taking up the rear of the party, was someone she knew: Ethan Jenkins, a Northshire boy she hadn't seen since he left for New York City after high school.

All wore the required hunter-orange vests over their clothes.

None of the strangers looked like they could hit the broad side of a barn with a gun, much less kill a deer with a bow and arrow. The only ones who seemed at home in the woods were the silver-haired couple. Even Daniel Feinberg appeared vaguely uncomfortable—and it was his woods.

Ethan looked like he'd rather be back in the city, though as a Vermonter he could not be a stranger to the forest, which covered nearly 80 percent of the state. Vermonters loved their woods. She wondered what could have turned a local boy into such an urban creature that the native woodchuck in him did not reassert itself when back home in the woods. As it did with practically everyone else born and bred here, no matter how far away they wandered.

Mercy caught Gunnar's eye, and he raised his thick blond eyebrows at her. She could feel Elvis shimmy with energy, desperate to join his rowdy canine friends at the base of the oak.

"Stay," she said sternly.

To his credit, the shepherd stood perfectly still, although his sleek fur rippled with anticipation and frustration.

The florid-faced guy in the group assumed a shooting stance with bow and arrow, standing at a right angle to his target, the bear in the tree.

"No!" bellowed Gunnar.

Florid-face nocked the broadhead tipped arrow.

Gunnar strode toward him.

Florid-face raised his bow, glaring at Gunnar.

Feinberg nodded at the groundskeeper and he called the elkhounds, and they withdrew.

With a gloved hand, the man pulled back his string to his chin and aimed.

Be the arrow, thought Mercy. *Not.*

Elvis leapt forward, startling the man. Florid-face wobbled as he released the string. The arrow flew toward the bear. Sort of. Falling short and striking a lower branch and finding its mark in the bark, not the bear. Missing its target by several feet.

Mercy doubted he could've hit the bear even had Elvis been playing dead.

The bear scrabbled down the tree. The man started yelling, his ruddy face a flaming scarlet.

Mercy bit back a smile as another line from Shakespeare popped into her head: *Thou canst not hit it, hit it, hit it, Thou canst not hit it, my good man.*

"Give me your rifle," the florid-faced man said to Gunnar. When the groundskeeper demurred, the man turned toward his host. "Danny, I want that bear."

Feinberg shrugged, and Gunnar handed the man his rifle.

Elvis raced past him and the bear, bounding out of the clearing. He disappeared into the thick of the forest, and the elkhounds chased him, abandoning the hunting party in a riot of barking. The big bear crashed through the brush in the opposite direction, lumbering away from them at a surprisingly fast pace. Florid-face hustled after him.

Bears could outrun man any day. If this one got away, he'd be deep into the thick broad-leaved forest and long gone. Until the next promise of an easy meal was too good to resist.

Mercy shrugged her apologies to Gunnar and ran after Elvis. She left behind the hunting party, the guests squabbling while the groundskeeper tried to restore order and get their hunt back on track.

She heard a shot. Seemed like Daniel Feinberg's unpleasant guest had tried to bring down the bear again. She hoped to hell he'd missed again. She couldn't believe Gunnar let him get away with it. He was the kind of hunter who killed out of ego, not for the meat that could see a family through a long winter, but for bragging rights. Like those trophy hounds who shot baby elephants on safari. For all she knew he was one.

With guys like him in the woods, Mercy was especially glad she was wearing her hunter orange.

She found Elvis and his Norwegian pals in a blowdown area a hundred yards south of Feinberg and his friends. The shepherd stood in silence at the end of a large fallen beech, while the elkhounds howled like they were on fire.

"What's up?"

Elvis held his position as Mercy made her way through the yowling frenzy of bear-hunting dogs. She couldn't imagine what could distract them from chasing that bear. Unless they were simply chasing Elvis. Who was chasing . . . what?

Elvis jumped up, laying his front paws on the log. His dark nose pointing to the other side of the fallen tree.

"Good boy." She stepped up to join him, looking past his paws to a reclining figure lying on the ground parallel to the downed beech.

It was a woman. A pretty young woman in dark brown leggings and a khaki field jacket. A flower-patterned yellow silk scarf was around her still neck.

An arrow pierced the breast pocket of her jacket.

Mercy leaned in for a closer look.

The point was buried in the woman's chest. The nocked end of the arrow rose straight into the air above the wound, its green helical fletching marking its human target like a bloodstained bull's-eye, right through the heart.

Fletching just like that on the arrow the florid-faced man had aimed at the bear. He had missed.

Whoever shot this woman had not missed.

She was dead. There was no question of that. Mercy looked away for a moment. She'd seen too many die too soon. Over there.

She didn't expect to see it here. But if the army had taught her anything, it was that the darkness could fall on anyone, anytime, anywhere.

Elvis nudged her with his cold wet nose. Bringing her back from the battlefields of Afghanistan to the Green Mountains of Vermont. Where the darkness had fallen on this young woman lying at her feet.

"Good dog," she said again, patting the dog's head.

The elkhounds swarmed behind him, yelping and jumping. Desperate to corner the corpse, as if it were a bear up a tree.

"Come!" Gunnar appeared at the edge of the blowdown. Thor bounded toward him, and the rest of the elkhounds followed. He looked at Mercy inquiringly, waiting for her to enlighten him. She knew he'd wait as long as needed. He was not a big talker.

"There's a dead woman over here."

"Who is it?"

"I don't know. Definitely not a Vermonter." She pointed at the elkhounds. "If you can get those dogs to stay put, come closer and take a look. Maybe she is one of yours."

Gunnar growled at his elkhounds, and they dropped to the ground in a collective down.

"Stay," he told his dogs, and loped over toward her.

"Not too close," she warned. The groundskeeper was at least six and a half feet tall, with enormous feet encased in enormous work boots, with which he could destroy what was now a crime scene. At least whatever was left intact after his dogs' ruckus.

Gunnar stopped in his tracks and looked past Mercy at the body. "Well?"

"I do not know her."

"Maybe your boss does."

"I do not think so." He shook his head. "She does not look like a hunter."

"At least not a local one." She squatted down again, the better to look at the corpse. "These are expensive clothes she's wearing."

"She does not look like a hiker, either."

"No hunter orange. No pack. No weapon." She looked over at him. "So what was she doing out here?"

He shrugged.

"Meeting her murderer."

"Accident."

"I don't think so." She rose to her feet and faced the groundskeeper. "That fletching matches the fletching on the arrows you and your hunting party are using."

Gunnar crossed his thick arms across his chest. "Only one arrow shot this morning."

"Florid-face."

"Mr. Farrow."

"He's reckless."

"His arrow landed in the tree. You saw."

"I saw. I saw you give him your rifle, too."

He ignored that. "We need to tell Mr. Feinberg about this."

"We need to tell the police about this."

The groundskeeper grunted. Mercy knew he didn't think much of local law enforcement. She didn't either, apart from Troy and his search-and-rescue dog Susie Bear.

"I'll stay here," she told Gunnar. "You go get your boss. And take your canine friends with you."

The big man nodded and strode off, the elkhounds on his heels.

While she and Elvis waited, Mercy checked her cell phone. No signal. No way to call Troy and let him know there was a dead body in his woods.

She knelt down next to Elvis, and he licked her cheek. She scratched his ears while examining the body more carefully, snapping photos with her cell phone.

The dead woman wore elegant gloves of butter-colored suede, which matched the thin suede belt she wore under her jacket. The belt held a slim pouch, probably for a phone, although if so it wasn't there now. The silk scarf tied loosely at her neck was the same color as her pale yellow hair, which framed her face and its empty blue eyes like a broken halo.

The shepherd stiffened at her side. Mercy came to her feet just as Gunnar led Daniel Feinberg and the members of his hunting party into the blowdown. Joey Darosa was not among them.

Leaving Elvis to guard the body, she went to meet her neighbor.

"I'm afraid this is a crime scene now, Daniel. I'll tape off the area. Meanwhile, keep these people away from here."

He nodded to Gunnar, who stopped the guests before they could venture any closer to the victim.

She led the billionaire over to the dead woman. "Do you know her?"

He didn't answer, his eyes on the dead woman. "I'm not sure, but I think she may be Alice de Clare."

"But you're not sure?" She could hear the skepticism in her voice. The Daniel Feinberg she knew was rarely unsure of anything.

He gave her a sharp look. "I've never actually met her in person. She's an architect. One of my weekend guests. She was supposed to arrive yesterday, but her flight was delayed." He paused. "I suppose we should call your game warden."

She could feel the heat rise on her face, blushing in spite of herself. Curse of the redhead. "He's not *my* game warden."

"The Montgomerys know her. She did their brownstone in Boston."

"The Montgomerys?"

He swiveled back to face Mercy, waving his arm in the direction of Gunnar and his guests. "They're here. Let me introduce you."

He guided her over to the hunting party, who stood in a small clutch, whispering amongst themselves. Silence fell over them as she and their host approached.

"What's happened?" asked the silver-haired man in a strong Boston Brahmin accent.

"This is Mercy Carr and her wonder dog, Elvis." Feinberg gestured to the silver-haired couple. "Blake and Katharine Montgomery."

Blake nodded and his wife murmured a greeting Mercy didn't quite catch as the billionaire proceeded with the introductions.

"Caspar and Cara Farrow," he said, indicating the florid-faced man and his much younger, much prettier wife, who looked vaguely familiar. Mercy smiled. Caspar glared at her in return while his better half gave her a cool smile.

Next to the Farrows stood the lady with the camera, a Nikon D5 by the looks of it. She stepped up to Mercy with an outstretched hand. "Lea Sanders."

Mercy shook her hand. A firm but friendly grip.

"And I think you know each other," said Feinberg, coming to Ethan Jenkins.

"Yes," they said in unison.

Ethan was Lillian Jenkins' son. Lillian ran the popular Vermonter Drive-In restaurant and, in her off-hours, virtually every nonprofit in Northshire. She and Mercy's grandmother Patience were old friends.

Mercy had known the family for most of her life. But she hadn't seen much of Ethan since he'd moved to Manhattan to work for Feinberg after getting his MBA at Harvard.

"What's going on?" demanded Caspar Farrow. "I've got a bear to get back to."

His young wife laughed. "You missed. Twice." She removed her cap and undid her ponytail, unleashing a waterfall of copper-colored curls that fell past her shoulders in shimmering waves. She had good hair and she knew it.

"I did not. That bullet hit him. Grazed him at the very least."

"We are not here to hunt bear," Gunnar said, as much to Mercy as to the florid-faced man.

"What's happened?" asked Blake again, the Boston Brahmin accent thickening.

"I'm afraid Mercy and Elvis have come across a dead woman," said Feinberg. "A woman we may know."

"Impossible," said Katharine.

"Who is she?" asked Cara Farrow, her bored expression replaced by a feral curiosity framed by all that shining hair.

"I think it might be Alice de Clare," Feinberg told them.

Mercy watched their faces as they absorbed the news. Blake frowned and lowered his eyes, staring at the ground. Caspar and Cara exchanged a glance.

"How horrible," said Cara, but in her voice was an odd note of triumph. Mercy wondered what that was about.

Lea looked angry. "How could that happen?"

Only Katharine seemed truly disturbed by the news. "Oh, no." She stumbled back, as if avoiding a blow. Her husband caught her, steadying her against his chest.

Ethan said nothing, his face gray as stone, his hands clenched into fists at his side.

"We'd asked Alice to refurbish a property for us. She was here to show us her plans." Feinberg's dark eyes, which usually held warmth or wariness, depending on the situation, folded into a weariness

Mercy had never seen before. He suddenly looked ten years older. "We'll need someone to confirm her identity."

Caspar blustered. "We didn't even really know the woman."

Blake stepped forward. "I can do it."

Katharine paled, and Lea went to her side, taking her husband's place as her consoler.

"We should wait for law enforcement," said Mercy.

"I'll do it." Ethan ignored her, pushing roughly past Blake. "I should be the one to do it."

"Whoa." She grabbed his arm as he approached the body. He tried to shake her off, but she held firm. "Not too close. This is a crime scene," she repeated.

"Right." He stuck his fists in his pockets, then leaned so far forward she worried that he might fall over onto the victim. He swallowed hard, looking down at the face of the woman stretched out in death beneath him.

His voice was hard. "It's Alice."

It was clear to Mercy that this woman Alice had meant something to him. "Are you all right?"

"I don't understand. I just saw her. She was fine."

"What do you mean?"

Ignoring the question, he turned to her. "What the hell happened here? Who did this?"

"That's what the police are going to find out. That's why we need to protect the scene." She nodded to Feinberg, who ushered Ethan back to Blake and Katharine. Lea was quietly shooting pictures again. No one stopped her.

Mercy slipped off her pack and pulled out her Swiss Army knife and the duct tape she always carried in an outside zippered pocket. You just never knew when you'd need them.

Like now. She ran the tape in long strips around the trunks of trees and the branches of bushes to isolate the body as best she could, feeling the eyes of the hunting party on her as she worked.

After securing the last of the tape, she turned back to the billionaire.

He was speaking into his sat phone. She was surprised he could get a signal up here, but then they weren't too far from the mansion on his Nemeton estate, where everything worked like clockwork despite its isolation. He probably had his own satellite.

"The game warden should be here shortly," he said. "Detective Harrington and his team may take a little longer."

Troy and Susie Bear were almost always the closest law enforcement around, whenever bad things happened in the woods.

And this was bad, thought Mercy, as she and Elvis stood sentry to the woman struck down on opening day.

CHAPTER THREE

It is illegal to take any wild animal by shooting with firearm, bow and arrow, or crossbow from any moving vehicle.
—VERMONT FISH AND WILDLIFE REGULATIONS

VERMONT GAME WARDEN TROY WARNER and his New-foundland retriever mix Susie Bear were bumping down one of the many unpaved roads to nowhere in southern Vermont on a perfect autumn morning, the kind that reminded him that he had the best job in the world. The windows were down, and Susie Bear had her square, shaggy black head hanging out in the fresh air, long thick tongue rolled out like a mottled pink rug.

The Green Mountains were ablaze with color, and the woods smelled like damp earth and decaying leaves and evergreen and fallen apples. This was their busiest time of year. Between the peepers and the hikers and the hunters—all of whom were out in force now, overrunning the roads, thronging the trails, gunning the wild game—he and his fellow game wardens all over the state were pretty much on call twenty-four hours a day.

Dispatcher Delphine Dupree had called him on the radio with an anonymous tip about a guy taking shots at deer from his truck up this way. Shooting from a vehicle was illegal, not to mention dangerous as hell for all concerned.

As for game wardens, hunting season was a dangerous time of year, period. Every time Troy approached a new situation, he was dealing with armed people who killed for sport. Most were lawful hunters who harvested game that would feed their families during the freezing cold winter ahead. Some were good old boys who thought of hunting as a kind of frat party, just another reason to get drunk and stupid and shoot at anything that moved. And the worst were the poachers who killed at will for profit—endangering the wildlife Troy was pledged to protect, for this generation and those to come.

These lawbreaking hunters could prove as deadly for him as for the wildlife. The good old boys because they were often inebriated and reckless, the poachers because they tended to be repeat offenders—the offenses being ones that carried significant fines and jail time they'd prefer to avoid—and because they tended to be very, very good shots.

The road took a sharp turn to the left, then stopped abruptly at a T fronting a small meadow. An unmarked road ran at right angles into forest on both sides. This was where the anonymous tipper had told Delphine they'd spotted the hunter shooting from his truck.

To the right was woods, and to the left was woods.

"Flip a coin," he said to Susie Bear, and hung a right.

About a half mile up, Troy saw an old gray pickup parked on the side of the road where the meadow met the woods. The description of the vehicle matched the one given to Delphine—as did the partial plate number. Two men stood at the back, lifting something into the bed of the truck. Something that could be a deer.

He pulled up behind them and got out of his Ford F-150. "Stay," he told Susie Bear, who was rocking the truck in her excitement to get out and go to work.

"Game Warden Troy Warner," he said by way of introduction. "How's it going?"

The two guys turned toward him. Sandy-haired twins in hunter-orange vests, brown flannel shirts, blue jeans, and well-worn duck boots, separated only by age. Father and son, that was Troy's guess. The father looked about forty; the kid was tall for his age, which Troy estimated at about fourteen.

The older one reached back and pulled up the tailgate as Troy approached. Not a good sign.

"Step away from the vehicle," he said.

"We just got a bear," said the younger. But he looked away from Troy as he said it.

"On our way to the tagging station now," said the elder with more confidence.

"I'll need to see your IDs and hunting licenses."

"In the glove box."

Troy looked into the bed of the truck as he followed them to the cab. A black plastic tarp covered a large object. His gut told him it was no bear.

"Where are your guns?"

"Just one rifle. In the back seat."

Troy watched as the older guy opened the glove box and pulled out a couple of wallets and two laminated hunting permits. He fished out the driver's licenses along with the hunting permits and handed them to Troy.

"Daryl Buskey." The game warden raised his eyebrows at the father, and he nodded. Then he addressed the son. "Tyler Buskey. You're sixteen."

"Yes, sir."

"Any relation to Johnny Buskey?" Johnny was a small-time poacher who'd been lucky enough to avoid jail time so far, despite several run-ins with law enforcement. Troy was determined to change that.

"Second cousin once removed or whatever." Daryl looked down at his feet. "We aren't close."

"Uh-huh." Troy was not convinced. Poachers ran in some families, like certain cancers. He examined the hunting permits, which were up to date. "All good. Let's see your firearm."

Daryl opened the back-seat door and retrieved a .22 rifle. He passed it to Troy.

Troy checked that the safety was on, but when he opened the action, he saw that the weapon was loaded. He emptied the chamber and slipped the ammo into his pocket. "You know it's illegal to have a loaded weapon in your vehicle. And it's dangerous. One bump in the road, and bang."

"Stupid. I know. Sorry." Daryl looped his thick fingers into the waistband of his jeans.

"That's one serious violation right there." Troy held onto the guy's gun, tossing his head in the direction of the truck bed. "I got a feeling that's no bear back there. When I pull up that tarp, you could be in big trouble. So why don't you just tell me what happened before I do that." While it was currently bear-hunting season and bow-and-arrow season for deer, rifle deer season didn't begin until next month. If, as he suspected, there was a deer in that truck bed, shot with that loaded rifle, that was another serious violation.

Neither father nor son said a word.

"If you tell me the truth, things will go better for you."

Tyler Buskey coughed, and stared down at his boots.

His father sighed. "We just came across this deer dead in the road. Didn't look like anyone else was gonna harvest it, so we figured we may as well. Didn't want it going to waste."

"We, huh?" Troy couldn't believe the guy was implicating his kid.

Daryl seemed to realize his mistake. "Well, me, I mean. Tyler here was just along for the ride."

"Yeah," said Tyler, without much conviction.

"Still warm," the father said. "So we gutted it."

Troy grabbed the edge of the tarp and tugged. The covering fell open, revealing a fair-size buck laid out on a green tarp. Two tips. Shot right in the boiler room, about where his heart and lungs should be. Gutted, and ready to be tagged. "Stay right there."

He walked back to the Ford F-150 and called in to check on the plates and any records the state may have on the Buskey boys. He secured the rifle in his truck and let Susie Bear out. "Heel," he said, and she trotted along next him, her nose at his hip.

"This is Susie Bear," he told the guys, who stared at the big dog with trepidation. "She's trained to find bullets and spent shell casings. I'm going to let her loose in that field, and she's going to find the casing from the bullet that killed that deer. And maybe the bullet, too, if it's not still in the deer. That's as good as a fingerprint for our forensics guys." Troy stared hard at Daryl. "Then I'll calculate the trajectory of the bullet—and I'll bet it will prove that the rifle that fired the shot that killed this deer out of season was fired from the road. Another violation." He paused. "Could be costly, when you add up all these violations. We're talking big-money fines and jail time, Mr. Buskey."

Susie Bear wagged her tail and barked.

"She loves her job." Troy smiled. "Search is her happy place." He reached down to unsnap her lead.

"I did it," said Tyler.

Troy straightened up and waited in silence, wondering if Daryl would really let his son take the fall for his own actions.

"No, you didn't." Daryl Buskey squared his shoulders and looked Troy in the eye. Preparing to accept responsibility. "We were just driving by, thinking about hunting bear. And we saw a couple of does in the middle of the meadow. We pulled over, and I got out the gun. The deer took off. But a beautiful buck followed them right across the field. I got him."

"Through the window."

"Yeah."

"I appreciate your telling the truth." Troy left Susie Bear to guard the guys and went back to his truck, where he checked their records. They were clean. No previous arrests or convictions. Unfortunately, being Johnny Buskey's second cousin once removed—or whatever—was not a crime.

There was also a report coming in from Delphine about a wounded big bear and a dead body—human—deep in the woods of the Nemeton estate. He was closest to the scene.

"Captain Thrasher says to watch yourself," Delphine told him. "Detective Harrington will be out there eventually, and he won't appreciate your being at his crime scene."

The head of the Major Crime Unit didn't think much of the game-warden service. Maybe because they sometimes solved his high-profile cases for him. Not that Detective Kai Harrington would ever admit that.

Quickly Troy wrote up the violations, walked back to the Buskey boys, and handed Daryl the paperwork. "Don't miss this hearing."

"Right," said Daryl.

Troy confiscated the buck and the gun and the ammo and both father's and son's hunting licenses and sent them on their way. He'd drop the deer at the tagging station on the way to the crime scene. The meat would go to a needy family; whenever possible, confiscated game went to local food banks.

Susie Bear whined.

"Sorry, girl."

The search for the bullets and spent casings would have to wait.

Bears—and murder—came first.

CHAPTER FOUR

Vermont has one of the densest black-bear populations in the country, approximately one bear for every three square miles, most commonly found in the Green Mountains and Northeast Kingdom.
—VERMONT FISH AND WILDLIFE REGULATIONS

WHILE THEY WAITED FOR THE WARDEN, Elvis continued his guard duty by the corpse as Mercy talked to the suspects. That's how she thought of them now, no matter how highbrow-Yankee the accent, as with the Montgomerys, or how good the hair, as with Cara Farrow.

Small talk, mostly, so as not to alarm them, and not to be accused of jumping the gun and doing law enforcement's job, as Detective Harrington would do regardless. He didn't like her or her dog. And he liked Troy Warner and Susie Bear even less.

She started with the women, who were gathered together on one side of the crime scene while the men talked in low voices with Feinberg on the other. Gunnar stood apart with his dogs.

An easy question first, she thought. She didn't want to upset Katharine, who seemed to have regained her composure, and with it, her natural reserve. "How long have you been hunting?"

"Since childhood," Katharine said, her eyes carefully avoiding the corpse. "Shooting, rather than hunting. I'm content to ride my horses, and to settle for clay shooting when I desire to shoot."

"But not your husband."

"No." Katharine looked at Mercy. "He's thrilled by the idea of big-game hunting, just as his father was. I'm sure he talked poor Daniel into this hunting party. And now look what's happened."

"It's not his fault." Lea took her friend's hand and squeezed it.

It's somebody's fault, thought Mercy. *Probably somebody right here.* But aloud she asked, "How well did you know Alice?"

"We met her in Boston." Katharine closed her eyes. "At a party held by our friends, Jean-Paul and Sandrine d'Arcy. She's Parisian, like they are. She redesigned their house on Beacon Hill. So beautiful, yet fresh and modern, and still *très chic,* as only the French can be." She sighed and opened her eyes. "Later, when we bought a penthouse in Trinity Place, Blake and I hired her to redo it."

"I see."

"Only four thousand square feet, but with views of the Charles River."

Four thousand square feet hardly sounded small to Mercy, whose own cabin was barely a quarter that size.

"It was a horror when we bought it," remembered Katharine. "No style at all. Alice transformed it into a postmodern Louis XVI gem."

Mercy couldn't even begin to imagine what that might look like. But her mother would know.

"Gorgeous," said Lea. "So gorgeous it was featured in *Architectural Digest.* I took the pictures."

"Vulgar, I know," said Katharine, her cheeks high with color. "But I did it for Alice. I—" Her voice caught.

"Katharine believed Alice could use the exposure," explained Lea. "She is—was—so young. Her career was just taking off."

"When we decided to renovate the inn, we immediately thought of Alice." Katharine's voice was steady now.

"The inn?"

"The Bluffing Bear Inn, at Bluffing Bear Mountain."

Mercy grinned. "We used to go skiing there when I was a kid."

Katharine sniffed. "Well, then you'll understand how much it needs renovation. I doubt it's changed a bit since you were there."

"Right." Mercy had always loved the ski lodge, which had a Jetsons space-age vintage kitschy appeal even back then. But apparently that wasn't postmodern Louis XVI enough for the likes of Katharine Montgomery.

"I thought this hunting party would be a great opportunity for Alice to show Daniel some drawings and design proposals for the inn," said Katharine. "Now that will never happen."

Mercy frowned. "What's Daniel got to do with it?"

"We're transforming the inn into a major resort. The biggest in Vermont. Daniel and the Farrows are our partners."

"So this hunting party was intended for business as well as pleasure."

"Yes," said Katharine sadly.

Mercy directed her next question to Lea, whose fancy camera still hung around her neck. "Do you hunt?"

"No, I'd rather shoot the foliage," says Lea. "I came to hang out with my friends. We went to school together. Katharine, Blake, and me."

"Caspar, too." Cara Farrow spoke for the first time.

"He was a couple of years behind us," said Lea.

"It was a lifetime ago," said Katharine.

"Before I was even born," said Cara.

"Indeed." Katharine made it sound as if that were her loss.

"Did you know Alice?" Mercy turned to Cara, whose brief interest in the proceedings had waned once more, if the bored expression marring her pretty features were any indication.

"No." She flipped her shiny hair over one shoulder. "But Blake and Katharine's penthouse is nice. I thought maybe she could redo our place in Malibu." She chewed on a long bright-blue fingernail. "I guess now we'll have to find someone else."

If looks could kill, the one Katharine and Lea both gave Cara would have made her the second murder victim of the day. Mercy changed the subject before the group broke up.

"How did you all meet Daniel?"

"Blake and Daniel are on the board of Atlas Oil with my husband," said Cara.

Mercy bit back a smile at the proprietary way she pronounced *my husband*.

Katharine nodded. "We introduced Lea to Daniel."

"They set us up." Lea smiled. "Very kind."

"And effective," said Katharine, smiling back.

"It will never last," said Cara to Mercy, as if Katharine and Lea could not hear her. Prompting them to walk off in the direction of the men.

"How long do we have to stay here?" Cara tossed her hair again, as if she knew how the sun filtering through the trees threw her and her hair into the spotlight. Maybe she did. "I need to go back to the house. I have work to do. For my TV show."

Cara Farrow, thought Mercy, with sudden recognition. Also known as Cara Tyler, model and host of the reality TV show *Be Hair Now*, where aspiring hairdressers competed for chairs at the top salons in the country. Mercy's mother loved that show, and was always pestering her to watch it, in the unlikely event that her daughter might take more interest in fixing her hair.

Cara paused, waiting for her to say something, anything, acknowledging her celebrity.

"Yes," she said finally, not wanting to encourage this line of conversation, which she suspected could become a long soliloquy on the virtues of hair product and the vagaries of her own messy tresses.

But Cara was already off and running on the latest trends in coiffure. The hair model was encouraging her to try *flamboyage,* whatever that was, when Mercy excused herself and went to talk to the men.

They were huddled together, speaking in low, tense voices, like ballplayers discussing the next play in a tight game with just seconds on the clock. Ethan stood apart, leaning against a trio of close-standing birch trees, each of his long arms grasping a branch, as if he were folding himself into the forest. For the first time, the veneer of city sophistication slipped. There was a wildness to him now. He looked like he belonged in the woods.

At her approach, Feinberg broke away from the huddle.

"I suppose there's little doubt that this is murder," he said quietly.

Mercy glanced over at the perfectly hit target that was this victim. "Very little doubt."

He grimaced. "You'll find whoever did this, won't you?"

Before she could answer, Caspar Farrow thrust himself between them, brushing his hand across the breast pockets of Mercy's hunter-orange vest in the process.

"Sorry," he said.

But she could see that he wasn't sorry at all.

"Danny, we can't hang around this forest forever."

"No one can leave until the police arrive." She used her MP voice, which in her experience was the only way to deal with a man like Farrow.

"That's absurd." He threw a harrumph her way before turning back to his host. "Isn't this your land?"

"This is my land, Caspar. And my policy is to cooperate fully with law enforcement."

"How well did you know Alice de Clare?" she asked Farrow.

"Not at all. The wife wanted her to do our place in Malibu. And of course she was under consideration for the project at the inn." As he spoke, his ruddy face reddened even more.

Mercy had the feeling he was lying. "You hadn't seen her either here at Nemeton or before in Boston?"

"No." Farrow was still lying.

"As far as I know, the only people here who'd actually met her in person are Blake and Katharine. And Ethan."

Blake stepped forward at the sound of his name. "We met her when she did our Trinity Place penthouse. Lovely girl. And talented." He leaned forward, lowering his voice. "Katharine can be, well, particular about such matters, though she was pleased with the results. So pleased that naturally we thought of Alice when it came time to redesign the inn."

"When was last time you saw her?"

Blake seemed taken aback at the question, and she wondered if that was because of the question itself or rather because she was asking it. He looked to Feinberg, who nodded for him to respond. "It must've been a couple of weeks ago. At the penthouse in Boston. We were showing Alice old photos of the inn in its prime."

"And you didn't see her this morning?"

"No, it was my understanding that her plane was late and so her arrival was delayed."

Mercy knew that law enforcement would ask all these questions and more to nail down the time lines of every suspect, but she still wanted to get some sense of everyone's relationship with the victim. Ethan aside, they all claimed that relationship to be strictly professional. But that hardly ever proved the case.

She moved onto Ethan. There was always a temptation to see the people you'd known from childhood as they were then, only taller. But that could be a dangerous assumption. He was half a dozen years older than she was, and he'd always treated her with a sort of distant benevolence, letting her tag along on walks in the woods or skateboarding through town to Lulu's Ice Cream Shoppe.

But this Ethan Jenkins was not the blasé teenager she remembered. This Ethan Jenkins was a strong-willed man trying hard to control his emotions.

"I'm so sorry." She took his hand and squeezed it gently. And he let her, although he did not squeeze back.

"I loved her," he said simply.

"Yes. I can see that."

"And now she's gone. I just don't understand how this could have happened." Ethan looked up through the trees to the sky as if the answer to his questions were hidden in the clouds. He turned a fierce gaze on Mercy. "I'm going to find out who did this to her. And they are going to pay."

"I understand how you feel."

"Do you?"

"Yes, as a matter of fact, I do."

He thought about that. "I suppose you do. Mom told me what happened to you in Afghanistan."

"Yes." Ethan's mother, Lillian Jenkins, and her grandmother Patience had been telling each other everything about their lives since before Mercy and Ethan were born. She changed the subject. "When did you meet Alice?"

"At the office. In Manhattan." He smiled a little. "I was her contact at the firm, you see, advising her on the portfolio she needed to present to Mr. Feinberg and other investors."

"For the redesign of Bluffing Bear Inn."

"Yes. I took her to lunch at the Jockey Club. We had martinis. She was . . ." Ethan's voice trailed off, and for a moment Mercy lost him to the memory of happier days. Finally, he looked back at her with hooded eyes. "She was . . . spectacular."

"You fell in love."

Ethan laughed, and Mercy heard the man's heart break. "I fell by the second martini. It took Alice a little longer."

"And when did you last see her?"

Ethan tilted his head back up to the sky. "This morning. We had a fight." He jerked his chin back down and stared directly into Mercy's eyes. "No one knows. Uh, knew. About us. Alice didn't want anyone to know. Not yet. I thought that was ridiculous."

"I'm afraid everyone knows now."

"So be it. I want everyone to know. And I want everyone to know I'm going to find her killer."

Elvis yelped twice, running for the edge of the blowdown. Abandoning his post.

"Excuse me," said Mercy, and jogged after him. Before she could catch up to the headstrong shepherd, he boomeranged back toward her, an enormous Newfoundland retriever mix on his heels. Susie Bear.

Troy Warner followed. He nodded at her, and in that brief nod of recognition Mercy felt a line of energy as straight and true as a well-aimed arrow hitting her right in the solar plexus.

The game warden grinned at her. "I should have known."

"Hi, Troy."

He held her gaze for a moment. She flushed, remembering what Brodie had said about Madeline Warner being back in town. When Madeline married Troy, she'd been the most beautiful girl in Northshire. But the marriage hadn't lasted. According to her grandmother, she'd run off with a flatlander from Florida a couple of years ago. Mercy wondered if Madeline were back in town to see her mother or Troy. Or both.

"If there's anything amiss on my property, we can always count on Mercy to find it." Feinberg joined them, while the rest of the hunting party regrouped, all together in one anxious cluster. Gunnar remained with his dogs, now leashed but none too happy about it. "Maybe I should put you on retainer."

"I still haven't found that last folly," she said, referring to an art installation hidden somewhere on the Nemeton estate. The artist had been murdered before he could reveal its location. Feinberg had asked her to find it, as she'd found his murderer, but so far she had failed to do so.

"You will," he said.

"Agreed," said Troy. "Now let me see the body."

He strode over to the duct-taped area. "Your handiwork, I presume?"

"Yes."

"I'll leave you to it." The billionaire excused himself and retreated to his guests.

Troy slipped on plastic gloves and handed her a pair while she filled him in on the day's events.

"Shot right through the heart," she said.

"Bull's-eye."

"Gunnar says she was at the wrong place, at the wrong time."

"An accident?" He shook his head. "You don't believe that."

"No." She waited for him to tell her why.

"To make a shot like that with a longbow, most archers couldn't be more than thirty, thirty-five yards away. And given how thickly wooded it is around the blowdown, he wouldn't have had a clear shot unless he were pretty close in."

"Tree stand?"

"The angle's wrong." He pointed to the arrow sticking out of Alice de Clare's chest. "Almost a perfect ninety-degree angle. Whoever shot her was not above her, but on the same plane."

"I'll be the judge of that." Dr. Darling, the medical examiner, greeted them with a big smile. She was a short, cheerful middle-aged woman who reminded Mercy of a pug. All charm and cleverness in one energetic little package. Elvis and Susie Bear loved her, telling her so with hard wags of their tails. She gave them big hugs. She wasn't that much bigger than they were.

"That was fast," said Mercy. You could wait for hours sometimes for the Major Crime Unit to show up, depending on weather and traffic and how busy they were attending other crime scenes.

"What Daniel Feinberg wants, Daniel Feinberg gets." She waved an arm at the Crime Scene Search techs who accompanied her. "Lovely to see you, Mercy. But does it always have to be a murder? We could just have lunch, you know."

Mercy smiled. "I would love that. Elvis, too."

"Better make yourselves scarce," warned the doctor as she suited up for her examination of the body. "Harrington should be right behind us." She grinned at them. "But he won't stay long. He's wearing a new suit."

Troy and Mercy stepped aside and let the CSS team do its work. Mercy introduced the game warden to the rest of the hunting party, biting back a laugh when Caspar Farrow complained to Troy that she and Elvis had sabotaged his chance at snagging the bear with bow and arrow. How he recovered quickly enough to take him down with a bullet instead.

"I know I hit it," said Farrow. "I would have gone after it and finished the job—if that woman hadn't gone and gotten herself killed."

"He missed," said Cara, giving Troy a shameless once-over that reminded Mercy how good-looking he was in that earnest way of his. Her husband didn't seem to notice, and if Troy did, he didn't show it.

"Stop saying that," Farrow told his wife. "You weren't even looking."

"Tough break," Troy told Farrow. "But there are plenty of bears in these woods. Gunnar knows what he's doing. Just stick with him and his dogs and I'm sure you'll have a successful hunting season."

Mercy watched as he told Lea Sanders that he'd need to see the photos she'd shot today. She nodded, and Troy turned his attention to Blake and Katharine Montgomery. He was asking about the plans for the inn that had brought them all to Nemeton when Detective Kai Harrington of the Vermont State Police barged into the blowdown with two uniforms. He wore his usual bespoke suit and handmade Italian shoes and did not look happy that the trek through the woods had soiled his ensemble. He looked even less happy to see Mercy and Troy.

He rearranged his sharp features into an approximation of amiability as he greeted Feinberg with a firm handshake. The billionaire introduced him to his friends, and Harrington played the role of handsome and brilliant homicide detective perfectly.

"He's good," she whispered to Troy. They stood on the other side of the crime scene with their dogs, watching the detective ingratiate himself with the rich and semifamous. Although she knew Cara Farrow would object to that characterization.

"Yeah. Too good."

Harrington told the hunting party to stay put, then oozed his way around the crime scene, speaking quietly to Dr. Darling and the CSS team while the uniforms stood sentry over Feinberg and company. Elvis and Susie Bear both growled as the detective neared them.

"We're going to get the boot," whispered Mercy.

"Yep." Troy did not lower his voice.

"You again." Harrington addressed her, ignoring Troy.

"Good morning," she said.

"You found the body?"

"Actually, Elvis did." She told Harrington how they'd come upon the victim.

He glared at the shepherd, and Elvis growled again. Susie Bear added a low rumble of her own.

Harrington fell back. "Get those dogs out of here. Warner, go help that groundskeeper with the bear."

"Sir."

Harrington turned his glare on Mercy. "That's it for now, but you're going to have to make a full statement later."

"Okay," she said.

The detective nodded curtly at Dr. Darling and his CSS team. He strode back over to the hunting party without a backward glance.

"Pay no attention to him." The medical examiner pointed to the arrow. "I'd say you were right, Troy, about the archer who shot this arrow. Definitely on the same plane. And probably came from that direction." She tossed her head south, across the blowdown, where a muster of CSS techs searched for evidence. "If there's anything there, they'll find it. You better go after that bear."

"I'm on it," said Troy.

If the bear were wounded, Troy would want to find him and assess his condition. If he could save him, he'd sedate him and bring him in for treatment. If not, the poor beast might suffer the fate of many a nuisance bear before him.

Mercy and Troy walked over to Gunnar and his elkhounds. All the dogs were dancing on their leads, desperate to get going. The groundskeeper was glowering at a young man in a hunter-orange jacket, who stood with his hands in his jeans, rocking back and forth on his heels. Joey Darosa, Gunnar's assistant.

"I lost him," Joey was telling Gunnar. "He was big—the biggest bear I ever seen—and fast. I tracked him as long as I could, but he took off across the creek and into the meadow. You know, the one by the county road. I heard the sirens. Figured I better come back."

"Huh," said Gunnar.

Mercy could tell he was not pleased. "Did Farrow manage to hit the bear?"

"I do not know." Gunnar sighed, and in that sigh, she heard the cold wind of his native Norway. "Idiot."

They all looked at Joey.

"Didn't look wounded to me."

"I can show Troy where you treed the bear," she said. "Gunnar, you and Joey better stay here until Harrington says you can go."

"Works for me," said Troy.

"Okay," said Gunnar, but again he did not seem pleased.

"Good luck," she said, and she swore the groundskeeper almost smiled.

Almost.

They waved their goodbyes to the medical examiner and Mercy led the way back to the clearing where she and Elvis had barged in on the bear. Susie Bear and Elvis brought up the rear, roughhousing with each other along the way, seemingly as glad to be free of Harrington as she and Troy were.

Mercy walked Troy through the incident, pointing to the large oak at the edge of the clearing. "That's where Gunnar's elkhounds treed the bear."

"Where Farrow claims he wounded the bear."

"Not exactly. This is where Farrow took the first shot at the bear, the one with his longbow and arrow. Elvis startled him, and he missed by a yard. Not that I'm convinced he would've hit it anyway."

He laughed. "Then what?"

"Farrow yelled at Gunnar to give him his rifle, so he could go after the bear. Elvis took off in the other direction, and the elkhounds followed him."

She walked over to the base of the tree, showing him the tracks of the bear making his retreat.

He dropped into a squat to get a better look. "This is a good one." He pointed to a perfect track in a small patch of soft mud, where a large square print was clearly visible.

"Front paw." She crouched down on her heels to join him. The length and width of the paw print were about the same, indicating that it was a front-paw print; had that print been longer than it was wide, it would have been a back-paw print.

"Right." He pulled his Leatherman tool out of his pocket and used the ruler to measure the width of the bear-paw print with his outstretched hand. "Nearly eight inches." He repeated the measurement for the length of the print. "Again, nearly eight inches."

"Big bear." She looked over at Troy.

"I'd say. Four hundred fifty, four hundred seventy-five pounds."

"Wow." Even bigger than she'd thought.

He duckwalked along the bear tracks. "There's been talk of a monster black bear on the warpath up here somewhere."

"Really?"

"It happens."

"Well, this guy was big and fast. But he didn't charge, he bolted."

"What happened next?"

"I'm not sure. I went after the dogs. I heard a shot behind me."

"Farrow."

"Yeah." Mercy shrugged. "Maybe he's a better shot with a gun."

Troy kept his eyes on the ground as he inched forward. "No sign of blood or injury so far."

"I find it hard to believe he made the shot. I'd bet money the bear is just fine. Deep in the woods around here somewhere, laughing his big bear butt off."

"Let's track this monster bear for a while just to be sure." He rose to his feet, holding out his hands to help her up.

But she was already on her feet. "Sure."

"If you've got the time." He seemed uncertain. An awkward pause.

She knew her mother would have told her to let him play the gentleman, but she was no good at that. Whenever she found herself in a situation like this, by the time she figured out what the guy was trying to do for her, she'd moved on under her own steam.

Like now. But she didn't mean to insult him, and she wasn't about to say no to a bear hunt. "We wouldn't miss it for the world. Would we, Elvis?"

The shepherd stopped playing with Susie Bear and trotted over to her, triangular ears cocked. Elvis was ready. As was his big furry friend lumbering along behind him.

Together the four of them tracked the bear through the forest for about a quarter mile, until they came to a rushing stream and the trail ended. No indication of any wounded beast, just a big bear on the run.

"We may as well go back," said Troy, "and see what if anything else they've found at the scene."

Mercy smiled. Technically it was Harrington's crime scene, but she knew the game warden wouldn't sit still while the staties searched for a murderer in *his* woods.

They made their way back with the dogs, skirting the perimeter of the clearing just within the trees, keeping out of the detective's line of sight. When they were within about thirty feet, they could see that Harrington had begun his interviews with the hunting party. They stopped to listen.

The detective had commandeered a large tree stump, covering it with what appeared to be a uniform's jacket, the better to keep the seat of his new suit trousers tidy. He sat there, spine imperiously straight, the king of crime fighters on his throne, lording it over his subject suspects.

An angry-looking Ethan paced in front of him while an anxious rookie named Becker took notes, sans jacket. Mercy knew Becker was afraid of the detective, whose disdain for subordinates was legendary. Not that he liked anyone else much, either, as far as she could tell.

Feinberg stood to Harrington's right, well within earshot of the detective as he questioned Ethan. If Harrington minded the imposition—and you'd think he would—he wasn't saying anything. Probably because he cared more about the billionaire's good opinion than his own integrity.

Just beyond them, the rest of the hunting party waited, restless under a copse of slim brilliant yellow maple trees. Cara Farrow was braiding and unbraiding her hair, her sullen husband fiddling with his cell phone. No signal out here, so maybe he was playing *Candy Crush*.

Blake and Katharine huddled together, while Lea kept to the background, shooting pictures with more discretion than Mercy had ever seen in a photographer.

"Do you think she's a wildlife photographer?" Mercy asked Troy. "You know, good at shooting skittish subjects out in the wild?"

"It would explain how she's managed to avoid Harrington's wrath," said Troy. "Or maybe she's just got influential friends." He nodded toward Feinberg.

They were close enough now to hear Harrington grilling Ethan. He'd obviously found out about his relationship with Alice, which Mercy knew would make Ethan a prime suspect in the detective's eyes.

"Tell me again why you kept your relationship a secret," said the detective.

"It wasn't my idea. Alice insisted." Ethan sighed. "Nonfraternization and all that."

"It was an open secret," said Feinberg, who'd obviously had enough of Harrington's haranguing of his employee.

Harrington turned his attention to the billionaire. "Why do you say that?"

"Everyone knew about it."

Not much they could do here. Mercy and Troy continued their out-of-sight circumvention of the crime scene. They found Dr. Darling and the CSS team still hard at work.

"Anything new?" asked Troy.

"One thing that might interest you," said the medical examiner. "She hasn't been dead that long, maybe an hour, maybe two, tops. I'll know when I get her back to the lab."

"That's what I figured," said Mercy. "When I found her, the scavengers hadn't really gotten to her yet."

"I'm thinking that broadhead ruptured her aorta. She would have been dead in minutes."

"I'm glad she didn't suffer too long."

"I'll make sure you know what I know. Just in case our friend Harrington tries to keep the maple bread pudding all to himself."

"Thank you," said Mercy.

"He's been busy chatting up the rich folks," said the doc quietly. "Especially Feinberg. He loves that man and his mansion. Not to mention his money."

Mercy laughed.

Troy did not laugh.

"You're smart to stay out of sight. He won't want any competition. He still hasn't gotten over your besting him last time."

The medical examiner was referring to their complicated history with Harrington, which nearly cost Troy his career and Mercy her life.

They fell back behind the trees and continued their search of the perimeter.

"They should be looking back here," she said.

"They're not trackers. They can't read the woods the way you can."

"Or you."

"Agreed." Troy grinned at her. "Let's see what we can find that they missed."

CHAPTER FIVE

A fishing house is a fishing shanty, bob-house, smelt shanty, tent, or other structure designed to be placed on the ice of the waters of Vermont for fishing or to be occupied for other purposes.

—VERMONT FISH AND WILDLIFE REGULATIONS

HALF AN HOUR LATER, Mercy pulled Troy behind a scrub of winterberry and pointed to a broken line of faint footprints in a narrow patch of mud. The prints led out of the clearing and were barely visible in the tangle of tracks made by the hunters and the dogs.

"Small," said Troy, referring to the footprints.

"Too small to belong to any of the hunting party."

"A child?"

"Maybe."

They followed the prints, the dogs on their heels, checking for broken twigs, disturbed leaves, crushed fern, and other minor disturbances.

"Look." She stopped short. "Something caught on that branch."

He followed the angle of her outstretched arm to a scrap of blue fabric caught on a fallen tree limb. He pulled out a new pair of plastic gloves from his duty belt and handed them to Mercy.

She slipped them over her long pale fingers and picked the torn fragment of cloth from the bramble. She held it up to the light dappling through the sugar maples.

"Is that Batman?" He pointed to the small black logo imprinted on the blue background.

"I think so." She shook her head against the obvious. "A child's Batman pajamas."

"I had a pair when I was a kid," said Troy. "I wore them day and night. I never wanted to take them off, even to let my mom wash them. Drove her crazy."

"I'm sure you were a very cute little boy." She'd first met him at the town pool when they were teenagers. He was the lifeguard and she was the fourteen-year-old summer girl crushing on him. He was cute then. As now.

Troy grinned. "All little boys are cute."

"What is a kid in pajamas doing in the woods? And why off-trail?" She frowned. "Maybe he's lost."

"Or maybe he's lost and scared."

"Do you think he could have seen what happened to Alice?"

"I don't know. Let's not get ahead of ourselves."

"Is this scrap big enough for the dogs to track with?"

"Even if it's not, Susie Bear should be able to find him." The Newfie mutt could follow a specific scent—tracking and trailing, nose to the ground—but she was also one of the best air-scent dogs in Vermont. Air-scent dogs specialized in blind search. They didn't look for a given scent, they followed scent they found in the air, noses up. The scent of someone out of place—someone scared or excited or anxious—carried by the wind.

"If Elvis doesn't find him first."

Troy laughed. "How's your training going?"

She and Elvis had been working with the Green Mountain Search and Rescue K9 Volunteer Corps, a highly trained group of civilians and their canines who showed up rain or shine or snow to help law enforcement find missing people in the wilderness.

As a bomb-sniffing dog, the Belgian Malinois had learned to detect more than two dozen different substances—far more than other kinds of working dogs. Air-scent work was different, but the shepherd was proving quite good at it as well.

"It's going great."

"But . . ." He paused.

"But what?"

"There's always a but when it comes to training dogs."

"Yeah." She kicked at a pile of leaves. "He's very smart. As good at nose-up as he is at nose-down."

"No surprise there."

"No, but as you know there's more to it than tracking and trailing and air-scent skills."

Troy smiled. "Sociability."

"Right." It took most civilians and their dogs a couple of years to certify for search and rescue. Mercy figured she and Elvis would fly through the certification. But she'd been wrong. The best search-and-rescue folks—whether two-footed or four-footed—had exceptional social skills. Amiability was especially important for the dogs, as they had to interact off-leash with all kinds of strangers, canine and human.

"What does Laura say?" Laura Dawson was the head of the organization. Mercy knew that Troy and Susie Bear had worked many searches together with her rescue Hemingway. Hemingway was a muscular brown-and-white dog—part Labrador retriever, part sharpei, part pit bull—as smart as he was handsome. He and Susie Bear were the best—and friendliest—air-scent dogs in the county.

"She says Elvis needs to be more like Hemingway and Susie Bear."

"He's not exactly Mr. Congeniality."

"It's not that he's not friendly. He's just reserved. He waits to see if someone's worthy of his friendship."

"Sounds like someone else I know."

Mercy frowned. "He's never going to be Susie Bear."

"He doesn't have to be. He just has to be approachable. Learn to mingle."

"It's not like it's a cocktail party." She suspected he was talking about her as well. She was no better at mingling than her dog was. In the army, you acted first and chitchatted later. If at all.

"He'll follow your lead."

He was definitely talking about her as well.

"'I will seem friendly, as thou hast advised me,'" she quoted aloud.

Troy laughed. "Shakespeare, the great mingler."

"Very funny."

After so many years away, coming home to the civilian world wasn't easy for her. And it was even harder for Elvis. He was a one-person dog. That person had been Martinez, his handler and her fiancé. When he was killed, they both lost their man and their mission. It took nearly a year and a couple of near-death experiences for them to form a strong bond. They were still working on it.

Troy nodded toward the dogs, romping around together around the clearing. "He likes Susie Bear."

"Everyone likes Susie Bear," she said.

"True. But don't worry. I know you'll figure it out." Troy whistled for Susie Bear, who was digging in a pile of yellow leaves. Elvis was watching his shaggy canine pal with his dark nose in the air, as if to say, *We have better things to do.* At the whistle, both dogs ran to Troy.

"Now let's put them both to work." He stepped aside, and let Mercy hold out the scrap of Batman fabric.

Susie Bear snorted enthusiastically while Elvis took a more re-strained approach, carefully sniffing the cloth as if he were directly responsible for the chain of evidence.

He sat on his haunches and waited, ears perked, waiting for her command. He was ready when she was.

The Newfie thumped her plumed tail wildly, scattering leaves with every *whomp,* her large shaggy head tilted to one side, as if wondering what was taking them so long to say the one word that they were desperate to hear.

"Search," Mercy and Troy said in unison.

And they were off.

"My dog is going to give your dog a run for her money," said Mercy.

"We'll see about that."

Mercy and Troy jogged behind the dogs. They all wore hunter-orange vests, and she knew Troy was watching for a flash of the bright blaze, hoping that the kid who'd gone crashing through the woods in his Batman pajamas was wearing a hunter-orange vest, too.

First a murder and now a missing child. It seemed impossible that the two were not connected. She hoped that whoever killed Alice de Clare wasn't also a threat to this kid.

She figured that one of the hunting party was to blame for the arrow piercing the victim's heart. One of them was a far better shot than he—or she—looked.

Alice de Clare had not been a Vermonter or a peeper looking for foliage or a trophy hunter out for big game. Even dead, she had looked as out of place in the woods as Mercy would look at a fashion show in Paris. And vice versa. Alice had the look of a European, and a chic, rich one at that.

"Ethan told me he met the victim in the woods just before the hunting party officially began. They had a fight."

"What about?"

"Their relationship. Apparently, she wanted to keep it a secret. Since they were working together and all."

"And he didn't."

"No. It wasn't much of a secret, as it turns out. At least not according to Daniel."

"People notice."

Mercy didn't say anything to that, but she could feel her pale skin flush. She changed the subject. "The question is, who else was out in the woods, then?"

"Harrington will track down everyone's movements. Maybe that will tell us something."

"Seems like they're all holding something back, if not outright lying, about their relationship with her." She slowed down a little so she could talk more easily. The dogs were moving fast, and they were huffing to keep up. Not easy, as they were off-trail, making their way across a forest floor crowded with roots and ferns and leaves and rocks and sticks, not to mention trees. "Alice had to be more than just the hired help to somebody in that hunting party. The only one I know anything about besides Daniel is Ethan Jenkins. And I haven't seen him since in years."

"I don't see much of him these days either."

At her inquiring look, he added. "We were Eagle Scouts together as kids."

"Always in uniform."

"Go figure." Troy slowed down, too, matching her pace.

"But not Ethan."

"No. When he went off to college, we lost touch. He's been living in New York for years now."

"Working for Daniel."

"Yeah," he said, as they picked their way through another blow-down. Elvis and Susie Bear barreled on ahead.

"He seems to be more New York than Northshire now."

"Gone to the dark side."

"Lillian doesn't talk about him much." Ethan was the one child Mercy hadn't heard Lillian talk about since he grew up and moved away. She was always bragging about her daughter, a baby doctor up in Burlington, and her son, an FBI agent down in Washington, D.C. But nothing about Ethan the financier. Maybe she didn't approve of his profession.

"She's more worried about Henry," said Troy.

"Ethan's son?"

"Yeah. He's a good kid but needs looking after." Troy held a low branch up and away from her face, so she could pass through a tight copse of birch trees.

"Thanks." *Always the gentleman,* she thought. That probably started in childhood, too. She'd never met his parents, but she hoped that she would one day. If only to confirm her theory.

"Have you met Henry?"

"Sort of," she said. "I saw him a couple of times at the Vermonter Drive-In this summer. He helps Lillian in the back when Ethan brings him home from New York to see her." Like everyone else, she loved Lillian's restaurant, home of the best burgers and milkshakes in southern Vermont, maybe the whole state.

"He gets lost."

"What do you mean?"

"He just takes off, apparently. Gets lost. Lillian blames his mother."

"Billie Whitaker?"

"Yeah. Well, Billie Whitaker Jenkins now. You know Billie?"

"We went to the same summer camp. She was a few years ahead of me. Very creative, artsy-craftsy. Kind of scattered." She tried to imagine the Billie she'd known as a grown-up mom with a child— and failed.

Elvis and Susie Bear disappeared into a stretch of wetlands. They scrambled over a pile of dead wood and plunged into the marsh's shallow waters, with no regard for the poison ivy, switchgrass and loosestrife that flanked the indistinct shoreline of small pools dotting the boggy plain.

She cursed as the game warden plowed ahead, his boots and uniform good protection from the elements. No such luck for her, as she'd run after Elvis in nothing but a pair of yoga pants and a long-sleeved T-shirt over which she wore only her hunter-orange puffer vest. On her feet were thin cotton socks and slip-on sneakers, cold and soaking wet now. Her grandmother was right. She should have changed into duck boots before running after a dog into the woods.

"Not really dressed for this, are you?"

"I was planning on spending the day on my couch, reading a good book."

"Let me guess." He grinned at her. *"Hamlet."*

Troy knew about her obsession, and he liked to tease her about it.

"Nothing by Shakespeare."

"Then what?"

She sighed, knowing she'd never hear the end of it. *"Shakespeare and the Hunt."*

He laughed. "You lied."

"I did not. It's not by Shakespeare. It's just about him."

"That makes all the difference." Troy grinned as he splashed along behind the dogs. "Sounds like a real page-turner."

Mercy felt her cheeks redden. "In honor of the hunting season."

"Of course."

A sudden round of barking echoed across the wetlands.

They slowed to a stop, standing side by side in the reeds, staring across the marsh. On its north side stood a shack where the ground solidified.

"Is that a bob-house?" From here, the ice shanty appeared typical of the ones New Englanders used for ice fishing on lakes and ponds in the dead of winter.

"Looks like it."

"A little early, isn't it?" she asked. "Not to mention it's on dry land."

"Can't put a bob-house out on the ice until November twentieth," he told her. "And you have to take it down by the last Sunday in March."

Always the game warden, she thought. Troy's job was to make sure everyone followed the rules and regulations designed to protect the flora and fauna of the Green Mountains. That he took his job so seriously was one of things she liked best about him.

Ahead, they could see the dogs—Elvis in front, a streak of tawny fur, and Susie Bear, a bouncing ball of black shag behind him—both headed straight for the hut.

"I'll go after them," said Troy. "You can take the long way."

"I'm fine."

"You're really not dressed for this."

"I'm fine."

He shrugged and waded across the marsh. She trudged on, up to her shins in the murky water, thick with water lilies and cattails, bulrushes and sedge.

"There's a large pond beyond the marsh northwest of here," yelled Troy over his shoulder. "That woods skirts it."

"Presumably that's where the bob-house belongs."

"During the season only."

"Right." The spongy bottom of the marsh suddenly dropped off, and she found herself hip-deep in water. Even Troy, who at six-foot-three was some six inches taller than she, was up to his thighs now.

She watched as he unhitched his duty belt and raised it in one smooth movement above his head before settling it deftly around his neck. In the distance, Susie Bear and Elvis swam toward the far shore, reaching solid ground in a rush of cattails. She held back a laugh as both the Malinois and the Newfie mutt scrambled onto the bank, wiggling and wriggling violently, spraying each other with marsh water. A couple more twists and shakes later, they disappeared around the back of the bob-house. She hoped they were still on the trail of the boy—and not just taking a detour through the nearest body of water. Both dogs were good swimmers, and they loved a good dip. Neither minded getting wet, no matter what the weather.

She and Troy quickened their pace. The sooner they caught up with the dogs, the better. A real challenge, at least for her, as her feet kept sticking in the sodden sludge, her slip-on sneakers sinking with each step, the mud sucking at the soles. It was like marching in glue. She wondered if—when—she'd lose a shoe. Or both.

Troy, on the other hand, seemed completely at home in the muck. Graceful, even, as he made his way across the wetlands, his fine brown hair tucked neatly under his orange cap, his broad shoulders easily carrying the weight of his duty belt. The only hint of possible discomfort was a splotch of perspiration darkening the collar of his forest-green uniform shirt.

He hit solid ground first, not far from the bob-house, then turned and waited for her. She stumped along, sludge pulling at her sneakers. At least she still had them both on her feet.

As she approached the rise of the bank, he held out his hand. She grabbed it, and he swung her up to him with strong solid fingers. Her hands were cold in the crisp air, but his were warm. He seemed impervious to the weather, just like shaggy Susie Bear. Probably a good quality in game wardens and search-and-rescue dogs. They made a good pair. The two were as grounded as the forest they protected.

She and Elvis made a good pair, too, in their way. But they were more high-strung, more high-energy, more hyper-focused.

"Thanks," she said as Troy helped her up to solid ground.

He smiled at her. That smile was one of the reasons she'd focused on Elvis's search-and-rescue training the past couple of months. A deliberate attempt on her part to slow down the growing attraction between them. Like that was working.

They stood a moment, hands clasped together. She looked down at the murky water, away from that smile. She felt him watching her. She raised her head just enough to look him in the eye and smile back.

Susie Bear interrupted, pushing her wet pumpkin head between them. Mercy laughed and dropped her arms to give the shaggy wet dog a hug. She was a friendly beast, even if she could take down a bad guy as easily as Elvis. Mercy had seen her do it. She wondered what she was after now.

Susie Bear gave her a lick with her thick tongue. "I know, we haven't had the time for a proper hello."

"And we don't have time now, either," said Troy. "Susie Bear, show us what you've got."

The Newfie mutt snorted her approval, then took off around the ice shanty.

Troy and Mercy trotted after her.

The bob-house was a hastily made affair of pallet boards. It was about six by four feet, with a flat plywood roof and a sled for a foundation. There were a couple of small windows cut high on the long side. On the shack's south side, they found Elvis lying in his classic Sphinx pose, paws at the opening at the bottom of a crude door. His alert position.

At the sight of them, he thudded his black-tipped curlicue tail. Not another muscle moved. Susie Bear jigged at his side, eager to breach the perimeter.

"Okay, let's see what you've found." Troy pushed in the flimsy door—and the dogs rushed past him into the shed.

He gave Mercy a look. Both dogs were trained to wait for a command. But neither had waited this time.

Mercy and Troy went in after them.

This was not one of those fully equipped, plush ice-fishing houses whose owners preferred to fish in relative comfort, with gas stoves, ovens, and PlayStations. Whatever amenities this place once had—if any—had been stripped and stolen away. Not even the odd empty beer can was left behind.

The only thing in the room was a big old gutting table that commanded most of the space. Susie Bear bound over to it, sliding to a dead stop right in front. Elvis stood behind the shaggy black dog, triangular ears perked.

"What is it?"

"I don't know." She leaned over to look under the table, peering past the dogs. Tucked under the table was a small boy curled into a ball, his thin arms wrapped around his knees. She couldn't see much of his face. His dark head was down, his chin tight against his chest, his eyes closed.

"It's Batman." Mercy turned to Troy. "I need to get closer." She pushed through the dogs, and dropped to a squat, pitching her head under the table.

The boy rocked on his heels, back and forth, shivering in Batman pajamas. He was mumbling.

"Hi there," she said.

The boy did not answer, only rocked harder and muttered louder.

"Do you recognize him?" asked Troy.

"I'm not sure."

"What's he saying?"

"I'm not sure." She twisted toward the game warden and put her finger up to her lips, then turned back to the boy and closed her eyes, listening. "Numbers."

The boy spoke in a soft voice full of rhythm, as if to a drumbeat only he could hear. "Two . . . three . . . five . . . seven . . . eleven . . . thirteen . . ."

She ducked further under the table, closer to him, and smiled. "Prime numbers."

The boy raised his head. His was a sweet face, framed with board-straight chestnut-brown hair that fell over his pale forehead. Dark solemn eyes and a freckled nose. Small mouth and pointed chin.

"Henry," she said. "You're Lillian Jenkins's grandson, aren't you?"

Henry stared at her, or rather past her. She scooted a little closer, careful not to scare him. "We met at your grandmother's restaurant."

He kept rocking and reciting numbers.

"I like prime numbers, too," she said. "Like three hundred thirteen. My birthday, March thirteenth."

Henry stopped rocking and looked at her with round dark eyes. "Palindrome."

"That's right." This was one smart kid.

Susie Bear pushed her shaggy mug past Mercy and gave Henry a lick on his cheek. The giant dog snuggled right up to him, using her pumpkin noggin to push through his hands. He released them, and when he did, Mercy could see that his pajama bottoms were torn, and that both of his little knees were scraped. The boy let his wounded knees fall open, sitting cross-legged. Allowing the New-fie mutt to crawl right onto his lap. Henry buried his head in Susie Bear's damp fur.

She tried another tack. "I know you're good at counting. I know you help your grandmother with the inventory in the back room at the restaurant."

He mumbled into the dog's thick coat just loudly enough for her to catch the words. "Fifty pounds of hamburger, thirty-three six-packs of hamburger buns, twenty-seven jars of bread-and-butter pickles, sixteen bottles of catsup. . . ."

"That's great."

Susie Bear licked both of the boy's cheeks this time, and he laughed. It was a halting sort of giggle that made Mercy suspect this serious boy didn't laugh much, or often. Elvis yelped and broke his position, slipping under the table and gently placing his dark muzzle on Henry's shoulder. He was practically enveloped by wet dog now.

It was getting a bit crowded under there.

"Come on out."

Henry did not respond, clutching at Susie Bear and Elvis.

"The dogs will stay right with you. Promise." She held out her hand. Elvis nudged Henry's neck with his nose.

He didn't move. Just tightly hugged Susie Bear.

"Okay, you don't need to take my hand. Hold onto her collar, and she'll lead you out."

She could see that this approach appealed to him. He unclenched his fingers, then felt around for the red leather collar fastened around the Newfie mutt's thick neck, mostly buried in her dense double coat. Susie Bear sat still as he tucked his hand around the wide band; she seemed to understand how frightened he was.

"Don't worry," said Mercy quietly. "You won't hurt her. She's as sturdy as a mule. And she's trained to help people out of tight spots."

Kids loved Susie Bear. She was large and cuddly, like an overstuffed teddy bear with a tongue. Elvis was not cuddly; he was kingly. But together the two dogs were irresistible.

Susie Bear licked the boy's chin, as if to reassure him, and then pulled him carefully along. Elvis flanked them, ever the vigilant guardian. They moved slowly along toward Mercy, the boy wrapping his legs around the big dog's torso, hanging onto her collar with both hands. His eyes were closed, and he was reeling off prime numbers again. Susie Bear was basically carrying him, as if she were a horse and he the rider. No problem for the good-natured mutt, given her strength and stamina.

Mercy backed up to the edge of the gutting table, and once free of it, rose to her feet. Troy stripped off his vest, handing it to her. Susie Bear emerged from under the table, the boy on her back, and Elvis at her side.

She gently removed the boy's clenched fingers from the dog's collar.

They were cold. His eyes were open now, but there was a glazed look about them.

"Say hello to Troy," she said.

The shivering boy hardly glanced at the game warden. She squatted down and pulled him off the dog and onto her lap. She rubbed his hands between her own to warm them. Not good enough.

Troy pulled a pair of thick gloves from a pocket and gave them to her. She smiled her thanks and then slipped them onto his small hands.

"I know these are too big for you," she told him, "but we need to warm up those fingers."

The boy finally stopped chanting primes. She wrapped Troy's vest around his thin shoulders.

"Not sure what we can do about his feet," she told Troy. "He'd stumble in my shoes. Or yours."

"His feet never have to touch the ground," said Troy. He squatted down to talk to Henry face-to-face.

"Henry, I'm going to carry you back to your father. He's not too far from here."

The boy shook his head, hard, straight brown hair flying. Susie Bear cuddled up to him, and he buried his face in her fur. Elvis dropped into his classic Sphinx pose, a furry footstool for the boy's slippered feet.

"Look, buddy, I can see you're upset." Troy's voice was calm and confident. "But it's cold in here. And I'm betting you're hungry. We can fix that, but we need to get you out of here."

"He's a game warden. An officer of the law."

"And she's a soldier. Military police. Let's get you home. And then you can tell us all about whatever has upset you."

"The dogs will come with us, too. They're smart. Elvis was in the army. Trained to go after bad guys."

"Elvis is almost as smart as Susie Bear," said Troy.

"Smarter," said Mercy.

"We've all got your back. No worries."

Mercy glanced at Troy, and he nodded. They waited, and let the dogs do their magic.

Finally, Henry raised his head, and looked up at Troy. "Ranger."

He smiled at the boy. "Close enough." Gathering the small boy in his arms, he stood up. Mercy rose with him.

"Bear," said Henry softly.

"That's your cue, Susie Bear. You lead the way."

She clambered out of the bob-house.

"I'm going to have to track down whoever left this shanty here out of season," said Troy over his shoulder as he prepared to follow Susie Bear. "Do you think you could get some shots of the bob-house?"

"Sure." Mercy pulled her cell from her pocket and snapped several shots of the ice-house interior. Elvis stayed with her, watching from under the gutting table. When she'd finished shooting pictures from every angle, she stepped outside after Troy, the shepherd at her side.

"Every bob-house is supposed to be marked with the owner's name and address," he said. "Get that if you can."

"Sure. Go ahead, Elvis and I will catch up."

Troy turned back the way they came, Henry in his arms and Susie Bear at his side.

"Wait," said the boy. "Wolf."

"You mean Elvis?"

The boy nodded.

"Don't worry," said Troy, walking on, "they'll be right behind us."

"Right behind you!" she called after them.

Mercy examined the ice-house exterior carefully, snapping several more photos with her cell. Elvis shadowed her.

"That should do it." She tossed her head at the shepherd and off they went to join Troy and Susie Bear.

They hadn't gone far.

"Henry insisted on waiting for Wolf," said Troy.

"Right." *Wolf. Ranger. Bear.* Mercy wondered what he would call her. "I didn't find any name or address on the bob-house."

"No surprise there. I'll have to come back here anyway. Let's get back."

They waded through the marsh again. Troy held the boy high above the water, as if making an offering to the gods. Henry did not hang onto Troy. He kept his thin arms tightly crossed against his chest, tucked into himself like a frightened hedgehog.

"We've got you covered, son." Troy smiled over the boy's head at Mercy, and she could feel herself flush.

They reached the edge of the marsh, and the dogs ran out of the water, shaking, shimmying and spritzing everyone else.

"Down," commanded Mercy and Troy in unison. Both dogs stopped in their tracks and dropped to the ground.

Henry laughed, another awkward whoop. While Troy held the boy, Mercy wiped him down as best she could with the dry part of her T-shirt, the section protected from the water by her vest. It was clear that he didn't like being touched, at least not by strangers. Fortunately, he hadn't gotten that wet.

"That will have to do," she said.

"Not too far now," Troy told Henry.

They tramped into the forest, single file, through fallen leaves and rattlesnake ferns. Troy started singing, his voice comfortingly deep and surprisingly resonant. She had no idea that he could sing. She realized there was a lot she didn't know about him. Their time together had been intense, as time together on a mission always was, whether overseas or in the wilderness of Vermont—and it fostered an intense closeness that in some ways was false. It made you think you knew each other better than you really did. Or maybe it meant that you knew parts of each other very well, and other parts not at all. She wondered about those other parts of Troy Warner.

He was singing one of the old Vermont traditional songs, the "Vermont Sugar-Maker's Song":

When you see the vapor pillar lick the forest and the sky,
You may know the days of sugar-making then are drawing nigh.

Frosty night and thawy day make the maple pulses play
Till congested by their sweetness they delight to bleed away.
Then bubble, bubble, bubble, bubble, bubble goes the pan
Furnish better music for the season if you can
See the golden billows, watch their ebb and flow
Sweetest joys indeed we sugar-makers know.

She chimed in on the chorus as they marched along to the beat of the song. *Bubble, bubble, bubble.* Troy knew all the verses, and there were far more than Mercy remembered from summer camp. Henry didn't sing along, but his legs relaxed, bouncing gently to the rhythm of Troy's stride. He uncrossed his arms and let them fall to his sides. He settled into the game warden's strong embrace.

How perceptive of Troy, she thought.

They sang the song three times, her soft mezzo complementing his deep baritone. At least to her forgiving ear. And maybe to the boy's, too, because he dozed off while they sang.

Sleeping to the sweet sounds of the maple sugar-making song.

CHAPTER SIX

"If you don't like the weather in New England now, just wait a few minutes."

—MARK TWAIN

WHEN HENRY FELL ASLEEP IN TROY'S ARMS, Mercy finally voiced the thought that had worried her ever since they found him in the bob-house. "Do you think he saw Alice de Clare get murdered?"

"I don't know. Something sure shook him up." Troy tightened his grip on the slumbering boy as they hiked on through the woods, picking their way carefully through one blowdown after another. "But it could've been hunters or hikers or even that big bear."

"Still."

"I know. It's one heck of a coincidence."

That was one thing she and Troy had in common. Neither of them believed in coincidence. "Taking him back to that hunting party may be a terrible mistake."

"You're assuming one of them killed her?"

"Aren't you?"

"It is a tempting assumption," he admitted, "but we have no choice but to take him back to his father."

"With his involvement with Alice, Ethan's going to be a prime suspect in Harrington's eyes. Especially when he finds out about that fight." She paused. "We could take Henry to his grandmother."

"Let's see what happens with Ethan." He looked down at Henry as the boy moaned in his sleep. "But it couldn't hurt to let Lillian know what's going on."

"I'll see to that."

When they got back to the crime scene, they found Dr. Darling watching as the Crime Scene Search techs zipped up the body bag. Harrington was interviewing Ethan Jenkins, his back to Mercy and Troy. But Ethan looked over the detective's shoulder and spotted them.

"Excuse me," he told Harrington, launching himself toward them, his eyes on the sleeping boy in Troy's arms. "Henry?"

Mercy raised a finger to her lips. "He's sleeping."

"I recognized the pajamas." Ethan stared at his son. "I don't understand."

Harrington strode across the clearing, Becker on his heels. "What are you doing back here, Warner? I told you to take care of that bear."

Feinberg and his friends followed at a discreet distance.

"Stay," ordered Harrington.

The police rookie stopped short.

"Not you, Becker," said Harrington, exasperated.

Unlike Becker, the hunting party paid no attention to Harrington, and continued across the clearing to see the boy. They formed a tight knot to the left of the detective, Feinberg at the forefront. They watched in an expectant silence, as if waiting for the curtain to rise on a theater stage.

Troy held Henry out to his father, who gathered him into his arms.

"Is he okay?" asked Ethan.

"I think so," said Mercy, "but he was very cold when we found him. We did what we could to warm him up, but I'm not sure it was enough. He could be dehydrated or hypothermic or both."

"He never wears a coat unless I put one on him. He doesn't think about the weather."

"Take him to Nemeton," said Feinberg.

Ethan started off, heading out of the clearing.

"Wait." She touched Ethan's shoulder. "We'll go with you."

"Jenkins, you aren't going anywhere." Harrington regarded Ethan with the haughtiness that had earned him the nickname Prince Harry. She wondered if he knew about it. She hoped for Becker's sake that he didn't.

Feinberg stepped up to Harrington. "The boy needs his father right now."

"This is a murder investigation," said Harrington evenly. "There are procedures to follow. We need to finish our interviews. We are counting on your full cooperation."

From imperious to ingratiating in less than sixty seconds, thought Mercy. The man was a marvel.

Feinberg ignored Harrington, addressing Mercy instead. "What happened?"

"I thought he was back at the estate," said Ethan. "He was asleep in bed when we left. The housekeeper was supposed to watch him. Give him breakfast. Take care of him."

Ethan sat down on a large fallen log behind him, where he could hold his son more securely on his lap. The dogs flanked father and son, twin sentries on guard.

"Maria Espinosa is very responsible and efficient," said Feinberg. "It would be unusual for her to shirk her duties in any way."

"And she loves children," added Lea. "She would never do anything to endanger Henry."

"Someone dropped the ball," said Troy.

"Henry likes to walk," said Ethan. "Sometimes he slips out the door and off on his own before anyone notices."

"We found him in an old bob-house, hiding under an old gutting table." Again, Mercy tried to keep her voice neutral. No judgment.

"He hides when he gets agitated," said Ethan. "Something must have upset him."

"Or someone." Harrington, who'd been uncharacteristically silent, now spoke with an authority that reeked of ambition. "I'll need to speak to the boy."

"Is that absolutely necessary?" asked Feinberg.

"Henry just went for one of his walks," said Ethan. "He has nothing to do with this."

"I'll be the judge of that," said Harrington. "I need to establish where he was and what he was doing. He might have seen something relevant to the investigation."

"Surely you can do that at Nemeton," said Feinberg.

Ethan smoothed his son's hair, brushing it back off his forehead. "He feels clammy."

"We need to get him back to the house." Lea stood at Feinberg's side, and Mercy was struck by what a handsome couple they made. Good for Blake and Katharine for setting them up.

Henry stirred in his father's arms.

"He could be a material witness," said Harrington. "And he's waking up now." The detective waved his hand, directing the group to fall back. "Jenkins, come with me and bring your boy."

"He probably won't tell you anything. He doesn't talk much, unless it's about math or video games or Batman."

Henry pulled away from his father and embraced the dogs.

"Come on, Henry." Ethan rose to his feet, pulling the boy with him. "You need to stay with me. We've talked about this before."

But Henry wriggled away from his father and slid down to the forest floor, tucking himself into a ball, just as he had under the gutting table in the bob-house. The dogs formed a shield around him, Susie Bear a big black shaggy boulder and Elvis an elegant fawn wall of fur.

"What's he doing?" Harrington glared at Ethan. "I can't talk to him down there."

"We can try." Ethan got to his feet and looked down at his son. "Henry, we need to talk about where you've been. You need to tell us where you went."

The boy patted Susie Bear with one hand, Elvis with the other. Ignoring his father, Harrington, and everyone else.

"You were supposed to stay at the estate," his father said. "But you didn't, did you? Where did you go?"

Henry began chanting.

Mercy listened carefully in the silence that followed, everyone straining to hear what the boy was saying. But this time, Henry was not rattling off prime numbers. He was mumbling, but what he was mumbling she couldn't quite figure out.

"What's he saying?" Harrington crossed his arms across his chest, careful not to wrinkle his double-breasted suit jacket.

"I don't know," said Ethan. "Usually it's numbers."

"Prime numbers," said Mercy.

"Yes." Ethan looked at her with appreciation. "Henry like prime numbers."

She squatted down next to Henry and the dogs. "It sounds like 'dark tree, dark tree.'"

"What does that mean?" demanded Harrington.

"I don't know." Mercy looked up at Troy. "But this isn't helping." She and Elvis and Susie Bear stayed down on the forest floor with the boy, forming a ring of protection around the boy. "It's okay, Henry. It's okay."

"Obviously, he's traumatized," said Lea. "I've photographed victims of trauma all over the world and I know it when I see it. We need to get him back to the house. Immediately."

Mercy looked up at Harrington. "Well, it's obvious he's not going to talk to you. Or his father. At least not right now."

"They're right, Harrington," said Feinberg, the one person there who could influence the man. Mercy had seen the billionaire wield that influence before, and she was grateful to him for it. "Maybe you'll have better luck when the boy has calmed down," he said.

"Fine." Harrington glared at Troy and Mercy. "The kid won't leave your dogs, so take him and the dogs back to Nemeton. Ethan Jenkins stays here. Along with everyone else. Until I say we're finished." He dismissed them with a curt nod.

"We'll take good care of him, Ethan." Mercy rose to her feet as Troy once again gathered the boy into his arms.

"Thank you." Ethan ruffled his son's fine hair. Henry did not respond. Just stared up through the yellow maples to the blue sky.

Elvis and Susie Bear led the way back to the estate while Troy followed, carrying the boy. As she rushed to join them, she glanced behind at a forlorn Ethan.

He raised his arm in farewell.

AS ALWAYS MERCY was struck by the sheer size of Feinberg's estate. Nemeton was a massive thirty-thousand-square-foot mountain lodge built out of native stone and lumber about halfway between Northshire and Stratton—and a good forty-five-minute walk through the forest from the crime scene.

Troy had led them out of the woods and down an ATV trail to the perimeter of the main grounds, where a broad expanse of lawn began. At the edge of that lawn sat the enormous house, as elegant as it was big, built to capitalize on the spectacular vista of the forest, the valley, and the mountains beyond. Water surrounded the estate on three sides, flowing from swimming hole to fishing pond to twin waterfalls cascading over granite boulders and feeding a rich landscape of ferns and flowers and trees and carefully manicured topiary, dressed now in the brilliant colors of autumn.

The reds and golds and yellows shimmered in reflections on the water in the bright October sunshine. It was chilly, but beautiful.

"Let's go to the side entrance," said Troy.

"Sure." Mercy knew that's where the kitchen was. Troy would want to talk to the staff, particularly the housekeeper, before Harrington showed up and started throwing his weight around.

They skirted the lodge, passing the wooden bridge that separated the fishing pond from the swimming hole and led to the lodge's three-car garage. Gunnar's quarters were above the garage. At the moment, there was no sign of the groundskeeper.

At the service entrance, Troy buzzed the intercom, equipped with a video camera. This was an update from the keypad system in place when Mercy had been here last, tighter security in the wake of a burglary attempt. Billionaires had a lot to secure, and this one was taking no chances.

"Game warden," Troy told the video camera, "delivering a lost boy."

They were buzzed in right away. They walked through a mud-room lined with a wall of padlocked employee lockers, to another door, which opened as they approached.

"Come in, come in." The housekeeper, Mrs. Espinosa, ushered them in with a chorus of what Mercy believed were *Hail Mary*s in Spanish. Martinez would sometimes whisper the prayer, too, under his breath when the going got tough in Afghanistan.

She blinked back tears. Funny how grief waxed and waned. It faded away until you thought you were safe and then a random word, sound, gesture brought you right back to the brink again.

"Are you all right?" Troy looked at her with those warm brown eyes.

"Fine."

"Don't tell the butler I let you in this door." Mrs. Espinosa was a short, friendly, curly-haired widow with the unflappable air of a woman who'd raised five kids on her own and now enjoyed the relatively leisurely occupation of running a billionaire's house. She reminded Mercy of a poodle—a smart and energetic protector who did not suffer fools gladly. "Guests come to the front door."

"We aren't guests," said Troy.

"Butler?" This was news to Mercy, who didn't think of Feinberg as the butler type. But then what did she know about the hopes and dreams of the very rich?

"*Si, Señor* George Wilcox, very British, very proper." Mrs. Espinosa wrinkled her nose.

"I see."

"Master Henry, we were so worried about you." The housekeeper hugged the drowsy boy. More *Hail Mary*s. "We didn't realize he was missing. We thought he was hiding again."

"Again?"

"Yesterday we found him in Mr. Feinberg's map room. I think he likes maps."

Mercy had never been in the map room, but if Henry liked it, she bet she would, too.

But first things first. "We need to get Henry into warm clothes right away," she said. "He'll need something to eat and drink, too."

"Of course. And maybe a sandwich? Some hot chocolate?"

"That would be great."

"Follow me." Mrs. Espinosa gave each dog a pat before bustling through the kitchen and through the massive dining room, leading them all up a spectacular stone and wood staircase to the second-floor landing, a space flooded with light from floor-to-ceiling windows and a breathtaking view of the mountains. The housekeeper turned down a wide hallway displaying eighteenth- and nineteenth-century American art, formal portraits of serious-minded men and women, grand landscapes of the American West and dark New England seascapes of determined fishermen in turbulent waters.

On each of the handsome walnut doors to the guest rooms hung gold frames with large calling cards listing the name of the visitor staying in those quarters. Mr. and Mrs. Montgomery commanded what Mercy imagined was the grandest of these rooms. They passed others marked as *Mr. and Mrs. Farrow, Ms. Lea Sanders, Mr. William Montgomery, Mr. Ethan Jenkins,* and *Miss Alice de Clare.*

Mrs. Espinosa opened the last door on the right, the one labeled *Master Henry.*

Henry was fully awake now, and he wiggled out of Troy's arms, rubbing his eyes. Elvis and Susie Bear immediately flanked him, and he put his arms around their necks.

Troy ruffled the boy's stick-straight brown hair. "We need to get you cleaned up a bit, buddy. Starting with those knees."

"Clean clothes should be in the bureau." The housekeeper pointed to a fine antique highboy next to the sleek modern metal king-size four-poster bed. "And there's an en suite bath on the left of the fireplace. Do you need any assistance?"

Henry shook his head hard.

Troy laughed. "I guess that's a no."

"I'll leave you to it, then." Mrs. Espinosa smiled at Henry. "I'll prepare something special for you, *pobre niño.*"

"Peanut butter," announced Henry, surprising them all.

"Peanut butter it is," said Mrs. Espinosa.

After the housekeeper left, Mercy looked at Henry. "I guess you're kicking me out, too?"

The boy stared down at the polished wide-planked floors.

"I suppose Elvis and Susie Bear get to stay." She looked at the dogs, who'd been shadowing the boy all the way from the woods.

Henry smiled.

"Just us guys," said Troy. "And the Newfie."

"Okay, see you downstairs." Mercy shut the door behind her. But instead of heading down the hallway to the stairs, she pulled out her cell and texted her grandmother, asking her to contact Lillian Jenkins.

"May I help you?" A well-built man of medium height stood outside one of the guest rooms on the opposite side of the hallway closer to the staircase. He approached with an air of quiet authority.

She slipped her cell back into her pocket, and met the butler halfway, hand outstretched. "Mercy Carr."

"I know who you are." He shook her hand. "I'm George, the butler."

He wore a smartly pressed, perfectly tailored navy suit (the kind her attorney father always wore to court) and spoke in a perfect British accent (only slightly less plummy than the Queen's). He had a full head of light brown hair and a matching, neatly trimmed full beard and mustache. His posture was impeccable, his manner polite, his smile welcoming.

"Nice to meet you." She'd never before met a butler up close and personal, but George looked just like how she imagined a butler should look, from the white silk handkerchief in his breast pocket to the gold signet ring he wore on the little finger of his left hand.

"Mr. Feinberg speaks highly of you."

"I was just looking for the restroom."

"This way."

"How long have you been here?"

"Only a fortnight. Two weeks."

"Not very long."

"Long enough to know that I will be quite content here. Nemeton is a lovely estate and Mr. Feinberg is a gentleman."

She wondered how many billionaires you could say that about. She often mistrusted the very wealthy as a matter of principle, but she'd found Feinberg to be a good guy. She was happy to have him as a neighbor, and proud to call him a friend. But she did wonder how her name could have possibly come up in conversation in just fourteen days.

"If you follow me downstairs, I'll show you to the ladies' room."

"Isn't there anything up here? I want to stay close to Henry."

"Of course." He gave her a knowing look and directed her to a guest room without a calling card, two doors down from Henry's room.

"Madame," he said, opening the door for her.

"Mercy, please."

"Mercy." He spoke her given name as if it were unfamiliar to his tongue. "Now, if that will be all . . ."

"I'm good. Thank you."

George gave a slight bow and disappeared down the hallway. She waited inside the door until the butler had retreated and descended the staircase before she slipped back across the hall and into Alice de Clare's room.

She found herself in one of the most elegantly feminine rooms she'd ever seen. A wall of floor-to-ceiling windows framed another glorious view of Vermont in autumn. A massive pink marble fireplace dominated one wall; across from it sat an elaborately carved Art Nouveau bed of walnut, whose floral filigree headboard was backed with pink velvet. Prints—oops, knowing Feinberg they could be originals—brightened the pale cream-and-gold papered walls. Mercy stepped closer, recognizing the art as a Virginia Frances Sterrett illustration from one of her most beloved books as a child, *Old French Fairy Tales* by the Comtesse de Ségur. She'd devoured every book of fairy tales she could find, but this one—a gift from her mother on her eighth birthday—remained her favorite. The magical stories of fairies and genies and princesses fascinated Mercy, and Sterrett's fanciful illustrations fueled that fascination.

As a child she would get lost in the fantastical forests and flora and fauna of the Comtesse's and Sterrett's imaginations. As she stared at them now, she was tempted to get lost there again.

But she wasn't eight years old anymore. Since Afghanistan she'd felt so old, older than her twenty-nine years and older even than these timeless stories of love and hate and good and evil. She had her own stories of love and hate and good and evil now. And no fairy tale could fix that.

Mercy turned her attention away from the enchanted paintings that had illuminated her childhood and began a quick search of the room. She heard the door squeak and stopped cold.

"What are you doing in here?" Troy poked his head into the dead woman's room, grinning at her. "Snooping?"

Caught.

"Maybe," she said.

Stepping in, he shut the door behind him.

"Where's Henry?"

"Right behind me. The dogs, too." He pulled another pair of plastic gloves from his duty belt and handed them to her. "Easy. This is my last pair. If I'd known I'd be spending the day with you, I would have brought along more."

"Very funny."

"At least be careful."

As she slipped on the gloves, she felt the weight of his brown eyes on her. They were warm but also all-seeing and all-knowing.

"Make it quick." He backed out the door again. "I'll go head off Henry."

She heard the door close behind the game warden as she headed for the expensive Louis Vuitton luggage on the walnut rack in the corner. In true butler fashion, Alice de Clare's belongings had been unpacked for her. Since she was French, she probably didn't mind. Mercy always unpacked her own duffle; she wondered what George the butler would think of that.

A week's worth of designer blouses, slacks, and skirts hung neatly in the walk-in closet, along with a black leather trench coat; two pairs of heels, two pairs of flats, and a pair of riding boots lined the floor beneath them.

In the antique bombe dresser next to the bed she found drawers filled with extravagant French lingerie and expensive jewelry. Thanks to her own uber-chic mother, Mercy recognized the best in clothing and accessories when she saw it—even if she herself lived in yoga clothes, cargo pants, and T-shirts. A small dressing table in the closet held an empty black satin evening clutch and a glamorous litter of toiletries—bottles and brushes and pots and perfumes, all Chanel. Nothing personal. Nothing of interest.

She moved onto the sleek kidney-shaped desk. On the cream-and-gold leather desk blotter lay a burgundy suede portfolio embossed with a silver rose, a matching daybook, and a black-and-platinum Mont Blanc pen.

The portfolio held designs for the remodel of the Bluffing Bear Inn, which if carried out to the letter would transform the campy ski lodge into a swank twenty-first-century version of itself. With Alice gone, Mercy didn't know if that transformation would still happen, but if an overhaul was inevitable, she hoped they used these plans.

She looked to the daybook, which might hold more promise. As she'd seen no cell phone or purse near the victim, this daybook could be the only clue to the dead woman's recent activities. Mercy flipped through it. Appointments, initials, doodles. The usual. Still, she felt like she was getting somewhere.

She retrieved her cell from the front pocket of her yoga pants. There was a text from her grandmother Patience, telling her Lillian was up in Burlington running a book fair, but that she would come home as soon as she could.

Mercy confirmed receipt of the text, then began snapping photos of pages from the daybook, starting with today's date and working backward through the calendar. She'd gone back about a month when Troy stuck his head back in the room. "Ready or not, here we come."

Henry pushed his way through the door, heading straight for her, the dogs on his heels. She tucked her cell back in her pocket and deposited the daybook back on the blotter, moving in front of the desk so Henry couldn't see it. He was out of his pajamas and slippers and was dressed in jeans, striped socks and sneakers, and a black sweatshirt emblazoned with a knockoff of the bright orange-and-pink Dunkin' Donuts logo that read *Dungeons & Dragons*.

She frowned at Troy. "Hi, Henry."

"It's okay. Henry isn't a tattletale." He punched the boy gently on the shoulder. "You can keep a secret, can't you?"

Henry wasn't listening. He was staring at the illustration behind her, which featured a boy in a red Robin Hood–style suit greeting an old monk in a black cloak holding a blue-and-gold book. They were up in the mountains, on a pass filled with big boulders, long vines, and tall flowers.

"Funny you should like that one," said Mercy, grateful for the opportunity to distract the child from any evidence of her snooping. "That's Good Little Henry. He's on a quest to find the magical plant that will save his sick mother. Do you know the story?"

Henry shook his head.

"Tell him the story later," said Troy. "Henry has something to show you."

"What's that?" She smiled to encourage the boy.

"Go on, show her."

Henry stuck his fingers in his pocket and pulled out a beautifully barred gray-and-white crumpled feather. He held it in his open hand and stretched his arm out toward her.

"May I?"

He nodded.

She plucked it from the boy's palm, straightened it as best she could, and held it up to the light streaming in from the large windows. "It's lovely. Where did you get it?"

He ignored the question, simply reached out for the feather. She gave it back to him, and he stuffed it back into his jeans pocket, turning his attention to Elvis and Susie Bear. The feather forgotten.

"It looks like a peregrine feather," said Troy. "I found it stuck in the waistband of his pajamas."

"I thought peregrine falcons were endangered."

"They were nearly wiped out by DDT. But since then we've been working with falconers to reintroduce them in the wild. It's been slow going, but it's working. Slowly. They're listed as a threatened species now."

"So Henry just found it in the woods?"

"I don't know. It's possible; they do molt. But there still aren't that many of them here. And they've got their own predators to worry about. Eagles, great horned owls, bears, foxes."

"Poachers."

"They sell the eggs and the feathers. But the biggest money is in live birds. Falcon racing is huge in the Middle East, and they'll pay big bucks for peregrines."

They heard a muffled noise outside down the hall.

"We better get out of here before Harrington shows up."

Henry started chanting again, and the dogs settled against him. Ballast for an anxious child.

"It's okay," she said. "You don't have to see him."

Henry stopped chanting as quickly as he had begun.

Mercy leaned over and whispered in the boy's ear. "We don't like him much, either."

She could have sworn the boy smiled.

DOWNSTAIRS, MRS. ESPINOSA had set out pitchers of cold milk and platters full of peanut-butter treats: peanut butter–and-jelly sandwiches cut into quarters, peanut-butter granola bars, peanut butter smeared on apple slices and celery, even peanut-butter cookies.

"I see you like peanut butter almost as much as I do." Mercy pulled out a chair beside Henry, who sat quietly at the long oak table with Elvis on one side and Susie Bear on the other. "And as much as your furry friends there."

Henry carefully arranged a plate with a peanut butter–and-jelly sandwich quarter, one celery stick, and a peanut-butter cookie. He ate around the crust of the sandwich, dividing the leftover crust between the dogs.

Mrs. Espinosa stood over the boy like the food police. "You can do better than that."

Henry slipped one celery stick into each hand and let each dog lap it up.

Mrs. Espinosa shook her head. "Boys need to eat."

Troy shrugged. "I never liked celery much myself."

"He didn't eat a bit of his breakfast," said Mrs. Espinosa, watching as Henry chomped down the cookie in two bites and washed it down with half a glass of milk. "That's much better."

Elvis stiffened into his alert position and barked once, loudly. Susie Bear shambled to her feet. Both dogs held their noses high in the air, in the direction of Nemeton's grand entrance.

"Harrington," said Mercy. Of course, the self-important detective would use the front door. She was sure he'd have a butler himself if he could afford George.

Henry stood up. "Nana."

"Nana?" asked Mrs. Espinosa.

He repeated the word. *Nana* became a chant, the incantation continuing as surely and precisely as a metronome.

"Let's go." Mercy put her arm around the chanting Henry and headed for the side door.

Harrington appeared in the doorway. "Where do you think you're going?" he bellowed behind her.

"We're taking Henry to see his grandmother." She used her army MP voice, the one that said *I'd rather die than retreat, and if it comes to that you're going down with me.*

She didn't turn around as the detective shouted after them to stop.

CHAPTER SEVEN

Ranger: warrior of the wilderness, reads the trees and speaks to the animals, protects the forest and all its creatures.

—HENRY'S GAME

GUNNAR GAVE THEM ALL A RIDE TO TROY'S TRUCK, and they piled in for the trip to Mercy's cabin, where Henry could hang out until his Nana Lillian could pick him up. Patience was still there, along with Amy and Brodie and the baby.

"We were beginning to worry about you." Patience raised an eyebrow at Mercy as she ushered the boy into the great room, along with Troy and the dogs.

"Long story."

"I bet." She looked up from the KitchenAid stand mixer, where she was spooning in boiled potatoes. "I figured sooner or later you'd all need to eat." Patience believed in feeding a crisis, like feeding a cold.

"This is Henry." Mercy waved a hand at her grandmother at the island separating the kitchen from the living area. Amy and Brodie lounged on the couch in front of the flagstone fireplace, and Helena played with blocks on the floor by a brightly colored cloth tunnel that ran along the pine-paneled wall on the other side of the room, the kitty Muse batting at the blocks as the baby tried to stack them up.

"Henry, this is my family. Extended." She looked over at Brodie, who dozed with Amy on her long butter-colored leather sofa, nested in the quilts she'd bought when she'd moved in here with Elvis. A maroon one for her, a teal one for the shepherd. That was then, this was now.

A mumble of sleepy hellos hailed from the sofa, accompanied by a cheerful greeting from Patience.

"Henry, we've met. I'm your grandmother's friend. You remember, we played with puppies at my office when she brought in her cat Bangor for a checkup."

Henry smiled, not at Patience, really, but seemingly more at the memory of the puppies.

"I hope you like cake."

The boy's small absent smile brightened into a beam at the word *cake*.

Mercy had never met anyone who didn't like her grandmother's desserts—or anything else she made. "He really hasn't had much to eat at all today. Peanut butter, mostly. Apparently, he's a picky eater."

"Huh." Patience wiped her hands on the Vermont moose apron she wore tied around her waist over her usual white vet's uniform jacket.

Mercy smiled. She knew that her grandmother did not believe in picky eaters, only inadequate cooks. She'd see feeding Henry as a challenge.

Elvis's dark-tipped tail wagged, and Susie Bear's feathery tail swished wildly at the sight of their beloved veterinarian. Patience scratched between the shepherd's elegant ears and patted the Newfie mutt's pumpkin head.

"Yankee pot roast in the oven," she said, as much for the dogs' benefit as theirs. Their tails wagged harder.

"Smells great." Troy was no more immune to Patience's pot roast than anyone else.

Patience squeezed Henry's shoulder as she lifted her cheek for Troy to peck. "Ready shortly." She gave Mercy one of her *This man could be yours for the taking* looks before whispering, "What's going on?"

Henry stayed close to Susie Bear as Elvis trotted over to Helena and the tunnel. Susie Bear whined.

"Susie Bear wants to play, too," Mercy told Henry. "Why don't you go on over?"

Henry held back. Helena clapped her hands, and Elvis sat at her feet, nudging her tiny toes with his cold nose. The baby squealed. Susie Bear clamored over to join the fun, and Henry followed. Muse darted away from the chaos and out of the room.

Amy untangled herself from Brodie and pulled herself up from the couch. She hustled over to the baby and the dogs. "Go ahead, Helena. Into the tunnel."

The baby crawled over to the north end of the fabric tube, disappearing inside. Elvis moved to the south end and sat back on his haunches, waiting for the infant to make her way through the tunnel to him. Susie Bear lumbered over to the opening as well. Helena's peanut gallery.

Amy pointed to the dogs. "They're playing hide-and-seek with the baby."

"You can play, too," said Mercy, joining them as Troy took Patience aside out of earshot to bring her up to date regarding the day's goings-on in the woods.

Henry looked away from the dogs and the baby as if he were not the least bit interested. He showed more interest in Brodie, who ambled over and slipped his arm around Amy.

The boy pointed to Brodie's D&D T-shirt, emblazoned with sword and the words *Let's Quest!*

"I think he likes my shirt." Brodie grinned. "That's cool."

"I don't get it," said Mercy.

"It's from *HarmonQuest*," said Brodie, as if that explained all.

Amy laughed. "It's a show on streaming about a group of gamers."

"But, dude, you're really not old enough to watch it."

Henry frowned.

"Maybe he's mature for his age." Amy punched Brodie in the shoulder. "Not like you ever watched anything you weren't supposed to when you were a kid."

Brodie ignored that, his hazel eyes on Henry. "I like your shirt, too, man."

Henry was still wearing the black sweatshirt with the orange-and-pink knockoff Dunkin' Donuts logo that read *Dungeons & Dragons*.

Brodie held up his hand to high-five Henry, but the boy did not respond. "Whatever."

Henry's attention shifted to Elvis, who dropped into his Sphinx pose. Helena emerged at the end of the tunnel, giggling when she saw Elvis. She reached out for him, and he licked her fingers.

"Your turn, Henry." Mercy opened her arms wide. "Only you've got the whole house to hide in." She pointed to the far side of the room, to the left of the fireplace, where a hallway led to the bed-rooms and the bathroom.

"Go on." Amy swooped down and picked up the baby. "Elvis will find you."

"Stay," Mercy told Elvis, and then turned to Henry. "We'll count to fifty, and then send Elvis to look for you."

Henry looked up at the ceiling. He stared at the thick hand-hewn beams that ran across the high ceilings for what seemed like a long time. Just when Mercy felt sure he was too timid or disinterested to play the game, he shuffled off to the rear of the house. Out of sight.

Mercy counted loudly but slowly, giving Troy time to discuss the day's events with Amy and Brodie. They gathered around the dining-room table, which sat between the island and the couch.

"Wow." Amy rocked the baby in her arms as she listened to Troy's story. Brodie pulled out a chair for her, and together they sat in a huddle with the baby.

"Epic," said Brodie.

"Poor Daniel," said Amy.

"Poor Henry," Patience corrected. "What did he see?"

"We don't know," said Mercy quietly in between counting loudly, "Twenty-eight, twenty-nine, thirty . . ."

"He hasn't said very much," said Troy.

"How come?" said Brodie.

"Man of few words," said Troy with an exaggerated patience Mercy knew was for her benefit. He knew she was doing everything she could not to roll her eyes every time the Dungeon Master spoke. Both Troy and Patience insisted that there was more to Brodie than

Mercy gave him credit for. For Amy's sake, she hoped they were right.

"Henry's scared," said Patience.

"This is the first time he's let Susie Bear out of his sight all day," said Mercy. She was running out of numbers. *Thirty-six, thirty-seven, thirty-eight . . .*

"He should see a doctor."

"I'm sure Lillian will see to that. She should be here in a couple of hours."

"We'll just keep him here until she gets here," added Mercy. "Feed him, keep him occupied."

"Well, it's obvious he feels safe with you two and the dogs," said Patience.

"Who wouldn't?" Amy bounced the baby on her knee.

"Indeed."

Mercy raised her voice again. "Forty-eight, forty-nine, fifty. Ready or not, here comes Elvis."

She looked down at the Belgian shepherd, who waited patiently for his orders, Susie Bear at his side. "Search. Go find Henry."

Off he sniffed down the hallway, the big black dog clambering to catch up to him.

Mercy and Troy followed at a discreet distance, not to ruin Henry's fun—or theirs.

"What do little boys smell like?"

Troy grinned. "Snips and snails and puppy-dog tails?"

She shook her head. "More like dirt and pine needles and peanut butter."

The dogs passed right by the yellow guest room with its twin white iron beds, which Amy and Helena now claimed, the small workout room where Mercy kept her yoga mat and her heavy bag, and the blue master bedroom with her great-grandmother's cherry four-poster bed, the one she never slept in, preferring to crash on the couch with Elvis.

At the end of the long hallway, Elvis pushed his way into the bathroom. There was only one bathroom, and Mercy had made the most of it. She transformed it into a spa-like space, splurging on a deep soaking tub with whirlpool jets. Her only real extravagance, apart from the floor-to-ceiling bookshelves in the great room. She loved a good long soak with a good long book—nothing had soothed her sore muscles or her bruised soul more in the lonely months after coming home from the war. Before she'd tracked down Elvis and brought him home, as she'd promised Martinez she would do.

A sea-blue shower curtain—the same pearlized color as the custom tile surround—hung across the edge of the tub. Mercy usually kept it gathered and pulled to one side, the better to display that custom tile work, and to slip unimpeded into a bath full of bubbles. Stretched open like this, you could read the pearlized writing that graced the curtain. Shakespeare quotes.

"Of course," Troy whispered. *"To thine own self be true."*

She put a finger to her lips. Elvis dropped into his alert position at one end of the tub, and Susie Bear settled into a sit at the other end. Each nudged the shower curtain with a nose, pointing to the great find inside the bath.

Henry barked his funny little laugh, the one that was beginning to win her over with its sincere if poignant brevity. She smiled at Troy, who smiled back. He understood this lonely little boy.

"I think it's safe to say you've been found," she said to the boy behind the curtain.

Henry laughed again—another quick yip.

At her cue, Troy tugged open the curtain and Henry stepped out of the tub. The dogs broke their alert positions and proceeded to embrace the boy. Henry sank to the floor, scratching Elvis's sweet spot between his ears and allowing Susie Bear to lick his face.

"Well done," she said.

"Dinnertime," called Patience from the kitchen.

"We'd better go."

Elvis tickled Henry's chin with his muzzle. Susie Bear thumped her tail against the sea-blue tile floor.

"*Dinner* is one of their favorite words," Mercy told Henry. "You'd better not keep them waiting."

Henry buried his face in Susie Bear's furry neck, then tucked his hand around the collar. The Newfie mutt rose to her feet, pulling the boy with her. Elvis sprinted forward, swiveling around to face them as if to say, *Follow the leader.*

Troy held open the door for them, and off they went, single file— Elvis, Henry, and Susie Bear—parading down the hallway and back to the great room.

Amy was setting the long antique oak dining table, which separated the living area from the island in the open-style kitchen, while Brodie secured Helena into her high chair.

"Love your pot roast," said Troy.

"There's not a man alive who doesn't love my grandmother's cooking," Mercy told Henry as she pointed to a Shaker ladder-back chair. "I don't imagine you'll be any different. Take a seat."

They gathered around the table as Amy helped Patience bring out the food: platters of pot roast and roasted carrots and turnips, bowls of butternut squash and mashed potatoes and biscuits, and boats full of gravy, the better to smother your supper in. As they passed around the dishes, Mercy noticed Henry eyeing every single one with an almost scientific skepticism before precisely doling out a small portion of each offering onto his plate, careful not to let any touch the other. She watched—by now, everyone was watching—as the boy smoothed his mashed potatoes into a perfect oval crater for a perfect lake of gravy.

"Awesome," said Brodie, admiring his handiwork.

Mercy wondered how Henry would manage to eat it without some of the gravy running into the other foods on his plate.

Amy laughed as she spooned squash into her little daughter's mouth. "I can't wait until Helena eats that nicely." The baby's chubby fingers were sticky with mashed potatoes and the corners of her mouth splotched with gravy.

"For a kid who gets so dirty in the woods," said Troy, "you are a remarkably neat eater."

Henry said nothing, focusing on the food before him. He ate the mashed potatoes and gravy without going outside the oval—a balancing act that impressed Mercy.

"A single-minded young man." Patience smiled. "You'll go far, Henry, mark my words."

Amy chatted about the baby and school and the annual wild-game supper, the social highlight of the autumn hunting season. Brodie tried to engage Henry in a conversation about their mutual interest in role-playing games. Mercy kept her eye on the boy, hoping the exchange might loosen him up.

But Henry never said a word. Brodie gave up, but Mercy was still hoping to get Henry talking. "Brodie, how's the game going?"

"What game?" asked Troy.

"Dungeons & Dragons," explained Brodie, as if talking to a child. "I'm the Dungeon Master."

"Brodie's created this really cool campaign." Amy beamed as she tried to coax Helena into eating some mashed turnip.

"You like D&D, too?" asked Troy.

"Dude, girls can play, too," said Brodie.

"And play well, I'm sure." Mercy grinned at Troy, enjoying his discomfort.

"I didn't mean to imply . . . I just didn't know Amy was into it."

"I'm into it, but not like Brodie. It takes a lot of time to do what he's doing. Create a whole story line, with orcs and elves and wizards and all kinds of creatures and characters and environments. You should see his vision board."

"Ranger," said Henry, pointing at Troy.

Everyone turned to stare at the boy.

"You can talk," said Brodie.

"He can talk perfectly well," said Mercy. "But he only speaks when he has something to say."

"Cool."

"That's the second time he's called Troy *Ranger* today," Mercy told Patience.

"You're right," said Troy to Henry. "Game wardens are like Rangers."

"What do you know about it?" asked Brodie.

"When I was a kid, my older brother and his friends used to play D&D all the time. I begged and begged before they'd even let me watch. And they only did it then because my mom made them." Troy laughed.

"Did they ever let you play?" asked Amy.

"At first, they only let me sub when one of the guys couldn't make it. But eventually I became a one of their D&D gang."

"Voted in by the nerd council." Mercy smiled at the thought of a young Troy playing medieval make-believe.

"Exactly."

"But you didn't keep it up." Brodie gave him a look of disapproval.

"No. Turned out I liked the real woods better than the pretend woods."

Amy waved her fork in the direction of Susie Bear. "And a real animal companion better than, like, a pretend one?"

"Absolutely."

Brodie considered this. "I get that."

"Bear." Henry spoke again, and again everyone turned their attention back to the boy. He ignored them and went back to sculpting his mashed potatoes, bite by bite. Mercy watched Henry as she finished her grandmother's wonderful pot roast, hardly listening as Brodie jabbered on about the campaign for his game.

"I'm going to give the baby a bath." Amy scraped her chair away from the table. Helena banged her spoon on the tray of her high chair, a clear sign she'd had her fill and was ready to move on to life's next adventure.

"Troy and I will clean up," Mercy told Patience.

"That you will." That was the rule in her grandmother's kitchen: You either cook or clean up. You don't do both.

"Meanwhile," Mercy said to Brodie, "maybe you could show Henry your vision board. I think he'd like that."

"Sure. It's in my car. I'll go get it." Brodie loped off toward the front door.

Mercy steered Henry to the couch, where Elvis and Susie Bear were stretched out, snoring, having sated themselves on their usual dinner of high-grade dog food—topped with Patience's homemade gravy. There was just enough room for Henry to squeeze in the middle, sitting between the two dogs.

Brodie returned with his D&D props and plopped onto the otto-man on the other side of the coffee table. He opened up the vision board—a trifold made up of three eighteen-inch panels, each illus-trated by hand with D&D characters, weapons, tools, and more—and laid it on the coffee table. He also carried a roll of laminated paper, which he unfurled below the vision board, revealing a detailed map of an island land called Annwn. It looked a lot like a map of Britain.

"This is Glastonbury." Brodie pointed to the mountain that domi-nated the map. Brodie leaned toward Henry. "It's where they say the real King Arthur was buried. You know, the Holy Grail."

"Ley line," said Henry.

"That's right. You're a smart kid."

"Of course, he's a smart kid," said Mercy. "Now enlighten the rest of us."

Brodie waited for Henry to explain, but the boy said nothing.

"No worries, bro. I can do it." Brodie punched his finger at Glastonbury on the map. "A ley line is a line of electromagnetic en-ergy that connects sacred sites." He ran his finger east from the tip of Cornwall on the western edge of the island through Glastonbury to the Norfolk coast on the other side of the island. "This is the English ley line, which connects lots of ruins of churches and shrines dedi-cated to Saint Michael and Saint George."

"Monster slayers," said Henry.

"I was getting to that," said Brodie. "Like the kid says, Saint Michael and Saint George were dragon slayers. Their ruins are, like, totally mystical and powerful places."

"Got it." Mercy waited for Henry to say something more, but he did not. He ignored her, huddling over the board and the map with Brodie. She retreated to the kitchen as Brodie launched into a long and complicated explanation of his campaign. She only caught bits and pieces of the one-sided conversation as she and Troy began the washing up.

"You've got this covered." Patience handed her a couple of aprons. "I'll go help Amy with Helena's bath."

Her grandmother excused herself and was gone in a flash in an all-too-obvious ploy to leave Mercy alone with Troy. As if she were supposed to seduce the game warden right there at the farm sink while the boys talked medieval monsters and mayhem and a teenage mother bathed her infant with the help of a senior citizen. Mercy could feel herself flush at the thought.

She avoided Troy's eyes as she tied the apron festooned with red clover around her waist, holding out the manlier apron—the one with the moose—for Troy.

"I'm good." He took the apron from her and hung it back on the hook on the side of the fridge. "I'll rinse, you load."

"Okay."

"I know how particular people can be about loading a dishwasher."

She grinned. "You mean women."

"I mean my mother. If anyone dares to load her dishwasher, she just waits until she thinks no one's looking and then she reorganizes the whole thing."

"No chores for the menfolk?"

"Oh, no, we had to set the table, clear it, scrape the plates, and stack them up by the sink. Then we'd rinse, and she'd load."

"Sounds like a fine system." Mercy turned on the tap, waiting for the water to warm up. She squirted soap on a sponge and scrubbed the sink. Out of the corner of her eye, she watched Troy scrape and stack the plates neatly on the shiny black quartz counter beside her. Right at her elbow, with military precision.

She loaded the sponge with more soap, handing it to Troy. Stepping over to the side of the dishwasher, she opened the door and pulled out the tray. "Ready when you are."

"Roger that." Troy rolled up the sleeves of his dark-green uniform shirt, exposing muscular forearms and strong wrists, and reached for the sponge. He grabbed the first blue stoneware dish on the top of the stack, scrubbing it and rinsing it.

She found herself staring at the play of the soapy water over his well-formed hands, with their long fingers and wide palms.

He offered her the plate. "This is all Mom let us do."

Mercy smiled, her fingers brushing his as she took the dish and slid it into a proper slot in the dishwasher. She straightened back up, in anticipation of the next plate, but he was already there, ready for her.

They fell into an easy rhythm, punctuated by a constant stream of running water, the lemony smell of the soap, and faint chattering of boys and baby in the background. She was so close to Troy that she could hear the in and out of his breathing, and she found herself breathing along with him while the late afternoon sun set slowly to the west. It lit up the sugar maples as it descended, lending an amber glow to Mercy's small world of cabin, barn, woods.

When the last glass and fork and dish were loaded, she closed the dishwasher door. Troy held up a dish towel, wiping his hands with one end while she dried her own on the other end. She curled her arms behind her to untie the apron.

"May I?" He stepped toward her, reached out, and put his hands around her waist. Gently he turned her halfway round, as if they were executing a slow spin in a slow dance. She felt the weight of his hands on her hips, the quiet touch of his fingers at the small of her back undoing the ties, the whisper of his breath on her neck.

Gently he swung her back round to face him. She felt the corners of her mouth lifting as he looked at her with those warm brown eyes. He lifted the bib string up and over her tangle of red hair.

Pulled the apron away from her.

Folded it deftly into a neat square.

Held it out to her like a gift.

He stood very still. She didn't move either, all the muscles in her body conspiring to anchor her to the spot. She stared at the apron in his hand. Her apron. In his hand.

After a long moment, she stretched her fingers out to touch it. Another part of her brain registered the sound of Elvis barking a warning and Susie Bear bellowing in response and both dogs scrambling from the couch and bounding for the front door, nails clicking on the hardwood floors.

"Someone's here." Mercy smiled. "Best alarm system ever."

Troy fell back, nodding, as a knock at a door proved the Belgian shepherd right.

"I'd better get that." She fled from the scent of lemon and the solid presence of the game warden.

Elvis stood guard as Susie Bear pranced in the entry. Both tails wagged, a sign their visitor was friend not foe.

Mercy opened the door and Captain Floyd Thrasher marched in, every inch the cool military man under fire. He was Troy's boss, and didn't always approve of his subordinate's fraternization with a nosy civilian who involved herself in matters that he believed were better left to law enforcement, even a former soldier like herself. Or maybe *especially* a former soldier like herself.

Thrasher patiently greeted the dogs, his blue-green eyes bright with affection for the four-legged beasts. Of French, English, and African-American ancestry, the captain was easily one of the handsomest men in Northshire, maybe all of Vermont. Those extraordinary good looks coupled with his commanding presence were more than enough to impress practically everyone. Of course, Elvis and Susie Bear judged him by other criteria; Mercy suspected it was his vigorous belly rubs and generous sharing of Pizza Bob's famous meat-laden cheese pies that won over the canines.

Troy joined them in the hallway. "Sir."

"A couple of developments." Thrasher left the dogs to amuse themselves, looking down the hallway. "Where's the boy?"

"In the living room. Looking at Brodie's D&D vision board."

"Good." He turned his full attention to Troy and Mercy. "Harrington has arrested Ethan Jenkins for the murder of Alice de Clare."

"That was fast," said Troy. "Even for Harrington."

"Based on what?" asked Mercy.

"Apparently they found Alice de Clare's purse in Ethan's room. With a Dear John letter inside. She was dumping him."

Mercy exchanged a glance with Troy. She knew they were both thinking the same thing: *If only we'd searched Ethan's room.* Not that they would have removed evidence. But if the purse had been planted, they may have been able to help establish that.

Unless Ethan did kill Alice. Which she refused to believe, at least not yet, if only for Henry's sake.

"Harrington wants the boy back at Nemeton to interview him."

"Henry isn't talking," she said.

"He isn't really a much of a talker even on a good day, and this has been a very bad day for him," said Troy.

"He's traumatized," she said. "He's relatively calm now, but Harrington will upset him again if he tries to interview him. Just like when he tried before."

"The detective wants full statements from you too as well." Thrasher turned to Troy. "He'll have to wait for yours. We got a tip on those night hunters. You'll need to go out on patrol. Delphine will give you the details."

Troy nodded.

Night hunters were poachers who harvested their illegal game after dark. Hunting at night was by definition poaching, since hunting was banned from one half hour after sunset to one half hour before sunrise. Catching poachers at night was difficult and dangerous work. Mercy knew that Troy was in for a long and treacherous night.

Another knock. Lillian Jenkins burst in without waiting for anyone to open the door. Lillian was Henry's grandmother and arguably Northshire's most industrious citizen, a tiny brunette whose enormous energy and big personality more than made up for her diminutive stature. When she wasn't running the Vermonter Drive-In, she was running everything from the Friends of the Library to the historical society. But right now, it looked like all she was running was worry. And there would soon be much more for her to worry about. Mercy dreaded telling her about Ethan.

"Where's Henry?"

"He's in the living room on the couch with Brodie," said Mercy.

"How is he?"

"He seems better now, but it's hard to know," she said. "He's been through a lot. How much we're not quite sure." She told Lillian about the events of the day. Including Ethan's arrest.

"My poor boys."

"Harrington wants to interview Henry back at Nemeton," Thrasher said. "I'm supposed to bring him there."

"Kai Harrington can kiss my ass," said Lillian.

"Understood," said Thrasher. "I often feel that way myself. Like now."

Mercy caught Troy trying to hide a smile, just as she was.

"But it's tricky," said the captain. "Henry may be a material witness to a murder."

"Or not," said Troy.

"Or not," agreed Thrasher.

"Harrington has no right to interrogate a traumatized child," said Patience.

"Patience is right," said Lillian. "You can't make me turn him over."

"I have no intention of making you do anything," said Thrasher. "But if Henry did see something, it's important the Major Crime Unit knows about it."

"Henry might be able to exonerate Ethan," said Mercy.

Thrasher looked at her as if that were wishful thinking.

"My son is no murderer." Lillian glared at the captain. "Harrington has the wrong man."

Mercy nodded. "Then the real murderer is still out there."

"We need to keep the boy safe," said Patience.

"I for one do not trust Kai Harrington to keep my grandson safe." Lillian looked at Mercy. "But I trust you and Troy. And those dogs."

"I'm sure we can come to some kind of arrangement," said Thrasher.

Lillian hurried into the great room, and they followed. Henry was on the couch, squeezed between Elvis and Susie Bear.

The boy looked up from Brodie's map.

"I'm taking you home with me, Henry."

"He really should see a doctor," Patience said.

At the word *doctor*, Henry raised up his hands in surrender and began flapping them.

"What's he doing?" Brodie stared at the boy. "Chill, dude."

"He's stimming." Lillian sighed. "Self-stimulatory behavior. It's what he does when he gets upset. The mere mention of doctors and hospitals sets him off."

Lillian moved in to comfort the boy, but Elvis and Susie Bear beat her to it. They snuggled closer to him, nuzzling under his arms, using their noses to slow the flapping of his hands. Slowly the stimming subsided. Henry tucked his fingers around their necks and buried his face in their fur. Mercy heard his muffled voice, chanting prime numbers to the dogs.

"I know a psychiatrist who works with traumatized kids." Patience gave Lillian's shoulder a squeeze. "Why don't I contact him and ask him to make a house call?"

"Would he do that?"

"He owes me a favor."

"Let me guess," said Mercy. "You saved his dog."

"Lovely Great Dane named Duke." Patience smiled. "Terrible twisted stomach. All good now."

"I don't think Henry's going anywhere without those dogs," said Lillian.

"How about this?" Mercy counted off the points of her plan on her fingers. "Elvis and I will escort Henry home with Lillian. We can even stay the night, if you want."

Lillian nodded. "Of course."

"Patience will call her shrink friend and have him meet us there.

That way, Henry is safe and gets the help he needs, and Troy and Susie Bear can go after those night hunters."

"What about Ethan?"

"I'll talk to Daniel," said Mercy. "Ask him to do whatever he can for Ethan, if he hasn't already. He has more pull than we do."

"And Harrington?" asked Patience.

"I'll deal with him." Thrasher shrugged as it were no big deal. Maybe it wasn't: He was a decorated Marine who could eat guys like Harrington for breakfast. "But I don't know how long I can stall him. Sooner or later he'll insist on talking to the boy. And to Mercy and Troy."

CHAPTER EIGHT

For each count of taking deer in closed season, offenders face up to $4,000 in fines and restitution and/or 60 days in jail.
—VERMONT FISH AND WILDLIFE REGULATIONS

TROY HATED POACHERS. The laws governing hunting and fishing were designed to allow good citizens to reap the harvest of the wilderness while ensuring the beauty and bounty of the land for generations to come. The majority observed the regulations in place, but the minority who did not were Troy's prime preoccupations. The hunters baiting deer with apples. The trappers stealing raptor eggs. The poachers selling bear gallbladders on the black market to the Chinese. These were the people who violated the sanctity of this sacred space. His sacred space.

These were the people Troy was determined to stop.

Night hunters were armed and aggressive, reckless at best and psychopathic at worst. Finding them in nearly four and a half million acres of forest wasn't easy. Hard enough to apprehend poachers by daylight, but wicked difficult by dark.

Troy had two significant advantages: Susie Bear and night goggles.

The anonymous tip Delphine passed along steered Troy and Susie Bear north to an isolated section of Feinberg's property, where it flanked the Green Mountain National Forest. Park Ranger Gil Guerrette had also reported seeing flashing lights in this part of the park the night before. But by the time he got there, the lights—and light bearers—were gone.

Troy thought they might be his night hunters of the anonymous tip. He and Susie Bear met Gil at the ranger station. In Vermont, jurisdiction—local, state, federal—often overlapped. Those charged with protecting and policing the state from border to border—rangers, game wardens, municipal cops, county sheriffs, staties—were spread pretty thin on the ground. Collaboration trumped interjurisdictional squabbles, at least when Harrington wasn't around.

As Gil had told Troy when they first met a couple of years ago, "I don't care who saves my ass—even if it's you."

Troy laughed, but in time he learned that when Gil Guerrette had your back, it was backup worthy of the name. Gil was a wiry, tough mountaineer from New Hampshire who'd climbed peaks all over the world. In between expeditions he'd lived alone in a small cabin in the woods, off the grid and out of touch. Even though now he was a married man with a mortgage, he still fancied himself a sort of modern-day Thoreau, and often quoted him, like Mercy quoted Shakespeare.

Gil had the best of both worlds: family time with his wife, Françoise, and their three lively little girls and alone time in the woods hiking and philosophizing and communing with nature.

It was the life that Troy had envisioned when he married Madeline. Although looking back, he couldn't imagine why he ever thought she'd be happy living such a life, with or without him. He'd about given up on the whole idea . . . until Mercy.

He and Susie Bear followed Gil through the deepening gloom of the woods. Both he and Gil wore night goggles, and the Newfie wore a lighted collar, so they could still track her should they need to remove the goggles.

Night hunters used bright lights to blind their prey. A classic deer-in-the-headlights cheat that startled deer into a temporary paralysis, immobilizing them long enough for night hunters to shoot and kill them. This was illegal, and to Troy's mind, immoral.

Going after night hunters was always dangerous, but especially on nights like this, when a new moon darkened the sky and low clouds obscured the stars. The blackness was nearly complete. Giving the night hunters nearly complete cover.

Troy and Gil hiked on, the glow of their goggles streaking the darkness with faint streams of light. The woods were quiet at night. But not thoroughly silent.

Troy loved the sound of the forest after dark: the high-pitched yipping of the foxes, the chirps and clicks of the bats, the screeching of the owls. And the bleats of does and the grunts of bucks.

Deer were crepuscular creatures who preferred to browse for food mostly at dawn and at dusk. Vermont law forbade hunting of most game between half an hour after sunset and half an hour before sunrise. Night hunters used the cover of darkness to poach their prey when all law-abiding outdoorsmen were at home in bed.

"A couple of five-point stags have been grazing around here. Poachers may be after them." Gil pulled off his goggles and pointed his flashlight at a pile of apples under a tall oak in a small clearing.

Troy did the same. "That's why they call you the Ranger."

At Gil's questioning look, Troy laughed. He told Gil about finding Henry and how the boy called him *Ranger*. "I'll have to introduce you to Henry someday, so he can meet a real Ranger."

Gil crossed his arms across his chest. "You were there at the murder scene. You've been holding out on me. Spill."

Troy filled his friend in on the many events of his day spent with Mercy Carr.

"Mercy." Gil pronounced it the French way, as if it were *Merci*. "You asked her out yet?"

Troy frowned. "She's still grieving the loss of her fiancé."

"It's been a long time. For you, too."

"Not a priority right now."

"Françoise saw Madeline at the hospital with her mother. Knee replacement."

"I heard she was back in town."

"You haven't seen her?"

"Why would I?" Troy threw up his hands. "The woman left me."

"And now she's back."

"To help her mother, who just happens to hate me. It's that simple."

"When it comes to the fairer sex, it's never that simple." Gil punched him lightly on his arm. "You can read the woods, Warner, but you can't read women."

"So let's stick to the woods," Troy said firmly. "We need to find these night hunters and whoever killed that poor woman."

"You don't think Jenkins did it?"

Troy shrugged. "You never know. But Ethan the Eagle Scout couldn't do it."

"People change."

"Yeah."

"Do you think the boy saw something?"

"I don't know. He hasn't said much. But he's definitely scared of something."

"What's this got to do with our night hunters?"

"Probably nothing. Alice de Clare was shot through the heart with an arrow in broad daylight."

"Not their style."

"No."

"They're not the only people capable of murder out here," said Gil. "You got your poachers, your drug dealers, your gunrunners."

"Your squatters and your crazies."

"To name a few."

"Yeah."

They laughed, and walked back over to the pile of apples, Susie Bear on their heels.

"These night hunters can't be that good or they would have bagged those stags by now." Troy kicked at the ripening fruit with his boot. "All this bait."

"These are smart bucks. They know better than to go straight for the bait. They'll hang around, checking it out until they feel it's safe."

Troy gave Gil a look. "Eventually, those bastards will spot them, blind them, and then just pick them off."

"Dousing themselves in scent killers first." The deer's superior sense of smell was one of the creature's few defensive weapons, so hunters used scent killers to keep the deer from smelling the predators out to get them.

"You can get anything off the Internet," said Troy. "A guy up north used an ozone generator."

Gil shook his head. "I heard about a guy down in Texas who got arrested for poaching, and the judge sentenced him to weekends in jail during hunting season for five years."

Troy laughed. "Some tough Texans, only poaching on weekends."

"Yeah. Yankee poachers are out all night, every night."

"Wish we could try that here. Think about how much easier our weekend patrols would be with these clowns in jail."

"True. I could take my Françoise out on a Saturday night for a change." Gil grinned at him. "You might even be able to spend some quality time with *la belle Mercy*."

"Very funny." Troy swept his flashlight back and forth across the small clearing. "There must be a recorder around here somewhere, a camera they use to track the deer's comings and goings. Let's see if we can find one. Maybe we'll get lucky and catch them on camera."

Gil began a sweep at his end.

"Search," Troy said to Susie Bear, hoping that she could catch the night hunters' scent on the camera or in the air. Although if they de-scented themselves sufficiently, the dog might not succeed. Susie Bear sniffed around desultorily, which told Troy that at the moment she was not excited by anything olfactory.

"Over here," said Gil.

Trapped in the cross of thick oak branches they found a small digital camera operating on sensors. They took off their gloves to manipulate the device. Gil checked it out while holding the light on the camera.

"The memory card's gone." Gil looked at Troy. "They must have heard us coming and taken off with the evidence. What do you want to do? Pursue on foot?"

"Well, they're probably gone for the night, but they'll be coming back sooner or later. Let's plant our own camera." From his duty belt, he pulled out a camera with a motion sensor, much like the one the night hunters were using, only smaller and lighter and dressed in camouflage.

Susie Bear watched them, dark eyes and nose glinting in the blackness, while they looked for the best spot to put the camera. Someplace close enough to capture the poachers in the act but far enough from their bait camera to avoid detection.

Troy and Gil found the perfect hiding place in a small opening in a bush. They set up the camera, then stepped back to examine their handiwork.

"*It's not what you look at that matters, it's what you see,*" quoted Gil.

Thoreau, Troy thought. "Well, let's hope we get something we can use."

"Do you think Susie Bear is getting something?" Gil pointed at the Newfie mutt as she scampered into a thick clump of scrub.

"Susie Bear! Come back here!" Troy knew she wouldn't go far without him, but with night hunters on the loose, he wanted her to stay in sight.

The shaggy dog reappeared as quickly as she'd disappeared. She danced around, a whirl of black fur barely distinguishable from the darkness around her until Troy turned the flash on her, spotlighting Susie Bear's jig. Her thick paws pounded the ground.

"What is it, girl?"

Troy focused the flashlight on the scrub and followed her. They found Susie Bear on her haunches in her usual sit, alerting to something indistinguishable from the leaf-strewn forest floor.

"What's she got?"

Troy bent down, shining the flashlight on the area in front of the dog. There was something there, something that did not belong. That's what Susie Bear was trained to find and that's what she'd found.

"What is it?"

Troy picked it up. "A dead bird, or part of one."

Susie Bear looked up at him, big brown eyes shining. Troy wished he could read her mind.

"There are a lot of dead birds in the woods," he said. "Not sure why she's set on these." He held the clutch of long feathers in his outstretched gloved hand, shining the flashlight on it so that both he and Gil could take a closer look.

Four beautiful feathers, ranging in length from about six to ten inches. Even in the small spotlight they glowed, long stripes of cream and slate shimmering in the dark.

"Not part of a dead bird. Just the feathers."

"They look like the falcon feather I found in Henry's pajamas." He told Gil about it.

"Peregrine falcon." Gil turned the feathers over with the tip of his gloved hand. "They're connected, sewn together in a patch held by a pin."

Troy stared at a small silver fastener, no bigger than a quarter, but in the shape of a flower. Maybe a rose, maybe not.

"These are feathers from a woman's hat. My wife collects hats." Gil ran a finger lightly along the rachis of the longest feather. "She has a beach hat from California, a blue beret from Paris, a black fascinator from London . . . you name it, she's got it."

"You seem to know a lot about them."

"Why not?" Gil shrugged. "An easy way to keep her happy."

Troy wondered what it would be like to be married to a woman who'd be content with just a new hat.

"*Live your life, do your work, then take your hat.*" Gil stepped back, leaving him standing there with the feathered fastener.

Thoreau again, thought Troy. "What kind of hat do you think this came from?"

"Françoise has a brown Tyrolean decorated with feathers much like this."

"Tyrolean?"

"You know, like Will Ferrell in *Elf*?"

"*Elf*?" Troy laughed.

"Or maybe a *chapeau à bec*. Like Robin Hood."

"No hat at the crime scene, but Alice de Clare was wearing the kind of fancy outfit that might go with a hat with feathers on it. *Elf.* Robin Hood. Whatever."

"She *was* French."

"Yes. From Paris."

"If the feathers are here . . ." Gil looked around, swinging his flashlight around the clearing.

"Maybe the hat is here, too."

Troy whistled for Susie Bear, playing around in a blowdown area nearby, chasing her tail.

"Search," he told her, and the three went to work again. They went farther afield this time, in concentric circles from the scrub where the dog had emerged with the feathers.

Susie Bear disappeared into a small copse of birches, tall slim ghosts reaching into the dark sky. A cool breeze rustled through the trees. If they weren't out looking for poachers and gunrunners and murderers, it would have been a perfect night.

They kept on walking their grid, but Troy knew their best bet was Susie Bear. The Newfie retriever mutt had been gone about ten minutes when she crashed back through the birches.

She did her usual enthusiastic clomp, then disappeared.

Troy and Gil hurried after her, finding the big dog again in her alert position, head held high, plumed tail *whomp*ing away.

A pale object sat just shy of her large paws.

"Good girl." Troy scratched the top of her pumpkin head as he leaned over to retrieve the object.

"Hat." He showed the hat to Gil.

"Tyrolean," the ranger corrected.

"Yep." He turned the soft butter-colored cap inside out, looking for a label. All he found was a monogram with the initials *ADC*.

"The fact that we found this hat—and the feathers—so close to the bait site . . ." Gil paused. "Maybe the night hunters killed that woman after all."

"Only one way to find out. Do you think there's enough scent on that hat for Susie to track?"

"Maybe," said Troy. "But even if there's not, she'll find something. She always does."

He held the feathers and the hat back to Susie Bear, put them under her thick cold black nose.

The dog snorted and sniffed, sneezed and wheezed, feathers tickling her nose.

"Search," he said.

Troy and Gil trailed in her wake—night goggles on, careful not to trip over logs—as the bouncing Susie Bear barreled through the dark forest. She was excited, always a good sign.

They watched for signs in the woods. Listening, all they heard were animal sounds. Eventually they came to a marsh. A muddy slope led down to the water. Susie Bear sat at its bottom, flailing her tail in the mud. She'd definitely need a bath when they got home. She barked once.

Two shots rang out. The cracking and hissing echoing over the water.

"Rifle," said Gil.

"On the marsh."

The forest rustled around them in response to the gunfire. Creatures everywhere took cover. Troy whistled, and heard what he hoped was an uninjured Susie Bear crashing back up through the woods. Safe under the canopy of the forest, with any luck.

He and Gil each readied their own rifles, then silently slid slowly down the incline. Tree by tree. The camouflage of trunks and foliage.

Susie Bear appeared to Troy's right, apparently unharmed, plumed tail swishing hard, brushing the scrub. *Whoosh. Whoosh. Whoosh.*

He raised his gloved finger to his lips, and she settled down. She could be quiet when she had to be, though she didn't like it. It was hard for Susie Bear to curb her natural enthusiasm, to contain her considerable energy.

Her wagging tail slowed to a stop, and she stood completely still.

Troy smiled. He put his hand out to his side, and swatted it back, commanding her to stay behind him.

Gil was closer to the marsh now, to Troy's left near the bottom of the slope. He and the dog continued down the bank, catching up to him. They paused before leaving the cover of the trees. They entered the marsh, crouching among the cattails, rifles at the ready.

Deserted. No one in sight.

All Troy could see was a gray gloom. All he heard was the faint slapping of paddles across the water.

They pulled off their goggles. Gil shone his flashlight along the bank, where they could just make out footprints leading down to the water.

"They must have taken kayaks from here," Troy said.

"That would explain how they got in here to begin with. This marsh funnels into a stream that eventually leads down to the lake. Easy access to ATV trails back to the trailhead."

"Do you have a kayak up here?"

"Yeah, but it's docked several hundred yards down. They're long gone by now."

"Well, at least we have the cameras. And the hat."

"Tyrolean."

"Right." Troy patted the sweet spot between Susie Bear's ears. "That definitely makes the night hunters persons of interest in the murder of Alice de Clare."

"What about Jenkins?"

"This will help cast some doubt, but you know Harrington."

Gil smiled. "Never let the evidence get in the way of a good collar."

"I'll show this to the captain and Mercy before I turn it in to Harrington. Make sure I know what we're looking at."

"Any excuse to see her is a good excuse."

"That's not what I meant."

"Uh-huh."

Troy and Gil headed back toward the ranger station, Susie Bear on their heels.

"Did I ever tell you about my first wife?" asked Gil.

"No." Troy didn't know that his friend had been married before Françoise. "Did she collect hats, too?"

"She collected favors."

Not knowing quite what to say to that, Troy said nothing.

"That's the secret to women," Gil told him as they made their way through the dark forest. "What they collect."

CHAPTER NINE

The objective of the game is simple: Win all the cards.

—WAR

LILLIAN JENKINS'S HOUSE WAS a big eighteenth-century white Colonial on the outskirts of town, the centerpiece of a two-hundred-acre farm that had been in her family for generations. Mercy smiled every time she saw the *ARDEN ACRES, EST. 1760* plaque by the dark-red front door. It reminded her of *As You Like It* and the Forest of Arden, where the banished duke escapes *and a many merry men with him; and there they live like the old Robin Hood of England.*

If Vermont had a Robin Hood, it was Lillian, who wrangled more money out of more of the state's richest citizens for more good causes than anyone else. It was said that the old house had been a stop on the Underground Railroad, and that Lillian's ancestors had hidden slaves in a cellar beneath the sugar shack where they made the farm's justifiably famous maple syrup. Good works were in her DNA.

She was waiting for them. Elvis led Mercy and Henry into the hallway.

Lillian crushed the boy to her chest, hugging him tight, as if she hadn't just seen him at Mercy's cabin. Henry went limp, allowing his grandmother to fully embrace him. He was a small boy, and Lillian was a small woman. They were locked together like two perfect puzzle pieces. Henry and Lillian reminded Mercy of her and her grandmother. Patience was the one person who understood Mercy best. Now that Martinez was gone.

The myth was that mothers understood their children, but Mercy's mother didn't understand her. Or maybe the problem was that she did, and she disapproved. To be understood and accepted, Mercy felt that was the true nature of love. Though she knew her mother still loved her. It just seemed so hard for both of them.

Henry wriggled out of Lillian's arms. Elvis stood at his side, ever watchful.

"Henry, why don't you show Elvis around," said his grandmother. "I'll see what kind of treats I can round up for you and your pal."

The little boy walked away without looking back, Elvis following. Then Lillian gave her a long hug, too.

"It's okay," Mercy told her. "I talked to Daniel Feinberg. He believes Ethan's innocent. He'll do what needs to be done for Ethan. Starting with bail."

Lillian brusquely wiped away the tears gathered in the corners of her eyes. "Patience called to say that Dr. Jacobs is on his way here."

"More good news." She knew that her grandmother could talk the surgeon general into making house calls. Great Dane or no Great Dane.

"Go find Henry and Elvis. I'll see to those snacks."

The boy and the dog were in the den, a large wood-paneled space with a wood-burning stove and a big dark-red leather sofa. On the walls were a collection of vintage Vermont signs. *Fiddle Head Old Tyme Beer. True Blues Ammo. Peche Reserve.*

Sitting at an antique oak game table, Henry was surrounded by maps, dice, and little figures of elves and dragons and dire wolves. He pulled out a nut-brown scroll that he spread out on the table, sweeping aside the other maps and scattering the dice.

He looked up at Mercy to see if she minded the mess, but she just laughed.

"Doesn't bother me. You can pick up your toys later. If you can wait that long." She gave him a pointed look.

Henry secured the edges of the scroll with the figurines, and then dropped out of the chair to his knees. Elvis roused himself from his Sphinx pose to check him out.

"I was just kidding, Henry. I know you like things tidy."

Henry gave her an inquiring look.

"I've seen you eat mashed potatoes and gravy."

Mercy watched as Henry retrieved the fallen objects and placed them in a woven basket. Elvis joined in, picking up folded-up maps and scrolls carefully in his mouth and dropping them—slightly damper than they'd been before—into the basket. The Belgian shepherd left the dice for Henry.

"Thank you." He placed the basket on the Windsor chair next to him, then pointed to the one on the other side.

She pulled a chair close to the boy, to his right, and sat down. Elvis stayed on the floor to his left. Henry traced his index finger along a ley line drawn across a map with the heading *The Sword of Saint Michael.*

This was the same kind of line that had appeared on the map Brodie had showed Henry earlier that day. But this was not the ley line that ran through Glastonbury on Brodie's map. This line—the sword of Saint Michael, if the heading were any indication—ran from Ireland to Israel. Seven monasteries were points on this line, from north to south.

Mercy read each out loud, hoping to get some response from Henry, her index finger marking each location as she made her way down the map, from left to right.

"Skellig Michael, off the southwest coast of Ireland." She looked at Henry, whose eyes were fixed on the map. "I know that one. *Star Wars,* right? Where Rey finds Luke Skywalker in *The Last Jedi.*"

Henry raised his head, regarding her with an air of expectation.

She frowned. "I don't know much about it, apart from the film."

The boy frowned, too. Disappointed in her.

"I'll look it up later. Promise." She moved her finger down to the next dot on the map. "Saint Michael's Mount, Cornwall. Don't know anything about that one. You?"

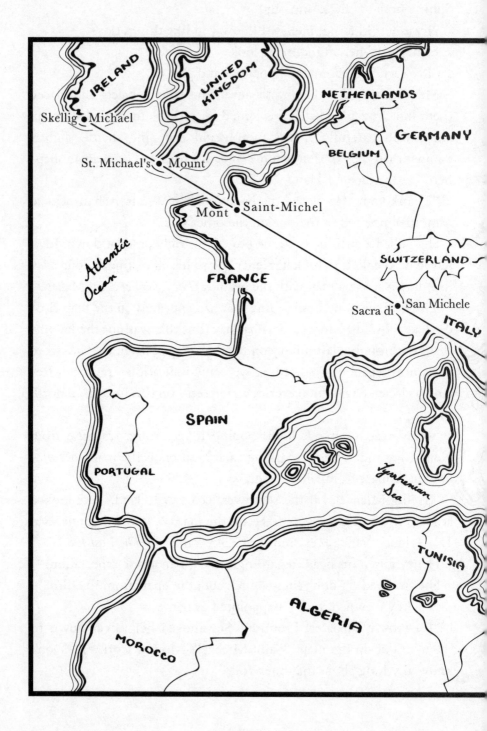

He ignored her question, so she moved on. "Mont-Saint-Michel in France. An island off the coast of Normandy. Even I've heard of that one. Wasn't it a prison once upon a time?"

Henry nodded curtly. Telling her in his nonverbal way to get on with it.

"Okay, okay." She tried the next location. "Sacra di San Michele. On the top of a mountain in Val di Susa, Italy."

The boy went back to examining his map, not bothering to look up.

She moved her finger on to the Sanctuary of Saint Michael the Archangel in Puglia. Still Italy. She looked over at Henry. "I got nothing."

He shrugged, so she pointed to Symi's Monastery, on the Greek island of the same name. No response. "Okay, on the last one. Stella Maris Monastery, on Mount Carmel in Israel."

Gently, Henry pushed her finger away from the map. He stabbed a stubby finger at Skellig Michael, at the far end of the Saint Michael line.

She studied the serious boy beside her. "What is it about this one, Henry? Does it have to do with your game? Or is it more than that?" She leaned toward him, willing him to tell her. Elvis cocked his triangular ears at her, feeling her intensity. He placed his handsome head in Henry's lap, comforting him. Helping him relax enough to answer her questions. At least she hoped that was what the dog was doing.

She pressed on. "Does this have to do with what happened today?"

Henry simply huddled more deeply over the map, his finger stuck on Skellig Michael.

"I want to help," she said quietly. "I think you know that. But you need to talk to me."

He lifted his head, lips quivering. He opened his mouth as if to speak.

The doorbell rang, a sonorous rendition of Westminster chimes.

Henry looked up at Mercy, round brown eyes widened. He started flapping his hands. She remembered Lillian saying he hated doctors.

And Mercy expected there was a doctor coming right now to the poor kid's door.

She hoped this shrink would have a soothing effect on him. That no shrink had ever had a soothing effect on her made Mercy somewhat less optimistic.

She got to her feet as Lillian ushered in Dr. Cal Jacobs. Elvis lifted his nose in the air, sniffing the newcomer.

To her surprise, the psychiatrist was a relatively young man, not much older than she was. Early to midthirties, with dark curly hair and the world-weary blue eyes of an older man.

He smiled at her, and he seemed young again.

"I'm Cal," he said, offering his hand. Tall, he wore jeans and a white button-down shirt open at the neck under a navy wool blazer. His handshake was firm. She found herself liking him in spite of herself. Especially since he meant for her to call him by his first name rather than by *Dr. Jacobs*. She found civilians who pulled rank even more annoying than their peers in law enforcement and the military.

She led Cal over to Henry. "This is Henry."

The boy didn't look at the doctor, just sat there, flapping his hands.

"Say hello, Henry," said his grandmother. But he ignored her, too.

Silence. Except for the *whish, whish, whish* sound of stimming.

The doctor waved his own hand as if it were of no account. Lillian excused herself, but didn't go far, positioning herself across the room in a paisley Bergère chair by the marble fireplace, where she commanded a good view of Henry and the game table.

"Nice to meet you," said Cal. "May I join you?" He didn't wait for the answer that they all knew wasn't going to come, pulling out the chair next to Henry, the one Mercy had just vacated.

In one smooth elegant movement, Elvis stretched to an alert standing on all fours. He remained at the boy's side, sniffed again, the verdict still out on the good doctor. Henry's stimming subsided, and he hugged the shepherd's neck, then sat back on his seat, his little fingers scratching the dog's ears.

"This is Elvis," Mercy said.

Cal held out his hand for the dog to smell.

Maybe this guy wouldn't be too bad. Elvis sniffed him up close and personal, then held up his nose as if to say, *You're okay.*

"Great map." Cal settled next to Henry. "Dungeons & Dragons?"

Henry meticulously rolled up the *Sword of Saint Michael* line map he'd shown Mercy, carefully placing it under his seat. He cleared the table with a sweep of his thin arm, sending the other maps and the figurines off the table in a waterfall of D&D paraphernalia.

Cal laughed. "Okay, no D&D. How about cards? You like to play cards?"

"You'll find cards in the drawer of the game table," Lillian said from across the room.

Mercy opened the drawer and pulled out a pack of cards whose plaid backs featured a large moose, placing the stack on the table.

"Thanks." Cal retrieved a deck of playing cards from his jacket pocket and held them out to Henry. His cards had backs emblazoned with Darth Vader. "I always bring my own. Shall we use yours or mine?"

Henry took the cards from Cal, turned them face up, and spread them in a perfect fan across the table. Each card showed a scene from one of the Star Wars films. He studied them without a word, then gathered them together in his small hands, and shuffled them.

"Okay, you deal." Cal smiled at Henry. "What would you like to play?"

Henry didn't answer him.

"He likes War," said Lillian.

"War, it is."

Henry dealt out the cards with precision. Mercy retreated to the paisley Bergère chair on the other side of the fireplace. Together she and Lillian sat and silently observed Cal and Henry quietly playing War, punctuated only by the occasional question from Cal. Henry didn't answer, whether he was asked about his breakfast or his dad or walking in the woods.

When the doctor asked him if he saw anything in the woods, Henry played on. War takes a long time to win, in cards as in life. Mercy knew that much.

The only time Henry looked up and responded to Cal was when he mentioned Mercy and Elvis.

"Ranger. Bear. Wolf," he said as matter-of-fact as an engineer. Then he went back to cards.

When he managed to win the game in less than an hour, Henry paused to ruffle Elvis's shiny coat, burying his head briefly in the dog's neck.

His way of celebrating his win, thought Mercy.

Elvis barked, his signal bark, and the doorbell rang.

"I'll get it," she said. "Elvis, stay."

The dog whined his disappointment.

"Friend, not foe," she told Henry.

The boy nodded, reshuffling the deck. Preparing to play another game of War with the doctor.

She excused herself and went to the front door. Given Elvis's reaction, she wasn't surprised to find Troy and Susie Bear on the porch. Susie Bear lumbered past her and disappeared down the hallway. En route to Elvis and Henry, no doubt.

"Let her go. Henry will be thrilled to see her." She ushered the game warden into the foyer.

"How's the little guy doing?"

"Better. He seems to be calming down."

"Good." he said. "Is he talking?"

"Not much. The doctor says Henry's scared, but less scared when we're around."

"Nothing we didn't already know."

"No."

"How'd it go with the night hunters?"

He told her about finding the hat with Gil. Shared the photos he'd taken of the fastener and the feathers and the cap before turning it in to Thrasher.

"These feathers are definitely a match for the one Henry found," she said.

"There were blond hairs on the hat. The lab will let us know if they belonged to the victim."

"That *is* Alice's hat."

"You seem so sure."

"It's her style. And it would complete the outfit."

"You sound like Gil." He told her about his friend the ranger and his wife, Françoise, and her penchant for hats.

"Gil sounds like a cool guy."

"He is, you'll have to meet him sometime. Henry should meet him, too, so he knows what a real ranger looks like."

She laughed, and he laughed with her.

Then she thought about what the hat could mean, and she stopped laughing. "Henry was there. He saw Alice."

"We don't know how he came to find that feather. Whether she was dead or alive or even there when he found it."

"We need to know."

"We could just ask him. Show him the hat. See how he responds."

Mercy shook her head. "He's had a very long day, and he's finally settling down. Can we wait until tomorrow?"

"Wait for what until tomorrow?" Lillian appeared in the hallway. 'What's going on?"

Troy handed her the pictures of the hat and the feathers.

"You may as well come on in and show these to Henry now. While the doctor is here. He doesn't seem to be getting anywhere, anyway. Maybe this will help." She looked from Mercy to Troy. "We have to do something. We need to know what happened to him."

"Okay."

Mercy and Troy followed Lillian back to the den. Henry and Cal were still playing War, and Henry was still winning. The dogs sat on either side of him, Elvis in erect posture as always, Susie Bear resting her shaggy pumpkin head right on the game table, her nose nearly touching the cards.

Henry looked up at Troy. "Ranger."

"Hi, Henry."

"Game Warden Troy Warner, this is Dr. Cal Jacobs."

"We've met," he said with what she thought might be a trace of disapproval.

"Troy," said Cal.

Mercy wondered how they knew one another. She couldn't imagine Troy ever going to a therapist and what business would a psychiatrist fairly new to Northshire have to do with the game warden. But they obviously knew each other. And she suspected they didn't like each other much. She'd have to ask Patience about that.

"Don't let me interrupt your game." Troy backed away from the table. "Go ahead and finish, and then we'll talk."

Henry nodded. He and Cal played for another half an hour, the doctor asking questions, the boy refusing to acknowledge them. Only an occasional shrug or a look up at the mention of Mercy or Troy or Susie Bear or Elvis.

Henry won again. He straightened the deck, pushing the stack of perfectly aligned cards over to Cal. Turning his attention back to Troy. Done with War. Done with games. Done with the doctor.

"Thanks, Henry. I enjoyed that. I hope we'll play again soon."

"May I?" Troy approached the table.

"Of course," said Cal, rising to his feet.

"No, please stay," said Mercy, joining them. "We have some photos we need to show Henry. We'd like you to be here when we do."

"May I speak to you privately before we proceed?" asked Cal.

"We don't have time for all that right now." Troy brushed him off. Cal frowned.

"Better us than . . ." She let her voice trail off, hoping Cal would heed her warning.

"Okay." But the psychiatrist did not look happy.

There were four of them at the game table now. Cal, Troy, Henry, and Mercy. The dogs flanking the boy, Lillian hovering close by.

Troy pulled a small folder out of his pocket and removed the picture of the cream-and–gray-blue feathers with the silver fastener, placing it before Henry. "Susie Bear and I were working in the woods with our friend Gil. He's a park ranger. Susie Bear found this." At the sound of her name, Susie Bear thumped her plumed tail against the highly polished wood floors.

The boy petted the Newfie, glancing down at the photo. "Falcon."

"Yes, Ranger Gil confirmed that these are peregrine falcon feathers."

"Like the one you hid in your pajamas," said Mercy.

"Peregrine falcons are birds of prey, the fastest animals in the world, clocked at more than two hundred forty miles an hour," recited Henry, as if he were reading right from Wikipedia.

They all stared at him, except for Lillian.

"Photographic memory," she said. "At least for things he's interested in."

Of course, thought Mercy. *A nine-year-old with a Wikipedia brain.*

"Right." Troy placed another picture down. The one of the hat.

Henry stared at the image of the crumpled yellow Tyrolean. Missing its feathers.

"Do you recognize this hat?"

He didn't say anything. He sat completely still. Unnaturally still. The color drained from his face.

"I think he's holding his breath," said Troy.

"He hasn't done that since he was a toddler." Lillian came forward and placed her hands on the boy's shoulders. "Breathe, Henry."

"Breathe, Henry," repeated Mercy.

Elvis put his paws on the seat of Henry's chair and leaned over to lick the boy's cheek. Susie Bear followed suit on his other cheek. He blinked, gasping for air. He shook off his grandmother's hands and dropped from his seat onto the floor, crawling under the table. The dogs went with him, pushing through the tangle of everyone's legs. Mercy pushed back her chair and squatted down by Henry. The dogs kept on washing his face with their thick tongues. Smart dogs; somehow, they knew he could not hold his breath and giggle at the same time. He ignored Mercy, focused on gathering up the RPG figures he'd scattered earlier with his usual fastidiousness. He was chanting again, too, a tense whispering of prime numbers. But at least he was breathing.

"Would you like a glass of milk, Henry?" asked Lillian. "And some cookies?"

Henry paused in his chanting and tidying up just long enough to say, "Cookies."

Taking their cue from Lillian, Mercy, Troy, and Cal left Henry in the fine company of the dogs, and they retreated to the marble-topped island that separated the den from the bright yellow-and-blue kitchen. Lillian put a blue crock cookie jar and a pitcher of milk on the island, along with glasses and a stack of blue-and-white plates.

She took her grandson his milk and cookies, and returned to the kitchen, where Mercy and the guys waited on ladder-back stools. Lillian stayed on the other side of the island, where she could monitor them all.

"Now what?" asked Troy.

"He recognized that hat," said Lillian.

"But he didn't say anything. We need to know what he saw." Mercy turned to Cal. "What do you think?"

"He's not a big talker, and it may take a while to get through to him in therapy." Cal washed down a cookie with a gulp of milk. "But Henry has other ways of communicating."

"You mean the stimming," said Lillian with a catch in her voice.

Not what she wants to hear, thought Mercy.

"Yes." Cal's tired eyes were kind. "He obviously saw something because he stimmed when Mercy told me about Troy and Susie Bear and tracking him through the woods to the ice shack. And then again when you showed him the picture of the hat."

"He held his breath," said Mercy.

"Yes. An extreme reaction."

"He hasn't done that for a couple of years. But when he was younger, he did it a lot. They had trouble keeping him in day care because he'd hold his breath until he passed out. Billie quit her job at the arts center to stay at home with him full time."

The beginning of the end of Ethan's marriage, thought Mercy.

"He didn't pass out this time," said Troy. "The dogs distracted him."

"Holding his breath is a regression," said Cal. "An indicator of his stress level."

"He likes Mercy and Elvis," said Lillian. "He feels safe with them."

"Exactly. I'd advise that you and the dog stick close by until Henry feels comfortable enough to open up about what happened today. If he ever does." Cal hopped off the stool. "Meanwhile, I'll plan to drop by tomorrow. The aim is to establish trust and hope that eventually that he will talk."

"If the hat belonged to Alice de Clare—and we believe it did— then he may have seen the murder."

"Or not," said Mercy, seeing the panic on Lillian's face.

"I think it's safe to say that something frightened him," said Cal. "But what that is and when he'll be able to tell us about it, that's hard to predict."

"Very helpful," muttered Troy.

"I'd better be going," said Cal. "I'll just say my goodbyes to Henry."

"Same for me," said Troy. "Night patrols."

They found Henry at the card table, his milk drunk and cookies eaten, napkin neatly folded to the side. The boy was again focused on the *Sword of Saint Michael* line map.

"Henry's really into ley lines," Mercy told Cal and Troy.

"Like in *The Da Vinci Code*?" asked Cal.

"Yes. But this line stretches from Ireland to Israel." Mercy noticed that Henry had covered the part of the map where Skellig Michael was located with his palm. He didn't want her to tell them about it. She wasn't sure why, but she figured he had a reason. His little secret, she supposed. Kids liked secrets. And it seemed clear to her that Henry expected her to figure it out. Which she must do, the sooner the better. "Or something like that."

Henry looked up at her with just a hint of a smile.

"Interesting." Cal gave a slight bow to Henry. "See you later."

Henry ignored him, but Cal didn't take offense. Mercy walked the handsome psychiatrist outside to the crescent-shaped driveway that ran in front of Lillian's house, where his Range Rover was parked. The night sky was cloudy, the crescent moon just a faint blur in the gloom. The wind was brisk and cold. It felt more like winter than fall.

"I guess there's not much we can do but wait," she said. "And try to protect him."

"He's really bonded with you and your dog. He may confide in you long before he confides in me."

"I hope so. Thanks again for coming out."

"No problem. I'll be in touch." Cal paused, and she could see that there was something else he wanted to say. But apparently, he thought better of it. Giving her shoulder a quick squeeze, he climbed into his Range Rover and drove off.

She waited there under the murky sky as the SUV disappeared down the road. She shivered, overcome suddenly by the feeling that someone was watching her.

That someone was Troy. The porch light was off, and he was standing in the dark on the porch, waiting for her.

"What are you doing?"

"Just checking to make sure you're all right."

"I'm fine. Why wouldn't I be?"

Troy said nothing.

"You don't like Cal very much, do you?"

He shrugged. "He's all right."

"Liar, liar, pants on fire."

"You're shivering. Let's go back inside."

She was hoping for an explanation, but she could see he wasn't going to give her one. She'd have to ask Patience about that.

THEY FOUND HENRY curled up on the floor of the den in front of the big-screen TV watching *Star Wars: The Last Jedi*. The dogs were his body pillows.

"It's Henry's favorite movie," said Lillian. "Apart from Batman movies, of course."

"Of course." Henry was nothing if not an intriguing little boy. But he was still a little boy.

Surrounded by Elvis and Susie Bear, he looked happier than he had all day.

"There's a boy who needs a dog," Mercy whispered to Troy.

"I heard that," said Lillian. "Don't even think about it. I've already got my hands full with Ethan and Henry. Besides, you know I'm a cat person."

Troy laughed. "Roger that."

But as soon as Lillian turned her back, he whispered back. "We'll think of something."

He clapped his hands and Susie Bear shambled to her feet. "We'd better get going. More patrols to do."

"First Cal, now Troy and Susie Bear." Lillian put her hands on her hips and addressed Mercy. "You aren't leaving, too, are you?"

"Of course not. Elvis and I are staying the night. As promised."

"And I'll check in with you first thing in the morning," said Troy. "Try to get some rest."

"We'll be fine," said Mercy. "You're the one who needs a break. Doesn't Thrasher ever let you sleep?"

Troy laughed. "I can sleep when hunting season is over."

LATER, AFTER TROY and Susie Bear left for night patrols, Mercy and Elvis watched as Henry—back in Batman pajamas, of which he had several pairs—curled up in his Batmobile bed. Lillian tucked him into his Batman sheets and pulled his Batman blanket up around his chin. His grandmother kissed him good night, which he tolerated with a quiet stoicism. Not willing to push him too far, Mercy settled for blowing him a kiss.

Elvis cocked his triangular ears at her, and she nodded. The handsome shepherd lay down at the foot of the Batmobile.

"Elvis wants to sleep with you tonight," Mercy told Henry. "If that's okay."

Henry nodded.

"All right then. Good night." She paused at the door. "If you need anything, just whistle."

Henry leaned up on his elbows, put his lips together, and tried to whistle. But only a faint toot sounded. He frowned.

She'd forgotten how literally his mind worked. "No worries. You can just yell."

Just as she closed the door, she heard a loud thump. Cracking it open again, she saw Elvis up on the bed, snuggling into the curve of the boy's legs. Henry barked his funny little laugh, and she sneaked one last peek at the boy and the dog in the Batmobile before shutting the door one last time.

Lillian put Mercy upstairs in Ethan's childhood room, done up as a ski lodge with a loft bed and slalom posters. There were also the usual textbooks, action figures, and video games, along with a TV and assorted electronics. Twin pine dressers lit by twin swing-arm lamps held books, photos, and school trophies. A blue beanbag chair sprawled in the corner, where Lillian had left a pair of neatly folded flannel pajamas and a new toothbrush for her. She'd also dressed the loft bed in soft cream-colored linens and a plush down comforter. The perfect hostess.

Mercy got ready for bed, but before climbing the ladder to the loft she checked out the closet and rifled through the books, then went through the drawers of the long dresser. There was just the usual teenage tangle of clothes, sports equipment, and board games.

She went back to the long dresser and took a closer look at the photos and trophies that littered the surface. There was Ethan with his mother, Ethan with his siblings, Ethan with his fellow Eagle Scouts, Troy among them, looking as earnestly handsome as always.

Ethan at his graduation, Ethan hiking, swimming, skiing. Ethan playing tennis and soccer and hockey. The trophies celebrated wins in debate, chess, and archery. Ethan had been a champion archer. Mercy had forgotten that, if she'd ever known it. Harrington would certainly use that as another nail in his indictment.

There were a couple of photos of Ethan with Henry as a baby and as a toddler, but no pictures of Ethan and Billie as a couple or the three of them as a family. Lillian must have removed those; or maybe Ethan did himself, as a way of sparing his son—and himself—the pain of Billie's absence. Apart from the more recent photos of Ethan and Henry, the room was a portal into the past. A typical young Northshire boy's past, seemingly unrelated to the successful Manhattan financier's present.

The key to Ethan's transformation must be Henry himself. Maybe his ambition was all down to providing the best he could for his son. Making enough money so that Billie could stay home with the little boy, when day care was not an option. Tough enough to support a family on one income in Vermont, much less Manhattan.

She climbed up to the loft and slipped under covers. Comfortable, but wide awake. Kicking off the comforter, she tried deep breathing. No good. She wasn't used to sleeping in a real bed anymore—and she missed Elvis. When she came home from the war, she hadn't the heart to sleep in the four-poster bed she and Martinez were supposed to share. She would curl up at one end of the couch instead—and the shepherd would join her at the other end of the couch, his head on her feet. Now it was a habit she was unwilling to break. The dog was her comfort and her anchor these days. And nights.

She went back down and settled into the beanbag chair. She pulled her cell phone from her pack and searched online for information about Skellig Michael. The uninhabited rocky island off the southwestern coast of Ireland had been home to a monastery during the Middle Ages. Storms and Vikings forced the monks to abandon their signature stone beehive huts for good in the twelfth century. Now the twin-pinnacled crag attracted pilgrims, Star Wars fans, and seabirds, serving as a breeding ground for storm petrels and puffins, kittiwakes and peregrine falcons, Manx shearwater and gannets. But she wasn't sure what any of this had to with Alice de Clare's murder. Apart from the peregrine falcon feathers on her hat. If there were some other meaning, it escaped her.

Mercy plugged her cell phone in to charge, visions of the spectacular Skellig Michael still dancing in her head. That would be one place worth leaving Vermont to visit, she thought.

She crawled up into the loft bed, but sleep still eluded her. The room was too warm for her to sleep—apparently Lillian liked her furnace working overtime—so Mercy opened the long window running the length of the loft space, just enough to welcome a slice of cool breeze and the not-so-distant calls of barred owls. She thought of Elvis guarding Henry in his Batmobile bed. She wondered if the boy counted prime numbers instead of sheep to go to sleep. Maybe she should try it.

Two. Three. Five. Seven . . . Mercy dozed off to the sound of the great streaky, brown-eyed birds of prey hooting their usual call, *who cooks for you, who cooks for you, who cooks for you.* She dreamed of raptors and green fletched arrows and boys who count in prime numbers.

CHAPTER TEN

ELVIS'S BARK GREETED Mercy the next morning. It was just
after dawn, and Elvis was a morning dog. They usually began
their day together hiking through Lye Brook Wilderness, but there
was nothing usual about the day following a murder.

Especially when the only witness to the murder might be the nine-
year-old boy who stood at the bottom of the ladder to the loft in his
Batman pajamas, clutching the shepherd's collar and saying, "French
toast, French toast, French toast" over and over.

"I guess you like French toast." Mercy climbed down to meet them.
She gave Elvis a scratch between his ears. Henry watched; then he,
too, scratched the dog between his ears. Elvis rewarded the boy with
a nudge behind his knees.

"He likes you. He doesn't nose-kiss everyone's knees, you know.
Elvis is a very choosy dog."

"French toast," said Henry.

She heard Lillian puttering down in the kitchen and could smell
the coffee brewing and French toast frying. As could Elvis, if his
twitching nose was any indication. He understood that until Mercy
had her morning coffee, his day did not really begin.

"Bathroom," she told Henry, escaping into the blue-and-white
fleur-de-lis wallpapered guest bath next to Ethan's room. Dog and

boy followed. She heard them outside the door as she ran her fingers through her messy red curls, always a tangle in the morning, and brushed her teeth. Swapping Lillian's red flannel pajamas for yesterday's clothes, Mercy made a halfhearted attempt to smooth her T-shirt, grateful that yoga pants never wrinkled.

That will have to do, she thought. As long as she didn't run into her mother.

Opening the door, dog and boy had their eyes on her, waiting.

"Okay, okay." She ushered them down the stairs and through the wide archway that opened onto the gourmet kitchen.

"Good morning." Lillian, bright as a penny in a copper-colored sweater and dark blue jeans, handed Mercy a steaming cup. "Pumpkin spice latté."

"Wow. Thanks."

"'Tis the season." Lillian grinned. "Ground from organic Vermont Coffee Company beans, and flavored with purée made from my own pumpkins and my secret pumpkin-pie spice recipe. Far better than any you'll find at any chain store, anywhere. If I do say so myself."

Mercy took a sip. "Outstanding."

Lillian beamed and sprinkled a little more cinnamon on top of the frothy latté for her.

"Have a seat."

Henry had already climbed onto one of the ladder-back stools at the marble island. He pointed to the stool next to him, and she took a seat. Elvis lay patiently at their feet, his fine head resting on one of the spindles of Henry's stool. He liked French toast, too.

Lillian placed yellow-and-blue plates piled with thick slices of French toast smothered in syrup in front of them. "French toast, Jenkins style, with eggs from our own chickens and maple syrup from our own trees."

"You baked the bread?"

"That goes without saying."

Mercy laughed. "Lucky us, huh, Henry?"

Henry nodded. The boy ate French toast the same way he ate mashed potatoes, carefully loading each bite with precisely the perfect amount of syrup before raising his fork to his mouth.

Elvis had no such manners, waiting only a split second after Lillian put down his plate before chowing down.

Mercy took her time, still finishing long after Elvis, and long before Henry.

The dog watched the boy and his diminishing stack of French toast as she brought her dish to the farm sink in the marble island. She and Lillian did the washing up while Henry meticulously cleaned his plate.

"Time for Elvis's morning constitutional."

At the sound of his name, the shepherd perked up his triangular ears.

"Walk." Henry pushed away his plate and slipped out of his chair, standing next to Elvis, ready to go.

"Okay, but you need to wear regular clothes," she told him.

Henry shifted on his feet, and for a moment she thought he might protest. Elvis leaned against his hip, nearly pushing the boy over, and Henry turned and trotted off to his room, the dog trailing behind him.

"And shoes," she called after them.

Lillian laughed. "That was easy. Maybe you and Elvis could take him with you every morning."

Mercy smiled. "Doesn't he have to go to school?"

The bright light that was Lillian Jenkins faded a bit. "His mother always homeschooled him. Since she left, Ethan has cycled through a parade of tutors. He's looking for the right school for him now. We'll have to see what happens." Her eyes filled with tears and she looked away.

"What about the Vermonter?"

"Victor and Lucas will cover for me until I can get there." Victor Santos was the grill chef at the Vermonter, and his son Lucas was his assistant. They'd worked for Lillian for years. "I need to find out what's going on with Ethan."

"Let me do that."

"Ethan really is in trouble, isn't he?"

She didn't know what to say, so she said nothing.

Lillian took Mercy's hands in her own. "You know he didn't do this. You need to find out who did. Before that detective locks up my poor boy for good."

"I'll do whatever I can to help. But that will mean poking around in your lives a bit." She felt uneasy enough about going through Ethan's closet, but it was going to get worse.

"Better you than Harrington."

"There's no stopping Harrington, I'm afraid."

"But you're smarter than he is."

She ignored that. "What can you tell me about Ethan's relationship with Alice de Clare?"

Lillian slid onto a stool at the marble island. "Not much. He never told me about her, but then he's never told me much about his love life. Even when he was a teenager. I think I was the last person in Northshire to know he got Billie Whitaker pregnant."

Mercy nodded. The Ethan Jenkins she remembered kept himself to himself.

"They were happy for a while. But Billie, well, you know Billie. Henry's too much for her. Hell, life's too much for her." Lillian slapped the marble with her palms. "When she left, Ethan did the best he could. Work and Henry—that was his life after she took off. Then he changed. He got happier. I figured there had to be a new woman in his life."

Mercy changed tack. "I'd forgotten Ethan was a champion archer back in school."

Lillian blanched. "That woman in the woods was killed by an arrow."

"Yes. But he's not the only guy in Vermont who can use a bow. This time of year, the woods are full of bow hunters."

They heard Henry down the hall, saying, "Walk. Wolf. Walk."

"Let us watch Henry. You go to work."

"I don't know."

Keeping busy might be the only way Lillian would get through the day without worrying herself to death, Mercy thought.

"Elvis is not leaving Henry's side, whether you're at work or not. You may as well go. You don't want to disappoint all those hungry peepers."

Lillian closed the dishwasher. "This *is* our busiest month of the year."

"Go on then."

"I've got paperwork to do here, then I'll head on over. After you're back from your walk."

"Deal."

Elvis bounded into the room, Henry on his heels.

"Looking good," said Mercy. He was wearing dark blue jeans, a green long-sleeve T-shirt with a yellow pi symbol on it, and Timberland boots. The blue puffer jacket he was carrying had the Batman symbol emblazoned on its back.

She grabbed her pack, her parka, and Elvis's lead. "Let's head out."

Outside, the sun shone brightly in a cloudless blue sky. The air was cold and crisp; a thin frost coated the long lawn between the house and the barn and silvered the fallen leaves littering the grass, still green but not for long. There were only a couple of other houses on the street, barely visible through the oaks and maples that formed a bower overhead.

Mercy headed to the right, toward town. Henry had spent enough time in the woods lately. Elvis stayed between her and the boy, the best kind of middleman.

They'd gone about a hundred yards when Henry bolted off the sidewalk and into the woods. Elvis chased him.

"Henry!" She ran after them, scattering leaves as she went. She found him sitting on a fallen log, Elvis facing him, his front paws on the boy's knees. He wasn't going anywhere.

"Good boy." She waved her hand and the shepherd dropped back. "Henry, you have got to stop taking off like that."

She grabbed his small hands and pulled him to his feet. "You're the one who needs a leash."

Henry looked away from her.

"Sorry. I didn't mean to hurt your feelings." But it was a good idea regardless, she thought. It might be the only way to get through this walk without losing this kid every five minutes. "If it's good enough for Elvis, it's good enough for you, right?"

The boy turned to face her. He grinned.

"Okay." She looped the leash around Henry's waist, snapping the carabiner onto the dog's collar. "Let's try this again."

She strode back to the road, confident that dog and boy were right behind her. When she reached the street, she slowed down and let them catch up. She slapped the outside of her right thigh, and Elvis stepped up beside her. Henry followed along like a pull toy dragged by a toddler.

They marched on toward town. Whenever the boy's attention strayed—he spotted a hawk in the sky or a chipmunk in the leaves or a wild turkey in the scrub—and he wandered off course, Mercy slapped her thigh and Elvis tugged Henry back to her. This *wandering, course correction, wandering, course correction* pattern continued the mile into the town center, where they stopped at the Northshire General Store to pick up a newspaper, half a dozen crullers, and three pints of milk. She also bought Henry a red whistle on a chain, which she placed around his little neck. "Just until you learn to whistle on your own."

Henry tucked the whistle underneath his shirt.

The mile back was the same, punctuated by doughnut and milk breaks. Henry and Elvis really, really liked crullers.

She was pleased with herself—and her partner, Elvis—as they guided Henry back to his grandmother's house. Lillian smiled at the sight of the boy tied off to the dog, then pulled Mercy aside. "Daniel called. He told me he's doing all he can to help Ethan."

"That's good news."

"He also asked if you could come by to see him at the inn, at your earliest convenience. Apparently, Harrington will be there. He won't be put off any longer. He wants to talk to Henry today."

Mercy agreed to take Henry to the Bluffing Bear Inn, with the understanding that Cal would meet them there. Lillian went to work at the Vermonter as planned, satisfied her grandson was in good hands.

Henry and Elvis riding shotgun, she set off in the Jeep for the inn. She called Patience on the way, asking her to brief her on the history of the old place. Her grandmother did not disappoint, providing an encyclopedic look that could give Henry a run for his money.

The ski resort owed its name to the original building on the property, a nineteenth-century hunting lodge built on a sweet piece of land on Bluffing Bear Mountain, not too far away from Stratton, in the southern Green Mountains.

But its name was about all that first lodge and its successor had in common. The midcentury-style complex she'd visited as a child was all retro space age with lots of wood, glass, and granite.

According to her grandmother, Bluffing Bear was one of the first ski resorts built in southern New Hampshire back in the Fifties. Part of the postwar ski boom fueled by soldiers, home from the battlefields of Europe and the South Pacific, now eager for adventurous outdoor sport. The brainchild of Blake Montgomery's grandfather, Barrington "Bear" Montgomery, the resort was a Disneyland of skiing and skating and swimming, with an indoor ice-skating rink and a heated outdoor pool, a reversal of the norm that flew in the face of conventional wisdom. "At the time, it seemed a bit risqué," cracked Patience over the Jeep's speakerphone. "Vermonters add layers in winter, they don't take them off."

The business had a good run until the Nineties, when bigger, slicker, more ambitious resorts with golf courses and spas and five-star restaurants—not to mention higher and longer ski runs with lifts to match—lured away the lodge's customers. By the time Mercy started coming here with her family, the resort had already fallen on bad times. They came anyway.

"One last question for you, Patience." Mercy glanced over at Henry and Elvis, who were gazing together out the window of the Jeep, a double handsome profile of boy and dog. "Your friend the shrink and Troy."

Henry looked up at Mercy at the sound of the game warden's name.

"Text me," Mercy told her grandmother. "We're pulling in the parking lot of the inn."

"Over and out," said Patience.

MERCY HADN'T BEEN to the inn in years. The place had a weary look about it now. Certainly, Alice de Clare's vision—the one revealed in her portfolio—would bring the lodge into the twenty-first century.

Feinberg was waiting for them in the lobby. His assistant, Jackie, a tall young woman with a skier's outdoorsy look, offered Henry the promise of a peanut-butter snack and a Nintendo Switch loaded with video games if he'd come with her to the kitchen, an obvious if effective ploy to get him out of the way so Mercy could talk to the billionaire alone. The boy slapped his thigh, as he'd seen her do, and Elvis stepped to the boy's side. Off they went, connected at the hip.

Smart kid, she thought, not for the first time. Her cell phone pinged and she read the text her grandmother sent her: *Cal was Madeline's therapist when she ran off to Florida with the orthopedist.*

Which explained why Troy was not overly fond of the psychiatrist. Maybe he'd encouraged her to bail on the marriage; maybe not. The Madeline she remembered from high school did what she wanted to do and let the chips fall where they may.

Mercy texted *Interesting* back to her grandmother and then put thoughts of the complicated triangle that was Madeline and Troy and Cal aside, turning her attention to the main lobby. The large, open space was a couple of stories tall with floor-to-ceiling windows. A towering black marble fireplace anchored the center of the room.

She remembered that fireplace, which still bore the massive carving of a bear chiseled right into the rock; a high-relief sculpture of a big male standing on his hind legs, upright, handsome and fierce. She'd spent hours gazing at that chiseled bear, drinking hot chocolate in front of the fire after a long day of skiing with her family: her brother, her parents, both sets of grandparents. Mercy's father loved this place, if only because his parents, too, had brought him here when he was a kid. Her mother preferred grander resorts, but in this one thing—skiing trips—she deferred to him.

Back then there were long curved banquettes in front of the fireplace; Mercy and her older brother, Nick, would plant themselves at opposite ends of one while their parents drank Irish coffees at the nearby bar. Nick was charged with watching her, but instead he'd ignore her and play video games. She'd curl up with a book. And contemplate the bear.

As night fell, flames would light the bear in flickering shadow. Mercy loved that bear, just the way she loved the lodge and her dad for taking them there.

"You aren't getting rid of Fluffy, are you?" she asked him. "I love Fluffy."

Feinberg looked puzzled. "Fluffy?"

"That's what we called him." She pointed to the fireplace. "The bear."

"That's what the old man always called him." Blake Montgomery appeared at her elbow. "He loved that bear, too."

At his inquiring look, she said, "We used to come here when I was a kid."

Blake snapped his fingers. "Of course. You're Duncan and Grace Carr's daughter."

"Yes." She smiled at him, but she didn't say more. She loved her parents, but her and their respective visions for the way she should live her life were poles apart. Getting along with them could be a struggle for Mercy. Especially with her mother.

Feinberg saved her. "Old Fluffy looks pretty good for his age."

She gave him a glance of gratitude for changing the subject. Her parents were among the many attorneys the billionaire had working for him, in one capacity or another. He knew them, and he liked them. As most people did. But he also seemed to understand their conflicted relationship, without her explaining it.

Blake regarded the sculpture fondly. "Fluffy was modeled after a bear Dad bagged in his youth. His first, and his biggest. Best day of his life, he always said."

She wondered what kind of man would rank the day he harvested a bear as the best day of his life—over the day his son was born, or the day he got married, or the day his ski resort opened. An obsessed hunter, she supposed. She wondered if Blake shared his father's obsession.

"I'm surprised he didn't have him stuffed," she said.

"Oh, he did. He was into taxidermy."

"What happened to the stuffed Fluffy?"

"When Dad died last spring, he had it buried with him. He left his likeness—the sculpture—to us."

That was one funeral she was glad she'd missed. "I was sorry to hear about your father."

"He was sick a long time. Cancer. He's in a better place now."

With the stuffed bear, Mercy thought, biting back a grin. "I'm glad that you're refurbishing this place. But only if Fluffy stays."

"Fluffy stays." Blake smiled. "Let me take you on a quick tour."

He led them through the rooms on the first floor. The dining room, the kitchen, the conference room, the business offices, all in various stages of disrepair. It seemed only Fluffy had survived the decades relatively intact—and the non-Fluffy trophy heads gracing the dark-paneled walls of Blake's office. There was a bighorn ram, a moose, another bear (smaller than Fluffy), and a couple of twelve-point bucks. Two low-hanging chandeliers were made of antlers.

"Quite a change from the rest of the place," she said.

"This was the smoking room in the original lodge. Dad kept it for his trophies. And a reminder of the good old days." He paused.

"When Dad got sick, he had his bed moved in here. He loved this room."

The smell of old wood and cigar smoke and a couple hundred years of mountain living was thick in here, she thought. The kind of place ghosts gathered to tell tall tales of hunts long past. "Are you going to keep it as is?"

"I was hoping to add a few trophies of my own. You know, harvesting my own bear." Blake shrugged. "I guess that won't happen, at least not at this hunting party."

Some party, she thought. Feinberg frowned at her, as if he could read her mind. He probably could. The man was a wonder—and not always in ways that made her comfortable.

As Blake ushered them out of his late father's smoking room and back to the lobby, she tried to reconcile the glamorous drawings she'd seen in Alice de Clare's portfolio with today's languishing Bluffing Bear Inn. "It seems like you have a lot to work to do."

"True," said Blake. "But we'll get it done."

"The sooner, the better." The billionaire frowned again, but this time he didn't seem to be frowning at her. "We have an aggressive schedule. This building is basically sound, we just need to hustle on the exterior, getting it done by the new year. The interiors we can work on regardless of the weather."

"We're upgrading the lifts and the runs as well," said Blake.

"We'll miss the lucrative Thanksgiving and Christmas skiing seasons," said Feinberg. "But conceivably we could make the winter and spring ski seasons. And we'll be good to go for weddings and summer sports come May."

"We need to finish the first phase of the remodel by the Bear Moon."

She smiled. *Bear Moon.* The month of January, so called by Native Americans because it was when bears gave birth to their young. "I remember the Bear Moon celebration at the inn. I loved the snowshoe hikes under the full moon. And the fireworks."

"Those stay, too. You'll have to come back when we re-open."

"I will." She looked up at Fluffy again, and changed the subject. "I guess you'll need to find a new architect. Sad for Alice."

"We're asking her protégé to take over the project. A talented young man named Owen Barker. He'll keep as close to Alice's original vision as possible."

"Her swan song." She wondered how close the relationship was between Alice and her protégé. She wouldn't be the first architect murdered for art. Or love.

"Yes. We'd like to honor that."

Blake made a show of looking at his watch, a vintage Rolex. He caught her glancing at it.

"My dad's."

"Nice." Despite the elegant man's success as an investment banker, he remained in his old man's shadow. Maybe remaking Bluffing Bear Inn in his own image was his way of stepping out into the sun.

"Will you rename the place?"

"Oh no." Blake pulled his sleeve back over his father's watch. "That stays. Just like Fluffy. And Bear Moon." He tapped his father's Rolex. "We've got that meeting with Owen Barker, Daniel."

"Go ahead. I'll join you shortly."

Feinberg touched Mercy's shoulder and gently guided her outside to the wide deck overlooking Bluffing Bear Mountain. She could see workers already cleaning up the ski runs up and down the mountain.

His dark eyes met hers. "You know more about Alice de Clare's vision than you're saying."

"I saw architectural drawings in her room," she admitted. No point in hiding it. He knew she couldn't help but investigate when circumstances demanded it. Maybe even when they didn't.

"I suspected as much."

"Your butler tattled on me."

"Yes."

"When did you decide you needed a butler?"

"Every house needs a butler. Butlers run a tight ship. After what happened this summer, I decided Nemeton needed one."

"You don't think Ethan did it." She figured self-made billionaires must be good judges of character.

"Of course not." He looked disappointed in her for even mentioning it.

"How is Ethan now?"

"I convinced Detective Harrington to keep him under house arrest at Nemeton. He's confined to the guesthouse. At least for now." He shrugged. "It won't last. Detective Harrington's like a dog with a bone. You need to exonerate Ethan before Harrington locks him up for good."

"Me?"

"Playing coy doesn't suit you."

Mercy smiled. "Agreed. But this is police business."

His eyes narrowed. "Harrington isn't up to the task."

"He hates me. Plus, he's already warned me off this investigation."

"You need something to do."

"I help Patience at the animal hospital," she said with a laugh.

"That's not a real job."

"Don't let Patience hear you say that."

"What I mean is that it's not a real job for you. Your talent lies in investigative work."

Mercy didn't say anything, because she knew he was right.

"Work for me. Starting with this murder. Find out who killed Alice."

"Lillian already asked me."

"All the more reason."

"But not *your* reason. I know Alice de Clare was your architect, but . . ." Mercy stopped midsentence. "You're worried about bad publicity. How the murder could affect the viability of this lodge."

"It's not just that. I liked Alice, what I knew of her. And her plans for the inn. And I like Ethan, and if that little boy really saw that murder . . ." He paused. "I know you'll want to keep him safe."

"Of course. But I'm already keeping an eye on him."

"You know that's not enough. Henry won't truly be safe until the real killer is in custody. Shall we say a hundred dollars an hour to start?"

"I'm already doing it for free."

"But you shouldn't. You need a job."

"Have you been talking to my mother?"

"I doubt this is what she had in mind for you."

Mercy grinned. "Which I admit is actually a point in your favor."

The billionaire grinned back. "Then it's settled."

"Hold on. I'm not sure I can deal with having a boss again. Even you. The army was enough boss for a lifetime."

"You'll be working for yourself, not for me. Just report your findings to me." His dark eyes warmed up, along with his pitch. "Everyone needs a job. Part of your recovery."

And Elvis's, she thought.

"Where I go, Elvis goes."

"Of course. A hundred twenty-five dollars an hour then, for the two of you."

That would keep Elvis in chew toys for a while. She changed the subject. "Your friends are all suspects. I'll be looking in their affairs."

"Understood."

"Speaking of your friends, there's something I don't understand."

"Only one thing?" He smiled at her.

"Caspar Farrow."

"I have friends, and I have fellow investors." Feinberg looked at her.

"And Farrow falls in the latter category."

"Precisely."

"You know that you're a suspect yourself."

"And if you think I killed her, you go right to Detective Harrington."

"You're not a murderer. You have more effective ways of dealing with difficult people."

He ignored that. "You notice things others miss. So does your dog."

"You don't miss much yourself."

"Obviously I missed something here." He cleared his throat, close to revealing emotion she knew he'd rather not let show. "Alice was a guest in my home. And Ethan is my employee. And my friend."

"Understood." She paused. "How well did you know her?"

"I wish that I'd met her. Ethan handled our dealings with her. What I know of her I know through her work." He closed his eyes just long enough for Mercy to imagine he was picturing Alice's dream of the new inn. He blinked and opened them again, the dream lost.

"Even if you had met her, odds are you wouldn't have known her well enough to predict what happened. Everyone has secrets."

"Find out what hers were."

"All right." Mercy was going to do it anyway, and she might as well get paid. Besides, Elvis would love it.

CHAPTER ELEVEN

*Blink Bear: a shaggy black magical animal companion with the
ability to appear and disappear whenever summoned by the Ranger.*

—HENRY'S GAME

WE'LL SAY THAT YOU and Elvis are here to help with Henry,"
said Feinberg.

"That's true enough." The best cover stories were always true
enough.

"Let's start with the meeting with Owen Barker."

He led the way to the south side of the lodge and a bright conference room with more floor-to-ceiling windows and a high slanted
ceiling with pine beams.

At a long glass-topped table surrounded by Queen Anne ghost
chairs sat the members of yesterday's disastrous hunting party: Blake,
at one head of the table, the regal Katharine to his right, queen to his
king. Lea sat to her right, the ever-present Nikon in her lap. Across
the table were Cara and Caspar Farrow. The hair model looked
bored and her husband looked belligerent, all per usual. Perched in
his seat next to the other head chair, presumably Feinberg's, was an
impeccably dressed young man who reminded Mercy of a whippet,
a sleek and elegant dog breed known as the poacher's best friend for
its ruthless chase of rabbits. He skittered to his feet when Feinberg
entered the room.

"I think you know everyone, Mercy. Except for Owen Barker.
Owen, Mercy Carr."

Alice de Clare's protégé, she thought.

As he settled into the head chair, the billionaire waved Mercy into the chair to his right, forcing Barker to move down a seat. He scowled at her, and she smiled back sweetly. She was no scared rabbit, but he didn't know that. Yet.

"I intend to preserve as much of Alice de Clare's vision on this project as is humanly possible," he announced to the group.

She wondered if that were really true. Architects were artists, and artists preferred their own visions over anyone else's. Now that Alice was gone, she figured it might just be a matter of time before the whippet made his move.

Feinberg looked pointedly in her direction, as if in rebuke. The man really could read minds.

Cara and Caspar beamed at one another at this pronouncement, as if their only child had just made honor roll.

"Mercy is here on behalf of Ethan, for Henry's sake," said Feinberg.

"The babysitter," said Barker. "I thought this was a professional meeting?" He spoke with a faux Continental air that made Mercy suspect he'd been born and raised in Newark.

Everyone at the table turned to stare at the man brash—or foolish— enough to question Feinberg.

"Mercy is former military police," said Feinberg, "having served with honor in Afghanistan and elsewhere. Given what has transpired over the course of the weekend, we could all use an extra layer of protection. She and Elvis will be around, watching over the boy— and us all."

"Elvis?" asked Barker with a smirk.

"Elvis served in Afghanistan, too," said Mercy. "Sniffing out explosives and taking down bad guys."

Cara drummed long blue fingernails on the glass tabletop. "Let's see your new drawings, Owen."

"New drawings?" Blake and Katharine spoke in unison, leaning forward as one direct challenge. "We didn't commission any new drawings," said Blake.

"Well, we did," said Cara, flipping her hair.

Barker rose to his feet, and with great ceremony spread across the long table the drawings that Mercy recognized from Alice's portfolio. "These are the original designs. Today I thought we might discuss my suggested changes."

"We never authorized any changes," said Blake.

Barker spread out other drawings. "Based on Caspar and Cara's input, I've been working up a few new ideas." Barker's designs were cartoonish, twisting Alice de Clare's elegant take on midcentury modern into a neon avalanche of kitsch.

Cara smiled and flipped her hair again.

She really needs another move, Mercy thought.

"As lovely as Alice's designs were, if this resort is going to be first-rate it needs much more pizzazz." Caspar beamed, his face redder than ever.

"Pizzazz?" Katharine repeated the word as if it were an obscenity.

"Alice is not even in her grave," said Lea quietly.

"We will not be so quick to abandon Alice's vision," said Katharine stiffly.

Good for you, thought Mercy. She was with the Montgomerys in principle, as well as in taste.

"I love Alice's drawings and I see no reason to *jazz up* the resort." Lea retrieved her camera from her lap and snapped pictures, documenting the travesty.

"Exactly." Blake straightened his spine, holding his silver head high. "This isn't Las Vegas. This is Vermont."

"This look will appeal to a younger demographic." Barker defended his vision. "Millennials will love it."

"Millennials want bargains and beginner slopes," said Blake. "Not tacky bells and whistles."

"And we cannot afford to alienate the parents and grandparents who still foot the bill for our family bookings," said Katharine.

Barker looked crestfallen. His flop of dark hair fell across his face. It wasn't quite long enough to flip, but she could tell by the adoring way Cara looked at the junior architect that she very much approved of his hair.

As a matter of course, Mercy never trusted anyone who flipped their hair. There was no hair flipping in the army.

Cara and Caspar stood up, too, blustering on about appealing to the beautiful people, whoever they were. Barker regrouped, continued his jabber on winning the hearts and minds and wallets of millennial skiers and snowboarders. Katharine and Blake droned on about preserving the integrity of Bluffing Bear Inn.

"No point in throwing the baby out with the bathwater," Blake insisted. Katherine agreed with him. Lea kept on taking pictures. Every once in a while, she would point to one of the new designs and say something like, "This doesn't work in terms of composition."

Tempers flared, and voices rose as everyone argued their points. Everyone except Mercy and Feinberg, who sat and observed. She wished she could read *his* mind. She suspected he used observation as a secret weapon, as she did.

Just as the meeting deteriorated into a shouting match, a newcomer breached the battlefield, prompting the billionaire to pound the table with his fist, instantly silencing the room.

Katharine beamed so beautifully at the new arrival that Mercy knew he must be her only child. With sun-bleached hair and stoner clothes, he looked more prepared for a skateboarding park than a business meeting.

"William, we're so glad you could join us," said Katharine. "We desperately need your feedback. You are a millennial after all. What do you think of these drawings?"

William glanced at the drawings new and old. Pointing to a large and ungainly neon tower on Barker's drawing, he said, "Cool."

"There you have it," said Caspar.

"I knew it," Cara chimed in.

"William, do be serious," said his mother.

"He's just saying that to be impertinent," said his father.

William grinned. Like a teenage boy, he lived to upset his father. But he was no teenager. Not anymore. He just dressed like one.

"We need a considered opinion, William," said Feinberg.

William looked at him. "Look, the only design I know anything about is boards. All I can tell you is that if you want me to bring in the hipster skiers and snowboarders, you're going to have to do better than this. All of this." With that, William gave a quick salute and left.

After that, all hell broke loose.

Feinberg slammed the table with his fist, ending the chaos a second time. Mercy figured three times was his limit.

"We'll have to convene again later. Jackie will arrange your transport back to Nemeton."

Jackie appeared on cue and ushered the squabblers from the room.

Looking unflappable once more, Feinberg looked at his watch and turned to Mercy. "The doctor and the detective should be here momentarily."

DETECTIVE KAI HARRINGTON arrived on time, a first in Mercy's experience. Prince Harry usually liked to keep people waiting. But Daniel Feinberg wasn't people, he was Rich People, and Harrington knew it.

Not that his timeliness mattered. They sat in vintage orange plastic shell chairs around a white Parsons table in a smaller version of the lodge's conference room down the hall. Henry was between Mercy and Cal on one side, with Elvis at his feet. Harrington sat alone on the other side. Feinberg reigned at the head of the table, eyes focused straight ahead, not looking at any of them. Not taking part in what everyone but Harrington could see was an exercise in futility.

Unsurprisingly, Henry refused to answer any of the detective's questions about what he saw that day. When Harrington pulled out the picture of the hat, the boy looked away, tucking his hand into Elvis's collar, chanting prime numbers.

It was clear that the detective was never going to convince Henry to talk. Mercy didn't know if he was completely lacking in emotional intelligence or just impatient. She did know he was a grade-A jerk.

Harrington glowered at Cal. "Can't you get anything out of him?"

"Henry does not seem ready to talk about this yet. He needs more time."

The detective tried Mercy. "What about you?"

"Maybe if we take him for a walk. He likes to walk."

"So let's take him for a walk," said Cal.

She shrugged. "We can try it."

Jackie passed out hunter-orange vests, and Mercy slipped Elvis's around his torso. Once outside the lodge, Feinberg looked up at the mountain. "They're working on the ski runs on Mount Northshire. But to the south, you'll find several hiking trails. One leads up to Bluffing Bear Creek."

"Thank you, Daniel," said Mercy.

"Good luck."

Mercy, Elvis, Harrington, and Cal set off for the creek. Overgrown with ferns and brambles, the trail was still easy enough to follow. The sun shone brightly through the golden bower of the trees, but the temperature had not climbed much since morning. A stiff wind from the west chilled Mercy even through her parka. She hoped Henry was warm enough.

The boy trotted ahead of them, Elvis on his heels. She hadn't tied him to the dog; she didn't want to embarrass him in front of Cal and Harrington. Besides, she was kind of hoping he'd give the detective the slip. Anyway, with the shepherd at his side, Henry wouldn't get too far away from them.

"We'll just go where he leads us," she told Harrington. "That's our best bet."

Elvis perked his ears and looked back at the trail stretching behind them for just a second before rocketing after Henry. Over her shoulder Mercy spotted a flash in the foliage behind them, a flash she recognized as Troy and Susie Bear following at a discreet distance. She wondered what they were doing here. It must be important for Troy to risk running into Harrington.

She smiled to herself. She didn't think Harrington had a clue they were following them. Some detective he was.

Henry dashed ahead, Elvis shadowing him. They'd only gone about fifty yards when Harrington snagged his suit on scrub and cursed out loud.

"This isn't getting us anywhere. He's not talking."

"It's just going take time," said Cal. "The wisest strategy is to let Henry hang out with Mercy. And maybe he'll say something. He trusts her."

Harrington snorted. "That's one of us."

"I'm sure you must have other avenues of investigation to explore," said the doctor genially.

"Fine." The detective looked at her. "If the kid says anything or does anything, I expect you to report back to me. Me, personally and directly."

"Absolutely," she said. *As if.* The overbearing man was the last person she would tell. Unless she had to.

She wasn't convinced he would put the boy's safety first. Not before his ambition. His ambition trumped everything else. He was a grandstander, and she hated grandstanders.

Harrington turned and stalked back toward the inn. Stopping only when he encountered Troy and Susie Bear. Mercy sneaked a peek their way and winced as he yelled at them, and then continued on, talking on his phone, yelling at some other poor subordinate. She hated yellers, too.

She let Cal and Henry go ahead, dropping back to meet Troy and Susie Bear. But up ahead Henry had halted in his tracks. Apparently, the boy was not moving on without them.

Elvis and Cal waited with Henry for them to catch up. When they did, Troy said to Cal, "Don't you have rounds?"

The doctor checked his watch. "In fact, I do."

"That's okay," she said. "We can take it from here."

"I appreciate all your help. If he says anything, let me know." Cal took out a card. "I meant to give this to you last night. It's my private cell number, as well as my office phone. Call me, day or night. Or text. Whatever works. I want to know what's going on with Henry. And you."

"Thanks." She felt Troy's eyes on her as she took the card from the psychiatrist, and his fingers lingered on hers. With a smile, she pulled her hand away.

He smiled back. She could sense Troy frowning.

Cal waved goodbye to Henry, making his way back down the path toward the inn.

Henry gazed up at Troy and they exchanged a look of derision. Mercy laughed. Seemed Henry didn't like Cal any more than Troy did.

They continued down the path, deeper into the woods.

Up ahead about a hundred feet, a fork appeared. Henry stopped, and they hustled up the trail to catch up. A faded wooden sign from the lodge's bygone days marked the crook. The arrow labeled BRIDAL WREATH PATH pointed toward the gazebo, and the arrow labeled THE PATH OF ZEN pointed toward the Japanese teahouse.

"I remember these venues. The gazebo is a pretty spot down by the creek where they perform a lot of weddings. Or they did at one time. No idea what shape it's in now."

"And the other one?"

"The Japanese teahouse. A meditation center, I think, where they did yoga and sat zazen and did tea ceremonies. Run-down now, I expect." Mercy frowned. "I'm surprised you haven't been down here."

"Private land. They have their own security." Troy shook his head. "For what that's worth. Probably rife with poachers during the off-season."

"Like now."

"I doubt they'd risk coming around in broad daylight with all the construction going on." Troy stepped over a large fallen log covered in moss. He held out his hand to help her over, and she took it. Her mother would be proud.

"Is the teahouse by the water, too?" he asked.

"Yeah. From what I remember, the creek winds around a lot. Both trails should hit the creek at some point."

"That's a safe bet. This area is loaded with streams, lakes, and marshes. Around here, all roads lead to water."

Henry knitted his brows together, his brown eyes fierce with concentration, set on the sign marking the fork.

"Which way should we go, Henry?" asked Mercy quietly. She didn't want to disrupt his focus.

Before the boy could respond, Elvis took off down the trail leading to the gazebo. Susie Bear lumbered after him, Henry on his heels.

"The little guy's pretty fast when he wants to be," said Troy to Mercy between breaths as they ran after Henry and the dogs.

She told Troy about looping Elvis's lead around Henry's waist. "I never should have taken it off."

Here the path was nearly invisible in many spots, ferns and saplings and scrub obscuring the trail and crowding out the little gravel still left. But that didn't slow down Henry or the canines. Mercy and Troy could still see the boy up ahead, but the dogs had disappeared.

Troy yelled for Susie Bear, and Mercy whistled for Elvis, but they didn't circle back.

"They must be on to something," he said.

Mercy and Troy caught up with Henry, and they jogged behind him as he raced forward on his thin spindly legs. The boy wasn't too steady on his feet, and she worried he would fall. If he did, she'd have to catch him.

The trail took a wide swing to the left, and the forest opened up onto a clearing. There sat the gazebo, a large, solidly built Victorian-style structure, the kind often seen gracing town commons across New England. Where a local band would play, and townspeople would gather to dance the night away. Another anachronism that Blake's father had let stand for the ages.

The octagonal-shaped gazebo's faded wood was peeling white paint and had loose and missing shingles on the roof. Its gingerbread trim in need of repair. Mercy could imagine brides meeting their grooms here to say, "I do," decked out in white satin and lace and lots of tulle, promising to love, honor, and cherish till death do they part as birds chittered and the stream gurgled and onlookers blinked away tears.

The dogs were waiting for them at the top of the stairs. Elvis sat on his haunches, absolutely still, triangular ears cocked. Susie Bear was next to him, plumed tail flying high but unmoving. Defenders on guard.

But guarding what?

Henry reached the steps before they did.

"Wait," she ordered.

Henry paid no mind. He charged up the stairs, which were in no better condition than the rest of the gazebo. She could see several of the boards on the stairs were rotted.

"Careful, Henry."

As soon as the boy reached the top, Elvis leapt to his feet, blocking Henry from the grandstand floor. The shepherd barked, and the Newfie mutt joined in. Together they made a lot of noise.

Henry put his hands over his ears, and walked around the dogs, heading for the center of the gazebo.

Mercy and Troy raced up the stairs, coming to a dead stop.

"Stop right there, Henry." She used her command voice, and Elvis stopped barking. Susie Bear followed suit.

Henry kept on walking.

"Whoa," said Troy.

A woman with long, dark hair stood in the middle of the gazebo. She looked up, and Mercy was struck by her beauty, her face a striking contrast of shapes, shadows, and cheekbones. Her black eyes had a haunted look.

At her feet was Caspar Farrow, laid out flat on his back, legs splayed. The belligerent florid-faced man stared straight upward. Shot dead with an arrow to the heart. Blood staining his shiny new L.L. Bean field jacket. Looking far more vulnerable in death than he did in life. Death being the great equalizer.

Just like Alice de Clare.

"Don't touch, Henry," said Mercy.

The woman straightened, then bolted across the grandstand. She leapt over the railing of the gazebo, a drop of about six feet. Mercy heard her land with a soft easy thud. She sprinted toward the creek. The woman was in good shape, she thought.

Henry rushed to the railing, as if he were going to leap after her.

"No, Henry!"

He didn't listen to her. He climbed over the railing and dropped out of sight with a *thwack* not nearly so light or graceful as the woman's landing before him.

Troy cursed.

The dogs vaulted after Henry, Elvis in a swift, elegant soar. Susie Bear in a slower, slightly less elegant leap.

Mercy ran for the railing, hurdling it easily and sticking her landing like the high-school gymnast she'd once been. Her coach would have been proud. Troy landed heavily beside her.

The gazebo was about twenty yards from the creek. The woman disappeared beyond the weeping willows lining its banks. Henry trailed her, the dogs flanking him.

Mercy and Troy darted after them, breaking through the weeping willows just in time to see the woman navigate several wide stepping stones running across the creek. Henry stood at the water's edge, watching her.

The dogs barked warnings.

"Don't do it, Henry!" She scrambled down the bank, just in time to see the boy take a first step. She yelled at him again to stop. The dogs tried to block his way, but he pushed through them. Henry stepped onto the first rock, then the second. Hearing her behind him, he briefly looked over his shoulder before turning his attention back to the creek. He jumped from stone to stone.

"Stop, Henry," yelled Troy, now at her side. The dogs plunged into the water after the boy. Mercy and Troy waded toward him.

Before they could reach him, Henry slipped. His feet flew out from under him, and he tumbled headlong into the fast-moving water. He came up, sputtering.

"Grab one of the rocks," she yelled.

The boy splashed around, flailing his arms, feeling for one of the granite boulders. He found one, and he grabbed on.

"Hold on tight."

But his little hands were wet, the rock was slick, and the current strong. Henry lost his grip.

She reached for him, but she was too late. The current quickly carried him downstream. She could see him floundering. Elvis swam after him, and so did Susie Bear. The big dog was as graceful in the water as a seal—and nearly as fast. She was catching up to the boy.

The long-haired woman was on the other side of the creek now, farther downstream, closer to Henry than they were.

"I'll get him," she yelled. Her Southern accent took Mercy by surprise. The woman ran alongside the creek until she was just ahead of Henry, then flung herself into the water. Seizing the child by one of his thrashing arms, she dragged him to the bank.

Mercy assumed the woman would stop there, to see if the little boy needed CPR.

But she did not. She threw the boy over her shoulder as if he were a sack of potatoes and disappeared behind the line of weeping willows. The dogs swam to the creek's edge, racing up the bank after her.

Mercy and Troy maneuvered the rocks, and then ran down the side of the creek to the point where the woman had fled with Henry into the woods. They could hear the dogs barking, and they followed the yowling.

Elvis would never let that boy out of his sight. And neither would Susie Bear. They'd lead Mercy and Troy to Henry and that woman, whoever she was.

She and Troy hurtled through the woods after the dogs. They

tracked the woman for about a hundred yards to a small glade near a blowdown in the forest. In the middle of the clearing was what must have been the Japanese teahouse. At least according to the dingy sign that hung crookedly from the top of the structure.

The glass was broken in many of the pagoda's wall and roof panels. Someone had boarded up these open spaces with logs, giving the place the odd look of a temple crossed with a tree house. A strange but somehow inviting retreat in the woods.

The woman disappeared into the teahouse with Henry through a makeshift door on the south side of the pagoda. Mercy and Troy and the dogs charged after her.

CHAPTER TWELVE

Wolf: a strong and sleek magical animal companion trained to protect, guard, and attack on command.

—HENRY'S GAME

THEY ENTERED THE PAGODA through the wooden door, which stood ajar. Henry's rescuer hadn't bothered to shut it behind her. Certainly, she wasn't afraid of the likes of them.

The room was about the same size as a one-car garage, but far cozier. The usual fire pit in the middle had been turned into a campfire, a circle of rocks in a freshly dug hole with a grate positioned neatly across the stones. At present it was unlit, but an old blue enamel coffeepot and a Japanese-style iron pot sat on top. Low black tables were battered remnants of tea ceremonies performed there in better days. And there were musty old tatami mats that Mercy would think twice before sitting on, although apparently the woman had tried to improve upon them with what looked like relatively clean cushions.

The woman laid the trembling boy down on an army issue–style cot, covering him in old quilts. Susie Bear and Elvis rushed to Henry's side, licking his face while she positioned him to lean forward, so she could massage his back.

The dogs paid no attention to the woman. She must be safe, Mercy concluded. If Elvis or Susie Bear believed she were a threat to Henry, they'd be all over her.

Henry coughed up water. Mercy knelt at the boy's side, brushing his brown hair away from his face. "Are you okay?"

He coughed again, then gave his trademark nod.

"Okay, let's warm you up." She helped the woman tuck the quilts around the boy's shivering body.

"I'll light a fire." Troy helped himself to the logs and kindling neatly stacked in one corner of the teahouse, starting a fire as quickly and expertly as you'd expect a game warden to do. He looked up toward the ceiling. Mercy knew he was checking for a smoke hole.

"It's okay. I didn't fix them all. Between the broken panels in the ceiling and the ones around the perimeter, there's plenty of air circulating in here." Yolanda pointed along the base of the pagoda, where several missing boards let in the cold air.

With the fire burning strongly, the teahouse's one room rapidly warmed up.

The woman was obviously living here, and she'd made an effort to make it as nice as possible. Mercy wondered how long she'd been here, and why she was hiding out. If that were what she was doing.

She gave them each a throw, and a couple of old army blankets for the dogs. The three of them huddled together, Henry tucked between Mercy and Troy, the dogs curled up at their feet, while the woman stood by the fire, watching them. The boy fell asleep at once, snoring softly. For a moment, they sat in silence, watching the rise and fall of his small chest.

Mercy looked up at the woman. "Thank you for saving Henry."

The woman smiled slightly.

She extended her hand. "I'm Mercy Carr, and this is Troy Warner. We're friends of Henry's."

The woman gingerly shook her hand. "Yolanda Yellowbird. Let me make us some tea."

While Yolanda filled the iron pot with water, Mercy looked around. There was not much in the teahouse. A few changes of clothes—jeans, T-shirts, socks, stacked neatly in a cheap plastic basket—a worn-out army duffel bag, a military-issue trunk, and food in zippered plastic bags. Crackers. Chips. Cans of chili and soup and beans. Plastic bottles of drinking water. All easily stored.

Mercy wondered how she kept the bears out.

Then she spotted the weaponry. A longbow and a quiver full of several arrows stood in the corner. She glanced at Troy, also staring at the bow and arrows in the corner.

Yolanda caught them looking. "I didn't kill that man in the gazebo. Or the other one. I'm done with killing."

"What does that mean?" asked Troy.

"Three tours in Afghanistan."

Troy nodded. Mercy knew he'd been over there too, just as she had.

"How'd you end up here?"

"I lost my job. I guess you could call me a squatter. I've been fine mostly, except for the creeps."

"What creeps?" asked Troy.

"Creeps are everywhere," Yolanda said. "All through these woods."

"How much of the forest do you know?" asked Mercy.

"I've been up and down and around this wilderness, from Northshire to Stratton."

"And you think poachers killed Caspar Farrow."

"That his name?" Yolanda shrugged. "Maybe poachers killed him. Maybe not. I didn't see anyone—just the body. And then the boy. The dogs. You all."

"What were you doing at the gazebo?" asked Troy.

"Foraging. Still lots of mushrooms around, if you know where to look." She pointed to an old basket in the corner. "Help yourself."

"What happened?" asked Mercy.

"I heard shouting at the gazebo, so I went to take a look. By the time I got there, there was only the dead guy."

"He was a guest at Daniel Feinberg's house."

"The rich dude."

"Yes."

Yolanda poured steaming water into three chipped blue-green *matcha* teabowls, dropping a tea bag into each one. "A while back, I ran out of the Japanese tea they had stocked here. All I got is Lipton."

She handed one bowl to Mercy, and one to Troy. The last she kept for herself. "Maybe poachers killed them both."

"Both?"

"Two people murdered, right?"

"You saw the first victim as well?"

"No. Just the cops and the forensics techs."

"What were you doing over there?"

"I was mushroom hunting, like today. I heard someone behind me, following me. I hid behind a couple of birch trees. Crouched in the ferns. Then I saw this little boy. He ran past me, and I tracked him."

"Did you see anyone else?"

"I only saw the boy."

"Did Henry see you?"

"I don't know." Yolanda sipped her tea. Her haunted look had faded, and her black eyes were brighter. Even more beautiful.

"What did you see, exactly?" asked Troy.

"I heard someone moving to my right—the kind of sounds poachers make when they're tracking prey. Weird because they usually only come out at night. Like vampires. And it was broad daylight. Maybe they were out checking their cameras or whatever. I don't know." She paused to sip her tea. "The boy must have heard them, too. I figured that's why he was running. I didn't know if he knew where he was going or not, but I didn't want those guys to find him. I made a racket, yelling and screaming, so they'd chase me through the woods. Instead of the boy."

"Weren't you worried they'd catch you?" Mercy appreciated what she'd done to protect Henry. But it was a risky thing to do.

Yolanda laughed. "They tried to run me out of here a couple of times. But they can't. I know these woods better than they do." She slurped up the remainder of her tea and put the empty cup on one of the long low tables.

"Have you seen poachers with bows?" asked Troy.

"No. They usually carry rifles." Yolanda took a seat next to Henry, folding her legs under her and sitting on her heels. "Whoever killed those people is a good shot. Although it doesn't take much to be a good shot with a crossbow."

She was right, thought Mercy. Most anyone could hit anything with a crossbow. It didn't take much strength. "Where did you learn to shoot with a bow and arrow?"

"I grew up in the South. With my mama's people. But my dad was from up here. He was a big archer. He was really good. A champion. You can see videos of him on YouTube."

"Why didn't you go back south?"

"Nothing for me there," she said with finality.

"What about your service weapon?" asked Troy, changing the subject.

"I got it. Legal for me to carry it."

Troy nodded. "That's true. As former military, you're allowed to keep your service weapon and carry it in the state of Vermont."

"I just use it for protection. There's lots of guys up to no good in these woods."

Troy leaned in toward her. "What kind of no good?"

"Everything, I expect. The usual illegal game, drugs, guns, God knows what else. I try to stay away from them. I don't trust them."

"Could you identify any of them?"

"No way. They cover up. Camo and bucket hats. Dark clothes and ski masks. Waders and trapper hats. I can't tell them apart." She clasped her hands together. "And even if I could, I wouldn't. I got no death wish."

"You're going to have to talk to Harrington," said Troy.

Yolanda cursed. "I've heard of that cop. I don't want to talk to him. I'm not talking to nobody." She looked around as if in a panic.

"Don't worry," said Mercy. "We don't have to tell anyone you're here."

Troy shot her a warning glance.

"We need to know if you saw something that's vital to the investigation. Someone is going around killing people. Someone who might be a threat to Henry." He lowered his voice. "Do you think the boy saw anything?"

"I don't know. But he was running for a reason. They were chasing him for a reason."

"We found him in an old ice shack huddled under a gutting table."

"Yeah, I know the place. Night hunters have been using that shack to store things in, off and on."

"Really?" asked Troy. "I'll put a camera on it."

"Who knows what you'll see," said Yolanda. "They're always up to something, those guys."

Henry roused, lifting his head and looking at Mercy.

"How are you feeling?" she asked. "Okay?"

Henry nodded. The dogs licked his face.

"He seems fine," said Troy.

"We need to get him back to the inn, get him in a change of clothes and warmed up." Mercy handed Henry her *matcha* bowl. "Have some of my tea."

The boy took the bowl into his small hands and raised it to his lips.

"You can't always count on us being around to rescue you every time you wander off. We can't protect you unless you stick close. Promise me you won't do that again."

Henry looked at her with solemn brown eyes, but he did not nod his assent. He just stared.

"Okay, let's get you back to the inn," said Troy. "Yolanda, you'll need to come with us, just to tell them what you saw. We don't have to tell them about where you're living."

The woman looked ready to run.

"Troy has no choice," Mercy explained to her. "He has to call the authorities."

"I need to get back to the crime scene," said Troy. "Secure it until the Major Crime Unit can get there."

"You're going to have to tell Harrington about this," said Mercy.

"Not looking forward to that."

And I have to tell Daniel what's going on right under his nose on his property, thought Mercy. *But not quite yet.*

Aloud, she said, "I don't want to put Henry through another bout with Harrington. I don't think he's up to it."

Troy sighed. "Mercy."

"You know I'm right." She paused. "I've got an idea."

"Uh-oh." He grimaced. "Whenever you get an idea, I get into trouble."

Yolanda laughed at that.

Mercy ignored it. "Go back to the crime scene. Do what you have to do. I'll take Henry and Yolanda with me back to Lillian's. We can set up a separate meeting to talk to Harrington."

"There's a murderer running around out there. I'd rather you all stay with me."

"We can take care of ourselves. We're both trained soldiers."

"I've got my service weapon," said Yolanda.

Mercy wished she had her own Beretta. But there was nothing she could do about that now. "We can say that we needed Yolanda to get Henry home. That he needed her. It's more or less true. Henry seems to trust her."

Yolanda shook her head. "I don't want to go anywhere near any police. No government."

"But you were a soldier," said Troy.

"Yes, I was a soldier." Yolanda smiled, and Mercy saw a world of hurt and heart in that smile. "In the army, we watch out for each other. But not out here in the world."

Mercy took Yolanda's hand. "We watch out for each other."

Troy placed his hand briefly on top of hers in a show of solidarity. "We do."

Mercy gently squeezed the woman's hand before releasing it. "So, we've got a plan."

"*You* have a plan." He shrugged in surrender. "I'm going back to the gazebo to call in Caspar Farrow's murder. You can follow me . . . or not."

"I'll take full responsibility."

"Like that matters to Harrington." He ruffled Henry's still-damp hair. "See you later, buddy." He gave her a hard look. "Stay in touch."

Mercy smiled her brightest smile. "Yes, sir!"

Troy rolled his eyes. "Come on, Susie Bear, let's go."

The Newfie retriever mutt whined.

"Come on." His voice was firm. The shaggy black dog shambled to her feet, gave Henry one last sloppy lick on his little nose with her long thick tongue, and ambled after the game warden.

The boy held up his hand in an awkward wave. Looking just like his father.

She turned to Yolanda. "Is there another way out of here? Where we get to the parking lot of the inn without bumping into Harrington at the gazebo?"

Yolanda stacked the now-empty teabowls. "We can circle back and skirt the gazebo completely."

"How will we get back across the creek?"

"There's an old bridge farther down the stream. We can take that route." Yolanda picked up the iron pot and poured the remaining water onto Troy's fire.

"You know they're going to find you here eventually," said Mercy. "They'll kick you out of here."

"I'll take my chances."

"The cops are going to insist on talking to you. It's better if you come in voluntarily."

Yolanda shook her head, her long, dark hair falling across her face like a shield.

Henry was listening. At the mention of Yolanda turning herself in, he started stimming.

"Let me talk to Daniel," said Mercy. "He'll help."

Henry flapped his arms harder.

So hard Mercy was worried he would hurt himself. "Henry, don't worry, we'll talk care of it. Yolanda will be all right. Promise."

* * *

YOLANDA LED HENRY and Mercy and Elvis away from the creek. Away from the gazebo. They weaved through a blowdown area marked by what had obviously been a fire. Countless trees scorched by a fierce blaze, left bare and black. Dark ghosts standing sentinel to the other side.

Mercy thought about Henry's dark trees. Maybe that's what he meant. Which still wouldn't explain anything.

Several hundred yards downstream, they came to an old wooden bridge, about twenty feet long, built in the same pagoda style as the teahouse. The floor of the bridge was worn but appeared stable enough.

"Watch your step," said Yolanda.

Mercy reached for Henry's hand, but he wouldn't take it. Instead, he reached for Elvis's collar.

"Okay, but the dog's in charge." She clipped a leash from her pack on the shepherd, handing the other end to boy. "Elvis will lead you. Let him go first. You follow in his footsteps. I'll be right behind you."

Elvis was not a service dog, but he'd done very well course-correcting Henry on their morning walk to the general store. She had every confidence he could handle this.

They made their way carefully across the shabby structure. Yolanda in the lead, followed by Elvis, then Henry, and finally Mercy.

The Belgian shepherd led his charge across the wooden bridge as carefully as any certified service dog. Henry wobbled a couple of times, but he had Elvis to steady him.

They made it across the bridge without incident, continuing down the overgrown trail. This part of the property had gone to seed. No forest management here; it was difficult to keep to the path among the saplings and the scrub and the fern threatening to obliterate it.

They picked their way deliberately across the messy forest floor, and eventually came to a wider trail. Henry was getting tired, but he refused to let Mercy carry him. He preferred to lean on his pal Elvis.

"Take this trail back to the parking lot," said Yolanda. "You'll see the pool area on the left."

"Got it," said Mercy. "Are you sure you don't want to come? You're innocent, you have nothing to hide."

"You know it doesn't work that way. I know it doesn't work that way. Y'all don't trust Detective Harrington. Why should I?"

"True enough. But we are on your side. And we have friends in high places."

"Like who?"

"Daniel Feinberg."

"Don't trust rich people."

"He's different. And Troy's boss, Captain Thrasher, is a good guy."

"I'm going back." Yolanda turned away from Henry, pushing her jacket aside so Mercy could see the service weapon she'd stuck in her waistband. "You should take this."

"Not necessary. We're nearly out of here, and you're going right back into the fray."

Mercy could see by the set of her jaw that Yolanda was not changing her mind. But neither was she. And she couldn't waste any more time. "You're going to need it."

Yolanda conceded. "Okay. Just get the boy home."

"Try to stay away from dead bodies."

Henry started stimming. Mercy wasn't sure whether it was the talk of Harrington or dead bodies that set him off.

Yolanda took him in her arms, and for the first time, Mercy saw Henry accept an embrace. He almost hugged back, leaning into Yolanda with his head against her chest.

He's a good judge of character, Mercy thought.

Yolanda gently pushed the boy away. "Go with Mercy now. She's good people."

Henry pointed at the dog.

"Yes, and he's good dog."

They watched Yolanda retreat into the deep forest. As soon as she disappeared, Mercy and Elvis ushered Henry along the path. This trail to the inn was far easier to traverse, and they made good time.

He was quiet. No stimming, no moaning, no apparent signs of distress or anxiety. He held onto the leash and Elvis walked beside him, head at his hip, the consummate gentleman.

The trees arched above them, a canopy of gold and red and yellow and purple and orange. If they hadn't been fleeing a crime scene with a possible murderer on their heels, it would have been a lovely walk in the woods on a beautiful October day. There was a slight breeze and the temperature was mild. For a moment, Mercy could almost forget the terrible events of the past twenty-four hours.

Fifteen minutes down the trail, the path opened onto inn's pool area.

"Okay," Mercy said. "We're going to run for the Jeep, which is to our left, about a couple hundred yards away." She pointed to her vehicle. "Elvis will run with you. All you have to do is stay with him. Don't look at anything, just keep running unless I say not to."

Henry stared up at her with big solemn brown eyes.

"Try to be quiet. Pretend we're deer, running quietly through the forest."

He smiled at that.

"Start out for the pool, then head for that dumpster. If it's all clear, we'll run for the Jeep. Got it?"

Henry nodded.

They skirted the edge of the parking lot, staying close to the trees.

The pool area seemed deserted. Blake must be saving that renovation for later.

As they passed the pool and drew closer to the porte cochere, she spotted people working in the distance. Closer to the entrance of the inn. Closer to her Jeep.

"Next time, we'll know never to park near the front door." She stopped at the edge of the dumpster, Elvis and Henry flanking her, peering at the construction workers. About a dozen guys in hard hats swarmed around the front of the inn, reframing the landing that fronted the porte cochere. She hoped they didn't go up on the roof, where they'd have a perfect view of her and Henry and Elvis. It may not matter, but there was always the chance Harrington was already searching for them, and had alerted the staff to be on the lookout for a red-haired woman accompanied by a small boy and a big dog.

Another hundred yards to the Jeep.

"We're going to make a run for it. Stay close to me and Elvis."

Henry held Elvis's lead tightly in his little fist.

"Ready?"

He nodded.

"On your mark, get set, go!"

They took off. Mercy kept one eye on Henry and Elvis, and the other on the workers. She didn't have to look for the Jeep; Elvis would lead them straight to it.

About halfway across the parking lot, Henry stumbled and fell to his bandaged knees. But he didn't cry out.

"Good boy," she whispered, pulling him to his feet. Elvis gave him an encouraging nuzzle. "We're almost there." She glanced at the entrance, but no one seemed to pay them any mind.

She half carried Henry the rest of the way, her long arms wrapped around his thin torso, his boots scraping the ground. His eyes were closed, his lips moving in what she assumed were silent expressions of prime numbers.

She didn't think anybody saw them.

She put Henry in the back seat with Elvis and fastened his seat belt. "We're going to go see your grandmother. Maybe we'll get her to make us one of her famous burgers, huh?"

Henry blinked. She supposed that was a *yes*. Poor kid must be hungry. She was hungry. And from the way Elvis snorted at the word *burger,* she knew the dog was hungry, too. There was no place better to eat than the Vermonter. That might be the one bright spot in what so far had been a rotten day.

She drove as quietly and slowly out of the parking lot as she could to avoid any attention. There was no sign of Detective Harrington and no sign of Captain Thrasher and no sign of Daniel Feinberg. A couple of uniformed cops were parked near the gate, but they paid her no attention. Maybe nobody knew about the murder at the gazebo yet.

Mercy pulled out along the road, deciding to take a roundabout way to the Vermonter.

She could have taken the faster route, but she did not want to encounter any police cars or other law-enforcement vehicles headed to the crime scene. This meant traveling on back roads, rarely used and with good reason. The majority of Vermont roads were unpaved and most people avoided them, especially as winter drew near.

She turned on the radio but couldn't get a station. She glanced in the rearview mirror, and caught sight of Henry, still whispering prime numbers.

Time to sing. She knew that Troy's singing had calmed Henry, and she thought maybe her singing might as well. She warbled out the opening lyric of her go-to kids' song, Randy Newman's "You've Got a Friend in Me" from *Toy Story*.

He ignored her. She switched to "My Favorite Things." She had high hopes for the *Sound of Music* classic, but Henry just primed on. Halfway through the chorus, she gave up.

"Okay, no singing." Mercy laughed. She was no Troy Warner. "We'll just take a nice, quiet ride then."

They bounced along in the Jeep, winding through the forest. Eventually the road took a wide curve, leaving the forest and entering a wide wetland.

"Hawk," said Henry, startling Mercy from her thoughts. He pointed out the window. Circling the marsh, looking for its next meal, was a broad-winged hawk.

"Beautiful." Mercy looked at Henry in the rearview mirror again. "How clever of you to know what kind of bird that was. You knew the falcon, too. Do you study birds?"

Henry didn't answer, but she figured the answer must be yes. He probably knew a lot about birds of prey and falconry and anything else figuring into the medieval fantasy role-playing world. She scanned the sky as she drove, looking for more birds that might interest Henry.

Elvis barked, his quick, urgent, scary, *pay attention now* bark. She glanced back at the shepherd. In the rearview mirror, she spotted a dark SUV pulling out behind them, off a logging road.

"Good boy."

Henry straightened up to see what was going on.

"It's all right, Henry."

Weird, she thought. They hadn't seen anyone else on this narrow road and hadn't expected to. Not this time of year. The only people out now were hikers and hunters. As nightfall approached, hikers would be sheltering in place. And hunters would be going home if they weren't there already, as hunting after dusk was forbidden.

The SUV raced up behind her. She honked, rolling down her window and waving the guy on so he'd pass her. The just barely two-lane dirt road was narrow, but Mercy thought he could make it.

But the SUV did not go around her Jeep. It pulled closer.

Tailgating closer.

Dangerously closer.

CHAPTER THIRTEEN

FORECAST: FALLING TEMPERATURES AS A FAST-MOVING STORM GATHERS OVER THE MIDWEST AND HEADS EAST TOWARD NEW ENGLAND LATE TONIGHT.

THE SUV'S TINTED WINDOWS were as dark as its charcoal paint. Obscuring the driver.

Elvis barked again.

"I hear you." Mercy stepped on the gas. There was nowhere to turn around and no side roads that she remembered. Her only choice was straight ahead, all the way to Route 7.

Night hunter, she thought. Maybe one of Troy's night hunters. Maybe a murderer.

"We've got company, Henry." She turned around and gave him a quick smile. He didn't smile back. "Could get a little rough. Just hunker down. Sit tight."

She floored it. The SUV came after her. Engine roaring. Bright lights on. Not slowing down. Not passing. Not playing nice.

He's trying to push us off the road, she thought. And the way the Jeep was careening down the road, he just might succeed.

"Hold onto Elvis and close your eyes."

She plowed ahead, hands gripping the steering wheel, foot firmly on the gas pedal, the Jeep jolting up and down on the potholed road. But she couldn't outrun them.

The SUV slammed into the back of the Jeep. As metal hit metal,

Mercy twisted the steering wheel hard, and veered away from the SUV, escaping the worst of it. She sped ahead, pushing the Jeep as fast as it would go.

The SUV had more power than her Jeep. It was gaining on her. On this road, she was at a clear disadvantage. She had to think of something. The only something that occurred to her was maneuverability.

Her vehicle was the more agile. What it lacked in speed, it made up for in tighter turning radius.

The Jeep jostled along, Mercy jerking the steering wheel back and forth. Zigzagging down the road, trying to stay out of the SUV's way.

She saw her opportunity about a quarter mile up the road where the wetland ended and the forest began again.

The road came to a fork. Mercy recognized the old fire tower inside the fork—one of many abandoned fire towers throughout the forest. Troy had converted a similar fire tower into a fine home. A beautiful place with a spectacular view.

No such luck for this fire tower, now in permanent disrepair. The forgotten structure had seen better days, although now it might signal her salvation, just as fire spotters signaled forest fires from its heights back in the day.

If she could just make it to the fire tower, take a hard left, and floor it, she might lure the SUV onto an old logging road with a notoriously bad bump. She'd been down it on her mountain bike more than once as a kid. A significant crack in the road that she knew had sunk more than one vehicle. And spun out lots of mountain bikers. She had a small scar on her left calf to prove it. She knew how to navigate that sinkhole. She'd done it before. She prayed that they hadn't.

Mercy raced for the fork, her eyes on that fire tower. She angled to the right, as if she were going to make a right turn, which is the direction most people would veer to avoid the sinkhole. At the last second, she wrenched the steering wheel to the left and hurtled down the other side of the fork.

The SUV couldn't react fast enough. The driver tried to make the turn, but was too late, and took the turn too slowly. In a screech of tires and squeal of brakes, the SUV rammed into the fire tower. The violent crunch of fender against beam was sweet music to Mercy.

But she knew that would not be the end of it. Their pursuer's vehicle was big enough and tough enough to survive a crash or two. Even if the SUV were disabled temporarily, it wouldn't be for long. She glanced back at the back seat.

"Don't look. Just close your eyes and keep on counting."

Henry did as he was told. He sat, facing straight ahead, eyes closed. Counting, counting, counting.

"Hang in there. We'll be rid of this guy soon."

In the rearview mirror, she watched the SUV back up, turn around, and start after the Jeep again. Its smashed front end did not appear to affect the vehicle's power. The driver was pushing the SUV to its limits. Putting on speed.

She hoped he was frustrated now, not paying attention, and that she could use that frustration and inattention to her advantage.

The sinkhole lay just ahead. Mercy drove as fast as she dared.

The deep depression fell in the center of the road. Over time, so many people had avoided the sinkhole that there were trodden paths along both shoulders of the road.

She sped forward, waiting as long as she dared. At the last second, as she approached the sinkhole, she jerked her Jeep hard to the right, onto the shoulder. Skirting the sinkhole, she kept up the speed so her tires wouldn't get stuck in the seeping muck.

The SUV barreled after them. She watched in her rearview mirror as it swerved to avoid hitting the sinkhole. Too late. The SUV's front tire caught the edge of the hole, sinking like a stone into the crevasse.

The tail end of the SUV flew up in the air and flopped back down. Hard. The vehicle lurched to a dead stop.

It was only about another half mile to the main road. She floored it all the way, ruts and potholes be damned.

Henry clutched at Elvis. The shepherd licked the boy's face. Unlike Susie Bear, Elvis wasn't much of a licker. Except with Martinez.

She was moved to see him licking the boy, comforting him as best he could.

"Just a little longer and we'll get that burger from your grandmother," she said with more confidence than she felt.

She grinned as Route 7 came into view. Once she hit the main road, she'd be back in cell-phone range. She could contact Troy and tell him what happened. He'd tell Thrasher, and Thrasher would send someone after that SUV.

She didn't know whether the driver was targeting her or targeting Henry. But she wasn't taking any chances.

Turning onto Route 7, Mercy whooped with relief. Henry joined in, whooping, too. Elvis barked.

Only twenty minutes down the road now to the Vermonter, and no SUV in her rearview mirror. She quickly texted Troy. She owed Daniel Feinberg a call, too, but that could wait.

Henry snuggled up to Elvis and started to hum "My Favorite Things."

She smiled. His way of thanking her. She hummed along. The boy lasted through the chorus before dozing off. All that adrenaline catching up with him. Within minutes, he was fast asleep.

Mercy was suddenly very, very tired. Elvis poked his nose over her seat and nuzzled her ear. The Vermonter was just around the next bend. The shepherd would be as glad to see it as she would.

"Time to eat," she told him. "It's been a long day and we're all hungry."

She just hoped they could all stay awake long enough to get through dinner.

CHAPTER FOURTEEN

Any person 50 years or older may use a crossbow during any season when the use of bow and arrow is permitted. Crossbow disability permits are required for those 49 years and younger. Includes archery deer, archery turkey, and archery moose seasons.

—VERMONT FISH AND WILDLIFE REGULATIONS

B Y THE TIME TROY GOT BACK to the gazebo and called in the murder, Harrington was long gone from the Bluffing Bear Inn and back to the office. A fact for which he was actually quite grateful. The detective would make his way back once he heard about Farrow's death, but for now Troy didn't have to deal with him.

The Major Crime Unit showed up about thirty minutes later, and Captain Thrasher came with them. He and Troy stood by the side of the crime scene watching as techs collected evidence. The diminutive Dr. Darling was her usual cheerful self. She called Susie Bear over for a quick belly rub. The Newfie mutt loved the medical examiner. They shared the same love of their work and good-natured temperament.

"That's it, girl." Doctor and dog got to their feet. She gave Susie Bear one last hug and started suiting up. Susie Bear knew the drill, settling at Troy's side for the duration. This was the boring part, at least for her.

Dr. Darling finally acknowledged Troy and Thrasher. "We got another one, huh, guys? And so soon." She regarded Troy with a sly smile. "Where's your better half?"

He patted his thigh, and Susie Bear leaned into him for a good head scratch. "Susie Bear is right here."

Captain Thrasher laughed. "I don't think she means the dog. But the fact that you thought she did worries me."

Dr. Darling approached the corpse, crouching down next to the recently departed Caspar Farrow. "This arrow's not the same as the one we pulled out of Alice de Clare."

"No," said Troy. "It's from a crossbow."

"Really." She grinned widely. "My first crossbow homicide."

"Congratulations," said the captain without a trace of irony.

"This one went all the way through the body," she said. "Another ruptured aorta is my guess. Although of course I'll question everything when I get the body back to the lab."

"How long has he been there?" asked Thrasher.

"Not long. Maybe a couple hours." Dr. Darling paused. "But don't quote me on that."

Troy nodded. "I suspect he was shot shortly before we came upon the gazebo."

"What were you doing out here?"

"We were trying to calm Henry down. The detective wanted to interrogate the boy and Henry doesn't like him much."

"Imagine that," she said.

"Cal Jacobs was there to make sure the interview went well." He tried to keep his voice even. "The psychiatrist."

"I know Cal," she said. "He's good with kids like Henry."

"Right." Troy didn't think Jacobs was good with Henry; hell, the dogs were better with Henry than he was. He sure wasn't any good with Madeline. Troy hoped his dislike of the man didn't show, but when the captain winked at Dr. Darling, he knew he'd failed. "Mercy thought a walk might do the trick. Henry likes to walk. Mercy and Elvis led the way."

"With Cal Jacobs," said Thrasher, with a grin.

Troy ignored that. "Susie Bear and I followed at a discreet distance."

"I bet you did," said Dr. Darling. "Harrington hates you."

"He hates everybody," said Thrasher. "Or at least everybody in a Vermont Fish and Wildlife uniform."

"What happened on your walk?"

"Henry walked."

"But he didn't talk."

"No. Harrington lost his patience and yelled at Henry to start talking, and the boy reacted badly."

"Poor kid. All that trauma and then Harrington on top of it." Dr. Darling shook her head. "Did that scare Prince Harry off?"

"A child in distress? No way. He bailed when he caught his suit jacket on a branch. Ripped it good."

"Ah," said the doctor.

"A man can only tolerate so much." Captain Thrasher paused. "Do we know how Farrow is related to the other victim?"

"Another one of Feinberg's guests," said Troy.

"Guess it doesn't pay to be a Feinberg guest."

"And yet his place is supposed to be so lovely," said Dr. Darling.

"You've never been to Nemeton?" asked Thrasher.

"I've only seen his woods," she said. "And his dead guests."

"Mercy could get you an invitation any time," said Troy. "He's a big fan of hers."

"Aren't we all?" she said, batting her lashes.

Thrasher laughed.

Troy laughed, too. What else could he do?

"I don't know which is more efficient, the crossbow or the longbow." Dr. Darling poked at the arrow that pierced Farrow's cold heart.

"I've seen hunters come to blows debating that very thing," said Thrasher.

"Either way they pack a fatal punch," said Troy.

"That little boy finds bodies wherever he goes," said Dr. Darling.

"Two in as many days," said Thrasher.

"Three." Dr. Darling looked up. "Alice de Clare was pregnant. About eight weeks."

Troy wondered what Mercy would make of that. "She was involved with Ethan. Odds are he's the father."

"What does he say about it?" asked Dr. Darling.

"We're not sure yet he even knew," said Troy.

"As far as we know, she was single," said Thrasher. "Apparently, Harrington is having trouble tracking down the next of kin."

"Two victims from the same hunting party," said Troy. "These murders have to be connected."

"What about Farrow?" asked the captain. "Maybe Alice de Clare was having an affair with him and his wife found out and killed them both."

Troy cast a doubtful glance at the corpse. "What would she want with this guy?"

"Well, checking to see if Farrow's the father will be easy enough," said the doc. "And Ethan Jenkins is in custody, so he should cooperate."

"Ethan couldn't have committed this murder," said Troy. "If the murders are connected, then he's off the hook."

"We'll see if Harrington agrees with you," said Thrasher.

The wind picked up, a sudden blast of cold air indicating that the day's perfect weather was about to change.

"It's supposed to snow later tonight," said Dr. Darling. "And it will be getting dark soon. We'll be wrapping up as quickly as possible."

"Once the snow starts, it's going to get progressively worse," said Thrasher. "Two storms in a row."

"Detective Harrington hates bad weather," said the doc.

"Flatlander," grumbled Troy. "He should move south."

"Not before he's senator," said Thrasher.

They all laughed at that, even though it wasn't really funny.

"Anything else?" asked Thrasher.

"Not right now," said Dr. Darling. "Harrington will want to get in and out of here fast. He should be here soon. You and Susie Bear should be long gone here before he shows up."

"I think I'll make my escape, too," said Thrasher.

"Thanks a lot." But the doctor smiled as she said it.

Troy waved a goodbye to the doctor and whistled for Susie Bear as his boss strode off down the trail. He and the dog caught up with him, and together they hiked in silence back toward the inn. Both checking their cell phones and radios, all dead in the woods. As they cleared the trees and the inn came into view, their devices came to life.

Thrasher checked his radio just as Troy got a text from Mercy.

"Delphine says someone tried to run Mercy off the road," said the captain.

"A dark SUV," said Troy, reading Mercy's message. "I'm going after it."

"We're on that. Why don't you go see if Mercy and Henry are okay?"

"What about Harrington?"

"I'll deal with him," said Thrasher. "Make sure they're all safe. Where are they now?"

"She was taking Henry back to his grandmother."

"The house or the Vermonter?"

Troy checked his watch. "The Vermonter is still open. Barely."

"Mercy will be headed there," Thrasher guessed.

"We're on our way."

"Report in when you get there. Meanwhile, I'll talk to Harrington about sending over some uniforms."

EVEN NEAR CLOSING time, the Vermonter Drive-In was busy. Its parking lot was full. Mercy was glad of it, as Henry was safer in public. Bad guys were less likely to strike if people were around.

Or were they? Whoever killed Alice de Clare and Caspar Farrow had done it in broad daylight. Twice. Deep in the woods, though, far from the enthusiastic crowds of peepers.

Officially, Lillian kept the store open only for breakfast and lunch. The restaurant's stated hours of operation were seven in the morning to three in the afternoon, every day, rain, shine, or snow, from

April to November. But she waived that rule every October, often staying open later to accommodate all the visitors who came from all over the world to bask in the colorful bounty that was Vermont in autumn. The state's population swelled in October, with more traffic than any other month. For many local businesses, this was the make-or-break month that would see them through the winter. Or not.

Not that that appeared to be a problem for Lillian. Even the tourists knew there was nothing better than a sandwich and shake at the Vermonter.

The place wasn't much to look at. The venue was less restaurant and more shack. It wasn't a true drive-in either, just an oversize lean-to built of thick planks and topped with a red metal roof and a vintage neon sign reading DRIVE-IN in bright white letters. Lillian had bought the sign at auction when the local drive-in movie theater went bankrupt. Where the names of films would have been listed, Lillian served up quotes from famous chefs.

Now it read:

> *You don't need a silver fork to eat good food.*
> —PAUL PRUDHOMME

Nowhere on the building did the words *The Vermonter* appear, except at the top of a chalkboard menu behind the counter. The home of the "Best Burger in Northshire" was a glorified shanty, with a large garage-size window where customers lined up to order.

"We're here," Mercy announced. The dog gave Henry a nudge with his dark muzzle. At that siren call, the boy woke up, rubbing his eyes with fists.

She pointed out the window. "There's your grandmother at the counter. She'll be happy to see you."

"Nana." Henry leaned out the side window and waved. Elvis joined him, tongue hanging out. Lillian spotted them and waved back.

Mercy bypassed all the cars crowding the lot and parked around back by the high cedar fence that secured Lillian's potager garden.

The fence kept deer and other undesirables from raiding the home-grown herbs and vegetables that were her pride and joy, as well as the source of the secret ingredients key to her culinary success.

They entered through the back-door staff entrance, saying hello to Chef Victor Santos and his son Lucas. Both were busy at the grill, slapping hamburger patties and Italian sausages and onions and pep-pers down onto the sizzling hot stove while Lillian held court at the counter, taking orders and ringing up sales.

Chef Victor, a fireplug of a man with the arms of a wrestler, looked up at Mercy without missing a beat in his persistent rhythm of *flip, fry, flip.*

Victor had been Lillian's right-hand man since her husband, Grant, went down to the Barn Store for a pack of cigarettes nearly twenty years ago and never came back. Some said he ran off with a ski in-structor from Norway; others said Lillian drove him away by focus-ing on her family business instead of her husband. Patience said he was a cheat and a gambler, and that Lillian was better off without him.

Lillian herself never said a word about her husband or his disap-pearance. So complete was her silence on the matter that people fi-nally stopped asking her about him. She kept his name and raised their kids, but he ceased to exist. Mercy wondered if Lillian's good works were meant to restore the solid-gold reputation her family had enjoyed before she married Grant. If so, it had worked.

She had wasted no time feeling sorry for herself. In true Vermonter fashion, she hired Victor—and eventually most of his extended family, immigrants from Brazil—and carried on. He was protective of his benefactor—and he'd expect Mercy to tell him if his boss or the boy were in trouble.

"Everything is okay?" Victor asked Mercy.

"Everything's fine," Mercy told the chef. "For now."

He nodded and turned back to his grill.

Lillian excused herself from the last of the customers. She gave her grandson a couple of tight hugs, looking up over his shoulder at Mercy.

Mercy mouthed *talk later* behind Henry's back. Lillian released her grip on him, and he scrambled out of her arms.

"Are you hungry? We're shutting down for the day, but I'm sure Victor and Lucas can rustle up a couple of burgers for you before they clock out."

"That would be great," said Mercy.

"Henry, why don't you do the inventory while we pull together something for you to eat?" Lillian said. "That would be very helpful."

Henry smiled—a small smile, but a smile nonetheless.

Lillian beamed. "Thank you, love." She shooed him through a saloon door to the back pantry, where he could count to his heart's content.

"Two burgers fully dressed, one plain," Lillian yelled behind her to Victor in a voice that would wake her ancestors.

The plain burger was for Henry; no one else—not even Elvis—would pass on Lillian's homegrown organic lettuce, tomatoes, onions, fresh herbs, and sweet bread-and-butter pickles, not to mention her special sauce. "Lillian's Sauce" was sold by the bottle for those who wanted to take a little Lillian home with them.

"We'll talk as soon as I serve these customers. It won't be long." She handed Mercy a white apron with *Drive-In, Northshire, Vermont* splashed across the front in big red letters. "Meanwhile, you may as well help out while you wait."

It was way past closing time by now. Mercy tied on the apron while Lillian settled up with the few remaining customers. Food service was second nature to Mercy. She got her first job at sixteen, at a pizza place in the North End. It was a relief to be here, in this familiar place, doing familiar things, things that had nothing to do with violence and murder and the dark side of human nature.

She was glad to help out. Lillian had that effect on everyone. You couldn't spend any time around the woman without wanting to help somebody do something. She was all about causes, her own and other people's. Whether that was due to her absent husband or her own good nature or some combination of both, the citizens of Northshire benefited.

Now Lillian was the one who needed help. She kept glancing back at Henry in the pantry, worry marking her usually cheerful face. And what Mercy had to tell her wasn't going to ease her anxiety.

When the last of her satisfied customers drove away, Lillian told Victor and Lucas to call it a day.

"Are you sure?" Victor asked.

"We're sure," said Lillian.

"We're sure," repeated Mercy. Thrasher was already tracking down the guys who'd tried to run them off the road.

Victor wrapped their burgers and put them out on paper plates while Lucas scraped the grill clean.

"Go on home." Lillian closed the counter window and pulled down the metal roll-up shade. "We'll do the rest. See you tomorrow."

Mercy heard the back door slam behind the chef and his son as she gave the counter one last swipe. She removed her apron and hung it on a hook.

She walked over to the saloon doors and observed Henry taking inventory. He held a steel clipboard in one hand and a red pen in the other, rocking back and forth on his heels as he counted. Elvis sat at his feet, nose in the air, alert to the value of inventory. Henry proceeded in his exacting manner, tapping the pen on the clipboard, counting packages of hot-dog buns, Ball jars of bread-and-butter pickles and sweet relish, bottles of catsup and mustard and hot sauce, rocking, rocking, rocking—stopping only long enough to record those numbers from time to time with great fastidiousness.

Lillian came up and stood beside her. They stayed still for a moment, shoulder to shoulder, listening to the boy count boxes of paper straws.

Quietly, Mercy updated her on Ethan and Caspar Farrow and then told her about the incident on the way home.

"Are you sure he's all right?"

"I think so. Hard to tell."

"Let's get you fed and then we'll talk." Lillian leaned over the saloon doors. "Time to eat, Henry."

The boy did not seem to hear. He went on counting, then paused to write something on the clipboard. "All done."

"Great," Mercy said. "I'm famished."

Elvis leapt to his feet. Henry laughed. He shuffled through the saloon doors with Elvis. Lillian handed them paper plates, along with a pitcher of lemonade, two glasses, and a bowl of water for the dog. "Why don't you all eat outside while I finish closing up?"

They settled in with their burgers at the old weathered picnic table at the edge of the potager garden, a beauty of knots and raised beds ringed by rows of fruit trees fronting the high fence that enclosed the entire space. This time of year, the bounty included carrots and kale and pumpkin and winter squash, along with grapes and apples and pears and her trademark herbs. The reds and golds and greens of the garden shone in the late afternoon sun, echoed by the reds and golds and greens of the forested mountains all around them, the high fence the only break in the riot of color that was Northshire in October.

Only a privileged few were allowed back here, according to the laminated sign in the middle of the table that read, RESERVED FOR VISITING DIGNITARIES ONLY.

In other words, grandchildren.

A ten-foot-high fence kept out most people and most animals. Except for the diggers.

If someone didn't tell you, you wouldn't even know the garden was there. In Lillian's private world, she raised the ingredients that made all the difference in her fabulous recipes. Whether it was a grass-fed beef burger or a veggie burger, a croque monsieur or a gyro, her sandwiches were the best, and this garden was part of the reason why.

Henry didn't say a word. But Mercy could see that he was glad to be back in his grandmother's garden. This was a safe place.

As they ate, the only sound was the snapping of Elvis's jaws as he inhaled his burger, followed by the slurping of water from his bowl. Henry consumed his burger with the same precision as he did his mashed potatoes and gravy, systematically nibbling around the perimeter. She ate her own meal at a polite pace; still, by the time she'd swallowed her last bite, Henry had made little progress with his dinner.

She watched the circle of bun and burger slowly shrink in diameter as the boy pecked his way around his meal, as fascinated by his constancy as she was frustrated by his lack of urgency.

It takes as long as it takes. That's what they said about training dogs. No rushing it. No rushing Henry, either.

Elvis sat at the boy's feet in his preferred Sphinx position. Patient as a dead pharaoh. Far more patient than Mercy.

Lillian had been inside for a while. Mercy figured she was busy closing up shop, cleaning up, and cashing out the register. She should probably go offer to help but didn't want to leave Henry, even with Elvis in attendance. They were all more rattled by the day's events than she'd realized.

The dog leapt up, barking madly.

"What's the matter?" She stood up, alert to any untoward sound or movement.

Nothing. Only Elvis's increasingly frenzied bellowing.

Henry looked up at her, fear plainly showing on his small face. His eyes dark with worry.

Elvis tore back toward the restaurant, and Henry ran after him.

"Wait!" Mercy sprinted after them. She made it to the back door before Henry. But not before Elvis. The shepherd jumped up on hind legs, tearing at the door with his claws.

"Down, Elvis, down!"

He didn't budge, so she grabbed the dog's collar and pulled him away. She pushed open the back door—and was greeted by billows of smoke. She fell back, raising her arm to keep the boy away. "Stay back. And don't move. Elvis, sit."

She jerked her cell phone out of her pocket and handed it to Henry. "Call nine-one-one. You know how to do that, don't you? Tell them the Vermonter is on fire and to send an ambulance."

Henry reached for the phone, his brown eyes huge.

"You can do it. Elvis will help you."

The shepherd whined. He wanted to come inside with her.

"No, Elvis, stay."

She pulled her T-shirt over her face and went through the door-way. Crouching down, she duckwalked past the grill toward the counter. The smoke was thick. It was hard to see.

She could feel the heat of the flames coming from the pantry.

No sign of Lillian.

Mercy dropped to her knees and blinked, peering through the smoke, eyes stinging. Through the blaze, she spotted Lillian sprawled on the floor of the pantry. She couldn't get to her, not through those flames.

There had to be a fire extinguisher around here somewhere. But where? She couldn't remember, although she was sure she'd seen it. The smoke was too thick to look for it, and she needed to stay close to the floor. She closed her eyes, and imagined the inside of the Vermonter kitchen, trying to remember where it was. She pictured the grill, the pots and the pans, the chopping block. And there, on the wall by the chopping block, she saw the fire extinguisher in her mind. She opened her eyes and crawled over to the fire extinguisher, stood up quickly, and pulled it off the wall, and dropped down again, coughing. She scrambled toward the pantry and aimed the stream of foam at the flames lapping at the saloon doors and spreading along the walls.

The worst of the fire was extinguished, at least enough to allow her to make her way into the pantry and over to Lillian. She cradled her in her arms.

Lillian was overcome with smoke. "Henry."

"He's fine. Don't talk."

She grabbed Lillian under the armpits. The woman moaned, then fell silent. Mercy backed up, duckwalking back toward the back door, dragging Lillian over the wide old oak plank floor. She'd have sore thighs tomorrow—and Lillian would have splinters.

Only a few feet more to the door. Mercy struggled to breathe through the thin cotton of her T-shirt. Her head swam, and she started coughing. Her butt banged the doorjamb just as she felt like she was going to pass out. She scooted to her left, into the open air, and struggled to her feet. She pulled an unresponsive Lillian out onto the deck.

Elvis bounded over, licking Mercy's face as she yanked her shirt off her face and gulped for air.

Henry started toward them, clutching her cell phone to his chest.

"Did you call nine-one-one?"

Henry nodded.

"Good boy. Now stay back. Let me get your grandmother out of here."

She dragged Lillian across the deck and down the main graveled path to the center of the garden, where two Adirondack chairs sat in front of a silver-blue gazing globe on a stone pedestal.

She laid her down on the gravel. Henry hovered over his grandmother, accompanied by Elvis, trying to lick Lillian's face.

"No, Elvis."

Whoever had set this fire might be nearby, even out front, watching the place burn. The arsonist must have thought the place was closed. Empty.

Worse, maybe the arsonist knew they were inside when he set the fire.

Mercy looked around the garden, but she didn't see anyone.

She smoothed Lillian's silver hair away from her brow. She felt for a pulse. Nothing.

"Okay, Henry. Time to count. Very fast. A hundred beats a minute."

She placed the heel of her right hand at the bottom of Lillian's sternum, and her left hand on top of her right, interlacing her fingers.

She pumped Lillian's heart, counting along with the compressions. "One and two and three and four . . ."

Henry counted with her in a small voice that grew louder with every beat. Whoever started the fire probably didn't know they were in the garden, thanks to that ten-foot privacy fence.

The boy was screaming the numbers now.

Lillian started coughing, and Mercy gently raised her up to a sitting position. "Quiet, Henry."

Henry stopped midscream. He stared at his grandmother as she continued a terrible hacking that subsided into gasps.

Mercy was conscious of holding her own breath as she prayed Lillian would breathe easily once again. Finally, the older woman seemed to clear her lungs. Inhaling and exhaling.

Henry put his head on his grandmother's lap. Elvis sat at Lillian's back, propping her up, the shepherd as spine.

Mercy rubbed the woman's shoulders and back. She thought Lillian looked a little better, less ashen. But she worried that she might be in shock. "Are you okay, Lillian?"

"Fine." She stroked her grandson's hair.

"What happened?"

"I don't know. I went into the back for Henry's clipboard, and I heard a *whooshing* sound. All of a sudden, the pantry was full of smoke."

"Henry called nine-one-one. Help should be on the way."

"Clever boy." Lillian managed a weak smile. Henry lifted his head and smiled back.

"Stay right there." Mercy ran to the fence and peeked through a small hole in one of the pine boards. She stared at her Jeep, whose tires were slashed. A nice complement to its smashed rear end. The tires on Lillian's Subaru were slashed, too.

She went back to Lillian and Henry and told them about the vehicles. "We're not out of the woods yet. Whoever set this fire could be watching right now. If we go outside this fence, he could be out there. And with our vehicles out of commission, we couldn't go very far very fast anyway."

"What do we do?"

"The safest thing to do is wait until help arrives." She looked up at the smoldering Vermonter. The fire seemed to be mostly out.

Lillian followed her gaze. "You saved it."

"I'm not sure about that. Maybe if the firefighters get here in time . . ." She let her voice trail off. She did not say out loud what she was thinking, that if the arsonist was out there watching, and realized the fire was not worsening, he'd finish the job. And find them.

"Is there a place to hide back here?"

"A garden shed on the other side of the property."

"Okay, we'll stay there until the fire department shows up. Shouldn't be too long. Wrap your arm around my neck and I'll help you to that shed. Come on, Henry. Elvis."

They made their way across the garden. The property comprised about an acre, and the shed was near the fence at the far southern edge, beyond several rows of corn.

When they reached the small shack, Elvis pushed the broken door of the shed open, and they all tumbled in. Their shelter was a glorified tin shed about ten feet wide and fifteen feet long, but it would have to do. On one long wall hung dozens of tools—rakes and shovels and spades and pruners. The opposite wall held a potting bench crowded with pots of all shapes and sizes. A wheelbarrow stood in one corner, and a crude shelf on the short wall held a collection of garden stones and ornaments.

Mercy eased Lillian beside a stack of bags filled with mulch, directing Henry to sit at her feet. "You two stay put."

"What about you?" asked Lillian.

"Elvis and I are going to hide in the corn. Guard duty."

Lillian nodded. "Okay."

"No screaming, Henry. Got it?"

"Got. It."

Mercy looked around and found a couple of old tarps, placing the green plastic sheets lightly over Lillian and the boy. "Sit tight."

She grabbed a shovel off the wall as she waved Elvis outside. The Vermonter was still standing, if a little scorched around the edges. Of course, there was no way of knowing the extent of the damage inside. For Lillian's sake, and the sake of burger lovers everywhere, she hoped it wasn't too bad.

Together she and the Belgian shepherd ducked through tall ears of corn. She crouched among the stalks with Elvis, the shovel between her knees. Waiting for the blessed sounds of sirens, hoping Lillian and Henry were all right holding tight in the shed.

Not for the first time that day, Mercy wished she had her gun.

CHAPTER FIFTEEN

FORECAST: TURNING COLDER AND WINDIER BY LATE
AFTERNOON. HEAVY SNOW EXPECTED TONIGHT,
WITH ACCUMULATION OF MORE THAN ONE FOOT
IN SOUTHERN VERMONT AND NEW HAMPSHIRE BY
MORNING, MORE IN THE MOUNTAINS.

TROY AND SUSIE BEAR huffed it back to the Bluffing Bear Inn parking lot in record time. He shooed the big black dog into the back seat, climbed in himself, and hightailed it out of the inn's lot and onto the main road. The route was packed with tourists, but it was still the fastest way to Lillian's burger joint.

All the main roads in Vermont were crowded. Troy turned on his siren and his lights, and the leaf peepers parted like the Red Sea. He passed Harrington on the road going the other way, toward the crime scene, Becker at the sedan's wheel. Sirens blaring and lights blazing. Becker honked, an obvious order from Harrington for Troy to stop and follow, but he ignored it.

He kept speeding toward the Vermonter, counting on Thrasher to run interference with Harrington. The detective was head of the Major Crime Unit, and as such he'd tried to get Troy fired the last time that he'd disobeyed a direct order. He might try to do it again.

Hell, of course he'd try to do it again.

Insubordination. The one thing Harrington hated most.

He turned onto Route 7. Susie Bear jumped up and down in the back seat, whining. She knew that when the sirens and the lights went on, the game was afoot. She wanted to get on with it as much as he did.

"Calm down, girl. We're nearly there."

As he approached a main intersection about two miles from the Vermonter, he realized all the peepers were pulling over to the side of the road—and not because of him. He slammed on the brakes as two fire engines lunged in front of him, careening around the corner through the intersection, their sirens clanging away.

He sped after them. They lumbered ahead of him at a surprisingly fast clip. But not fast enough.

He needed to go around them, like it or not. And they wouldn't like it.

"Hold on, Susie Bear," he said as they flew ahead, the fire engines seemingly in pursuit. The fire trucks laid on their horns as Troy overtook them, passing them on the left and barely missing a startled tourist in a minivan.

He barreled past the fire engines. They kept honking. Everyone was honking at him today. He was going to hear from Thrasher about that sooner or later.

He figured he'd just outrace the firefighters, but when he took a left onto Depot Street, the fire engines took a left, too.

"I've got a bad feeling," he told Susie Bear as they roared past the hotels and businesses packing this main thoroughfare.

The Vermonter was just up on the left, around a long curve, hidden behind a stretch of maples and oaks and birches aflame in color, lit by the setting sun. As Troy tore around the bend, he heard the sirens still behind him.

Then he saw why.

MERCY AND ELVIS sat in the corn, waiting. A cool breeze blew through the stalks and the silk. Which might have been a good thing if the wind did not refuel the dying flames threatening the Vermonter. If the arsonist wasn't refueling the fire himself, as she sat here doing nothing.

Elvis kept nuzzling Mercy's ear, his way of telling her he'd just as soon get the hell out of there. He didn't like doing nothing either. The determined shepherd wanted to go back to the shed. He didn't understand why they were stuck in a cornfield while the people they should be guarding were elsewhere.

But she'd told him to stay and so he stayed. Elvis had to trust that Mercy knew what she was doing. She scratched that sweet spot between his triangular ears. He could be a patient soldier when he needed to be. The army taught him that. The army taught her that, too. Still, it was a lesson she had to learn over and over again.

It was getting dark. Pretty soon the raccoons would be trying to get to this corn. She could see that Lillian had planted peppermint and summer squash around the corn in hopes of repelling raccoons. But some of the ears were nibbled at the top, meaning some kind of corn lover had been feasting on the sweet kernels.

Elvis was twitching, in anticipation of the critters who might be able to scale that fence or burrow under it. Mercy didn't know how deep the fence went, and how many creatures would try to breach it to nibble on the sweet corn that lay beyond it. The chipmunks and squirrels were probably asleep by now, or maybe the fire had scared them away. But raccoons stayed out forever; they were fearless annoyances of the first order.

And they liked corn.

She heard sirens in the distance. She thanked Saint George, patron saint of the cavalry, and one of Martinez's saints. He'd had a saint for everything: Saint Anthony for lost things, Saint Valentine for luck in love, Saint Jude for lost causes.

"Help is on the way," she told Elvis.

She assumed those sirens were for the Vermonter. Any other option was unthinkable. She hoped Henry and Lillian would stay put until she came and got them. Which she would only do when she was sure they were safe. She kept her eye on the door of the shed, which she could just make out through the cornstalks.

She figured they were probably as desperate to move as she was. She'd been crouched down, sitting on her heels in a squat for ages now, and her legs were starting to ache. She could feel the sweat in her hair and at the base of her neck, trickling down her back. She welcomed the breeze, although now it was growing colder as the sun went down. Snow was in the air.

If help truly were on the way, then the sound of the sirens should scare off anyone who was around. Namely whoever set this fire. She waited for the sound of the sirens to grow closer, but they seemed slow in coming. Farther away rather than closer.

She heard a thump. She listened hard and heard a bang, the gate opening and closing. Elvis stiffened, and she could feel him tense up, ready to pounce. She put her hand on his head, steadying him. He needed to be quiet and so did she.

She heard footsteps.

Someone was walking along the gravel path. Maybe more than one someone. She heard the crunch of boots. Accompanied by shuffling. She closed her fingers around the shovel, the only weapon at hand. Besides the Malinois.

The arsonist would not be pleased to find Henry and Lillian alive. Or her and Elvis.

The sirens were back. Elvis's ears ticked up at their return; he knew help when he heard it.

They remained perfectly still. The footfalls got closer. The sirens grew louder, the footsteps grew louder. She could feel Elvis trembling with the relentless urge to move.

"Stay," she whispered fiercely. To his credit, the shepherd didn't move. He sat on his haunches, ears cocked, but he stayed quiet. Still the good soldier.

She heard movement, the rustle of the stalks as someone stepped into the corn. The stalks crashed and tumbled and split open. Mercy crouched, ready to attack, waiting.

Susie Bear's big pumpkin head broke through the corn. Elvis nuzzled her neck.

Mercy laughed in relief and, as soon as she laughed, the dogs ran out of the corn, playing together like the carefree canine pals they were.

She looked up, and there he was, silhouetted against the setting sun. Troy Warner.

"Hi." He reached out to her, taking the shovel in one hand and pulling her up with the other. "Are you all right?"

"Fine." She smiled at him. "Where are the fire engines?"

"Right behind me. No worries. What about Henry and Lillian?"

"Hiding in the shed. Did you see anybody out there? I was worried that whoever started this fire might be watching."

"I didn't see anybody. No vehicle, nothing."

"Okay."

"I think you're okay. If there's a bad guy out there, he knows I'm here. And he's not going to come after me."

He held open the broken door of the shed for her. Inside, the dogs barreled toward the tarp and sat nicely, tails thumping, waiting for them to pull the tarp off.

"Come on out," she said.

Henry jumped up, and Mercy hugged him. She didn't care whether he liked it or not.

LILLIAN WAS NOT happy. Mercy stood next to the unwilling patient's hospital bed in a private room on the second floor of Northshire Medical Center, where they'd moved her from the emergency room. The small space was already filling up with flowers and balloons from well-wishers. Word spread fast in a small town, and Lillian was one of this small town's favorite daughters.

Against Dr. Sharma's orders, the patient wanted to go home. Mercy frowned as she listened to the earnest young doctor try to talk sense into the woman. Lillian lay there, hooked up to oxygen, looking small and vulnerable even as she argued right back. Elvis sat at her side, his head on the bed at her hip. Usually dogs were not allowed in the hospital, except for service dogs, but Dr. Sharma was a fan.

Giving up on Lillian, the young physician turned to Mercy. "She must be staying overnight," he told her with an air of certainty that only the likes of Lillian Jenkins would challenge. "We need to be running a lot of tests."

"I know." Mercy also knew that keeping her down while her grandson was in danger was going to be next to impossible.

"Not only is the fire itself containing dangerous chemicals, but she is also inhaling other potentially toxic chemicals released during the burning of materials in the restaurant environment." Dr. Sharma leaned in toward Mercy, his dark eyes full of warning. "At her age, it is important that we are being very thorough in our examination."

"I'm right here," said Lillian, her voice still hoarse from the fire. And with an unfamiliar crankiness. "And I'm not old."

Dr. Sharma ignored her. "She should be staying at least two days so we can be taking X-rays and doing blood tests."

"She's worried about her grandson."

"The boy is doing fine," said the doctor. "Very well considering what he is going through."

"We both need to go home," said Lillian. "Now."

Mercy took Lillian's hand in hers and squeezed. "You know that's impossible. You need to take care of yourself. We'll take care of Henry."

"His parents?" asked the doctor.

Lillian shook her head.

"His mother's not around," explained Mercy. "And his father is . . . unavailable."

She looked down at her phone where a new text had appeared. *Speak of the devil.* Mercy looked at Lillian and grinned. "Daniel Feinberg has persuaded Harrington to allow Ethan to come for Henry. Two police officers will accompany him."

"Police officers?"

"Don't worry. The fact that Caspar Farrow was murdered while Ethan was in custody should cast serious doubt on his guilt."

"I hope you're right."

Dr. Sharma smiled. "So all is well." He gave a little bow. "I am going now. Coming back this evening for rounds. Meanwhile, please be cooperating with the tests."

Lillian muttered a gruff goodbye.

Mercy accompanied Dr. Sharma to the door. "There should be a uniform sitting outside this room," she told him. "I'll find out where he is."

The doctor nodded and went on his way. Patience strode past him down the hall.

"Thank goodness you're here." She kissed her grandmother on the cheek.

Patience smiled. "I'll stay with Lillian for the duration. Make sure she does as she's told. She's stubborn. Always has been. But I'll keep her in line."

"Thank you."

"And you, please be careful."

"No worries. I'll have Elvis with me."

Grandmother in tow, Mercy returned to Lillian's hospital room.

"You look much better than I thought you would, oxygen tank and all." Patience smiled at Lillian. "Though certainly not good enough to leave."

"But Henry—"

"Mercy's got that covered." Patience made herself comfortable in the orange plastic seat at her friend's bedside. She fished a pair of playing cards out of her voluminous if battered wine-colored leather backpack. "Gin rummy. I'll deal."

Lillian sighed. "Jokers wild."

"I prefer deuces wild," said Patience.

"I nearly died," said Lillian.

"Whatever."

* * *

MERCY AND ELVIS snuck out while the two old friends were still bickering. She headed to the reception area, where Troy and Captain Thrasher waited with Susie Bear. An elderly couple was across the room, holding hands and watching an all-news channel on the television, but otherwise the waiting room was empty. The pair paid no attention to them or their dogs.

"I talked to the fire investigator," said Troy. "It was definitely arson. But your quick thinking with that fire extinguisher paid off. The Vermonter will still need significant repairs, but it's not the total loss it could have been."

"Well done," said Thrasher.

High praise from the captain. Troy gave her a thumbs-up behind the captain's back and she stifled a laugh.

"Thank you, sir."

Thrasher cleared his throat. *Uh-oh.* Mercy knew him well enough by now to know that usually meant he was about to announce bad news.

"Harrington has warned us off the investigation."

"What else is new," said Mercy.

"He also sent a team into the woods to bring in Yolanda Yellowbird," said Thrasher. "There was nothing I could do to stop him. He's convinced she's up to more than mushroom hunting."

"She saved Henry," she said. *"Twice."*

"All you can do is prove him wrong." The captain grinned. "You're good at that."

"I still think the night hunters are behind all this," said Troy. "I'm going to check that camera and put another one at the bob-house. I have to go out on patrols anyway, and with the storm coming tomorrow, there'll be plenty to do."

"The night hunters are up to something, but I'm not convinced that it's murder."

"Why not?" asked Thrasher.

"Follow the money," she said. "And the money leads to Nemeton. I've got to get back there and do some more digging."

"I didn't hear that," said Thrasher.

"You have no tires," said Troy.

"Daniel Feinberg had a rental delivered here for me to drive," she said. "When will Ethan arrive?"

"He's on his way," said the captain. "Becker and Goodlove are bringing him. They'll stay with Ethan and the boy for the duration."

"Goodlove?" She knew Officer Becker, but not Goodlove.

"A good officer, top of her class at the academy."

"A rookie?"

"She's new," admitted Thrasher.

She frowned. "Newer than Becker? Seriously?"

"Becker's a good officer," said the captain. "He and Goodlove make a good team."

"You can't do everything yourself," said Troy gently.

"Not to mention that you are a civilian," said Thrasher dryly.

Troy jumped in, probably to make sure that she ignored that remark. "Ethan will take Henry home to Lillian's house. And stay there with Becker and Goodlove until we figure out who is behind this."

"What about Lillian?"

"There's a uniform on the way," said Thrasher. "Even Kai Harrington knows that letting anything happen to the grand dame of Northshire would be a bad idea."

"Did they chase down the SUV that tried to run us off the road yet?"

"Not yet," said Thrasher. "It seems to have disappeared into thin air."

"Whoever they were," said Troy, "they knew what they were doing."

"They could be on their way to Maine by now. But we'll keep looking."

Dr. Sharma joined them. "Henry is okay to be going home."

"Elvis and I will stay here with him until his father shows up."

The doctor nodded and excused himself.

"Then I'm going to back to Nemeton," she told Thrasher and Troy.

"I suppose there's no stopping you," said the captain. "But stay out of trouble. That blizzard is on the move. Just the mention of snow and the peepers all panic. We're going to be very, very busy."

By which he meant Troy and Susie Bear would be very, very busy, and possibly unavailable, should she need help.

"I'll be fine."

Thrasher left as soon as Lillian's uniformed guard arrived. Troy and Susie Bear stayed behind in the reception area with her and Elvis just long enough for him to tell her that Alice de Clare had been pregnant.

"Dr. Darling can test for Ethan and Farrow," said Troy.

"But what about the rest of them? The sooner I get back to Nemeton, the better."

"Anyone could be the father. It doesn't have to be someone in this hunting party."

"You mean it could be a *coincidence*." She raised her eyebrows and waggled them at him.

Troy laughed. "Yes, Groucho, that's exactly what I mean."

"Private joke?" Thrasher rematerialized as if from nowhere.

She bit back a *yes, sir!* and said simply, "Sort of." She felt her face flush.

"Mercy doesn't believe in coincidences," Troy said. "At least not when it comes to murder."

"Neither do I." The captain looked from Mercy to Troy. "Not when it comes to anything. Time for patrols, Troy." He nodded at her, then exited, clearly expecting Troy to follow.

Which he did, after grinning a goodbye at her and calling for Susie Bear.

The shaggy dog lumbered after him, and Mercy sat in one of the thinly stuffed blue armchairs designed to make patients and family feel comfortable while they waited for good and bad news. Elvis settled at her feet.

She watched Troy and Susie Bear disappear through the wide hospital doors into the dark night. The elderly couple still sat in front of the television, still taking no notice of them, still holding hands.

Elvis lifted his head, resting it on the seat of the chair, nose nuzzling her thigh. Even so, Mercy felt alone. Whether this feeling was down to another sudden wave of grief over her fiancé's death catching her unawares again or the insistent tug of attraction to a certain game warden, she wasn't sure. Elvis licked her hand and she smiled. As long as she had Elvis, she was never really alone.

She slapped her thigh to rouse the shepherd to her side, and together they went to find Henry. Fifteen minutes later, she was back in the reception area with Henry and Elvis, waiting for his father.

Henry sprawled on the orange couch across from her; the shepherd sat to his left. Elvis leaned into the boy, his head on Henry's knobby knees, alert and attentive as ever.

The snow flurries had begun, and even though the driving conditions weren't near as bad as they would be once the storm arrived in full, she knew that accidents would be piling up as tourists spun off roads, slipped into ditches, and plowed into their fellow drivers. Law enforcement would be short-staffed and overworked, especially with three of them guarding the Jenkins family.

"What should we do to pass the time?" she asked Henry.

The toys in the corner of the reception area were for toddlers. There was a stack of coloring books and a box of crayons.

"We could color."

Henry just looked at her, big brown eyes aghast. He scrambled to his feet and went to the tall window on the left, one of the soaring glass panels flanking the hospital's entrance.

Coloring was not challenging enough for this little genius.

"Okay, no coloring." She joined him at the window. Elvis wriggled between them, and the three of them stood there, watching the snow fall, white sparkles in the dark night.

"They say every snowflake is different."

Henry shook his head *no*. "Crystals."

"Crystals," she repeated, trying to think like he would. "Oh, I get it. You're saying that snowflakes aren't really flakes at all. They're crystals."

Henry nodded. He got up and retrieved the box of crayons and one of the coloring books from the corner. *Cinderella.*

He took out a black crayon and opened the coloring book. In the blank corner of one of its pages, a page featuring the pumpkin carriage, the boy drew an arrangement of six-figured water molecules in the ice-crystal lattice. Hexagons.

"I'm guessing that's the molecular structure of a snowflake. *Er,* crystal."

Henry nodded, and continued to draw, detailing the molecular structure of different kinds snowflakes and labeling them as appropriate: stellar dendrites, bullet rosettes, sectored plates, twelve-branched stars, radiating dendrites. Quite a vocabulary, even for the Wikipedia kid.

"Impressive," she said. "You should be a meteorologist when you grow up. I could watch you on the news every night. You could wear a bow tie."

Henry smiled at that.

BY THE TIME Ethan Jenkins showed up with Officer Becker and Officer Goodlove, Mercy knew more about the complex structure of snowflakes than she ever thought she would.

"Henry!" Ethan gathered his son into his arms and Henry hung there, arms limp at his sides, letting his father embrace him.

Becker was a good cop for a rookie. Although she supposed that when he was paired with Officer Goodlove, she was the rookie, and he the seasoned veteran.

Goodlove was a pretty woman with a moon-shaped face framed by dark curly hair and blue eyes that gazed upon her new partner with admiration.

"Heartbreaker," Mercy said to Becker under her breath. He blushed.

She turned her attention to Henry.

"I know you'll miss Elvis, but two police officers are better than one police dog." She smiled at Becker and Goodlove. "At least that's what they say."

Henry lowered his head, staring down at the highly polished floor. Refusing even to acknowledge her presence. She squeezed his shoulder and left quickly. Elvis barked a goodbye, following on her heels.

The snow was falling more steadily now, and she had to spend a couple minutes clearing off the Land Rover Daniel Feinberg had rented for her. Fluffy snow, wet and heavy. She knew from her conversation with Henry and her own winter wisdom that as the temperature fell—and it was falling fast—the snow would grow lighter and drier, more powdery. No matter what its molecular composition, the white stuff was piling up.

She'd have to hurry to get to Nemeton before the roads needed plowing.

Elvis bellowed in the back seat. Cocked his triangular ears as if to say, *Where's Henry?*

"Henry couldn't come," she told the anxious shepherd. "Becker and Goodlove are with him. Don't worry about it."

But Elvis was going to worry about it. Just as she was.

BEFORE GOING OUT on patrol, Troy and Susie Bear dropped by the office to handle paperwork that couldn't wait. Then at the captain's request—read *order*—they joined him for dinner at Pizza Bob's Wood Fired Pie Company.

It was a command pizza. Which made him nervous, since he did not know what burr was under the captain's saddle this time. The man was nothing if not enigmatic.

Susie Bear was excited, not nervous, as *pizza* was one of her special people foods, right up there with *steak* and *sandwich* and Patience O'Sullivan's *pot roast*. All the way from the truck to the restaurant, she pranced in front of him. Despite her size, she was light on her feet. She stopped several times to enjoy the attentions of children and grown-ups alike. The dog's happy-go-lucky personality was a beacon, allowing Troy to shine in her light. He wasn't that good with people, but thanks to Susie Bear, most people never noticed.

He smiled at her many admirers as they made their way into

the restaurant. With all the peepers in town, the place was more crowded than ever. Pizza Bob—a big man with a big smile who always smelled of garlic and pepperoni—greeted him with a bear hug and Susie Bear with a breadstick from his back pocket. She loved Pizza Bob's breadsticks.

Pizza Bob's was not a fancy place, which was one of the reasons Troy and Susie Bear liked it so much. The other reason was the pizza. The best in town, thanks to a massive one-of-a-kind stone oven Pizza Bob and his brothers had built with their own hands back in the Sixties and embellished with colorful graffiti true to that time: peace signs and flowers and rainbows and *Give Pizza a Chance.*

In good weather, they could sit outside with the other human and canine customers. The rest of the year, they counted on Captain Thrasher to commandeer a quiet booth in the back with room for a hundred-pound dog to stretch out nearby. Even at peak peeper season, Thrasher did not disappoint. Pizza Bob led them through the throngs to him.

"I've already ordered," Thrasher said. "The usual."

That meant an extra-large Howl—a hand-tossed pie with pepperoni, sausage, bacon, meatballs, and ham—and fresh root beer on tap for them and a large bowl of water for the dog.

"Thanks." Troy slipped into the bench across from his boss and waited.

"An interesting day."

"Yes, sir." Although their relationship was friendly and their usual interactions fairly casual, he knew at times the captain needed to lay on the formality. This was one of those times.

"I read your report. Two murders. A child witness. A hat with peregrine feathers. Quite a story."

"Sir."

"What do our night hunters have to do with this?"

"Maybe everything, maybe nothing."

"We know that there's more illegal activity happening in the woods now than ever," said Thrasher. "In addition to the usual drug dealers and poachers, we've got those gunrunners to worry about."

The recent flood of illegal handguns on the streets of Toronto pointed to smugglers buying up handguns at gun shows down south, sneaking them over the border, and selling them on the black market. The Canadian authorities had been pushing Vermont law enforcement for results.

"No sign of them yet."

"With all these criminals operating in our woods, sooner or later we're going to catch them. And sooner or later, they're going to run into civilians. And we know what happens when civilians find themselves in the wrong place at the wrong time."

"Murder happens."

"Maybe. We don't know enough to make even an educated guess at this point."

"And much of what we do know doesn't make much sense."

"So we keep working until it does make sense." Thrasher steepled his fingers and raised them to his chin. "The name *Mercy Carr* appears several times in your report."

"She discovered the first victim. She tracked down the boy. She found the second victim. She got run off the road. She pulled Lillian Jenkins from a burning building. She—" He stopped when he saw the smirk behind his boss's fingers.

Thrasher laughed, a deep baritone that rolled through the restaurant like a tidal wave, sweeping away everyone in the place. It was an infectious laugh, one that made every man want to be his friend and every woman want to be his, well, woman.

Troy knew without looking that all of Pizza Bob's patrons were staring at them. Dying for an invitation to join the party.

"What's so funny?"

"Something's changed," said the captain. "You and Mercy Carr. Tell me about it."

To Troy's relief, Pizza Bob appeared with a steaming meat-laden pie and a pitcher of root beer. "I'll be back with the big girl's water."

Thrasher helped himself, and Troy put a plate piled with three thick slices under the table for Susie Bear, and one with another three slices on the table for him.

Pizza Bob set the Newfie's water down on the floor. "Enjoy, all of you."

For the next several minutes, neither of them said a word. The captain was completely focused on his food—he took eating very seriously—but Troy was distracted.

It was unlike Thrasher to pry into his private life. God knows the captain guarded his own privacy with a ferocity few dared to breach. His wife, Carol, had died of cancer two years ago, and he never spoke about it. Troy's wife, Madeline, had left him not too long after that, and they'd grieved their losses together over many pizzas and pitchers of root beer without mentioning their wives at all.

"None of my business, I know that." The captain wiped his mouth and hands carefully with a thick stack of napkins Pizza Bob always knew to supply, removing every trace of grease and sauce from his person. "But I have my reasons for asking."

Troy wished he would just come out and say what he meant.

"You'll just have to trust me."

"It's not that." He trusted the captain. The man had gone to bat for him more times than he could count, most notably with Harrington.

Thrasher pushed his empty plate to the side, placing the stack of dirty napkins in the middle of it. He leaned against the red uphol-stered back of the booth, folding his arms. The captain was a patient man. That patience had worked against Troy more than once—and it looked like it would again.

"Nothing's happened between us, if that's what you're asking," Troy said finally.

"*Something* happened." Thrasher uncrossed his arms and placed his elbows on the table, leaning toward him.

"Nothing happened."

The captain waited.

He sighed. "We just washed the dishes."

"Your fate is sealed. Did you wash or dry?"

"I rinsed, she loaded."

"They always have to load it their way."

"Yes, sir." He relaxed.

The captain smiled. "I knew the first time I helped Carol do the dishes, I was going to marry her."

"Hold on."

Thrasher studied him. "Does Mercy know you're still married?"

He looked away, away from the captain's penetrating stare, away from the worry that had preoccupied his every waking moment since he'd helped Mercy wash dishes and lost his heart.

"I don't know."

"What kind of a detective are you?"

He laughed, a short bark of a sound that he knew sounded as bitter to Thrasher as it did to him. "Mercy's the detective. I'm just a fish cop."

The captain frowned. "It's a serious question."

"I haven't told her, if that's what you mean. I just assumed that Patience or Lillian or somebody would have said something to her by now."

"If any assumptions have been made, it's probably that you divorced Madeline when she left you, what, nearly two years ago now?"

"Not that long." Madeline had bolted for the Sunshine State sixteen months ago nearly to the day, though Troy now realized that she'd left their marriage long before that.

Thrasher studied him. "I think it highly unlikely that anyone in Mercy's circle would say anything to her about it, even if they knew. Which I very much doubt."

Troy stiffened under his captain's scrutiny. Thrasher knew that he remembered the very day, the very hour, the very minute he'd found the note that she'd written in red lipstick on the bathroom mirror: *So sorry. Must go. M.*

"I hear Madeline's back in town," said Thrasher. "You're running out of time."

"I know." He meant to tell Mercy a million times. Hell, he meant to file for divorce a million times, too. But it was easier just to go out on patrol.

"Being a game warden is a job, maybe even a calling," said Thrasher quietly. "But either way, it's not an escape. You can't hide out in the woods forever."

"Sir." He'd learned that the quieter the captain's voice, the tougher the conversation.

"Using your professional life to avoid dealing with your personal life eventually compromises both." Thrasher slid down to the edge of the booth and stood up. "This time's the bill's on you."

CHAPTER SIXTEEN

FORECAST: BLIZZARD CONDITIONS.

Mercy cursed the snow aloud while carefully steering the Land Rover back to Nemeton. At this outburst, Elvis lifted his head, then flopped back down to sleep. He knew the vehicle was going nowhere fast.

It was slow going. Her friend the billionaire had built his own road up a mountain to his mansion. That was a good road.

But getting to that good road meant first traveling public thoroughfares. Crowding those streets were cars not meant for winter weather operated by people unfamiliar with winter driving methods. They were all trying to get home, or at least to a hotel. Several buses were stranded, full of leaf peepers perplexed by the incongruous sight of autumn's red, gold, orange, and yellow foliage dressed up in a coat of white.

Many of them weren't making it home anytime soon. They'd be lucky if they got out before the blizzard hit. All signs suggested that this was just the prologue.

Accidents slowed traffic to a standstill. The cops were out in force. But Mercy knew there weren't enough law-enforcement folks to go around.

It was nearly eight o'clock by the time she and Elvis got to Nemeton. George let them in, ushering them immediately to the billionaire's book-lined study. A deep and abiding love of books was one of the things they had in common. He was one of the few people she knew whose library held more volumes than hers did. Of course, more of his were first editions.

Feinberg rose from his desk to meet her, waving her into a Hepplewhite chair. Elvis stretched out on the Aubusson carpet at her feet. After she filled him in on the day's events, Mercy had to assure Feinberg that she was just fine, despite attempts on her life.

"I spoke to Detective Harrington at length over the phone," he said. "He's convinced Yolanda Yellowbird is somehow responsible for the murders."

"I don't believe it. What possible motive could she have?" She paused. "Troy thinks it might be the night hunters. The ones he's been chasing down in the woods. Yolanda thinks so, too."

"But you don't."

"No, but the night hunters are definitely up to something, and it might be something far worse than poaching."

Feinberg raised an eyebrow. "Like what?"

"Drugs. Guns. You name it. According to Troy, criminal activity is on the rise here."

"When I bought this place, I thought the worst that could happen was the occasional bear. I had no idea what goes on in these woods."

"Like Patience says, 'Where there's wood, there's wacky.'"

"This is beyond wacky. I take it that you don't think Caspar and Alice were killed by poachers or gun smugglers."

She shrugged. "It seems to me these murders strike closer to home, Daniel."

His brown eyes darkened with concern. "What do you mean?"

"These murders were personal: their timing, the choice of weapons, the fact that Alice was pregnant."

"I didn't know that."

"Any idea who the father was?"

He shook his head. "I'd assume it would be Ethan. You should talk to Katharine and Lea. They knew her better."

"I will. But first I need to see your security tape."

"Harrington has it all. But I'm not sure it matters. We've got cameras at the service entrance and the front door, but if you really wanted to get out, there are a lot of other ways to get out of the building without being seen."

Mercy frowned.

"We're really more focused on keeping people out than keeping them in. That said, George keeps track of everyone's comings and goings. He may be able to help."

She leaned forward. "I need to talk to all of them again. Casually. So they don't know I'm doing it."

He checked his watch. "Dinner is at eight thirty. It's eight now. We're putting out a big spread. It's been a long day, and everyone needs a good meal. I'll tell George to add a place for you, and to keep the wine flowing. Loosen people up. If there's anything to find out, I have every confidence you'll find it."

"In vino veritas."

"Indeed." He rang for the butler, and George promptly appeared.

She suspected he'd been standing just outside the door the whole time.

"Mercy needs to know what the security tapes revealed."

"Inconclusive, sir." George looked from his boss to Mercy. "The guests all appeared to be out of the house at the time of Ms. de Clare's murder. Except for William Montgomery. Who had not yet arrived."

"Everyone was at the inn for the meeting with Barker the morning Farrow was killed," she said. "When did they come back to the house?"

"Not until later," said the butler.

"We reconvened for lunch at the inn. But everyone was on their own between the meeting with Barker and lunch. About an hour, I'd say." He looked to George.

"Yes, sir. During the time that Detective Harrington said Mr. Farrow was killed."

"That narrows it down," she said. *Not.*

"I'm sure you'll learn more at dinner tonight." He explained their strategy to George, who promised to serve alcohol with all that evening's several courses.

There was something mysterious about George. Something elusive. Something she'd like to get to the bottom of. Feinberg seemed to trust him, but she didn't, at least not yet. Everyone was a suspect—until they weren't.

The butler had a backstory. Mercy needed to track down what that was. She needed to track down all of the backstories of all of the guests.

George coughed. Butler code for *I need to say something.*

"What is it?"

"Mrs. Farrow is still quite upset, sir. Mrs. Montgomery, Ms. Sanders, and myself—we've all tried to calm her down, but with little success. I worry that she might be spending a lot of time online, on Facebook and Instagram and Twitter, sharing her woes with the world."

"Uh-oh," said Mercy.

"Quite right," said Feinberg. "Bad for all involved. We don't want a swarm of reporters descending on the estate."

"The weather will keep them away for at least a little while," said Mercy. "But as Mrs. Farrow is the queen bee of social media, I doubt you can keep them away forever."

"What do you propose we do?"

"I thought perhaps Ms. Carr here could have a word with her," said George.

"Good idea." Feinberg grinned at her. "If anyone can talk sense into her, it's you."

She wasn't so sure. "I can't imagine I'll have any more influence with her than Lea or Katharine, but I'll give it a try."

"Thank you."

"I'll take you to Mrs. Farrow's room."

She followed George up the magnificent staircase to the wing with the guest rooms. She quietly knocked on Cara's door.

"Good luck," said George, making a quick exit.

"Yes?" called a wavering, high-pitched voice.

"It's Mercy Carr. Are you all right?"

"Mercy Carr." The voice trailed off. "I don't know a Mercy Carr."

"We spoke in the woods, after Alice de Clare's body was found?"

"Oh, yes, of course! You found my poor Caspar. You must come in."

Mercy could practically hear the drumroll. She opened the door and found Cara Farrow in full makeup, sitting up in an elegant antique hard-carved Art Deco bed tufted in cream linen. The hair model herself was resplendent in a blue silk dressing gown. She'd set up her iPad and was Skyping. Despite the remote location and an approaching snowstorm, Cara was having no trouble getting online. You could always get a connection at Nemeton.

Cara tapped the screen and whoever was on it disappeared before Mercy could get a good look.

"It's so very important that we speak. Is it really true someone murdered my husband?"

"I'm afraid so." Mercy felt awkward standing by the woman's bedside, so she pulled over a matching Art Deco chair and sat down.

"Oh, of course, do sit down. Where are my manners?"

Mercy felt sure her manners came and went like the wind.

"Who would do such a thing?"

"That's what we're trying to find out. Did your husband have any enemies?"

"No, everyone loved Caspar." Cara flounced her luxuriant hair. She did have incredible hair.

"Somebody killed him."

"None of us." Cara gave her a shrewd glance. "I mean, I didn't know Alice de Clare. But she couldn't have killed him, right? She was already dead."

"That's true."

"Do you think the same person killed them both?"

"I don't know."

"OMG. I could be next." She widened her eyes as if auditioning for a horror movie. "I really need to get out of here. Get *him* out of here."

"That won't be possible, I'm afraid. They'll have to do a full postmortem."

At her blank look, Mercy added. "An autopsy. It could be several days before they release your husband's body."

"And what will I do until then?" Her voice rose into a shrieking wail. Not a true keening; Mercy had seen that up close and personal before. This was a manufactured sound, like electronic music of mourning. She wondered how much this woman really loved her husband, and how much she was enjoying the dramatic notoriety of it all.

"Caspar's killing is all over the Internet. The most wonderful people are posting their condolences all over social media."

"That's great," said Mercy. "I think."

"Oh yes, Caspar was incredibly respected and popular. Lots of friends and colleagues. And of course, *my* fans have rushed to my side at this terrible time."

Just the way she said it, Mercy knew she'd rehearsed that last line over and over again.

"I don't want to talk to any more policemen. I didn't like that Detective Harrington. He's coarse."

"He's just doing his job."

"I don't think so." Cara smoothed the satin bodice of her dressing gown with a perfectly manicured hand. "He seems to think I murdered my husband. But why would I kill the world's dearest, loveliest man? He supported all my endeavors. Did you know that he was helping to raise financing for a film of my own? A Rita Hayworth biopic."

"I can see that." She had the hair, anyway.

"I know, right?" Cara flashed a starlet-worthy smile. "And that's not all." She leaned forward conspiratorially, revealing the results of a perfect boob job. "We were working together on my one-woman show."

"Wow." She wondered how you could get a ninety-minute show out of one head of hair.

"Caspar backed a lot of Broadway shows."

"By all accounts, your husband was a very wealthy man."

Cara narrowed her heavily mascaraed eyes. "What are you saying? I know that detective thinks I killed Caspar for his money. It's totally ridiculous."

"Is it?"

"Of course, it is." Cara held up her pointer finger. "Number one, I signed a prenup." She paused dramatically. "Just like all his other wives. Except wife number one. She took him to the cleaners. That's why he does prenups now. Uh, did." She waited while two perfect tears rolled down her cheeks. "Poor Caspar. He'll never need a prenup again."

Maybe she was a better actress than the world gave her credit for, thought Mercy.

Cara wiped away the tears with her pointer finger, then raised her middle finger as well. "Number two, without Caspar, my movie deal might fall through." She held up a third finger.

She waited, but Cara didn't say anything.

"And number three?" she prompted.

"Everything might fall through." Cara curled her fingers into a fist and pounded the bed.

If she were telling the truth, then no wonder she was more focused on the potential her husband's murder could offer her in terms of temporary notoriety than on his actual murder. Her goal was to make that notoriety stick. In lieu of her scotched one-woman show.

If anyone could do it, it was Cara. She had the resourcefulness of a Kardashian.

Mercy scooted her chair closer to her bedside. "What's your strategy going forward?"

"I don't know what you mean."

"I'm just wondering if you're holding out for the A markets."

"I'm getting interview requests all across the board from blogs, websites, podcasts."

"That's all online, and that's great, but I'm picturing you talking to Gayle King or Stephen Colbert, maybe Ellen?" She let those glorious images sink into Cara's hair-heavy head.

Her baby blues lit up at this pretty thought. "Don't you just love Ellen?"

"Everybody loves Ellen."

"Right. That would be the best."

"Let me text my agent. Tell him to hold out for the biggest shows." She tapped at her phone. "You know, I really should get a new agent."

"One thing at a time."

"I know, right?" She sighed. "Caspar was my manager. I consulted with him on all things." A true shadow of grief passed over her fine features. Then it was gone.

"You're going to have to take care of yourself now."

"I know," said Cara. "The good news is, with all the stress, I've lost two pounds."

Mercy felt the corners of her mouth pull, but she wouldn't let herself smile. The happy side of misery: weight loss.

"Mr. Feinberg has arranged a special dinner tonight. A sort of remembrance for Alice and Caspar."

"Oh, I couldn't face all those people."

She choked back a laugh. Cara was talking to the world on the Internet, but she couldn't face her husband's friends and colleagues. "Maybe you should just take a hot bath and go to bed. George has left something to help you sleep, if needed. You don't want bags under your eyes."

Cara shrieked. An authentic cry, this time. "I have to look my best for the camera. HDTV is the worst, you know. Shows every blemish."

Mercy handed her a glass of water from the crystal pitcher by the bed, along with one of the sleeping pills the butler left for her. She watched Cara take the pill.

"Now get some sleep."

Cara lay back against the mountain of pillows, then shot back up again. "You don't think the power will go out, do you?"

She laughed. "Not here. Daniel has plenty of generators up and running, ready to go should the power go out. I don't know about the rest of the woods, or the state, or even the country, but Nemeton will be fine."

"Having money is good," Cara said, in all seriousness.

Not knowing what to say to that, Mercy patted the woman's shoulder and retreated, pausing at the bedroom door. She looked at Cara, and she had to admit that she was impressed by the hair model's poise. Cara looked camera ready. She probably didn't have a bad side. And that incredible hair.

Mercy watched the young widow slip a satin pillowcase over the top pillow on her side of the bed.

"This is the best for wrinkles, you know," she told Mercy. "Always sleep on a satin pillow."

"I'll remember that." Any wrinkles she had she'd earned the hard way: on the battlefield. She thought of them as battle scars worth celebrating.

Cara fastened a satin-padded eye mask around her beautifully coiffed head and lay back on the satin pillow.

"Good night, Mrs. Farrow."

"Good night, *um* . . . Mercy."

MERCY SHUT THE door quietly behind her and turned to find George waiting for her. It was kind of creepy the way he always seemed to know where she was. There was a house full of guests here, so why focus on her?

"Is everything all right?" he asked.

"I got her to take the sleeping pill and to stay off social media for a little while, but the press will be here eventually, no matter how bad the weather."

"Understood. But Mr. Feinberg has his ways."

Those ways usually included bodyguards. But she hadn't seen them around much lately. "What happened to his bodyguards?"

"They're here. They keep a low profile."

Feinberg had come into some criticism over his use of bodyguards over the summer, when they had failed to prevent a burglary. But Mercy liked the guys anyway.

"There's a police presence, too. Harrington has gone, but he left two officers behind as backup. At least for now."

"Okay."

"Everyone will be at dinner but Owen Barker. Mr. Feinberg sent him back to New York."

Mercy grinned at the banishment of Barker.

George nearly grinned back, but seemed to catch himself just in time. "I'll take you down to dinner when you're ready. I assume you'll want to change."

"I've got nothing to change into." She looked down at the yoga pants and T-shirt she'd been wearing for two days. "I've been on the road."

"You've had a busy forty-eight hours," George said dryly. "Mr. Feinberg always has spare wardrobes for his guests. I've brought you a few things that might work."

She followed him to a room where he had laid out three outfits way beyond her style grade. "Have you met my mother?"

"I'm sorry?"

Mercy laughed. "Nothing. Thanks. I can take care of the rest."

George bobbed his head at her and left.

On the bed were three ensembles: one black, one blue, one red. All looked like something her mother would buy her. If she were going to keep hanging out with billionaires, she guessed she'd have to get all that stuff out of storage.

She chose the blue: a simple tunic with matching pants. Silk, she thought. Felt good against her skin. Maybe Cara Farrow was onto something.

She took a quick shower, washing the smoke out of her hair, and brushed her teeth. Slipped into the tunic and pants. She glanced into the mirror. Her hair was a red-hot mess per usual. She fetched lip gloss out of her pants pocket, borrowed some translucent powder from the makeup kit in the bathroom, and powdered her nose. It would have to do.

CHAPTER SEVENTEEN

In the huge dining room downstairs, the elegantly appointed, custom-made mahogany table could easily have seated thirty people. But gathered around it this evening were only Blake and Katharine; their son, William; Lea; and Feinberg himself.

Always the gentleman, he rose when she entered the room. "Mercy. We're so pleased you could join us."

Blake came to his feet as well, followed by the young man, who stumbled to his feet in a delayed showing of decorum, cell phone in hand.

George frowned.

"I think you know everyone here," said Feinberg. "William you met briefly this afternoon."

"Our son," Katharine said with obvious pride, despite the fact that the young man was obviously nursing a hangover, still drinking heavily, and even now didn't bother looking up from his phone.

To be fair, from the looks of it everyone had indulged in a generous cocktail hour. All their faces were flushed and animated. Except for Feinberg.

"Nice to see you again, William," she said.

"Ditto," said William, his eyes on his phone.

George pulled out a chair for her between Katharine and Blake. The men settled back into their seats.

Lea turned to her. "How's Cara doing?"

"She's taken something to help her sleep."

"I'm sure she needs the rest. What a dreadful day."

"A dreadful couple of days," said Katharine.

"What do you think about all this, Mercy?" asked Blake. "You're the trained investigator."

"We've all heard how you helped save this spectacular art collection." Katharine waved her arms extravagantly around the room, indicating the fine nineteenth- and twentieth-century paintings hanging on the walls.

"Dinner is served." George appeared at the entrance of the dining room, and distributed champagne to the guests.

Just in time, thought Mercy.

Feinberg stood up again, raising his glass. "To Alice and Caspar."

"To Alice and Caspar," they repeated gravely.

After a moment of hushed silence, he sat back down.

The courses began. George announced each course—and every single one featured a significant alcoholic ingredient. Starting with pumpkin soup spiked with hard apple cider, bourbon, and maple syrup, followed by escargot in garlic and wine sauce. Every course came with a wine pairing.

As the courses went on, tongues loosened, and the wagging commenced. She was surprised anyone could speak at all, given the amount of alcohol consumed between cocktails and dessert. She was careful not to drink anything, and her abstinence did not escape notice. Katharine pointed to her glass several times and told her, "Drink up, my dear!"

Over the third course—sea scallops in Grand Marnier sauce—their host steered the conversation toward the good old days. Everyone toasted Alice de Clare and the inn, then plunged into what amounted to an obituary for Caspar, listing his Broadway business triumphs. But all his successes didn't make him any less loathsome in Mercy's eyes.

He'd been a wolf. She'd come across them from time to time in the army and had been forced to protect herself more than once. She knew how to handle them. Their civilian counterparts were usually sheep, comparatively speaking. That said, she'd gotten a bad feeling about Caspar Farrow and was not entirely surprised to find him dead. Nor would she be surprised to find out that a woman killed him. Time to shake the pot a bit.

"I know you were at school together, but frankly I'm surprised you were all so close," she said. "Caspar Farrow seemed so different from the rest of you."

Katharine smiled. "You mean he was crass."

"He had his faults, but he was a loyal friend," Lea said.

"He was like a little brother," added Blake. "He drives you crazy, but you know he'd lay down his life for you. So you love him anyway."

Mercy couldn't see Farrow laying his life down for anyone. She wondered how these people managed to convince themselves otherwise. The blind loyalty of childhood friendships, she supposed.

"We'd heard the rumors, of course," said Katharine.

"Rumors?"

"Of sexual harassment," said Lea.

"All unproven," said Blake.

"A dozen lawsuits settled out of court," said Lea. "Not to mention five wives."

"I don't know why a babe like Cara would stand for it," said William.

"All his wives were beautiful," said Katharine.

"Some men aren't cut out for marriage," said Blake. "But Caspar seemed to settle down when he married Cara."

If that were true, she thought, it was only because he'd met his match in his enterprising fifth wife.

Feinberg guided his guests back to the subject of Alice de Clare. "The authorities need to notify her next of kin. But they're having trouble finding family members."

"I'm not surprised," said Katharine. "I believe her parents died in a car crash a couple of years ago. She struck me as a lonely young woman."

"She was adopted," added Lea. "As far as I know, she had no brothers or sisters."

"Did she ever make any effort to find her birth mother?" asked Mercy. "Her birth parents?"

"Not that I know of. But she may have. Many adopted women do look for their birth parents when they get pregnant."

"So you knew?"

"I guessed." Lea shrugged. "I spend my life taking pictures of people. I notice things."

"Did she tell you who the father was?"

"It must have been Ethan," said Blake.

"Not necessarily," said Katharine. "She was as lovely as she was ambitious. Alice had many admirers. And let's remember, she *was* French."

"Katharine," said Blake, with a note of warning.

"Don't be so provincial, darling. I certainly wouldn't think any less of her."

By the time the braised beef in tawny port arrived, everyone was in their cups. Time to take them back in time to the beginning.

"I understand you were all at school together."

William, a sullen drunk if there ever was one, looked up from his phone long enough to groan. "Oh God, don't get them started."

"Now, William, be nice," said Katharine, in that chirping way indulgent parents have of chastising their children to no effect. "We were inseparable," she said to Mercy. "Blake and I, Lea and Max."

"Max is gone now," said Lea quietly. "He died in 1985."

"I'm sorry."

"He was the loveliest man," said Katharine. "A genius, really. So talented."

"Max was an artist," said Lea.

"A very gifted sculptor," said Blake.

"You met at college?"

"Prep school."

"Elliott Academy," said Katherine.

Elliott Academy was a famous—some would say notorious—boarding school about fifteen miles north of Northshire. The academy was founded by villagers for public education in the early 1800s and transformed into a progressive powerhouse by radical educators in the Sixties. New England was a hotbed of boarding schools, the kind of schools where foreign dignitaries and princes sent their kids to be educated with the offspring of the most popular entertainers, the most powerful politicians, and the most ruthless business tycoons. Royalty: American, European, and otherwise.

"That must have been an amazing experience," said Mercy. Vermont had its share of these institutions, some more than two hundred years old. But Elliott Academy was one of a kind, known for its liberal views, flexible schedules, and unorthodox curricula. Prep school for millionaire hippies, some called it.

Lea laughed. "It was fun."

Katharine laughed, too, a drunken giggle that seemed incongruent with the self-possessed woman she usually presented to the world. "We were young and free and more or less unsupervised."

Even Blake grinned. "It was a wild time, and we were wild, too."

One of Mercy's best literature professors at Boston College was an Elliott graduate. He claimed that his alma mater produced more MacArthur genius grants than any other high school in the country. "You must have had very inspiring teachers."

"I suppose," said Blake. "But we didn't spend much time in class. We'd meet with our advisors in the morning, then pack a picnic and hike into the woods, spending afternoons smoking dope and skinny-dipping."

"We would stay up half the night playing games," said Lea.

"You girls always beat us at Scrabble and Boggle," said Blake.

"And you boys beat us at poker."

"We didn't just play games," said Katharine primly. "We'd have long debates on philosophy, art, politics. Those were the most interesting conversations of my life."

"We solved all the problems of the world," said Lea.

"Caspar Farrow, too?"

"Eventually," said Blake. "He was younger than we were, so we mostly ignored him at first.'

"Just another freshman adoring us from afar." Katharine laughed. "He had to try harder."

Blake and Lea laughed with her.

"I can't believe he's gone," said Katharine, looking at her husband and her friend, grief marking her fine features. "How can it be?"

They sat in silence for a moment.

"It seems like just yesterday we were at school together," said Blake.

"And you've stayed close all these years?"

"Yes," said Lea.

"We got married and had William," said Katharine. "Max and Lea got married. We stood in each other's weddings."

"Then Max got sick," said Lea. "AIDS."

"It was early on. No one knew what it was," said Katharine. "She started documenting Max's illness."

"Lea always took pictures," said Blake.

"But the ones she took of Max were the ones that made her famous," said Katharine.

"She changed the world with those photos," said Blake. "Nobody was doing anything about AIDS and her pictures helped change that."

"She won the Pulitzer Prize," said Katharine. "Max near the end."

"I've seen that picture," said Mercy, remembering the devastating portrait of a dying young man.

"Max was very brave," said Lea.

"So were you," said Blake. "You cared for him all that time."

Lea smiled gratefully at her friends, and Mercy was moved by the strength of their bond, even after all these years.

George and Mrs. Espinosa brought in dessert: drunken pear cobbler with sherry and brandy. Served with port.

"Lea also photographs children," said Blake between bites. "Kids all over the world."

"It started with children with AIDS," explained Lea. "And went from there."

"She takes happy pictures, too," said Katharine. "Like our wedding."

"I am a sucker for a good wedding," said Lea.

"And you?" Mercy turned to Katharine and Blake. "How'd you two get together?"

"I fell for Katharine the first time I saw her. She was on a horse."

Her confusion must have shone on her face. Blake laughed.

"Katharine was a talented equestrienne even back then," he said. "She came to Elliott on a full scholarship."

"They have a very prestigious horse-riding program," explained Lea, "and the school dressage team is among the best in the country. Katharine was captain of the team senior year."

"She worked hard," said Blake. "Half the time when we were out fooling around, Katharine was on her horse. Sometimes I thought she loved that horse more than she loved me. Sometimes I still do."

"It's a toss-up," said Katharine. "I do love my horses."

Mercy could picture the slim, elegant woman astride a horse, picking out fancy steps with poise, being one with the horse. "Do you guys ride, too?"

"I grew up riding horses here at the inn in the summer," said Blake. "But I'm not the professional that Katharine is."

"William rode when he was small," said Katharine. "He was good, too. But then he discovered snowboarding."

William raised his glass to his mother. "Cheers."

"The men in my life are not as passionate about horses as I am," Katharine said with a trace of bitterness.

That was the wine talking, Mercy thought.

"I run my own stables, breeding and training dressage horses."

"Sounds wonderful." Mercy wondered how Katharine had managed that, along with raising a family and being the wife of a man like Blake, although she figured being rich helped. "You must be very busy. Your own business, and now the inn."

"That's Blake's thing."

"She'll be the inn's official hostess," said Blake. "But Katharine has her horses."

The way Blake said it, Mercy felt he was trivializing his wife's interests. Mercy wondered why he felt compelled to do that, and how she felt about it.

"And what do you do besides snowboard?" she asked William.

The table felt silent, and Mercy realized she'd asked an awkward question.

"I'm a trust-fund baby," William answered with a smirk.

"William is a champion snowboarder," Blake quickly corrected.

"Was." William tapped his left leg with his fork. "I blew out my knee last year at the X Games." He said it lightly, but his sarcastic expression was gone.

"William is playing an active role in expanding and redesigning the snowboarding runs here," said Blake. "He's taking an interest in the family business."

If his parents had their way, William's trust fund–baby days might be over. Mercy wondered how he would feel about staying close to home. If he had been really a champion, he'd be a definite draw to the inn. If he didn't spend all his time partying. He'd spent most of dinner texting and grinning to himself. She'd love to get a look at his phone.

"We're just thrilled to have him involved." His mother beamed.

Katharine didn't come from money, she thought. It must be Blake's trust fund supporting William. Supporting them all.

"Did you go to Elliott Academy, too?" she asked William.

"No way."

"William had a full ride at the Rockies Preparatory School in Colorado," said Katharine. "Followed by Colorado State."

"Good times," said William.

Dinner was winding down. Maybe it was the drunken pear cobbler, or maybe it was Mercy's inadvertent faux pas, but suddenly everyone was ready for bed.

William was the first to excuse himself. Blake and Katharine followed quickly. Lea bade her and their host good night shortly thereafter.

Leaving only Feinberg and Mercy at the table.

"I need to check out that school."

"Really?"

"Backstories."

He sipped the last of his port. "I'm on the board of trustees. I'll make a call."

CHAPTER EIGHTEEN

FORECAST: UNSETTLED, WINTRY MIX, FOLLOWED
BY ANOTHER FAST-MOVING STORM FROM THE GREAT
LAKES BRINGING FALLING TEMPERATURES, SNOW
SHOWERS, BLUSTERY WINDS.

T ROY WAS TIRED by the time he pulled the truck up in front
of the fire tower. Susie Bear, having the benefit of a full-time
chauffeur, was snoring on the back seat. A loud and yet sonorous
snuffling that amused him, and even comforted him. Not that he
would ever admit that to anyone. Except maybe Mercy. She would
understand.

He roused the dog with a quick, "We're home, girl. Time for
stew!"

Stew was one of the Newfie retriever mutt's most anticipated
meals. Troy made it from scratch in his Crock-Pot, with beef chuck,
chopped carrots, celery, potatoes, vermicelli, and bullion. A treat for
them to come home to a hot meal waiting for them after a long day
of patrols. When he wasn't too weary to eat.

Of course, Susie Bear was never too weary to eat. She scrambled
into the front seat, slapping his shoulder with her thick plumed tail.
He leaned over and opened the car door for her, and she bounced
out of the truck, a soft landing due to the thick blanket of snow that
covered the ground. She rolled around on her back, giving herself a
snow bath. She loved a good wash in the cold white stuff.

Troy laughed, pulling himself out of the truck with his pack and shaking off his fatigue long enough to stomp through the snow to the red door, a spot of scarlet in a world of white. "Come on. You've had your fun. Now it's my turn to wash up." Although he preferred a hot shower to a snow bath.

Susie Bear lumbered to her feet, shaking the snow from her shaggy coat with a slow-motion shimmy. But instead of heading toward the door, she pranced through the drifts like the snow queen she was and headed round the fire tower to the back.

He watched her go, and for a second thought about going after her. He decided against it. He was dead on his feet. It was all he could do to drag himself into the house and dump his stuff on his kitchen floor. He left the door open a few inches so Susie Bear could nose her way in when she was ready. It wouldn't be long, as the sweet smells of beef stew overpowered Troy's olfactory system. He could only imagine its effect on Susie Bear, whose nose was some ten thousand times more sensitive than his.

The kitchen and the bathroom were on this ground floor. The living quarters—a den that doubled as a bedroom—were on the second floor. Which meant he didn't have to climb the stairs to get that hot shower.

A chill swept in through the front door, and Susie Bear blew in with it.

"About time," he told the dog, slamming the door behind her. He measured out two cups of stew into Susie Bear's bowl and topped off her water. She ignored him and her dinner and clambered up the stairs.

"Suit yourself," he said, and headed for the shower.

Troy stood under the hot running water until his skin turned pink. Then he dried off and climbed the stairs, a towel wrapped around his hips. That's when it finally hit him: the delicate scent of tuberose and jasmine, with a bass note of Rangoon creeper. Gucci Bloom perfume.

Madeline.

He hit the last tread and stepped into the room. Susie Bear sprawled on the sectional sofa, her pumpkin head pointed to the other side of the room. Her muzzle was closed tight in the closest thing the normally cheerful dog had to a grimace.

Troy turned, and there she was, lounging on his bed. His Murphy bed, which had been hidden in the wall behind cabinet doors when he last left the house. But the bed was down now, its blue sheets pulled tightly across the mattress, the perfect frame for Madeline Renard Warner, in her pink dress, long bare legs crossed at the knee, toes painted the same pearly blush as the dress. Her long black hair falling across her pale face, her red lips curled in a half smile, her dark blue eyes a deep lake in which he'd already drowned more than once.

"Hi, handsome."

She was as lovely as ever. The most beautiful woman in the county— back when she still lived in the county. Before she took off with the flatlander from Florida.

"How did you get in here?"

She smiled, full wattage this time. "I live here."

"Not anymore. I could arrest you for breaking and entering."

Laughing, she raised a graceful hand and dangled a silver key from a black-and-gold Chanel ring. "It's not breaking and entering if you have a key."

"Trespassing, then."

She frowned. "We're still married. This place is as much mine as it is yours."

"You hate this house."

"Don't be silly. I've always said that it has a certain je ne sais quoi."

"Madeline." He used his game-warden voice. The voice that could stop a poacher in his tracks. Not that it had ever worked on her.

She patted the bed. "Come on over here, and let's talk."

He crossed the room, stepping inside his small walk-in closet and shutting the door. Dropping his towel and slipping into blue jeans and an army sweatshirt.

"Are you going to hide in there all night?" Madeline laughed, that tinkling sound that alarmed him more than the sound of shots fired.

Fully dressed, Troy stepped back into his living room—*his* living room—and closed the door firmly behind him.

"You're leaving now."

Madeline rose from the bed and walked toward him in a subtle sashay that said, *I'm worth whatever trouble I cause and more.*

But he knew that wasn't really true. He held out his hands to stop her. She paused just as her breasts brushed the life lines of his palms.

"I'm sorry," she told him. "I didn't mean to hurt you."

"Out."

"Troy."

"Don't make me haul you down those stairs and dump you outside in the snow."

Madeline laughed, more tinkling, and it was clear she didn't think he was serious. He snapped his fingers, and Susie Bear tumbled off the couch and over to his side. She sat right in front of him, blocking Madeline. The Newfie weighed nearly as much as his so-called wife did.

Madeline straightened up and moved away. "Okay, I'm going."

She paused at the top of the stairs to turn. "I'll be back."

"The locks will be changed."

"We're not over until I say we're over, Troy Warner."

Susie Bear growled softly, and Madeline started down the stairs. The world's friendliest dog followed her at a not-so-friendly pace.

Troy heard the front door slam. He went downstairs and found Susie Bear waiting in the kitchen. Alone.

"Good girl." He smiled as he scratched the dog's shaggy head.

Whatever spell Madeline had once cast on him was broken.

For good.

THE NEXT MORNING, Troy stood in the gray-and-white waiting room of McGrath & Sons, the law firm that had handled what little legal business he'd had during his life: the drawing up of his will when he was deployed overseas, the changing of that will when he married Madeline, and now the filing of his divorce.

"Stay," he told Susie Bear, who was stretched out along the foot of a black leather club chair, her shaggy black head resting on its tufted seat. She was the only other visitor in the reception area at this early hour. Northshire was a small town, and Troy preferred to conduct his private affairs in, well, private. The office didn't officially open until nine o'clock, so with any luck, no one but his lawyer would see him there.

Nancy McGrath swept into the room from her inner sanctum, offering Troy a bejeweled hand.

He shook it, wondering as he always did how she managed to be so engaging in person and so intimidating in the courtroom. All charm on the outside and all brains on the inside, the sleek raven-haired attorney was the McGrath of McGrath & Sons, a fact that surprised no one who knew her and mostly everyone who did not. Troy was glad she was on his side.

"Come on in," she told him, calling "good dog" over her shoulder at Susie Bear as she escorted him back into a tasteful suite, which looked more like a living room out of a decorating magazine than a law office. Nancy waved him into a deep purple club chair as she slipped gracefully into a high-backed version, crossing her long legs under a massive mahogany desk, so highly polished Troy could see his reflection.

"It's about time," she told him, dark eyes disapproving. "I was beginning to think you'd slunk off to Bennington rather than come to me about your problem."

Troy risked a small smile. "Better late than never?"

She did not smile back. "You can ruin your life long before *never*."

He sighed. He wasn't sure if Nancy knew Mercy Carr or not, but she definitely knew his mother and Patience O'Sullivan and Lillian Jenkins. All women who wanted him free of his estranged wife, the sooner the better, for one reason or another. Most of which had to do with Mercy. Although he suspected none of them had ever liked Madeline. "I'm here now."

Nancy pulled a legal-size pad of cream-colored paper from a drawer in her shiny desk and popped the cap of a fancy cream-and-gold fountain pen. Pen poised in her fingers, she gave him a quick nod. "Shall we get started?"

An hour later, he was sweating from the exhaustive postmortem of his failed marriage.

"Now what?" he asked, desperate to escape this chic office and get home to his fire tower for a long nap. After that, he would lose himself in the wilderness, with nothing and no one but Susie Bear for company.

"We'll get the paperwork going." Nancy pushed back her chair, rising to her feet. "Since you've been living separately for far longer than the required six months, there should be no problem." The attorney paused. "She'll need to sign the papers, of course."

He frowned. Until last night, he'd believed that she was in Florida with that orthopedist she'd run off with. Nancy knew all about that. All of Northshire knew all about that.

"Will that be a problem?"

"No."

"I hear she's back in town." Nancy regarded him with something like concern. "Women like Madeline don't like sharing. Even when it's something they don't want anymore."

He thought about Mercy and Thrasher and washing the dishes. And about Madeline showing up at his place uninvited. "I don't care what it takes. I want a divorce."

"Good." At last, Nancy favored him with a smile.

CHAPTER NINETEEN

Live to learn. Learn to live.

—THE ELLIOTT ACADEMY MOTTO

E LVIS RODE SHOTGUN AS Mercy steered the Land Rover along snowy Sussex Road to Elliott Academy. Few vehicles were on the road; most people were probably still digging out. A thankless task with another storm on the way. They passed a few lonely snow-plow trucks, but that was all.

About fifteen miles northeast of Northshire, the school dominated the village of Sussex. Apart from the pizza place, gas station, and post office, most of the buildings lining both sides of the one-street town belonged to the academy. A hodgepodge of styles from at least three centuries—Colonial clapboard and Georgian brick and solar-paneled dorm—formed a campus of extraordinary beauty, thanks to the one common denominator that made all the difference: money.

Mercy was grateful to George, who had once again played fairy godmother and supplied her with another attractive outfit: slouchy dark-gray wool trousers and a pale-pink cashmere sweater, black leather riding boots, and a black wool car coat. Not her style, but her mother would approve, especially given the venue.

One year of tuition here cost twice Mercy's annual army salary. What was it Cara Farrow had said? *Having money is good.*

The rich kids who went here probably thought having money was good, too. There weren't many about; maybe they were all in class studying or at the ice rink skating or on the mountain snowboarding.

She wondered how many high schools besides Elliott boasted their own ski slopes. Maybe William's Rockies Preparatory School.

She braked the Land Rover at the crosswalk and studied two young women in jeans, down jackets, and hiking boots giggle past her. No uniforms here. They looked like teenagers everywhere.

She wasn't sure she'd ever been that young. Although it wasn't so long ago, she felt like she'd lived several lifetimes since she was a teenager. She pulled into the parking lot flanking Elliott Hall, an imposing nineteenth-century Federalist building that served as the public face of the three-thousand-acre campus.

She parked, and she and Elvis set out on a quick tour of the grounds, taking the long way to administration, winding around dormitories and laboratories, the dining hall and music conservatory, the performing-arts center and the woodshop.

Mercy could picture Blake and Katharine and Lea and Max here thirty years ago, looking much like the students now, skipping class and disappearing into the woods to hang out and smoke dope and talk about life. It was more difficult to picture Caspar Farrow here. He seemed too coarse for a place that prided itself on civility.

An efficient-looking woman of indeterminable age led Mercy and Elvis into the headmaster's high-ceilinged, darkly paneled sanctuary as soon as she mentioned the magic words *Daniel Feinberg*.

Mike Robbins was a tall, fit man with a big smile who looked more like a politician than a headmaster. He waved her into a black leather Eames chair as he stood across from her, leaning back against the edge of his Shaker-style desk. "You'll have full access to our archives. But you should know that a lot of our files from a few decades ago are missing."

"Why's that?" She mistrusted people who claimed information had gone missing.

"Fire in the late Eighties. Destroyed a lot of documentation." He gave her a rueful smile. "Before computers, you know."

Mercy thought about that. "Is there anyone who was around back then I could talk to? A teacher, staff member, maybe a former student?"

Mike pursed his lips. "Our alumni are scattered the world over. Leading good lives, doing big things."

"Right." She bounced to her feet. "Well, then, let's hope whatever files you have left prove useful. I'd hate to tell Daniel that I've come and gone empty-handed."

Headmaster Robbins blanched. He tapped his fingers on his Shaker desk, then abruptly stopped and snapped them. "There *is* someone who might be able to help you. Dr. Ruth Marie Wright. She taught biology and chemistry here for many years. She's retired now from teaching, but she still works part-time in the library."

Mercy had great affection and admiration for librarians, part-time or otherwise. She'd never met an unhelpful one. "Where can I find her?"

THE LUDLOW LIBRARY was a renovated nineteenth-century barn two hundred yards west of Elliott Hall. Inside, the space was warm, bright, and peaceful, with towering windows and a solar-paneled roof and row upon row of books. Quiet, too, with students tucked into corners with open books and laptops.

Dr. Wright sat surrounded by thick volumes at a long table at the back of the building in a former tack room that now served as the archive. There was a large orange tomcat on her lap and an elegant old-school fountain pen in her hand. The freshman who'd guided Mercy and Elvis to the library waved goodbye and quickly retreated, as if cowed by the elderly educator's very existence.

Mercy could see why. Dr. Wright was a short Boston bulldog of an old lady, with a shock of white hair and blue eyes that looked right through you. The kind of tough octogenarian New England was famous for.

Dr. Wright watched the girl depart. "All earnestness and entitlement."

She wasn't sure if the older woman was talking to her or not.

"Cat got your tongue?" The professor's voice was as strong and sharp as a new whip.

"No, ma'am." She choked back a laugh.

"Do you find something amusing?"

"No, sorry. You just remind me of someone."

"Who?"

"Ezekiel Watkins. My drill sergeant at Fort Leonard Wood."

She appeared pleased by that. "I'm Dr. Ruth Marie Wright." She stroked her cat. "This is Newton."

"And this is Elvis."

The dog stood quietly at her side. Watching the cat. As the cat watched him.

"Mercy Carr." She held out her hand, and the old lady firmly gripped it. She probably still chopped her own wood.

"The headmaster said you were a soldier. Did you see combat?"

"Two tours in Afghanistan. Military police. And Elvis here served as a bomb-sniffing dog over there."

"Well done, you." The professor paused. "And now you're investigating these dreadful murders in the woods. Which somehow leads you here."

"One of the victims attended this school."

"Caspar Farrow." She frowned.

"That's correct."

"An altogether unpleasant young man. Did you know him?"

"We met briefly."

"I don't suppose he improved much with age?"

"I don't think so, at least not that I could see in the short time I knew him."

"One always hopes that the deficiencies of character one takes note of in the young are softened if not corrected by the erosion of time, but sadly that rarely proves the case." Dr. Wright sighed. "We do our best here to mold our students into finer versions of themselves, but as often as not we fail. Of course, it's possible that without Elliott Academy they would turn out even more unsatisfactorily."

"Sergeant Watkins would agree with you."

Dr. Wright laughed, a surprisingly youthful sound that was almost a giggle. Newton purred loudly. Elvis cocked his triangular ears. "How can I best help you?"

"I'd like to see all the records that you have for the victim. And for Blake and Katharine Montgomery, Lea and Max Sanders, and anyone else around the academy at that time who interacted with them."

"I understand all, with the exception of Max, were at Mr. Feinberg's estate at the time of the murder."

"Yes, at his invitation. A hunting party."

"How very Victorian. Do please elaborate." She waited for Mercy to enlighten her, practically purring along with her cat.

Apparently Dr. Wright was not above a good gossip, as her grandmother called it. Mercy changed the subject. "Where do you suggest we start?"

"Most of the original source material that might interest you was lost to fire long ago. Report cards, administrative forms, medical records, et cetera. I've gathered together what little is left."

"Thank you."

"There is a wealth of secondary source material to sort through—school newsletters, student newspapers, literary journals, club notes, that sort of thing—that could reveal something." Dr. Wright pointed to a stack of boxes in the corner. "You'll find those in there." She looked at Mercy with something like relish. "Secrets. I suppose that's what you're after."

She smiled. "It would be great if you could give me a sense of what they were like as students."

"I've pulled out the pertinent yearbooks for the years in which they attended the academy. Let us take a look. We should begin with 1982, the year they were all here at the same time."

The Elliott Academy yearbook was a richly produced, leather-bound volume with gold lettering that spelled out *The Peak 1981–1982,* with a gold embossed pine tree set against a mountaintop. The profile of a falcon—the school mascot—perched on a limb.

They flipped through the yearbook together. Mercy was struck by how little the students and the campus itself had changed. This was the kind of continuity only the rich could sustain for any length of time.

The opening pages chronicled school activities on campus and around the world that helped justify the exorbitant tuition: an athletic program that included sailing, mountain biking, and lacrosse, field trips to Europe and South America, volunteerism at home and abroad.

"We have mandatory studies abroad devoted to art and literature and good works," said Dr. Wright with pride. "Students receive customized courses of study designed to help them realize their unique potential. They spend time at our campus near Lake Geneva, from which they explore the European continent and another at our campus in Oxford, from which they explore Great Britain. We do our best to instill an appreciation for the arts and dedication to service so that all that money might end up doing something good."

"There seems to be an emphasis on sports as well."

"We're keen on exercising the body as well as the mind at Elliott. All students must participate in both team and individual athletics."

"Archery?"

"Of course. Any activity that challenges the mind, body, and spirit."

"So I've heard." This meant that all the Elliott alums in the hunting party were at least familiar with the bow and arrow. Not just Ethan Jenkins.

On the following pages came tributes to the school's most significant benefactors. One featured the Barrington Lodge. Two men stood in front of the striking modern take on a mountain cabin.

Dr. Wright tapped the photo with her fountain pen. "Blake Montgomery and his father, Barrington Montgomery. On opening day of the new Elliott Academy ski area—a gift from the Montgomery family."

She recognized a young, good-looking Blake with surfer-blond hair. She recognized Barrington, too, as the man hosting her childhood vacations at Bluffing Bear Inn.

"What was Blake like as a young man?"

"An excellent skier. An adequate student." She turned several pages and came to a group shot of several kids. The tallest, skinniest boy of the lot stood in the middle, holding court. He had long black hair, dark eyes, and an air of intensity that screamed *artist*.

"Let me guess. Max Sanders."

"Maximilian Graham Sanders III," corrected Dr. Wright. "Rebellious but brilliant. A truly original mind. One remembers those rarities."

"I'm sure."

"He was a leader from the day he set foot on campus, although I doubt that was ever his intent. Even then he wanted to change the world, not one person at a time, but one defiant work of art at a time." Dr. Wright looked away. "You know," she said quietly, "he was discovered here, at our annual student exhibition. He had his first show in Soho when he was only a senior. Galleries were clamoring for his work, and he was still in his teens."

"He died too young."

"Yes." Dr. Wright's voice cracked. "AIDS. Terrible what happened to him. To all of them."

She waited for the professor to regain her composure. She knew how grief worked, how a photograph, a song, a smell, a conversation could trigger a memory out of nowhere and overwhelm you even years later.

Dr. Wright turned the page. "This is the seniors section for 1982. Here we should find Max and Lea, Blake and Katharine."

There were eighty-six graduating seniors that year, each with a full two-page spread in *The Peak,* appearing in alphabetical order. First in their group was Katharine Butts, better known to Mercy as Katharine Montgomery.

"No wonder she wanted to marry Blake Montgomery. If only to change her name."

"She was a talented equestrienne, and there were the inevitable adolescent jokes about posteriors and saddles and so forth."

"She must have hated that."

"If she did, you would never have known. Katherine held herself above all that."

The largest of the dozen photographs was taken outdoors in a grazing pasture, with quarter horses in the background. Katharine in the foreground, behind the fence, leaning over, staring straight into the camera, her fair waist-length hair shining in the sun. Blinding blondness. Very Lady Godiva. A boy stood to the side, next to a graceful chestnut Arabian, his hand glinting on the horse's neck, his eyes on Katharine rather than the camera.

"Who's the boy?"

Dr. Wright peered at the picture. "The stable boy. I can't recall his name. He wasn't here long."

"Looks like he had a crush on Katharine, too."

"They all did."

The professor traced the curve of Katharine's curtain of hair with her pen. "As you can see, she was a stunning young woman."

"She still is."

"Yes, she would be. She's the sort who takes good care of her assets."

"She was a scholarship student."

"Equestrian scholarship." Dr. Wright nodded. "I keep my eye on the scholarship girls, as I was once one myself. Katharine was the daughter of a dairy farmer from up north. She not did see cows in her future."

"So, Blake's good name was not his only appeal."

"No. She was disciplined and ambitious. More ambitious even than Caspar Farrow. But far subtler. Always a Katharine, never a Kate."

"I can see that."

"She had her eye on Blake from the beginning. Beauty is currency, and she spent hers wisely. That young man didn't have a chance. I suppose they've been happy?"

She shrugged. "They have a son, William. A good life together, at least from the outside."

Dr. Wright nodded. "The Boston Brahmin keep their unhappiness under wraps."

She flipped to Blake Montgomery's page, remarkable only for the striking photo of the young man surrounded by slalom trophies. Next up was Lea Sanders, née Person, whose two-page spread was a gallery of photos of Elliott Academy, the woods and the lake and the ski slopes, and her fellow students. The only picture of Lea herself was a small self-portrait, in which she looked decidedly uncomfortable, despite a well-executed pose against a beautiful backdrop of blue lake and white clouds, the Elliott crew rowing in the distance. Lea's features were sharper than they were now, her face having softened over the years. She reminded Mercy of a Modigliani model, all angles and curves and guarded emotion.

"Lea was in my biology and chemistry classes." Dr. Wright rustled in her seat, disturbing Newton, who stretched every direction, then curled back into a circle on her lap. "Compared to the others, she was quiet and low-key."

"She looks uneasy here."

"She was always happier behind the camera than in front of it." Dr. Wright pointed to the self-portrait. "I did worry about her when Max died. He was the sun and she was caught in his orbit, like everyone else. I wondered how she'd cope on her own. But she found her way."

"She still mourns him." She told the professor about the conversation at dinner the night before. "They all do."

"The four of them formed a very tight clique." Dr. Wright kept going through the yearbook, moving onto the sophomores and Caspar Farrow. "He was two years behind the others. They were the proverbial cool kids, and he was . . . not."

She could see why. At sixteen, he looked like the same florid-faced bully he'd been as a middle-aged man. Thick lips, broad features, dull eyes under bushy brows, and a sour expression.

"He had an unerring understanding of power."

"And the other kids were the power?"

"In the social hierarchy of the student body, they were at the top. The peak, as it were."

Mercy smiled. "What did Caspar do to try to fit in?"

"He was a pest. He dogged them wherever they went. I seemed to recall there was some kind of incident." Dr. Wright shook her head. "I can't remember the details. But maybe you'll discover it in these files." She shooed Newton off her lap and rose to her feet. The cat flounced past Elvis, who ignored her. Two could play that game.

"And now I have a question for you."

"Shoot."

"Whatever happened to your Ezekiel Watkins?"

"He was killed in a training exercise gone wrong. He died saving a new recruit."

"I'm sorry to hear that." Dr. Wright nodded. "I thank you for your service and for that of your sergeant."

Mercy bowed her head. "Much appreciated, ma'am."

Elvis bent his head, too, and Dr. Wright laughed. "That is a rather extraordinary dog."

"He is that."

Dr. Wright gave the shepherd a good scratch between the ears. "While I prefer the company of cats at this stage in my life, I do so admire a good dog."

"Thank you for your help."

"I hope you find whoever committed these horrible murders and that none of our alumni played any part in it." Dr. Wright hesitated. "One never knows. One watches and over time one sees that the rivalries and resentments of childhood often cast long shadows."

MERCY SPENT THE rest of the afternoon going through the yearbooks and box after box of other material, snapping photos on her cell and taking notes. She learned that Blake and Max climbed Mount Kilimanjaro, Katharine served as the captain of the Elliott Academy's equestrian team, Lea took a nature photography workshop during spring break in the Alps, Caspar Farrow broke his leg snowboarding, and they all spent a semester sailing from New England to the Caribbean on Elliott Academy's schooner, *Victory.*

Nothing like high school as she remembered it. At the Catholic girls school she'd attended, they played volleyball and basketball and tennis. Helped the nuns with charity work. Snuck out to meet boys at football games at the public high school on the weekends. Although she rarely did that, library nerd that she was.

She was repacking the last box when Elvis leapt to his feet, curlicue tail wagging. The door opened and Dr. Wright peeked her head through. She was wearing a bright orange toque, and her face was flushed from the cold. "I've remembered something. Are you about finished here?"

"Yes."

"Then let's take a walk."

"If you don't mind, I'd like to borrow this one." Mercy slipped into her coat and pointed to *The Peak* 1982 yearbook.

"Certainly. I know I can count on you to return it in good order."

"Yes, ma'am."

She and Elvis followed the professor out of the library into the wintry weather. Dr. Wright wore a warm green wool coat and sturdy snow boots. She navigated the shoveled sidewalks of the campus with a confidence that belied her advanced age. They walked north, passing several modern dormitories built out of steel and glass and wood.

The paved sidewalk ended, and they trudged along a gravel path leading to a big equestrian compound. Elvis ran ahead, circling back to make sure they stayed on track. There were stables, an indoor arena, an Olympic-size paddock, and a fenced pasture beyond. The place seemed empty now, the horses all inside out of the cold and the wind.

"Not much happening here at this hour of the day," said Dr. Wright. "The students have to feed and exercise the horses every morning, take their riding lessons in the afternoon after classes, then groom the horses. And of course muck out the stables."

"No stable boy?"

"We do have a stable boy who helps out our trainers, but they'll all be at lunch about now." Dr. Wright pushed open the door of the stables and Elvis rushed by, startling her.

"Sorry," said Mercy, steadying the professor. "He loves horses."

"So do I." The professor stopped to stroke the nose of a good-looking bay in the first stall to the right.

Elvis trotted up and down past the stalls, checking out his fellow four-legged friends.

"Speaking of stable boys. You remember the stable boy in the picture with Katharine."

"Yes."

"I think his name was Richard. Williams or Wilson. Watson, maybe. Something like that." Dr. Wright fed the bay an apple from the bucket hanging on the outside of the stall. "Anyway, apparently he took his crush on Katharine too far. She accused him of assaulting her. She credited Caspar Farrow with rescuing her."

Mercy thought about that. "That would explain how he went from stalker to insider so quickly."

"Indeed."

"What happened to the stable boy?" She dipped into the bucket and plucked out an apple for the dapple gray in the stall across from the bay.

"He took off." The bay nuzzled the professor's neck, pushing her toque akilter. "Preferred that to getting sacked, I suppose."

"And no one ever tried to find him?"

"Why? I'm sure everyone was relieved he was gone."

Elvis trotted back up to them, settling into his Sphinx pose right next to Dr. Wright, his nose pointing toward the bucket.

"What's he doing?'

"He's alerting to something."

"Does he like apples?"

"He loves apples."

Dr. Wright retrieved another apple from the bucket and held it out to Elvis in her gloved palm. "I think this is the last one, Elvis. Enjoy."

The shepherd politely removed the apple from her open hand and then chomped it down in two bites.

"That was fast," said Dr. Wright.

Mercy's jacket pinged and she pulled out her cell. A text from George, asking that she return to Nemeton as quickly as possible.

Billionaire-speak for *911*.

CHAPTER TWENTY

FORECAST: CONTINUOUS SNOW SHOWERS THROUGH-
OUT THE EVENING AND EARLY MORNING, WHITE-
OUT CONDITIONS.

S NOW WAS FALLING heavily again. As Mercy parked the Land
Rover in the back of Daniel Feinberg's mansion by Gunnar's quarters, the blizzard was raging in Northshire. By the time they made
it to the service entrance, both she and Elvis were covered in snow.

George greeted her as she stepped into the locker room that led
from the service entrance to the kitchen. "Follow me."

"Come on, Elvis." The shepherd sprinted after them.

In the kitchen, she found Ethan Jenkins and Henry, flanked by officers Becker and Goodlove. Henry raced forward, embracing Elvis.

"What are you doing here, Ethan?"

"Henry kept freaking out," he said.

"He seems fine."

"*Now*," said Ethan. "Now that he's here with you and your dog."

She turned her wrath on the rookies. "Becker, you were supposed
to keep them safe at home. You too, Goodlove."

"Sorry, Mercy."

"Harrington told you to stay put."

"Jenkins is right," said Becker. "The kid kept freaking out."

"He kept yelling, 'Paladin, Paladin, Paladin,'" added Goodlove.

"Why would he say that?" Paladins were holy knights who protected the weak, meted out justice, and fought evil at every turn. "What's it mean?"

Ethan regarded her with surprise. "He means you."

"Me? How do you know?"

"He compares everyone he meets to characters in his game."

"Henry's Game."

"Yes."

She looked at Henry, who'd curled up on the floor next to Elvis. This child was full of surprises. "Mrs. Espinosa, do you think you could get Henry a snack? I need to talk to the grown-ups."

"Of course." The housekeeper bustled over to the boy and Elvis. "Henry, sit down at the breakfast nook. Time for you and the big puppy to have a peanut-butter treat."

The Belgian shepherd jumped up at the word *treat,* and Henry laughed.

"We'll be right over here, Henry."

"I'll leave you to it, then," said George, disappearing with characteristic speed and stealth.

"Ethan, we discussed this," she said, moving the group out of the boy's hearing. "You've got to get Henry out of here. It might not be safe."

"Then you have to come with us," said Ethan. "It's not *safe* for him to be this upset. You've seen what happens. He starts stimming. He holds his breath. He runs away."

"I understand, but—"

Ethan cut her off. "I don't think you do understand. Not really. Henry only feels safe with you and Elvis. After all he's been through, I think he deserves to feel safe. Don't you?"

She didn't have an answer to that.

"We barely made it here through the storm," said Becker. "And Detective Harrington says we've got to get back to Lillian's now, before it gets worse."

"Detective Harrington believes Yolanda is a person of interest," says Goodlove.

Becker nodded. "He sent a team after her, but then the storm blew in. They couldn't find her. Now there's a warrant out for her arrest."

Mercy made a fist and punched her palm. "Yolanda didn't kill anybody."

"Detective Harrington says—"

She cut Becker off. "Harrington's wrong."

Becker and Goodlove exchanged a glance.

"Okay," said Becker. "What's done is done. And we have our orders."

"Detective Harrington says he needs us back," said Goodlove.

"People are stranded everywhere, and we're spread too thin on the ground as it is. Henry should be perfectly safe here with you and Elvis and Feinberg's bodyguards. I'm sorry," Becker said.

"Look at Henry," said Ethan. "He's not stressed or scared. He's calm and, well, happy."

"He's *your* son," said Mercy.

"You know I'm right. I called Dr. Jacobs, and even he said you're the one Henry needs right now. You and Elvis."

Mercy didn't like it. But she knew that Ethan had a point. "Okay. But just until we can figure something better out."

"Let's go talk to Daniel," said Ethan. "Henry, bring those peanut-butter treats with you."

In the dining room, happy hour was in full swing for what was left of the hunting party. Mercy noticed they'd all been drinking heavily, not too surprising under the circumstances.

"Hello, Henry," said Feinberg. "Ethan, we're so glad you could join us."

The little boy sat down, his attention strictly on peanut-butter brownies.

Everyone *ooh*ed and *ahh*ed over Henry, but he ignored them all. Mercy loved him for that. He simply ate his peanut-butter brownies in his precise manner, while everyone else sampled the spectacular spread of hors d'oeuvres George had put out.

All eyes were on Ethan as he helped himself to the port. He'd lost the woman he loved, maybe even a child, Mercy thought. But every-one here—herself and Feinberg excepted—looked at him as if he'd already been tried and convicted of murder. They seemed to forget that he couldn't have killed Caspar.

Ethan raised his glass to them. "You don't care about Alice. Not one of you really cares."

Mercy stood up, and she placed a hand on his arm. "Let's get Henry to bed."

He slammed his glass down. "Good idea." He gathered his weary son into his arms, striding out of the dining room without a second glance. She followed father and son up the long grand staircase to the guest wing. At her request, Henry and Ethan were now sharing a room. The name on the door read MASTER JENKINS AND SON.

The large room boasted two brass double beds dressed in navy and gold, one for each of the male Jenkinses. Paintings of naval vessels at sea hung above the gleaming headboards, and antique steamer trunks stood at the footboards. An altogether manly room for father and son.

Henry was sound asleep now.

"Let me put him to bed," she told Ethan. "Why don't you take a shower and cool down."

"Fine." Ethan headed to the bathroom.

Mercy deposited the sleeping boy on the nearest bed and pulled off his sneakers and socks. She rummaged through the highboy across the room and pulled out a pair of kid-sized navy pajamas. Cour-tesy of George, no doubt. She removed Henry's jeans and sweatshirt, slipped on his pajamas, and tucked him under the covers. Elvis curled up at the foot of the boy's bed. Henry slept on.

"Good boy," she told him, with a quick pat. The dog was a wonder.

She settled into a red wingback chair by the fireplace opposite the beds to wait for Ethan to come out of the shower. She didn't have to wait long. He joined her at Henry's bedside, wearing one of Ne-meton's signature terry-cloth bathrobes over navy pajamas much like the one his son now wore.

"Are you okay?"

He raked his hands through damp hair. "I'm just so angry. I know one of those bastards killed Alice. And I can't let them get away with it." He sat on the navy-and-gold ottoman opposite her.

"You really loved her."

He stared at her. "She was the one. My one."

"Did you know she was pregnant?"

He shook his head as if to clear it. "Yes."

"Was the baby yours?"

"Of course." Ethan ducked his head, holding it in his hands. "I wanted to marry her, but she kept putting me off. Said she wasn't ready. She even wrote me a letter telling me it was over between us. But I didn't believe that for a minute. I was hoping that this weekend she'd change her mind, and we could announce our plans."

"*Our* plans?"

He raised his head. "Well, my plans. But she was going to come around. I know she was."

"Look, I know how hard it is to lose someone you love," said Mercy. "I've been there. But this anger is a luxury you cannot afford. It won't do you any good, and it certainly won't do Henry any good."

"I've got to do *something*."

She softened her tone. "Focus on your son. I'm sorry about Alice, but she's gone. Henry is still here and he needs a father."

"I know."

"Try to get some sleep," she said firmly. "George can give you something to help if you need it."

"What are you going to do?"

"I'm going to find out who killed Alice and Caspar."

"Thank you."

"Don't thank me. I'm not doing this for you. I'm doing this for Henry. And for Lillian."

She stood up, heading for the door. Elvis barked.

"Stay," she told him. "Guard Henry."

With the fierce Belgian shepherd stationed at his bedside, she knew the boy was safe. She slipped downstairs, for once not encountering the omnipresent George. She found him in the dining room, overseeing the replenishment of the hors d'oeuvres and port.

Feinberg welcomed her back with a grin. No one else paid much attention as she slid into the seat next to William. The others were all feeling very relaxed despite the circumstances, thanks to food and booze. They lounged around on the generously sized upholstered chairs, as if they were at a pool rather than the formal dining room of the richest man in Vermont. Relaxed enough to talk openly about the murders as they kept eating and drinking.

Murder is a hungry—and thirsty—business, she thought.

"So, Mercy, tell us who you think killed Alice and Caspar." William took his eyes off his phone just long enough to pose the question. But whatever she said, she figured he'd tweet it out to all the world.

"It's a little premature to be making accusations."

"That didn't stop Detective Harrington from arresting Ethan," Blake pointed out.

"Lea says the murders must be connected," said Katharine.

"In which case, Ethan couldn't have done it," said Lea.

They finally figured that out, she thought.

"Does that mean it's one of us?" asked William. "Epic."

"Don't be ridiculous," said his mother sharply. "It's hunting season. The woods are full of hunters. That's where Detective Harrington should be focusing his investigation." She turned to Mercy. "And your game warden."

"I'm sure that they're doing all they can."

"I can understand that Caspar may have had a few enemies," said Lea. "Now that I think more about it, as many people hated him as loved him."

"He was not an easy man to love," said Katharine.

"Cara did," said Lea.

"But Alice?" asked Blake. "She couldn't have had any enemies."

"A lovely girl," said Katharine.

The conversation faltered at the thought of the beautiful architect with the arrow through her heart. One by one, the guests excused themselves, until just as had happened the night before, only she and Feinberg were left at the table.

"If you could loan me a laptop," she told him, "I've got work to do."

"Of course. This must be resolved. The sooner, the better."

AS REQUESTED, HER room was next to Ethan and Henry's. There was a laptop set up on the antique French kidney desk in the corner. And a crystal decanter of red wine with a matching glass.

Thank you, Daniel. Thank you, George.

Mercy sat cross-legged on the four-poster bed with the laptop on her knees and a full glass of wine in her hand. She was worried about Yolanda out there in the storm. She consoled herself with the fact that the army vet had weathered many storms before and survived.

She stared out the picture windows. Snow fell steadily, and according to the weather report the worst was yet to come. This was one of those storms that would last throughout the whole weekend.

Which was not necessarily a bad thing. She'd have this sequestered time to watch these people. The rub was, she'd have to know who the murderer was by the time the storm passed. And she'd have to keep Henry safe until then.

She started with Lea Sanders. Everything she pulled up confirmed what she already knew about the Pulitzer Prize–winning photographer. In the early days, Lea's husband, Max, was the star. There were several photos of the four of them—Blake and Katharine, Max and Lea—at art shows and galleries and parties celebrating Max's work. During the later stages of his illness, Lea's career took off. Her photos documenting his heartbreaking decline were the catalyst, but her success continued after Max's death. She took up the cause of children, documenting their suffering due to war and famine and disease.

Mercy moved on to Blake and Katharine. Lots of pictures of Katharine on horseback. Cutting a fine figure as an Olympian, where she brought home the bronze. If its website were any indication, her business, the Epona Dressage Center, was equally impressive. Mercy wondered how profitable her work was. And how much she relied on Blake.

Blake came from a long and storied Vermont family. They had been around here since the 1600s, building their wealth in successive waves of farming, industry, and tourism—and securing it by marrying into Boston Brahmin families even richer than their own. Blake broke that pattern of marriage-as-merger when he wed Katharine.

Whether young William Montgomery would follow his heart as well remained to be seen. Photos of the playboy athlete partying with actresses and singers were all over the Web. Here in the wilds of Vermont, he'd have to settle for ski bunnies. If William's injury really sidelined him for good. But it seemed Katharine's fair-haired boy might have bigger problems than injuries. He'd been in and out of several very expensive rehab centers for drug addiction. He'd been charged with possession and trafficking more than once, but so far the charges hadn't stuck. Mercy supposed he could thank his trust fund for that.

Last but not least: Caspar Farrow and wife Cara. She was exactly who she pretended to be: a hair model who'd made a fortune as the host of *Be Hair Now.* Her florid-faced husband was as much of a ladies' man as William. Five wives, like Cara had told her, but no children. Not that marriage seemed to sideline him. Online photos of Caspar with attractive women abounded. He was accused of sexual harassment and supposedly paid off a number of young women. One Web site predicted that he'd be kicked out of his own company within a year.

Then where would Cara Farrow be, she wondered. And where would Cara Farrow be now that he was dead?

On the *Today* show, Mercy answered her own question with a laugh.

Enough of the lifestyles of the rich and famous. She closed the laptop and finished her wine. The snow continued to fall, the wind howling around Nemeton, as solid a structure as a billionaire could build.

She couldn't help but think of Lillian in the hospital and Henry in his bed, Elvis at his side, his grieving father in the bed next to him. She thought of Alice de Clare and her unborn baby and Caspar Farrow, who unlike Alice and her child probably deserved his grisly end.

If anyone deserves such an end.

And finally, she thought of Troy. That smile. That grace under pressure. That down-home moral compass. Troy was the kind of man you could depend on. He'd proven it today, just as he'd proven it before.

She hoped he'd prove it tomorrow when she called him and asked him to come help her find the murderer.

ONLY HE CALLED her first. Half an hour later.

"I'm downstairs," he said.

She raced down to the kitchen, where Troy and Susie Bear were waiting for her.

"I checked the tape of the night hunters last night. No sign of them, but there was interesting footage of a suspect in a balaclava and a crossbow."

"So you're right and it's the night hunters after all," said Mercy.

"You don't believe that."

"I don't believe that the people here at Nemeton are innocent, which is not the same thing as saying they are guilty of murder."

"There's something else." Troy pulled a long cream-and-slate-barred feather from his pocket. "Remember the bob-house?"

"Where we found Henry. Where Yolanda said she'd seen night hunters."

Troy nodded. "I went back to hide a camera there during patrols last night, and I found this tucked under the gutting table."

"Another peregrine falcon feather."

"Yes."

"Why didn't we find it the first time?"

"We were looking for Henry."

"Or it wasn't there."

"I'm going back tonight to check the camera."

"I'm going with you."

Troy grinned. "I suppose there's no stopping you."

"No."

"What about Elvis?"

At the sound of her friend's name, Susie Bear leaned against Mercy.

"May I be of any assistance?" George appeared at the kitchen door, as if he'd been listening all along.

"Elvis and I need to go out with Troy and Susie Bear for a while. Could you ask Daniel if one of his bodyguards could guard Henry until we come back?"

"Of course. Right away."

She ran upstairs to fetch Elvis. Henry was sound asleep, as was his father.

"Come on, Elvis," she whispered. The shepherd hesitated, reluctant to leave his charge.

"Come," she said firmly, and he trotted over. She shut the door softly behind him, nodding to the bodyguard already waiting outside in the hall. Henry would be safe.

George appeared again, handing her a pair of gloves, a knit cap, and a pair of snow boots.

"Thank you," she said.

The dogs raced ahead to the truck, eager to be on the job together. Mercy was eager, too. She grinned at Troy as he opened the back cab for the dogs, who scrambled onto the back seat. He opened the passenger door for her, and she climbed into the front seat, greeted by the not-unpleasant smell of forest, man, and dog.

Troy drove down the long drive that led to Nemeton, parking on the other side of the gate that marked the entrance to the estate proper.

"Shortcut," he told her. "This way we can avoid getting wet."

When they all piled out, he handed her a pair of night goggles and a rifle. "Just in case."

He fastened a lighted collar onto Susie Bear; she did the same for Elvis.

"Good to go?" he asked, without looking at her.

"Good to go."

Mercy followed Troy and the dogs into the woods along a trail leading to the back of the marshland where they'd found the bob-house. The night's temperature was below freezing—and only a sliver of a moon peeked out from dark clouds obscuring most of the stars. They had crunched along in the snow for nearly a mile when the trees began to thin. The forest gave way to wetland, quickly icing over.

They didn't speak, just stomped along, watching the bouncing lights that were Elvis and Susie strobe the way ahead. That was one of the things she usually most appreciated about Troy. He never rushed to fill the quiet. He was comfortable with silence. She was comfortable with him. But tonight was different. He was quiet, yes, but there was no peace or companionability in his silence. He was tense, holding his shoulders high and tight.

"Are you all right?" she asked.

"Fine."

But she knew he was lying. Usually he was honest to a fault. "What aren't you telling me?"

"Nothing." He pointed ahead. "There it is."

She peered through the gloom and could just make out the shadowed shape of the ice fishing shack on the edge of the ice-covered marsh. "Did you ever find out who it belongs to?"

"Nope. But maybe this camera footage will tell us."

Elvis and Susie Bear raced for the shed and disappeared. She and Troy were about twenty feet away when she heard the first bark. Elvis. A second bark. Susie Bear.

Mercy and Troy sprinted for the bob-house. A shot rang out, barely missing Troy and splintering a birch behind him.

That was close, she thought. The shooter must be wearing night goggles.

Another shot, closer this time.

Mercy hit the forest floor. Troy followed suit. He turned to her, motioning for her to put on night goggles and ready her rifle. He put on his own goggles and pulled out his pistol.

He waved his arm and together they crawled on their bellies over the frozen marsh toward the bob-house. When they reached a stand of cattails, the only shield between them and the shed, he said, "Stay here and cover me."

Before she could protest, he was off. She squatted behind the cattails, her weight splitting the ice. She sank into cold shallow water, cocked her rifle, and raised the barrel through the cattails. Aimed for the bob-house.

Troy ran pell-mell toward the shed.

Silence. All she heard was the cracking of the ice under Troy's boots.

A figure in black eased around the corner of the ice shack, and Mercy caught sight of a glint of metal.

She aimed. Fired. Watched the figure fall.

Troy dropped to the ground. A frenzy of barking. A horrific yelping. A terrible silence.

The hell with this, she thought, and ran for the bob-house.

Troy was on his feet, too, and she caught up with him just as they came upon the figure on the ground.

A man in camouflage hunting clothes and night goggles.

"You shot me," he said to Troy.

"*I* shot you," said Mercy. "And I'll shoot you again if you hurt my dog."

"I've got this." Troy kicked the man's gun away, then squatted down to get a better look at him.

Troy rolled him over to cuff him and the man squealed in pain. Once he'd secured the cuffs, he removed the perp's night goggles, revealing an angry-eyed guy in his thirties with a crescent-shaped scar above his left eyebrow.

"You'll live," Mercy heard Troy tell him as she rushed into the bob-house. She found Susie Bear in the corner lying down. Elvis sat next to her, licking her thick pumpkin head.

"Oh, no." She fell to her knees. "Let me see, Elvis."

The shepherd backed away. Mercy carefully examined a welt on the Newfie's crown. The big dog whimpered.

"Poor baby. Don't worry, we'll get you to Patience right away." Mercy stroked the good side of her shaggy head, and Susie Bear wearily thumped her tail.

Elvis growled as Troy pushed the man ahead of him into the shed. He was tall and fit and probably a flight risk.

"Easy, Elvis," she said.

"What's wrong with Susie Bear?"

"She's got a nasty cut on her head. That bastard must have hit her with the butt of his gun."

Troy released him and knelt on the floor next to his dog.

The guy started to head for the door.

"I wouldn't do that if I were you." She looked at Elvis. "Guard."

The shepherd leapt for the door, and the man shrank back, flattening himself against the wall of the bob-house.

"That's better." She turned back to Troy. "How's she doing?"

"Okay."

As if to prove his point, Susie Bear shambled to her feet.

"Do you think she can make it back to the truck on her own?" The Newfie retriever mutt weighed a hundred pounds. And they had the wounded suspect to contend with.

"She'll tough it out."

"What about him?"

"Flesh wound. He'll be fine."

"Who is he?"

"I don't know. No ID and he's not talking." He started toward the door. "Let's go."

Mercy and Susie Bear followed Troy and the guy out of bob-house. Elvis did not follow. Nor did he come when she called.

"Elvis." She went back into the ice shack and found the shepherd under the gutting table where they'd found Henry, in his alert position. "What's up?"

She squatted down under the table and saw a black backpack. The top was open, so she shone her flashlight on it and peeked inside. A hunter's leafy bucket hat lay on top. She pushed it aside with the tip of the flashlight to see what lay underneath.

Handguns.

Lots of them.

"You're going to want to see this, Troy."

IT WAS A long night. By the time they secured the scene and tramped back to the truck with the suspect and the backpack full of handguns in tow, Mercy and Troy were both exhausted.

Troy dropped her off at Nemeton, where she texted Patience to tell her he was on his way with Susie Bear. Thrasher would meet him there and take custody of the suspect.

"Are you sure you don't want me to come with you?"

"Thanks, but no." He moved toward her as if to give her a hug, but then pulled back. "You and Elvis need to stay with Henry."

CHAPTER TWENTY-ONE

FORECAST: GUSTY WINDS, HEAVY SNOW, SQUALLS,
FOLLOWED BY FRIGID TEMPERATURES.

Back in bed at Nemeton, Mercy dreamt of snow, black bears, and little boys lost in the woods. She jerked to consciousness before dawn with Good Little Henry and the old monk in the mountains still in her head, just like in the Virginia Frances Sterrett illustration in the *Old French Fairy Tales* book she'd loved as a child. The same one that hung in dead Alice de Clare's room.

She took a quick shower to wake herself up thoroughly. Elvis would need to go out. He was an early dog, with early-dog habits, just as she was. And she wanted to check on Henry anyway. Last night when they got home, the bodyguard watching Henry and Ethan's room had gone back to guarding Feinberg, with Elvis taking up his position as sentry at the foot of Henry's bed.

She knocked on their door, but there was no answer. Weird. Elvis would know she was there before she even held up her hand to knock. The shepherd always knew when someone approached the door, and always warned her—even when the person on the other side of the door was Mercy herself.

She knocked again. Not a sound. She pushed the door open. There was Ethan, still in dressed in the navy pajamas, sleeping on top of the bedsheets, snoring. Henry's bed was empty. No boy, no dog.

Maybe Elvis had gotten Henry up. Maybe they were playing hide-and-seek. Maybe Henry was letting Elvis out.

She shook Ethan roughly by the shoulders. "Wake up."

He jolted upright. "What?"

"Where's Henry?"

"What do you mean?"

"Where. Is. Henry."

"He's right there. In bed." Ethan pointed to the empty bed across from his own. When he realized his son was not in it, he bolted to his feet. "He was right there. With Elvis."

"They're gone."

"Where's my son?" He tore the linens from Henry's bed. Still no little boy there. He looked at Mercy as if it were her fault. "Where's your dog? You were supposed to watch over him. You and your dog."

He was right. It was her fault. "We need to find them. Now."

"Let's get moving," he said.

MERCY AND ETHAN searched the unoccupied rooms on that floor. As they came downstairs, they ran into George.

"We can't find Henry or Elvis," she told the butler. "Have you seen them?"

"No."

"When did you get up?"

"I've been up since six thirty. It's nearly seven now. If any of our household staff had seen them, I'd know about it."

She didn't doubt that. George ran a tight mansion. "Any other guests up? Daniel?"

"No."

"I'm not surprised. Lot of drinking going on last night."

"I could neither confirm nor deny that."

Mercy gave him a tense smile. "We don't have time for misplaced diplomacy right now."

"I'm sorry. Occupational hazard." George straightened his already straight spine. "I can help you find him. We'll organize a room-by-room search."

Joining in were the bodyguards, whom she knew only as Smith and Jones. They checked all exits. The back door. The staff and service entrance. The massive front door that dominated the entrance at the porte cochere. The French doors that opened onto the pool.

No sign of exit or entry. No footprints. Although between the snow and the wind, Mercy wasn't sure there would be. Finally, a hidden door in a wardrobe at the very end of the house. Shades of C. S. Lewis.

"Nobody knows about this entrance," said George. "It's the new security entrance. I suppose that it's possible Henry could have wandered in here."

"A good place to hide if they were playing hide-and-seek." Ethan looked at her with hope.

"Henry likes to play hide-and-seek with Elvis. Elvis is really good at it."

"I have no doubt."

Mercy whistled for the dog, and they all called for Henry. No answer. Even if the boy were hiding and refused to come out, the shepherd would answer her call. He knew her voice, which was tight and anxious now.

"What about the bedrooms?" asked Mercy.

"The guest rooms?" The butler seemed shocked at the suggestion that they disturb their guests.

But they checked anyway, George discreetly opening each door and looking in. Katharine and Blake, sleeping on opposite sides of the king-size bed. Cara Farrow, lightly wheezing in her sleep, blind to the world under her purple satin eye mask. William Montgomery was passed out on his bed, fully clothed, phone in hand. Lea's room was empty, and her bed had not been slept in.

"I'm glad Daniel has found someone," she said. "Lea seems like a nice woman."

George refrained from comment. But she could tell he was pleased. "I can wake Mr. Feinberg."

"Only as a last resort."

"Let's search the grounds first," said George. "The sun is rising now, and Gunnar will be up. He'll help."

"I know where his quarters are. If you could tell Daniel when he wakes up, that would be great. And just make sure Henry's not in your boss's suite somewhere."

"Done."

"I'm coming with you," said Ethan, in a firm voice.

She nodded. They bundled up—gloves, hats, boots, packs—and went out in the brightening gloom to brave the blizzard. The snow was falling softly, but she knew that this was just a lull. Local meteorologists were already calling this the storm of the century in a decade marked by storms of the century—in reality, two storms piggybacking each other, one right after the other, dumping another foot of snow or two by evening.

She stomped through the snow, about a foot deep at this point, drifting high in the corners. Some places were only two inches deep, other drifted a couple feet. She stomped over to the three-car garage, climbing the stairs to Gunnar's quarters.

His Norwegian elkhounds started barking as she approached the landing. Gunnar opened the door, coat and pack on, ready to go.

George, the super butler, thought Mercy.

"We'll find them," the groundskeeper said.

She texted Troy.

They searched the estate grounds, about a five-acre parcel before the trees took over and the forest reasserted itself. A winter wonderland wherever you looked. But today, she did not see the beauty of Vermont, she only saw the cold reality of a little boy lost in a blizzard. The good news was that Elvis would do everything possible to bring him home. They searched the outbuildings one by one, Mercy whistling for Elvis, Ethan calling for Henry, the elkhounds racing around. Gunnar had a set of dog whistles, too, and he blew those, but they couldn't find Henry and Elvis anywhere.

At least Henry's coat and boots were missing, which meant he was dressed more warmly than usual. Still, in weather like this, he could quickly get frostbite and hypothermia. Not to mention that neither Henry nor Elvis were wearing hunter orange.

Troy texted her that he and Susie Bear were on the way, and not to leave without them. He said she was as good as new, thanks to Patience's ministrations.

Mercy hated waiting, and Ethan kept threatening to leave on his own, but she knew their best bet was Susie Bear, the most experienced search-and-rescue dog in the county. And Troy was the most experienced woodsman. While they waited, they packed enough supplies for what could prove a long and difficult journey. Mrs. Espinosa brought thermoses of coffee and hot chocolate, sandwiches, and extra clothes for Henry. Gunnar added everything else they might need in a blizzard, from a portable shovel to glove warmers.

By the time they were good to go, Troy showed up with Susie Bear, snowshoes, and trekking poles.

She gave the Newfie mutt a big hug and a look-over. Apart from a butterfly bandage you could hardly see for all her fur, she seemed fine.

"Where do we look next?" asked Troy.

"The only thing I can think of is that he's gone to see Yolanda Yellowbird."

"But he'll get lost." Ethan's voice as high with strain and sorry. "Henry's always getting lost."

"I don't think so. It's the way he looks at the world. Mathematically." She told them about the snowflakes, how Henry recreated the molecules. "I think he sees the forest the same way."

"So all these times he's never been lost?" Ethan shook his head. "I don't get it."

"Not all those who wander are lost," she said.

"What?"

"She means that he doesn't get lost, he wanders off," explained Troy.

"If he gets scared, he hides," she said. "Just like he did in the bobhouse."

"He may as well be lost if he's hiding," said Ethan. "It's not safe for him to be out there, especially if bad weather or bad people find him before we do."

"We just have to find him first." Mercy patted Ethan's shoulder. "We *will* find him first."

"It's a long way from here to that pagoda," said Troy. "A couple of miles, as the crow flies. And it's up and down most of the way. You're talking a couple hours to get there. When do you think he left?"

"I checked in on him when we got home last night from our outing with you and Susie Bear. Long after midnight. I found him missing this morning around six-fifteen."

"Henry wouldn't go out on his own if it were too dark outside. He does his wandering in daylight," said Ethan.

"He's got Elvis with him."

"Still." Ethan frowned. "Unless someone's snatched him."

"They would have had to kill Elvis first."

Ethan considered that. "So assuming you're right and Henry took off to see Yolanda, how could he possibly make it that far?"

"I don't know, but it's the only thing I can think of. We've looked everywhere else. He may still show up asleep somewhere."

"We could call search and rescue, but everyone's already out on operations," said Troy. "Everything's shut down, and there's no getting in or out."

"We're on our own," she said.

"What's the fastest way there?" Ethan looked more worried than ever. "Driving?"

"Driving back to the inn is taking the long way around." She shook her head. "And the roads are a mess right now."

"We'd still have to hike to the teahouse from the inn," said Troy.

"And it's not the way Henry would go," she said.

"What about snowmobiles? Daniel must have some," said Ethan, brightening slightly.

"But Henry isn't following a trail, is he?" Troy looked at Mercy.

"No, he's on foot, following the map in his head. He won't stay on a trail."

"The most sensible thing to do is follow him on foot," said Troy. "And hope Mercy is right about where he's going. Either way, Susie Bear will find him."

"It's not snowing hard right now." Ethan stared out the windows that flanked the kitchen, framing a dangerous if beautiful woods gone white.

She could only imagine what the poor man was thinking.

"The little guy probably thought it was no big deal," said Troy, "given the lull in the storm, but the weather's going to change, and it's going to change fast. And he's got a head start on us."

"We can catch up with him," said Ethan. "He's just a little boy."

She said nothing to contradict that, and neither did Troy. Ethan was worried enough already.

"We don't have much time," said Troy. "The storm's going to kick up again soon. There'll be blizzard conditions again within the next hour or two."

They put on their snowshoes and off they went. The snow had stopped, and the sky was a pale blue. The winter sun glinted on the snow. Hawks soared above, taking advantage of the lull in the storm to nail their next meal.

The predators were out. Henry could be wandering right into their path.

IT WAS SLOW going in so much freshly fallen snow, even while they were still on the grounds of the estate. It would be even slower going once they hit the woods.

"Search," Troy told Susie Bear. "Elvis. Henry."

Susie Bear charged ahead, her hunter-orange vest bright against her black shaggy coat. The Newfie retriever mutt loved snow. And fresh snow was to her as exciting as a chew toy full of peanut butter was to Elvis. For Susie Bear, only thing better than playing in the snow was working in the snow.

"With that fur coat, she'll never get cold," said Mercy.

"Neither will we, as long as we're moving."

Ethan trudged along several feet behind them, benefiting from the tracks left by their snowshoes. Out of his earshot, Troy told her the latest on Alice. Harrington still hadn't found her next of kin, although they had actually called law enforcement in Paris.

"The Parisian police say she's originally from Gstaad. I'm not sure how eager the Swiss authorities are to help us," he said. "They certainly don't seem to be in any hurry."

"Elliott Academy has a satellite program in the Alps," she said. "And Alice was born the same year everyone in our hunting party went to Elliott—less than six months after the older ones' graduation. They all would have spent some time at the Lake Geneva campus, depending on their specialized courses of study."

"Could be another coincidence. But we hate coincidences."

"We do. Have you identified that suspect we caught yet?"

"He's still not talking, but we ran his prints, and came up with a match. His name is Macon Boone, from Red Hill, Georgia. Released from Georgia state prison six months ago after serving time for armed robbery and aggravated assault." He told her about the gunrunning operation they'd been trying to crack.

"Looks like you've got your man."

"But not our murderer."

"Hard to believe a gun smuggler would resort to a bow and arrow."

"True." He recounted the captain's theory about run-ins between criminals and civilians in the woods.

"I can see that. But Alice and Caspar's murders must be linked. And why kill Caspar? Two unfortunate run-ins seem unlikely."

"Agreed." Troy glanced back at Ethan, who stomped along several feet behind them. "Henry is the key. If only he could tell us what he saw."

"We have to find him first."

Deeper into the woods, she let Troy lead the way. He knew this part of the world better than she did. Mercy struggled to hide how very worried she was. She knew Elvis would take good care of Henry, but she also knew Henry was sometimes clueless and often stubborn. He may or may not listen to Elvis.

The Malinois was trained to keep people in place. He knew his job was to take care of Henry. She was surprised that he didn't bark when Henry took off. She should have heard him; she was just in the next room. Or maybe he did bark, and in that big solid house, she just didn't hear. Or maybe she did hear him, and that's what had interrupted her dream.

She knew that as long as the temperature didn't dip below zero, Susie Bear should be able to do her job. The human trio kept up with the dog as she plowed ahead, pausing now and then for Ethan to catch up. The big shaggy dog was generally not the most graceful creature, except under two conditions: in the water or in the snow. She swam like a river otter, and she romped in the snow like a bear.

"Maybe we'll see that big bear," Mercy said.

"One thing at a time," said Troy. "It's only morning, and we've already had enough excitement for one day."

"True. I'm just hoping night hunters haven't got that bear yet."

"So far he's proven to be a good escape artist."

Prey animals hated snow. They hated change. They tended to buckle down and hide when it snowed. But predators loved snow. They loved new situations. Just like man, the ultimate predator.

They moved at a consistent pace, mostly in silence. Talking took too much effort and it slowed them down. Instead, they just hiked at a good clip. Troy was taller than she was, but Mercy managed to keep up, two strides for every one of his. He was in great shape, but then, so was she. They made a good team. Ethan, not so much. Sitting behind a desk in New York City had made a flatlander out of him.

"I walk miles each day in the city," he told them, huffing and puffing, "but it's been years since I hiked in snowshoes."

"You're doing fine," she said.

The woods were quiet. No sound but wind blowing and leaves falling and the crunch of the snow under their feet. Autumn's colors drifted into white.

The snow started falling again.

"We have to move faster," said Troy. "How are you doing?"

"I'm fine," said Mercy.

"Ethan?"

"Fine," he managed between breaths.

They settled into the steady rhythm of snowshoeing, using trekking poles, as much to test the ground in front of them for fallen logs, exposed roots, and granite boulders they couldn't see as for support.

As the snow started to fall again, so did Mercy's spirits. She needed to find Henry.

"He called me Paladin," she told Troy. "That's what Ethan said."

"He's right. You *are* a paladin."

She smiled at this flattery, but she was no holy knight. She had failed Henry. She had failed Elvis. She had failed Ethan, Lillian, and Feinberg. She had failed Martinez.

"Saint Anthony," she said.

"The saint of lost things," said Troy.

Alas, poor world, what treasure hast thou lost, Mercy thought. But aloud she said, "If I believed in saints."

They'd hiked over a mile when they entered a small glen. And that's when she saw it. A telltale lump in the snow. Splatters of blood.

Mercy stopped cold. "Troy."

Susie Bear raced over to the snow-covered bulge, slipping down into an alert position.

A bulge about the same size as a Malinois—or a little boy.

"What is it?" asked Ethan behind her.

"Stay back."

He lunged forward, but she caught him.

"Let Troy go," she said quietly.

She stood as solid and still as a column of snow, holding Ethan back. Together they watched as Troy approach the fallen object. He bowed his head and squatted down. He turned around.

"It's a deer."

Ethan cried out, letting her go and falling back against a towering pine. Mercy thanked Saint Anthony and Saint Francis of Assisi and Saint Jude and all the saints in the heavens. She stumbled over to Troy. Susie Bear was sniffing a doe's dead carcass.

"Night hunters. Odd that they left a deer here."

"Maybe they got caught in the snowstorm."

"I don't know. In this cold, it'll last until the scavengers come out. But it hasn't been de-gutted, so it's no good to anybody. This doe is a decent size. They would have taken her with them or at least gutted it so that they could come back and get her later, at least what was left of her. The predators would be out, and they would have gotten to her, so this is pretty fresh."

Out of the corner of her eye Mercy glimpsed a splash of bright blue. She headed over to a log splayed at the edge of the glen. "Look."

She reached out and tugged at the bright-blue cloth. She held it up for Troy.

"It looks like part of a puffer jacket."

"Henry's Batman puffer jacket." Ethan laughed with relief. "He's alive. You were right, Mercy. He *is* going this way." He bounded ahead, buoyed by a parent's desperate optimism.

For once she was happy Henry never paid any attention to where he was going, which was why he was always snagging his clothes on branches in the woods. Happy he was within reach. Unless. . . . She took Troy aside. "Are you thinking what I'm thinking?"

"Henry could have interrupted the night hunters, and that's why they abandoned the deer."

"Oh God."

"It's okay. We'll catch them. Him."

"He must have been running. He's no good at running." She felt hot tears behind her eyes.

"We're close. Come on, Susie Bear, let's go."

Snow was falling heavier now, and the wind was picking up. The blizzard would soon be back in full force.

Susie Bear sprinted ahead to join Ethan, and they followed her, adrenaline and the prospect of a little boy in a torn Batman puffer jacket alone in the woods spurring them on.

But Henry wasn't alone. He had Elvis with him. And Elvis would keep him safe. But who was going to keep Elvis safe?

"I guess the good news is that he really is wearing a jacket this time."

Troy smiled at her. "He's going to be okay. So is Elvis."

"Promise?"

"Promise."

And they kept on going.

IT WAS COLDER now. Another bomb cyclone could be on the way. Wherever Henry was, she hoped he was warm. The air was thick with snow. She couldn't see much more than a yard in front of her. She was glad they brought the trekking poles and glad for Susie Bear, her black, thick, shaggy fur and hunter-orange vest easy to follow in the whirl of white.

Ethan had fallen behind again. Mercy hooked her lead to Troy, so she wouldn't lose him, and then hooked another lead to Ethan.

"Do you think it's possible he could have made it to the teahouse already?" asked Ethan.

"I hope so." She raised her voice to be heard over the wind, which was picking up now, driving the snow in sheets. "I hate thinking of him out here. I'd feel better if I knew he was with Yolanda. I'd feel better about both of them."

"Your instincts were right on the mark," said Ethan. "You said he was going toward the Japanese teahouse, and that's where he's going. The scrap of his jacket proves that."

She was not so sure about that.

Susie Bear barked. A whining yowl they could hear despite the wind. The sound echoed through the forest.

No, thought Mercy, *that was no echo. That was another bark.*

She stopped, pulling on both leads to alert Troy and Ethan. "Listen."

Susie Bear disappeared from view. But they could hear her bark. And they could hear an answering bark, faint but unmistakable.

"Elvis!" Mercy unsnapped the leads tethering her to the men and jounced ahead, following the dueling banjos of barking.

She stumbled into a small clearing and found Susie Bear nuzzling Elvis.

"Elvis!" The shepherd was tied to a tree with rope. Left there to die of the cold or starvation or worse.

She ran over to the dog and buried her face in his neck. He licked one cheek, and Susie Bear licked the other. Troy joined her, pulling out his hunting knife and cutting Elvis loose. The dog leapt in the air, then raced off. Susie Bear followed suit.

"He's going after Henry," she told Troy.

"Is he all right?" asked Ethan as he caught up with them.

"He's fine. Now let's go find your boy."

They came to the fork that marked the paths leading to the gazebo and Japanese teahouse. But the dogs zoomed down the path to the gazebo—not the teahouse.

"What do we do?" asked Ethan.

"Trust your dog," said Mercy and Troy in unison.

"What does that mean?"

"It means that when in doubt we follow the dogs," said Mercy.

Their steps quickened, and soon they were sprinting through the forest on snowshoes. They could no longer see the dogs, but they could track them by their prints in the snow.

Through the howling wind she heard the roar of a snowmobile.

Oh no, she thought. If whoever tied up Elvis and left him to die had taken the boy, they could be getting away with him right now on that snowmobile. The gazebo was straight ahead. She made out two guys in ski clothes and balaclavas, one on the snowmobile and the other pushing Henry toward the big machine. Their backs were to them, so they couldn't see her.

But she could see rifles slung over their shoulders.

Elvis and Susie Bear had nearly caught up with them. Mercy yelled, "Attack!" but between the wind and the snowmobile's motor the command was lost to the storm.

Not that it mattered. The Belgian shepherd sailed through the snow, chomping on the wrist of the guy holding Henry. The guy yelled as he went down, but the scream came seconds too late to warn the driver on the snowmobile. Susie Bear tackled that dude, knocking him off the machine. Henry pulled out his whistle and blew and blew and blew.

Both Susie Bear and Elvis looked toward the boy. The driver scrambled to his feet and climbed back on the snowmobile. The guy on the ground punched Elvis with his free hand and wrestled away from the dog.

Mercy, Troy, and Ethan all sprinted toward Henry and the dogs.

"Game Warden! Stop!" yelled Troy.

The driver grabbed his buddy and pulled him onto the snowmobile. The buddy pulled his rifle off his arm, turning around and aiming at them, as the snowmobile zoomed off in a sweep of snow.

Troy fired a couple of shots at the speeding snowmobile, but visibility was poor and they were soon out of sight.

Mercy nodded to Ethan, who ran for Henry. She went to Elvis, who was stumbling to his feet. She checked out his head and neck, seeing no sign of injury. He nuzzled her chin and she scratched his sweet spot between his ears. He was wet with snow, but she didn't mind. Susie Bear shambled over for her fair share of attention.

"What do we do now?" Ethan had Henry in his arms.

"Are you okay, Henry?"

The boy nodded.

"Nice whistle," said Troy.

Henry grinned at him.

"There's no going anywhere in this storm," said Troy. "It's getting worse and it's supposed to last all afternoon and through much of the night. I think we should find shelter and wait it out."

"Here at the gazebo?" asked Ethan. "We'll freeze to death."

"We're not far from the teahouse," Mercy said. "I'm sure Yolanda will let us in."

"We'll have to cross the creek," said Troy.

"It might be frozen," said Ethan. "Or at least thick enough to cross without falling in."

"Maybe, maybe not," said Troy.

"We don't have to chance getting wet. There's a wooden bridge farther down," Mercy said. "Yolanda showed us on our way back. No risk of Henry falling in the water again this time. Let's go that way."

CHAPTER TWENTY-TWO

FORECAST: THE FIRST OF THE TWIN BLIZZARDS PUM-
MELING THE MIDWEST AND THE NORTHEAST ROLLS
OUT INTO THE ATLANTIC, TAKING THE SNOW AND
WIND WITH IT. CLEAR AND COLD UNTIL THE SEC-
OND BOMB CYCLONE ARRIVES, BRINGING ICY COLD
AND DRIVING SNOW.

THE TEAHOUSE WAS in sight. Barely. The wind had blown huge drifts around it. It looked like a snowbound enchanted cottage in a fairy tale.

Mercy stumbled in the snow as she clamored up the steps, pounding on the door.

"Yolanda! It's Mercy. I'm here with Troy and the dogs. We have Henry and his father with us. Let us in."

Elvis howled, and Susie Bear howled in return.

Yolanda opened the door, and they all piled in. Mercy told her what had happened.

"We don't think we can make it back to Nemeton in this weather."

"You're not going anywhere," said Yolanda. "You were right to come. Y'all can ride out the storm here."

Despite the fire, it was cold in the teahouse. Too cold.

"We need to heat this place up," said Troy. "We start by stacking as much snow around the house as possible. To insulate it so we can stay warm." He turned to Yolanda. "Do you have enough firewood?"

"I think so."

"Okay. We'll do the best we can. We brought provisions, and that should help. Henry, stay inside with Yolanda, okay?"

The boy nodded, snuggling under the blankets with Susie Bear and Elvis.

Mercy, Troy, and Ethan went back outside and started stacking snow against the sides of the teahouse.

"The more it looks like an igloo, the better off we are," Troy said.

Mercy was tired after the long hike to the teahouse. Ethan looked thoroughly exhausted. She was sure Troy was tired, too, but he didn't show it. They soldiered on, rolling snowballs, pounding them into squares, and piling them up against the teahouse.

"Be sure that you don't block the openings where air can circulate," said Troy.

They worked their way around the pagoda, packing snow tightly around the drafty structure.

"That's the best we can do," said Troy. "Even with whiteout conditions and gusting winds, we'll be as safe as we can be in this little igloo now."

They tramped inside and stomped the snow off their boots.

Yolanda stoked the fire, the smoke escaping from the broken glass in the pagoda's ceiling that served as a smoke hole. She'd also made tea. Mercy unpacked their provisions and helped her make lunch.

"Courtesy of Mrs. Espinosa," she said. "Here, Henry, all the peanut-butter sandwiches, cookies, and brownies you can eat."

Yolanda laughed. "I guess you like peanut butter."

"If you don't like peanut butter, Yolanda, we've got ham and Swiss and roast beef and cheddar. On Mrs. Espinosa's homemade bread. We also have thermoses of hot coffee and hot chocolate."

They huddled around the fire, eating sandwiches and drinking coffee and hot chocolate.

"It's going to be a long haul," said Troy. "The storm's not supposed to break until the wee hours of the morning. We should shelter in place all night."

Henry ate his sandwiches, cuddling with the dogs. Feeding them peanut-butter cookies when he thought no one was looking.

"I saw that, Henry," said Mercy.

The boy flushed.

"I don't like giving Elvis treats unless he earns them. Although lately I've been pretty remiss about this rule." She waved her hand down and the shepherd sat. She waved it up and he stood up again. "Make him work for it, Henry."

Henry tried it, and he liked it. He did it again, much to Susie Bear's chagrin.

"I don't make Susie Bear work for her treats," said Troy. "But if Elvis has to train for a treat, I guess she can train, too."

Henry waved his arm up and down, and Susie Bear lumbered up to her feet and lumbered down again, cocking her big pumpkin head as if to say, *Really? All this for a peanut butter cookie?* The boy laughed. The game went on with the dogs until he was out of cookies.

"That's enough," Troy said. "You'll ruin their supper."

At the word *supper,* both dogs jumped to their respective paws, tails wagging.

"We've got dog food in our packs," said Mercy. "But we have to feed them separately. Elvis doesn't like to share."

Henry watched as she and Troy filled the dog bowls. She handed the boy Elvis's bowl, and he placed it carefully at one end of the teahouse. Troy gave him Susie Bear's bowl, and he carried it to the opposite end. Both dogs attacked their bowls as if they hadn't just inhaled a baker's dozen of peanut-butter cookies.

Mercy and Troy repacked their packs while Yolanda stoked the fire again. Henry settled down with his father near the blaze, wrapped in blankets, the dogs as pillows.

"Time to hunker down for the afternoon," said Troy.

"We'll have to find a way to amuse ourselves," Mercy said.

"Henry loves games," said Ethan.

"Numbers especially. Right, Henry?"

Henry looked up at them. "Five one three nine five."

Yolanda shrugged. "Don't know that game."

"Three four two zero zero." He looked at them expectantly.

"What does he mean?" Troy turned to Ethan.

"I don't know."

Mercy thought about it.

"Two six zero five zero," said Henry.

"They're not prime numbers," she said.

Troy laughed with recognition. "They're license-plate numbers."

Henry nodded.

"Five-number sequences you find on specialty plates here in Vermont."

"License-plate numbers," said Mercy. "It makes perfect sense."

"I don't see how," said Yolanda.

"Henry is always looking out the windows: at home, in the car, everywhere," said Ethan. "I thought he just likes looking at things."

"I thought he just likes cars," said Mercy. "But maybe it's the license-plate numbers he likes. Do you remember them, Henry, the way you remember prime numbers?"

Henry nodded.

"Lillian says he has a photographic memory for things he's interested in."

"Like some kind of math genius," said Yolanda.

"Exactly."

Troy leaned forward. "This means he may remember all the license plates he's seen this week."

"That's right."

"It would be helpful to know the license-plate numbers of all the cars in the parking lot at Nemeton, all the cars that went in and out, on the morning of Alice de Clare's death," said Troy. "And all the cars that have been back and forth since. And the number of the license plate on the SUV that was following you."

"That plate was caked over," she said. "I couldn't see."

"Four five three," said Henry.

"Is that the partial that you saw, Henry? Four five three?" Troy grabbed his pack and pulled out a notebook and a pen. "Okay, Henry. Tell me the numbers of the license plates that you saw on the morning that Alice de Clare was killed."

Henry rattled off a list of numbers, and Troy wrote them down. "Great, I'll track them down first chance I get."

"What a memory," Yolanda said. "I've never seen anything like it."

"It's phenomenal," said Mercy. "Henry can list prime numbers, too. And I'm betting he knows pi to a zillion places."

"Two hundred fifty," said Ethan.

"Get out," said Yolanda.

Henry started rattling off the numbers on pi. The recitation seemed to go on forever.

"I bet you can add and subtract numbers, too," said Yolanda. "What's three hundred forty-three plus one thousand twenty-six plus four hundred eighty plus ninety-seven?"

"One thousand nine hundred forty-six," said Henry.

"Don't ask me," said Mercy.

"Don't ask me," said Troy.

"We'll have to take it on faith that you're right."

"He's been adding and subtracting numbers in his head since he was little," said Ethan. "But I haven't seen him do it in long time."

Yolanda proposed another list of numbers, but Henry shook his head.

"You don't know how to do it?"

"I don't think that's it," said Mercy. "Maybe he doesn't want people think he's a one-trick pony."

"Sorry," said Yolanda.

"Good Little Henry," Henry said.

"The story?" asked Mercy. "You'd like to hear the rest of the story?" He nodded.

It was cozy in the teahouse now. A blur of blowing snow outside, huddled inside an ice palace, trapped in a snow globe. A perfect place for storytelling.

"It's quite a long story, but I'll see what I can remember of it," she said.

Troy sat cross-legged close to her. Henry snuggled with the dogs and his dad and Yolanda.

Mercy began as all storytellers began:

"Once upon a time, there was a little boy named Good Little Henry. He lived with his mother in a small house in the woods. He loved her very much. When she fell ill, and the doctor told Henry there was nothing he could do, he called upon the Fairy Bienfaisante. She told him he must travel to the top of the mountain, where a holy man would give him the Plant of Life. Only that could cure his mother.

"And so Good Little Henry set out for the mountain. He traveled many miles and still the mountain seemed as far away as ever. He encountered many obstacles. Raging rivers to cross. High walls to scale. Wild beasts to outwit. Along the way he saved a crow from a fox, and the crow carried him across the raging river. He harvested grapes for a giant, and the giant crumbled the high wall with the sounding blows of his terrible voice. He helped a wolf feed his family, and the wolf gave him a magic stick to carry him home. But Good Little Henry could not go home without the Plant of Life.

"So he kept on, using the magic stick as a walking stick, and after many days and nights he came to the base of the mountain. And he began to climb. He was tired and hungry and thirsty, but he kept on climbing. Finally, he reached the peak, where to his surprise he found a lush garden full of strange and wonderful plants. But how was he to know which was the Plant of Life? And then he remembered the Fairy Bienfaisante, and the holy man who would give him the Plant of Life. He searched the garden thoroughly, and there in the middle of a maze he found the monk. He told the holy man about his mother, and the monk gave him the Plant of Life. But the holy man warned Good Little Henry that he must hold it in his hands at all times, and if he should drop it, it would disappear, never to be seen again.

"Good Little Henry thanked the monk. But as he began his descent, he wondered how he could hold the Plant of Life all the way home if the journey back was as challenging as the journey to the mountain had been. And then he remembered the magic stick that the wolf had given him. He mounted the stick, and off he flew, the Plant of Life in hand, all the way home. Whereupon he pressed the Plant of Life against his sick mother's pale lips. She sat up, fully cured, and hugged Good Little Henry.

"And they lived happily ever after."

Henry smiled.

She smiled back. "Now it's your turn to tell a story."

Henry shook his head.

"Hard for a kid who doesn't like to talk to tell a long story," said Yolanda.

Mercy considered this. "You like to draw. Why don't you draw us a story?"

Troy pointed to his notebook and pen.

"I've got something better." Yolanda pulled paper and colored pencils out of an old, battered suitcase. She placed the suitcase in front of Henry to use as a desk. "Go ahead."

The boy took the pen in hand and started drawing. It looked like a map.

"That looks like a ley line," said Ethan. "Henry's into ley lines."

"What's a ley line?" asked Yolanda.

"A line connecting special places." She explained about Skellig Michael and how ley lines had inspired Henry's Game.

They all watched in silence as the boy worked on his map.

"I think it's a map of the woods here," said Mercy. "Look, there's the bridge that goes over the creek and there are the stepping stones farther up the creek, where Henry fell into the water. There's the Japanese teahouse and there's the gazebo. There's Nemeton and there's the glen where we found Alice."

Henry drew an arrow there and an arrow in the gazebo, to show where Alice de Clare and Caspar Farrow died. But there were other marks on the map as well. Marks that Mercy wasn't sure she understood.

"What's this, Henry?"

Troy and Yolanda leaned forward. It was a stick figure of a cat and a jagged object.

"Is that a trap?" Troy asked.

Henry nodded.

"A bobcat trap," said Troy.

Henry shook his head.

"Lynx?"

Henry shook his head again.

"Marten?"

Henry beamed.

"What does that mean?" asked Mercy.

"It means that night hunters are illegally trapping marten," said Troy. "Their fur's worth a fortune."

"I didn't think there were any martens left anymore," said Ethan.

"They've made a comeback in southern Vermont," said Troy. "But no one should be trapping martens. They're endangered, like lynx and mountain lions. There's no trapping them at any time."

"What about bobcats?" asked Yolanda. "I've seen them around."

"Bobcat season is only two weeks in December. And you're never allowed to use a toothed foothold trap. Which is what this looks like." Troy pointed to the line drawing of the jagged-edged object.

"So maybe the night hunters aren't running guns," said Mercy, "they're trapping."

"What about the guy you caught at the bob-house?" asked Ethan.

"Macon Boone," said Troy. "But it looks like he's more into gun smuggling."

"Two separate groups of offenders," said Mercy.

"Or one very enterprising group," said Troy.

"Vermonters are nothing if not resourceful," said Ethan.

"Boone is from Georgia," she said with a smile.

"Marten is one of the most expensive furs in the world," said Troy.

"I didn't think anybody wore real fur anymore," said Yolanda.

"Maybe not here. But there are lots of places in the world where fur is as popular as ever."

"How do you know about the traps, Henry?" asked Ethan.

"Dark trees."

"I still don't know what that means, Henry," said Mercy.

"Monster slayer."

"Like you were talking about with Brodie."

Henry nodded.

Troy looked at Henry. "Like tree monsters."

Henry nodded again.

"Tree monsters?" asked Yolanda.

"Dark trees are a kind of tree monster. The kind you find in enchanted forests, only not the good kind. The bad kind."

"Poachers are dark trees." Mercy pointed to the traps on Henry's map. "You saw them setting traps. That's how you know where they are."

"Which is why they're after him." Ethan looked worried.

"We can find the traps using Henry's map," she said. "Henry has an ability to construct maps in his mind. He reads the woods, just like we do. Only in a completely different way."

"Lucky you," said Troy to Henry.

"Well, that's the best story ever," said Yolanda.

Troy drew his finger along Henry's map. "Look at the pattern. The night hunters seem to be going north. Which would make sense. The higher elevations are where martens like to go. The deep snow areas. And the hunters seem to be going higher as time goes on, as they go deeper into the woods. Now is the best time to hunt marten. The fishers compete with them for food and prey on them. The martens are safer in deep snow, where they can survive better than the fishers. We just have to look higher up the mountain and we can catch those bastards. Oops, sorry, Henry."

The wind picked up again and the snow howled around the little teahouse. Henry yawned.

"I think you should take a nap, son," said Ethan. "You've had a pretty busy day."

"That was a long walk you took with Elvis through the woods," said Mercy. "And it wasn't your first. Exactly how many times have you been out in the woods by yourself?" She looked at Ethan.

"I don't know," Ethan admitted. "At least twice that we know of this week."

Henry ignored her and his father and went back to his map, sketching trees and rocks and trails. She watched as he continued working, going back to where he'd drawn the arrow in the clearing where Alice de Clare's body was found. Henry drew a stick figure lying next to the arrow.

"Is that Alice?"

Henry started flapping his hands. Elvis and Susie Bear flanked him, nudging his arms with their noses until he calmed down.

"The night hunters must have killed her," said Yolanda.

"If Alice caught them trapping martens, they'd have a strong motive," said Troy. "Have you ever seen them set traps?"

"I've seen them with rifles, hunting deer and bear and whatever else they find. I haven't seen any traps. But I wouldn't put anything past them."

Henry yawned again.

"One more thing before we put you to bed, Henry," said Mercy. "Why did you go out in the storm to see Yolanda?"

Henry shook his head. "Morning constitutional."

"What does that mean?" asked Ethan.

Mercy smiled. "It means he took Elvis for his morning walk."

"Don't ever do that again," said his father.

The boy curled up with the dogs as bed warmers. In minutes, he was fast asleep. *Good Little Henry.*

Yolanda and Ethan joined Henry and the dogs and soon they were both dozing off.

Darkness fell quickly during a blizzard. It got colder. Even Troy's fire wasn't enough.

"I guess it's going to be a two-dog night," said Mercy.

Troy laughed. "The dogs are taken. I guess we'll just have to rely on human warmth."

It was very unlike Troy to say such a thing. Or maybe she didn't know him as well as she thought she did.

Between Henry and Yolanda and the dogs, the mats covering the floor were mostly occupied.

Only one mat left.

"We'll have to share," said Troy. To keep warm, they curled up together.

There was no escaping it, thought Mercy. It had to be done. He wrapped his arms around her, and they spooned. She felt his heart beating against hers.

He was careful to keep his hands around her waist. Careful to be as polite as a man could be, hanging onto a woman for human warmth in the middle of a blizzard. Mercy appreciated that he was a gentleman.

He was a good man. Patience was right. Lillian was right. Even Amy was right. Mercy should let this man love her. If he wanted to.

Everyone said they'd make a perfect couple. Now she was beginning to believe that they just might.

Maybe it was the cold. Maybe it was the proximity. Maybe it was just human nature. That they should be drawn to one another in a time like this. Mercy felt a longing that she hadn't felt since Martinez died.

She tried to put that feeling out of her mind. She needed to think of something else. Mercy could hear the dogs snuffling. Yolanda and

Ethan were tucked together like two longtime lovers, and Henry was a cuddle bug in a rug of dogs. Talking in his sleep. Chanting prime numbers even as he dreamed. Mercy wondered what it would be like to have a brain like Henry's, to see the world the way he did.

He was a remarkable little boy. She wondered how his mother could have left him, where she was, and if she should try to find her. She thought about Alice de Clare and wondered if she would've made a good stepmother for Henry.

Poor Troy. Mercy knew he didn't get much sleep this time of year. She'd have to keep still and be quiet. In a minute.

"Gunnar told Daniel there's at least one bow and quiver of arrows missing from the estate's hunting equipment. He thinks Alice took it, meaning to join the hunting party."

"So her murderer killed her with her own bow, and then got rid of it?"

"I don't know."

"Let's figure it out tomorrow," he whispered in her ear. Brushing her earlobe with his lips.

"Tomorrow," she whispered back.

So much for thinking about something else. Or sleeping. She longed for Troy, not just physically, but emotionally. Dangerous territory.

Dangerous, and yet she still felt safe, as the wind howled around them and snow dumped from the sky, and a sad little boy and a grieving father and a wounded soldier and two good dogs slept nearby.

Mercy was grateful for their presence. If the others hadn't been there, she wouldn't have trusted herself with Troy. It was hard to lie here beside him, feeling the warmth of his body against hers—and not hope for something more.

It was going to be a long night.

CHAPTER TWENTY-THREE

FORECAST: CLEAR, COLD, AND SUNNY. SNOW FLUR-
RIES LATE IN THE DAY.

As SLEEP-DEPRIVED AS he was, Troy didn't sleep, at least not much, and he didn't think Mercy did either. He lay next to her in a state of heightened awareness that he simply could not shut off. He spent long hours listening to wind howling around the teahouse, wondering what it would be like to spend every night with his arms around Mercy Carr. It was one of the most painful and pleasurable nights of his life.

As soon as he got Henry and his father back to Nemeton and figured out who the murderer was and caught the night hunters, when this was all over, he was going to do whatever he needed to do to make this woman happy. Forever.

Of course, he'd have ask her out on a regular date first. No kids, no cops, no dogs.

Just the two of them, a good steak dinner, and a bottle of Big Barn Red.

By around five in the morning, the storm abated. No more sheets of snow pounding the teahouse. No more wind howling around its ice-packed perimeter, or thunder booming and cracking above their heads.

It was deathly quiet, and he could hear her breathing. It rang in his ears. A siren call.

Susie Bear knew he was awake. She shuffled over to him, rousing Henry in the process. Elvis jumped up and joined them; they were desperate to go outside. Yolanda and Ethan slept on, wrapped in each other's arms as if they'd been together forever. He wondered how they'd made that jump so quickly. And why he and Mercy shouldn't make the same leap.

Mercy turned over and looked up at Troy as he lay supported on one elbow.

"Good morning," she said.

"Good morning."

"The dogs need to go out."

A tangle of red hair fell across her face, and it was all he could do not to brush it away. Henry trotted over to join them, pulling a blanket tight around his torso. "Out."

"Don't move, I've got this." He scrambled to his feet. "Okay, guys, come on. You, too, Henry."

Troy pushed the door open hard, dislodging a foot and a half of snow outside. Drifts of much deeper snow marked the clearing. The dogs ran off, playing in the snow, wrestling each other as Troy guided the little boy through the predawn gloom about a hundred yards away from the house. "Okay, do your thing."

Henry looked up at him.

"There's no bathroom," said Troy.

Henry stared at the ground.

"You've never peed outside before?"

The boy shook his head.

"There's a first time for everything, and we're in the middle of the woods so better make do. Or you can wait until we get back to Nemeton."

Henry started stimming. Troy wasn't sure if it was the thought of going back to Nemeton or the thought of peeing outside that set him off. The dogs rallied round the boy and he calmed down. *Now or never,* Troy thought.

"Just do what I do." He did his business while the boy and the dogs watched. "Your turn."

Henry did his business, too. Very seriously.

"Good job. Now we have to get you back to the estate. Mercy and Elvis and your dad will go with you. I'm going to go after those night hunters. Thanks to you, I have a good idea where they might be."

He walked Henry back with the dogs, observing how he noticed everything around him. The kid didn't miss a trick. But he never seemed to have much fun.

Troy leaned over, packed a snowball, and threw it. Susie Bear wouldn't chase it; she didn't see much point in fetching anything other than people who needed rescuing. But Elvis took off after it like a bat out of hell. When the snowball disintegrated upon impact, the Belgian shepherd sniffed the ground, then raced back to Troy.

Henry laughed. Troy threw another snowball, this time at the boy. Henry scooped up his own snowball and tossed it at Troy.

He needed to teach this kid how to throw a ball.

The snowball fight continued while the dogs leapt around them. Troy hadn't seen Henry this animated—in a good way—since he'd met him. He'd have to tell Mercy.

"Okay, let's not get too wet and cold. We've got a long way to go."

They went back to the cabin, where Mercy and Ethan were up, packed, and ready to go.

Mercy was trying to convince Yolanda to come with them. "There's at least one murderer running around in these woods. Probably more. You'll be safer with us."

"I can take care of myself. And what about Harrington?"

"You don't have to worry about Harrington," added Troy. "He'll back off once we tell him about the hunters trying to take Henry."

"We could really use your help," said Ethan.

"Yolanda," said Henry.

That clinched it. They waited while Yolanda tossed the bare necessities into a backpack.

She slung her bow and quiver of arrows over her shoulder, and handed her service weapon over to Mercy. "Better safe than sorry."

"Good," Mercy said. "We can give the bow and arrow to Harrington. It'll help prove you didn't kill anybody. And it's always good to have another weapon."

"I'm surprised you're not carrying your gun," Troy said to Mercy.

"I haven't had time to go home and get it."

They started the long hike back. It was early, and the woods were steeped in shadow.

"This is prime feeding time for deer," said Troy. "So be on the lookout."

It was slow going in deep snow, even with snowshoes. Which Henry didn't have.

"Mercy, can you take my pack?" Troy asked.

"No problem."

"Come on, Henry, you're going to crawl on my back and I'm going to carry you."

"I can do that," said Ethan.

"We'll take turns. I'll go first." Troy squatted down, and the boy wrapped his arms around his neck, his little legs around Troy's torso. Troy straightened up, his arms under Henry's knees. "Onward."

The way back to Nemeton was more challenging than the way to the Japanese teahouse the day before.

"I know a shortcut," said Yolanda, leading them deeper into the woods.

The birds started to chatter, the forest coming back to life after a long, hard storm. Troy and the others did their best to avoid the deeper drifts, but it wasn't easy.

As they approached another blowdown, Henry started chanting prime numbers.

"Something's wrong," said Mercy. The dogs stopped, and they stopped, too.

Yolanda kept going.

"Stop, Yolanda."

Troy trusted Mercy's instincts. He handed Henry over to Ethan.

"Stay here," he said quietly.

Mercy handed Yolanda back her service weapon.

"No, you keep it."

"You need to protect Henry."

Yolanda kept the gun, but she handed Mercy her bow and arrow.

Troy and Mercy proceeded carefully into the blowdown, dogs at their heels. In the middle of a pile of downed tree limbs stood a pair of night hunters, dressed all in black and wearing ski masks. The taller of the two poachers cocked his rifle, aiming it at something they could not quite make out in the gloom. Two steps nearer, Troy spotted the poachers' target.

A very big bear. Probably the very same big bear that Caspar Farrow had tried to take down before he died. Troy looked at Mercy, and she nodded.

The big bear was still here.

"Game warden!" he yelled.

The night hunter spun around, gun in hand, but he pivoted too quickly, slipping in the snow. Mercy and Troy dropped to the ground, Susie Bear and Elvis at their sides. The poacher dropped his rifle and it discharged, the bullet flying toward the bear, missing it by a whisper.

Troy pulled his weapon and pointed it at the hunter on the ground. The other hunter turned tail and ran.

Mercy drew her bow, and Troy wondered how good she was at shooting it. If she was half as good as she was with a rifle, that would be good enough.

The bear stood on his hind legs and roared. Usually that was a bluffing move.

But the bear did not retreat. He charged.

The man on the ground screamed, but Troy didn't move. He wasn't going to shoot that bear if he didn't have to. The bear rambled right by the night hunter—away from him, away from Troy and Mercy, away from Yolanda and Henry and Ethan.

Way to go, thought Troy. He smiled, thinking of the poacher who'd fled. The bear was traveling in his direction. The poacher might have thought he made a clean getaway, but only time would tell.

Back to the night hunter on the ground. Troy cuffed the guy's hands behind his back, then jerked him to his feet, pulling the balaclava off his face. "Johnny Buskey. Fancy meeting you here."

Johnny hung his head and cursed. Troy read him his rights. "Okay, we're going to walk back to civilization. Which basically means jail for you."

"I didn't do nothing."

"Really? You were about to shoot a bear."

"It's bear-hunting season."

"The sun hasn't risen yet. You're poaching. You're a poacher and a murderer."

"Murderer! What are you talking about?"

"And you're trapping endangered species. Should I go on?"

"I didn't kill nobody," said Johnny. "Animals are one thing, people's another."

Troy looked at Mercy. "Let's get going. The sooner we get him into custody, the better."

"What about the other guy?"

"Maybe his cousin, Daryl. We'll catch him later. If the bear doesn't get him first."

Johnny shook his head. "You can't let that bear get him."

"He's armed."

"He didn't do nothing."

"Once upon a time he was clean. Not anymore, thanks to you." Troy sighed. "You're in some real trouble now, Johnny. You and your cousin."

"It was self-defense."

"Right. You were pointing your gun at a bear."

"What would you do if a bear charged you?"

"Come on, let's go." They walked back to Yolanda and Henry and Ethan, Troy pushing Johnny ahead of them. The dogs flanking the suspect.

"You're going to have to ride with your dad this time," Mercy told Henry. Ethan pulled the boy onto his back, and they trudged through the woods.

Mercy slipped ahead of the rest of them to join Troy.

"I think they're poachers who should go to jail, but I don't think they're murderers."

"And Macon Boone?"

"Nope."

"That's a lot of innocent criminals." Troy laughed. "So who did it?"

"I'm not sure." She lowered her voice, so Henry wouldn't hear. "But I worry that Ethan could be in danger now. Maybe Alice's baby wasn't his. Maybe that's what they were actually fighting about."

When she leaned toward Troy, the memory of their spooning together the night before nearly laid him flat.

"While you were out with Henry and the dogs, I was looking through my cell phone at the photos I took of Alice's diary. Most of the entries were straightforward. You know, appointments with her clients, architects, suppliers, people she worked with. The usual doctor appointments, hair dresser, manicurists, that kind of girlie thing." She paused. "The Montgomerys, the Farrows, Lea, Daniel, they're all in there. Ethan hardly appears at all. She may have loved Ethan, but I don't think he was the reason she was here."

"I'm not following."

"Alice wasn't here only to design the inn. She had an ulterior motive."

"Like what?"

"She was pregnant, and she was adopted. Many women adoptees go in search of their birth parents when they find out they're pregnant. Maybe that's what Alice was doing. Remember, she was born just around the time they were all going to the Elliott Academy."

"How did she make that connection?"

"I don't know. It's just a theory."

"Assuming your theory is correct, the trail led from Elliott to the hunting party."

"Exactly. The Farrows claim they hardly knew Alice, and yet their initials are all through her daybook, especially Caspar's."

"Do you think he might have fathered her baby?"

"I don't know."

"Dr. Darling will figure it out, if she hasn't already." He looked at Mercy. "Why would a woman like Alice de Clare sleep with a guy like Caspar Farrow?"

"No idea. But then, different strokes for different folks. There's no explaining attraction."

Troy grinned, thinking of the night they'd spent together, not sleeping, not making love, just breathing. "True enough."

As soon as they crossed onto the grounds of the estate, he called Thrasher. The captain was happy to hear from him, but worried about Harrington.

"He won't be pleased that you've made another arrest that should have gone to him."

"Nothing I can do about that."

"I'll have him send a couple uniforms over to pick up Johnny Buskey as soon as the plows can get through. And I'll put an APB out on his cousin Daryl Buskey."

"Thanks."

"As far as Harrington is concerned, the case will be closed."

"That's not what Mercy thinks."

Thrasher laughed. "Of course, it's not."

Troy told the captain about Henry and the license-plate numbers. "I'll send you a photo of the list."

"Okay. I'll try to get out there as soon as I can. In the meantime, keep that kid safe. And it might be best if you kept the poacher with Gunnar."

"Great idea," said Troy. "It will be good to have him out of the way."

* * *

DANIEL FEINBERG GREETED them at the service-entrance door. That was a first, thought Troy.

"Thank goodness you're back and all is well."

Ethan excused himself and took Henry off to get into a clean and warm set of clothes. The dogs went with them.

"Who's this?" asked George, turning to the prisoner.

"Johnny Buskey," said Troy. "He's under arrest, for poaching, and maybe more."

"Shall I call Detective Harrington?" asked Feinberg.

"Sure, I already called Captain Thrasher, so you can do those honors."

"Consider it done." The billionaire regarded Yolanda with interest.

"This is Yolanda Yellowbird," said Troy.

She extended her hand. The billionaire shook it solemnly. "A pleasure."

Gunnar arrived at the door, followed by his dogs. "I'll take the prisoner off your hands."

"If you don't mind," Yolanda said to Troy, "I'll stay with Gunnar. Help him guard Buskey."

"I do not need help."

"Go ahead. Save me the trouble of backup." He suspected she did not feel comfortable in the billionaire's house. She'd feel more comfortable with Gunnar, who was the kind of guy who looked like the woods itself. Besides, the more people paying attention to anything Johnny Buskey may say or do, the better.

Yolanda went off with Gunnar, and Mercy turned to Feinberg. "I know it's still relatively early for your guests, but I wonder if it's possible for you to get them out of their rooms for a while?"

"I won't ask," he said. "Consider it done."

Troy escorted Mercy to the staircase, waving an arm to indicate she should go first and then following her up the stairs.

He liked the way she moved.

* * *

SHE COULD FEEL his eyes on her as she made her way up to the second floor. She went back to her room, took a hot shower, and changed clothes, giving George time to get everybody out of their rooms. The butler had put out a new outfit for her. Where he found them, she had no idea, but the black wool pants and nubby cream-colored sweater were just her size. She ran her fingers through her hair and brushed her teeth and put on lip gloss. She didn't look too bad for a woman who'd spent the night wide awake in a blizzard, in the arms of a man she'd never kissed.

Mercy knew the key to these murders must lie with Alice and her baby. She needed to find the fatal connection between the hunting party and Alice.

She started with Cara's room, but the grieving widow was still there. Mercy heard her inside doing a Skype interview.

"I'm not feeling well," Cara said to her through the door, but she knew that was a lie.

Not that Mercy thought she was the murderer. If Caspar were the father of Alice's baby and if he left her for Alice, Cara would happily challenge the prenup, take half of everything and more—milking the divorce drama in the tabloids. She'd come back to the grieving widow later.

She moved on to Lea's room. Nothing but clothes and toiletries in the closet and bathroom. On the dresser there was a framed photograph of Max and Lea, Katharine and Blake, on one of those picnics they'd talked about, lolling on a blanket by the lake on a bright spring day, looking very stoned, very free love, very hippie commune.

She wondered if they'd ever swapped partners. Supposedly it was like musical chairs back then.

But Blake had made it clear that he fell for Katharine right away, and hard. They had obviously paired off early.

If Alice suspected that a pair of early-1980s Elliott students were her biological parents, she would check out those people. And she had met the Montgomerys first, at the d'Arcys' party in Boston—and maybe she'd engineered that meeting on purpose to meet Blake and Katharine. Blake and Katharine, who were high-society and aspiring high-society, and for whom a baby out of wedlock would be a faux pas. And who went on to have William. That was a lot of maybes.

Or maybe Max and Lea were the biological parents. But Max died of AIDS and he and Lea had no children. Then again, they were both dark haired and dark eyed and Alice was a fair blonde like Blake and Katharine. Not that either was conclusive proof one way or the other.

Mercy stopped herself. Too many variables. No point in more conjecture until she had more to work with.

Next to the picture was Lea's camera bag. Inside she found the Nikon camera, the one she'd been using since Mercy first met her, in the glen where she'd found Alice de Clare's body.

She flipped through the photos on the digital camera. Pictures of this weekend, mostly. Dinners. The woods. The couples. The crime scene. Nothing Mercy had not seen before.

She put the camera back where she'd found it and closed the bag. Time to search Blake and Katharine's room.

Their corner suite was down the hall, situated to command the most spectacular views Nemeton had to offer, from the pool and waterfall behind the house to the forest and mountains beyond. It was a space that even the discerning Katharine could appreciate. How had she described the apartment Alice de Clare had designed for her? A postmodern Louis XVI gem. Well, this was more like something out of Versailles itself. Cream-and-gold paneled walls, an intricately carved and gilded black marble fireplace, and an elaborately corniced king-size bed draped with yards and yards of Wedgewood blue silk.

Mercy checked the walk-in closet, where his-and-her designer Montgomery wardrobes hung pristinely, shoes lined up neatly below, and suitcases empty. George at work again.

In the room proper she went through the drawers of the antique Louis XIV armoire and found little of interest, apart from obscenely expensive sweaters and lingerie. In the black-and-white all marble en suite bath, Blake's grooming essentials were laid out between the double sinks. Katharine had commandeered the dressing area, its gilded vanity topped with three mirrors.

The better to see you with, my dear Katharine, she thought. A mirrored tray held all manner of toiletries—creams and lotions, Oriflame makeup, perfumes and colognes. Dr. Wright was right. Katharine took good care of her assets.

A freestanding cream-and-gold jewelry chest held her enormous collection of jewelry. And this is only what she traveled with. One drawer held rings, a second bracelets, a third necklaces. Two drawers were devoted to earrings alone.

No nostalgia here. Katharine had happily left her dairy-farm past behind, and if Dr. Wright were to be believed, Blake Montgomery was her best memento from Elliott Academy.

Only one place left to search.

This would be tricky, given George's apparent gift for surveillance and sudden appearances. Carefully she made her way to the butler's room, in the lower level of the house where the service quarters were. Even down here, each room had a door with a plaque.

MR. WILCOX, it read. His room was nicely appointed. Not as nicely as the upstairs rooms in the guest wing, but nicely appointed, nonetheless, reflecting George's position in the household.

An antique highboy, four-poster bed, nice Berber carpet, and mahogany paneling. A man's room. Suitable for a butler. A suite with a sitting area and a private bath.

She quickly searched the room and found nothing. In the bathroom, she found an elegant leather Dopp kit. She went through it and realized it had a false bottom. She lifted it up; in that false bottom lay an old faded color photograph of a young Katharine Montgomery wrapped in nothing but a white bedsheet, a man's arm draped over her shoulder. Mercy couldn't see the man. The photo was cut off, but she saw a man's hand. On his hand was a signet ring just like the one

BLIND SEARCH   299

the butler wore. She looked closer and saw they were surrounded by hay.

Hay. Horses. Stables.

She pulled out her cell phone, swiping through the pics she'd taken doing research at the Elliott Academy. There it was: Katharine on the pretty Arabian chestnut, the stable boy at her side. The boy was not George; he was much taller, with deeper set eyes and a narrower jaw. She zoomed in on the young man's left hand. Barely visible but recognizable nonetheless: a gold signet ring.

Why would George have this photo? What was his connection to Richard, the long-lost stable boy from the Elliott Academy? Why was he really here at Nemeton?

She snapped photos of the kit, its false bottom, and the photo on her cell.

Now it was time to talk to Feinberg.

And his butler.

CHAPTER TWENTY-FOUR

Paladin: a combat-trained adventurer sworn to fight for justice, protecting the innocent and battling evil wherever it is to be found.

—HENRY'S GAME

WHEN MERCY SLIPPED OUT OF GEORGE'S ROOM, to her great relief, the butler was not standing outside the door. She went to her room and grabbed the Elliott Academy yearbook and went to find George.

She found him in the kitchen, where he was supervising the imminent serving of an elaborate brunch, designed to keep the guests out of their rooms and out of trouble.

"I need to speak to Daniel right away."

George raised an eyebrow, and for a moment she thought he was going to balk. But then he shrugged and said, "Follow me."

He led her to the study, where the billionaire was at his desk. George bowed, preparing to leave, but she blocked him from the door. "Stay. We need to talk to you."

"What's this all about?" asked George with a hint of irritation. "What's that book you have there?"

"First things first." She gave George her *I'm an MP and you're not* glare of intimidation, and he didn't even blink. Which meant he was former law enforcement or military or both.

"Who are you? Really?"

"I'm George Wilcox. Of Lancashire."

"Wilcox." She remembered Dr. Wright. *I think his name was Rich-*

ard. Williams or Wilson. Watson, maybe. Something like that. "And how are you connected to Richard Wilcox?"

"I know no Richard Wilcox."

"Who is Richard Wilcox?" asked Feinberg.

"The stable boy at Elliott Academy when your hunting party were students there. According to Dr. Wright, he assaulted Katharine. Caspar Farrow rescued her. Wilcox was going to be dismissed, so he ran off."

"Nonsense." George stood tall against the accusation.

Mercy pulled her cell from her pocket and swiped to the photo of Katharine and the stable boy. She showed Feinberg the photo. "I found this in his room, hidden in his toiletries kit. In a very slick false bottom. Note the signet ring on the boy's hand. Just like the one George wears. On his left pinkie finger."

"George?" The billionaire gave George a look that would freeze the heart of most mortals. Icier even than Mercy's MP glare.

Still didn't faze this tough-as-nails butler.

"Does that look like assault to you?" asked George, his plummy English accent broadening with emotion.

"No, it doesn't," she said quietly. "Why don't you tell us about it?"

"He was in love with her. He wanted to marry her. That's what he wrote home to his mother. My sister-in-law Marian." George's eyes clouded for a moment. "My brother died of cancer quite young, when Richard was ten years old. The boy was devoted to his mother, and she to him. She missed him terribly when he went off to America. He wrote her every week for two years. Then nothing. That letter was the last time she ever heard from him. The last time any of us ever heard from him."

"You looked for him." It was a statement, not a fact.

"When the letters stopped coming, I made the usual inquiries. All the school would say was that he'd been fired for cause, and that he disappeared before they could file charges. He'd sent me the photo, a bit of bragging, I suppose, about his beautiful American lover. I knew there must be more to the story than the school would admit.

I reckon the girl's parents found out and had him fired. That's usually how it goes at places like that, isn't it? The rich kids get a great education, and the poor kids get sacked." He looked at his boss. "No offense."

"None taken. Please go on."

"Marian never believed the accusations against him, but the worry killed her anyway. She died six months later."

"Why come looking now?" she asked.

George hung his head for a moment before lifting it again. "After she died, I put it out of my mind. I was a young police officer in Lancashire, busy with solving cases right there at home. But when I retired, I decided to find out once and for all what happened to Richard. I felt I owed it to Marian. And to my dead brother."

"You're not a real butler." Feinberg's voice was incredulous. Mercy understood why; George did seem every inch a true butler. At least the PBS kind of butler she was familiar with. But then he'd fooled the billionaire, too.

"I did a lot of undercover work. And I knew the Montgomerys traveled in rich circles. It seemed a good way in."

"You came highly recommended." Feinberg shifted in his seat. She thought he looked embarrassed. She couldn't imagine it was an emotion he experienced often.

"I had some assistance there. My chief inspector put in a good word with the agency."

"It worked," said Feinberg.

"Troy will check him out for us." Mercy was growing impatient. She wanted to get to the bottom of this. "What have you found out?"

"There's no record of Richard anywhere. If he did disappear, he did a bloody good job of it."

"But you don't believe that."

"I can't believe that Richard would let his mother suffer that way. He may have been a bit barmy, but he was a good son." He reached inside his jacket and retrieved something from the hidden breast pocket. "You should see this. I found it in Alice de Clare's room."

George handed her an old postcard, featuring the wildflowers of Switzerland. *Alpenblumen,* read the caption on the address side. *Alpine flowers,* translated Mercy. The rest of the card—where you'd write a note or the address of the recipient—was blank. She passed it on to Feinberg.

"You tampered with evidence," she said to George.

"It was before she died. While I was unpacking her things. I was going to return it. But then . . ."

"But then she was murdered."

"Correct. And I wasn't going to give it to that wanker Harrington. Not before I figured out what it meant. If anything."

"And did you?"

"No," he admitted.

"Anything else you'd like to share?"

He shook his head.

"Really?

The faux butler squared his shoulders. Mercy knew he was holding something back, but she also knew he wouldn't spill until he was good and ready. If ever.

"That will be all, George." As soon as the butler had gone, Feinberg turned to Mercy. "I'll deal with Wilcox. Now what?"

"We keep on digging. Meanwhile, you keep an eye on your butler."

FEINBERG ACCOMPANIED MERCY down to the dining room, where George was ushering in the guests for brunch. At the long formal dining table, Ethan sat on one side of Henry, Troy on the other. The Montgomerys were there, along with Lea and William. All looking weary and bleary-eyed. Between the murders and the booze, the elegant façade of the hunting party was slipping. And the free-flowing champagne at this brunch wasn't helping. Cara was having breakfast in bed, her façade undoubtedly intact.

"Henry, how are you feeling?"

The boy did not answer her; he was too busy feasting on peanut-butter toast and slipping the crusts to Elvis and Susie Bear under the table.

"That's enough people food for Elvis," she told him.

George brought her a breakfast plate and she placed it on the table but did not sit down.

"Could you spare a minute?" she said to Troy between bites of a Danish. "Henry, stay here with your father and the dogs." Mercy glanced at Feinberg, who nodded.

"Sure," said Troy.

They excused themselves and went to the map room, the room Henry loved. They shut the door, stepping into a darkly furnished library full of freestanding antique globes. Vintage maps graced mahogany-paneled walls. Finely crafted architectural desks rimmed the room, undoubtedly full of rare maps. She could see why Henry loved this space. They stood next to a beautiful globe that must date from the early Forties, given the changing shape of Europe at the time.

She told him about George and his nephew. She showed him the old postcard George found in Alice's room.

"What does it mean?"

"I don't know. All of them spent time at the Elliott Academy campus in the Swiss Alps, not far from where Alice was born. There's got to be a connection. Since she's adopted, the simplest explanation is that she's related to someone from Elliott."

"You think Katharine and Blake were Alice de Clare's parents?"

"It would explain some things, though not why she or Caspar Farrow were killed. And why give up baby Alice for adoption? Blake had plenty of money."

"Maybe they weren't ready."

"Maybe Katharine wasn't ready to give up her chance at Olympic gold. Blake said himself that she loved her horses more than anything or anyone."

"That doesn't explain why Alice was murdered. If she is their daughter, why kill her? And why kill Farrow?" Troy placed the post-card next to one of the globes. "I think the Buskey brothers are our best bet. We know they've gone after Henry. Because he saw them kill Alice."

"Maybe. But that doesn't explain Farrow. I feel like I'm missing something." She spun the globe absently. She gazed at the globe, running her finger across the Swiss Alps. *"Alpenblumen."*

"What?"

She reached for the postcard. There were three photos on the decorative side of the card, each a close-up of an Alpine flower. "There's a reason Alice kept this."

"Alice liked flowers." Troy shrugged. "Her scarf had flowers on it, and there was a flower on the pin that held the peregrine feathers on her hat."

"Tyrolean." She grinned at him.

"Right." He grinned back.

"There was a flower on her daybook, too."

"It's got to be more than her just liking flowers." She examined the postcard again. "She kept this old postcard for a reason. And she wore that silver flowered fastener with the peregrine falcon feathers on her hat for a reason."

"Not just fashion?"

"I don't think so. All of her other clothes and accessories and accoutrements—from her daybook to her lingerie—are twenty-first-century chic. No vintage—except for these two items."

She pointed to the photo on the left of the postcard, which featured a small white star-shaped bloom. "This is an edelweiss."

"I recognize that one."

"Do you?"

"Even I've seen *The Sound of Music.*"

She laughed. "Okay." She tapped the picture on the right, the one of a pretty bloom with purple petals and a yellow center. "And this is an aster."

"And the one in the middle?"

"I think it's an Alpine rose."

"If you say so." Troy stared at the image. "It looks like the flower on the fastener."

"Yes. Alice brought the postcard and that fastener with her all the way from Paris here to Nemeton. Why?"

"You got me."

"If she were looking for her birth parents, wouldn't she bring whatever clues she might have to their identity with her?"

"That would make sense."

"Blake said they played Scrabble and Boggle all night, and that the girls always won," she said, as much to herself as to Troy.

"The girls?"

"Lea and Katharine. Apparently they're both really good at word games." She looked around, desperate for a pen and paper. "Is there anything to write on in here that's not worth a fortune?"

Troy pulled a small notebook and pen from his shirt pocket and handed it to her. "And you call yourself a detective."

"No, I don't." She grabbed the notebook and the pen and sat in one of the leather upholstered chairs flanking a long map-reading table.

He sat beside her. "What's up?"

She tore three sheets of paper from the notebook, laid them on table, and printed out the words: *Edelweiss. Aster. Alpine rose.*

"What are you doing?"

"Lea studied nature photography in Switzerland."

"I still don't see the connection."

She scribbled down the letters of the word *edelweiss*, shuffling them around in her mind and on the page. If Henry could see letters the way he saw numbers, he could solve this in a minute. But she was no Henry.

"What exactly are you doing?" Troy looked bewildered.

"I'm trying to figure something out."

She wasn't getting anywhere with *edelweiss*. She thought about *aster*, and came up with *tears, stare, taser, rates.* She tried *Alpine rose*, drawing a blank. Too many possibilities, none of which fit properly.

"I'll help you if you just let me know what you're doing."

"Doesn't matter. Dead end." She sat there for a moment, feeling defeated. She picked up the postcard again. "I know I'm missing something."

"Relax. You'll figure it out." Troy smiled at her. "You always do."

She smiled back. "I appreciate your faith in me, however misplaced." She turned the card over to the address side and read the caption again: *Alpenblumen.*

She dropped the card onto the table and snapped her fingers. "It's *Alpenrose,* not *Alpine rose.*"

"English, please."

She laughed. "Exactly. *Edelweiss* and *aster* are the German words for edelweiss and aster. But *Alpine rose* is *Alpenrose* in German."

"That explains it." He rolled his eyes.

"Hold on." On the sheet marked *Alpine rose,* she crossed out that word and wrote *Alpenrose* underneath it. She shuffled the letters around in her head and on the page. She whooped. "Yes!" She looked at Troy. "It's an anagram."

"Show me."

She tapped the pen on the paper where she'd printed LEA PER-SON in block letters under the *Alpenrose.* "*Lea Person* is an anagram of *Alpenrose.*"

"Lea Person?"

"Person was Lea's maiden name." Mercy smiled. *"Alpenrose."*

Troy's phone beeped. "Hold that thought." He read the text, looked up at her. Thrasher sent me the list of the license plates associated with the full numbers Henry gave us. They're still working on the partial from the SUV that tried to run you off the road."

"That was fast. I guess we have Feinberg to thank for that."

"And the captain." He pulled up the list on his phone, and they looked at it together. The phone listed all the times and comings and goings of cars in the parking lot. One car was on the list that shouldn't have been there, the car that was supposedly *not* there that morning, William Montgomery's Escalade. License-plate number 26050.

"George told us that William had not yet arrived that morning." She gave the globe another spin. "I knew he wasn't telling us everything. He lied."

"Why?"

"I think I know." She showed him the photo of Katharine in bed with the man with the signet ring. "According to George, this picture proves that she was sleeping with his nephew Richard. Maybe Richard is William's father."

"Not Blake?"

"It was the early Eighties. Everybody was sleeping with everybody."

"It fits." He gazed at the photo of the young lovers. "That would make the butler William's granduncle. Is that why George gave him an alibi? To protect his grandnephew?"

"I think so. And he's still protecting him." She paused. "There's more here than meets the eye and I can't seem to figure it out."

"You will."

"You go back to Henry and Ethan," she said. "I want to search William's room while everyone is still downstairs at brunch."

He pulled a pair of plastic gloves from his pocket and handed them to her. "Be careful."

Troy left her, and she made her way to William's room at the end of the hall. His was one of the smaller rooms, though nicely decorated with twin beds dressed in Ralph Lauren plaid and navy linen walls. She slipped on the gloves and carefully searched the messy space. Clothes on the floor, jewelry cluttering dresser tops, snowboard magazines strewn about. Lots of hair product. Porn magazines tucked under the mattress.

Trust fund playboy, she thought.

In the walk-in closet were snowboards, snowshoes, and a large sports-equipment locker. The locker had padlock on it. She pulled her Swiss Army knife from her pocket and retracted its thinnest tool. Picking locks was one of the things Martinez had taught her to do between missions. Something to do when there was nothing else to do but wait. She got pretty good at it. Sliding the tool in the lock, she jiggled it just right—and tripped the lock. She pulled the shackle out, removed the lock, and opened the door. Inside the locker were cross-country skis and boots and poles. Stuffed into the boots she found pharmaceuticals. Opioids.

So much for rehab, she thought.

There were several ski sleeves as well. She unzipped them one by one, and inside she found skis. Until the last sleeve, which held a longbow. Maybe the longbow used to kill Alice.

She snapped photos on her cell of the boots, the drugs, the longbow in the ski sleeve. She left everything as it was, replacing the lock and slipping her knife back into her pocket.

She searched the closet and the room again for the missing quiver of arrows, but she found nothing. Still, she now had some of the proof she needed. Troy would help her sort out the rest.

MERCY SLIPPED OUT the door into the hallway—and ran right into William Montgomery.

"What were you doing in my room?"

"I'm going downstairs." She continued past him down the hall, ignoring him.

He caught up to her and grabbed her by the shoulder to swing her around. "What did you take?"

She gripped his arm with her free hand and squeezed until he let go. "I didn't make off with your drugs, if that's what you mean. Although you really should hide them better."

William stared at her. "What do you want from me?"

"I want you to tell me why there's a longbow in a ski sleeve in your closet." She whistled for Elvis. Just in case the snowboarding playboy tried to take off.

"I don't know what you mean," he stammered.

George appeared at the top of the staircase. He was carrying a silver tray, loaded with a full tea service, probably for Cara, who was still ensconced in her room. For once, Mercy was glad to see the butler arrive without warning.

"Leave him alone," he said, putting the tray down on a Hepple-white hall table.

She realized that he wasn't coming to help her; he was coming to help his grandnephew. "It's time to stop protecting him, George. You know that."

"I don't understand, and I don't want to. I'm out of here." William stepped forward, but Mercy blocked him.

"No way." She could hear the soft padding of Elvis's paws as he flew up the stairs and down the carpeted hallway behind the butler.

"Let him go." George squared off against Mercy. For once the butler mask slipped, and the tough constable shone through.

"Elvis won't like that," she warned.

"Go on, William," said George. "Go downstairs to your mother."

Elvis came to a dead stop between George and Mercy, his muzzle dangerously close to the fly on the butler's perfectly creased trousers.

Nobody moved.

Troy bolted down the hallway, followed by Ethan, Feinberg, Blake, Lea, and the bodyguards, all clamoring up the stairs to see what had happened. Troy glanced over at Mercy.

"We were just discussing the contents of William's room," she said.

William started to move toward the staircase, but he stopped when Troy shook his head at him. "Stay a while and talk."

"I didn't kill anyone," said William.

"Yes, you did, and your granduncle here lied to protect you." She addressed Troy. "You'll find a longbow hidden in a ski sleeve locked up in the closet. Along with a considerable stash of opioids."

"Good to know."

"That's not true," said William. "I swear, Dad, it's not true."

"You promised, son," said Blake. "No more drugs."

"She's crazy, Dad. Don't listen to her."

"I think it's about more than drugs, Blake," said Feinberg. "Let Mercy explain."

Mercy let him have it straight. "It's a long story. But it starts with William. He is not your biological child."

"That's preposterous."

"I'm afraid it's true."

William laughed. "You're saying the butler is my father?"

"No. The butler's nephew. Richard Wilcox. He worked at the stables at Elliott Academy."

"The stable boy?" Blake seemed astonished.

"Yes, the stable boy." *Rich people,* Mercy thought.

"The stable boy, as you call him so derisively, was my brother's child," said George. "A good son and a good nephew."

"That Wilcox boy was a monster," said Blake. "He assaulted Katharine, and then ran off."

"Nonsense," said George.

"I don't think that ever happened." She showed Blake the photo of Katharine in bed with the man with the signet ring. "When you married Katharine, she was carrying Richard Wilcox's baby."

"I don't believe it."

"You were all sleeping with each other. Katharine slept with the stable boy and you slept with Lea and Max Sanders slept with everyone."

"Impossible."

"But as it turned out, free love wasn't so free, after all. Katharine got pregnant and Lea got pregnant and Max got AIDS."

"William is right. You *are* crazy." Blake turned to Feinberg. "Stop this."

"Hear her out."

"Lea had your baby, and she gave her up for adoption. Alice de Clare was your daughter, and she was going to tell you. That would make *her* your blood heir, not William. She could inherit at least half of all that lovely Montgomery money."

"That can't be true," said Blake. "It makes no sense."

"Oh my God." Lea backed up against the wall.

Mercy's eyes met Lea's. "When you gave your baby up for adoption, you gave the adoptive mother that *Alpenblumen* postcard and that silver rose pin with the feathers. The one that adorned Alice's Tyrolean hat. *Alpenrose.*"

"They made me sign her away. Made me promise I'd never return, never contact her, never see her again." Tears gathered in the corners of Lea's dark eyes. "But when she grew up, I thought she might try to find me. It happens. I knew the odds were against it, but just in case, I left her *Alpenrose*. I always hoped that someday it would lead her back to me."

"*Alpenrose* is an anagram of *Lea Person*. The clue you left behind for your daughter to find you."

"I don't understand," said Blake.

"It's true," Lea told Blake. "I got pregnant, and I didn't know what to do. It was your baby. I went to Switzerland after graduation to think about what to do. Katharine was my best friend and I knew she had her heart set on marrying you. I wasn't sure if I loved you or Max." She wiped tears from her cheeks with the back of her hand. "I thought of telling you, but then Katharine was pregnant, and you two were already planning to get married." Lea sobbed. "I had the baby there and gave her up for adoption."

"Alice's adoptive parents died in a car crash. Her adoptive mother must have kept the postcard and the silver rose fastener all those years, bequeathing them to Alice upon her death. She must have started looking for her birth parents then," Mercy told Blake. "Her search took her to the Elliott School and the class of 1982. She started checking out possibilities, and eventually she came to you and Katharine. She arranged to meet you, to get to know you better, hoping she could find some answers. Remodeling your apartment was the perfect opportunity to do that. She grew to like you, and especially Katharine. She trusted her. When she got pregnant, her desire to find her biological parents intensified. She must have confided in Katharine, hoping she could lead her to her birth parents. Katharine figured out that she was your daughter. She loved being a Montgomery and wasn't going to give up a dime of it to some upstart bastard child."

Mercy turned to William. "She told you, didn't she? And she encouraged you to put a stop to it. That's why you killed her."

"It was all Mother's idea. She told me to find out what Alice was up to," said William, wrangling against the bulk of the bodyguards. "*Take care of her,* she said. She sent me out to the woods after her. But—"

She interrupted him. "Where *is* your mother?"

"Katharine took Henry outside for some fresh air," said Blake. "A walk in the woods."

"Oh no." Mercy yelled for Elvis and dashed past them all and down the steps. She raced through the kitchen, grabbing her orange puffy vest at the door and Yolanda's longbow and arrow. Not as good as a gun, but it would have to do.

She and Elvis tore through the snow, the shepherd far more gracefully than she. She could hear Troy and Susie Bear huffing behind them.

Now that the storm was over, the sun shone brightly, and the snow glinted like diamond dust. Henry's small boot prints and Katharine's larger ones were visible. Mercy tracked them easily until they got to the woods. There the tracks were harder to follow.

But Elvis leapt ahead, hot on Henry's scent.

Mercy caught up with him just in time. The Belgian shepherd alerted, stopping short as they approached a blowdown, dropping down into his Sphinx position. She crouched behind the fallen log at the perimeter of the blowdown. About ten feet away from Elvis. About thirty feet away from Henry and Katharine.

The boy stood there, transfixed, staring at a six-foot stone arch set between two massive oak branches. The branches were supported by a mandala of rock nestled into the lap of the old tree. It was the art installation Feinberg had hired Mercy to find earlier that summer. Henry had found it.

"I know you're out there," said Katharine. "I can hear you."

The slender woman stood behind Henry. She stepped up closer, placing her gloved hands on his small shoulders.

"It wouldn't take much, you know. All I'd have to do is push. His head would crack like an egg."

She could crush his skull against the stone, thought Mercy. And she'd do it. *She wouldn't think twice about it.*

"Why on earth would you do that?" She wanted to keep Katharine talking.

"The boy saw what happened out there in the woods. To Alice."

"Alice was going to ruin everything, wasn't she?"

"She was a bastard child carrying another bastard child. Unworthy of the Montgomery name."

"Caspar Farrow knew, didn't he?" Silently, she pulled the arrow from the quiver and drew the bow. "He was always following you around, watching you. Wanting you."

"He was a foul man."

"He knew about you and Richard Wilcox. He knew about the baby. He helped you come up with the assault accusation, and he backed up your story. Your ploy worked. Richard ran off, and Caspar kept your secret . . . for a price." She pulled back the string and aimed for the center of Katharine's back. "But being part of the inner circle wasn't enough for Caspar. He wanted you, too. All those years of sexual blackmail. When Alice showed up and told you her story, you knew that it was all going to come out. The secrets, the lies, the betrayals. You knew that in the end Caspar would sacrifice you to save himself—and you would lose everything. He had to go. So you killed him."

"You can't prove any of this."

Be the arrow, Mercy thought.

"Stay where you are. The dog, too."

She released the arrow. It hurtled forward. Katharine twisted unexpectedly, pivoting, pulling the boy in front of her, placing Henry between her and the flying bolt.

Mercy whistled the command to attack. Startled, Katharine turned toward the whistle.

Elvis sailed out of the bushes. Going right for Katharine.

"Hide, Henry!" yelled Mercy.

Katharine stumbled out of Elvis's path. Henry wrenched free and scrambled away. Elvis followed Henry.

The arrow missed the intended bull's-eye of Katharine's back, clipping her right bicep instead. She cursed.

The tip collided with the stone wall.

Henry ran.

The arrow broke.

Katharine slogged after Henry in the snow, holding her bleeding arm. Mercy huffed after her.

Katharine ran about a dozen steps, then abruptly stopped at the sound of a terrible crunch. A terrible shriek echoed through the forest.

Mercy realized Katharine had stepped in one of the night hunters' traps, the sharp teeth snapping shut on her foot with a devastating crunch.

She ignored the woman's wailing and went after Henry. She found him hiding behind a fallen log rocking back and forth, chanting prime numbers, Elvis standing guard.

"Henry, it's safe, you can come out now." The shepherd licked the boy's face and nuzzled his neck with his nose.

The boy went limp as Mercy lifted him into her arms and carried him back to the blowdown. The others had followed Katherine's harrowing howls. Feinberg. Lea. Blake. Troy and Susie Bear. The bodyguards.

Ethan ran to Mercy and scooped Henry from her arms. He hugged his son tight. Henry let him and for the first time, she saw the boy hug his father back. The dogs licked the faces of father and son.

Katharine, still caught in the trap, on the ground, was silent.

In shock now, Mercy thought.

Blake ran to help his wife. He looked up at the rest of them. "She's going to bleed to death."

"Don't you dare help that woman." Lea pulled a small pistol out of her pocket. "She deserves to die."

Blake edged forward. He opened his hands in a silent plea to save his wife. "Stop."

"She murdered my child," Lea told him. "Our child. And our

grandchild." Her face was still wet with tears, but now her warm brown eyes were cold with grief.

"Lea, please." Blake stepped forward, getting between the two women.

Just as Lea pulled the trigger.

He cried out, wobbled on his buckling legs, and crumpled to the ground.

Pistol in her trembling hand, Lea seemed stunned by her actions. Mercy carefully approached her. Out of the corner of her eye, she saw Troy rush to Blake's side.

"Give me the gun, Lea. It's over." Mercy reached out and removed the weapon from Lea's hand.

Lea sank to her knees in the snow. Feinberg went to comfort her.

"Dark trees," said Henry.

TROY AND MERCY stood behind the Nemeton mansion, about a hundred yards from the helicopter pad. They watched as EMTs loaded Blake Montgomery into the helicopter, headed off to fly him to Tufts for surgery. Katharine was on her way to a local hospital under police guard, her arm wrapped, her mangled foot released from the trap. William was in police custody, still insisting that he was innocent, and that it was all his mother's fault.

Lea was also under arrest, although Mercy believed that she'd get off in the end. Feinberg was determined to hire her the best defense attorney money could buy. And he had a lot of money.

"I can't believe Katharine fell into a bear trap," she said. *"Are these thy bears? We'll bait thy bears to death. And manacle the bear-ward in their chains, If thou darest bring them to the baiting place."*

"Well said."

"Aren't those traps illegal here in Vermont?"

"Yep. They should be illegal everywhere. Another nail in the Buskey boys' coffin."

Troy's phone pinged, and he read the text to her. "They ran that partial plate. Matches one Johnny Buskey."

"So Johnny tried to run me off the road."

"Do you think he set the fire, too?"

"I don't see how. That SUV was pretty beat up."

"He probably put Daryl up to it. We should know soon. If anyone cracks, it'll be Daryl."

Together they watched the helicopter disappear from sight, and gazed into a bright blue sky, the promise of a better day, a better tomorrow.

"You did it again," he said.

"I was too slow. It took me so long to figure everything out."

"You need to give yourself more credit. You were brilliant." Troy smiled at her, taking her hand. He squeezed it, and she squeezed back.

"Let's go see Henry."

Henry was in the kitchen with Elvis and Susie Bear. Mrs. Espinosa was showering him with peanut-butter treats, which he in turn was sharing with his canine pals.

"You really have to stop feeding them so much people food," Mercy said.

Henry had been drawing again.

"Working on something new?"

The boy nodded, pointing to three drawings of stick people. There was a picture of a woman, with a bow and arrow and a hat with feathers. Henry had printed the words *monster slayer* above her.

Poor Alice de Clare. She'd died protecting Henry. Which suggested that her motives were pure, after all. Odds were that all she wanted to do was protect her unborn child. She wanted her medical history so that she could deliver a healthy, happy baby. She didn't care about the money. She didn't care about the legacy. That was all Katharine and William.

Another stick figure labeled *Assassin* wore a crude ski mask, carrying a crossbow. And the last was a figure that was part tree, part person. With leaves covering its face and head. This one was called *Dark Tree*.

Mercy tapped the Dark Tree figure with her index finger. "Is this who shot Alice?"

Henry nodded.

"Troy, you should see this." She showed him Henry's handiwork.

"It's one of those tree monsters we talked about." He crossed his arms against his chest and leaned back. "Go ahead, enlighten me. What does it mean?"

"It means all of William's protests of innocence may be correct. Remember the leafy bucket hat and mask we found in Macon Boone's backpack with the guns?"

"Yeah."

"That's what Henry saw. Macon Boone wearing that leafy bucket hat and mask. He killed Alice."

"Dark tree," said Henry.

"You're a mind reader," said Troy as he checked another text message from Thrasher. "The captain says they found a bow and arrow under the bed in Macon Boone's hotel room, along with a cell phone they believe belongs to Alice. It's got what looks like a rose on the case."

"Alpenrose."

"Anything else you'd like to wrap up for Harrington today? He's going to be here soon."

"Time to get out of here."

"Susie Bear and I will give you a ride. Anywhere you and Elvis want to go."

"I've got the Land Rover."

"Feinberg can get it back to you."

She looked up at him and smiled. "There's one more place we need to go first."

LAURA DAWSON AND her dog Hemingway met Mercy and Troy and the dogs in front of the stables at the Elliott Academy. Dr. Wright was there waiting for them, her bright orange toque covering her white hair. She watched the three dogs—one handsome Malinois, one big shaggy Newfie retriever, and one Lab–shar-pei–pit bull mix—greet each other with enthusiasm and lots of rude sniffing.

"This is why I have a cat," she told Laura, as Mercy introduced the professor to the leader of the Green Mountain Search and Rescue K9 Volunteer Corps. Laura was a feisty, middle-aged woman with a big smile and a big voice. The counterpoint to Dr. Wright's sharp reserve.

Laura laughed, then turned to Mercy. "Tell me why we're here. What are we looking for?"

"I think there's a body buried in the stables. Elvis alerted the last time we were here. I thought he was just jonesing for an apple from one of the treat buckets hanging on the stalls, but now I think I may have been wrong."

"We haven't done any cadaver training with Elvis."

"That didn't stop him and Susie Bear from finding that shallow grave in the woods last summer," said Troy.

"True," said Laura.

"That's why you're here. Your Hemingway is the best cadaver dog in the state. Before I embarrass myself by telling Detective Harrington my theory, I'd like some confirmation."

"How long do you think this body has been in here?"

"Since the Eighties."

"Wow. Long time. But if it's there, Hemingway will find it."

"You believe that this body is Richard Wilcox." Dr. Wright stiffened, sticking her hands in the pockets of her green coat. "And you think one of my scholarship girls killed him."

"Katharine slept with him, and she got pregnant. He wanted to marry her."

"She would never agree to marry down," said the professor. "Katharine was determined to marry up. To marry Blake Montgomery."

"Richard Wilcox threatened to tell Blake, and she killed him. Caspar Farrow saw it happen, and he helped her cover it up."

"In return, he was granted access to the circle of power," Dr. Wright shook her head, the bright orange toque bobbing up and down.

"It was easy enough once Katharine told the others that Caspar had stopped Richard Wilcox from raping her. They were happy to make him one of them."

"I can't imagine Caspar Farrow was content with just that. He wanted Katharine, too."

"Yes. She was forced to grant him all sorts of unsavory favors over the years."

"Deplorable." The professor pursed her lips. "I suppose she'd finally had enough."

"It all came to a head when Alice de Clare decided to find her birth parents."

"Lea and Blake."

"Yes. When Katharine realized who Alice really was, she knew that her days as Mrs. Blake Montgomery were numbered. As were her son William's days as the only heir to the Montgomery fortune. Unless she did something about it. So she convinced William to kill Alice. And she killed Caspar."

"But William didn't kill Alice," said Troy.

"No, he couldn't do it. He knew his mother would be furious with him, so when Alice turned up dead, he let her think he'd done it. That's why she tried to hurt Henry. She knew he'd seen Alice's murderer. With Alice and Caspar dead, the boy was the last link to William's guilt. Or so she thought."

"Murder, blackmail, infidelity, betrayal. It would seem that the class of 1982 has a lot to answer for." Dr. Wright shook her head.

"I'm sure it's an anomaly," said Mercy.

"Let's hope so.

"That is some story. Let's find out if it's true." Laura clapped her hands, and Hemingway bounded over, Susie Bear on his heels. Elvis followed at a leisurely pace, as if to say, *Calm down, guys.*

"If Mercy says it's true, it's true," said Troy.

"I must confess that I find it all too believable," said Dr. Wright.

The professor led the way into the stables. They'd moved the horses to the indoor paddock, so the building was empty. All of the stall doors were open. It was a clean, well-maintained stable, but nonetheless the scent of horse and hay and manure was very strong. Mercy couldn't imagine how the dogs could smell anything over that. But she knew they could.

She and Troy stood to one side with their dogs, while Laura and Hemingway stood in the middle of the center aisle. Hemingway looked up at Laura, his mouth twitching, ready to go. He was an intimidatingly muscular, brown-as-dirt dog, but the splashes of white on his nose and chest gave him a friendly look. And he *was* friendly, Susie Bear's equal in charm and likability.

Mercy hoped Elvis was paying attention. Which meant she should be paying attention, too. Learning the art of congeniality.

"Okay, let's see what Hemingway can do." Laura glanced down at her happy dog, panting with joy at the prospect of playing his favorite game. "Search."

All three dogs took off. And all three nosed around. Elvis went straight to the stall where he'd alerted last time, settling into a Sphinx pose in the middle of the stall. Hemingway trotted in after him, with Susie Bear lumbering along behind him. Hemingway sat down on his haunches near Elvis, and Susie Bear squeezed in between them, stretching out her big body along the hay-strewn floor.

"I think we have a consensus," said Laura.

CHAPTER TWENTY-FIVE

I T WAS A beautiful day for a barn raising. Although technically it
was more of a burger-joint reno, thought Mercy. She and Elvis rolled
up to the Vermonter in her repaired Jeep on four brand-new tires,
courtesy of Daniel Feinberg. He wanted to buy her the Land Rover,
but she demurred. She liked her red Jeep just fine.

The parking lot was packed, so she had to pull up on the side of
the road onto the grass behind a long line of other vehicles stretching nearly a mile in either direction. The snow was all gone now,
and autumn was again at its shining best. Everyone in town seemed
to be here, all heeding the call to help Lillian Jenkins get her restaurant up and running again before all the peepers went home until
spring. They'd been at it for a week now, and today was the last
push before the popular eatery opened to hungry customers again
tomorrow.

She reached over and opened the passenger door for Elvis. The
shepherd leapt out, waiting like the gentleman he was for her to join
him. Together they walked down to the torched Vermonter, where
dozens of people swarmed around queen bee Lillian's hive like devoted worker bees. There were painters slathering thick red paint on
the exterior, roofers swapping out the fire-warped metal panels for
bright new white ones, vendors carrying in new appliances, electri-

cians and carpenters and firefighters ordering the volunteers about in an impressive show of energy and enterprise.

Elvis ran ahead to greet Mr. Horgan, the elderly retired restaurateur manning the refreshments table. His late wife had been the town librarian for many years, and like everyone else in town, Mercy had loved her. As had Mr. Horgan. He still visited her grave site every day.

The old man patted the shepherd between his dark triangular ears.

"Shakespeare girl," he said by way of greeting.

"Good morrow, sir."

He grinned at her, tapping his cane in appreciation. "Would you like some root beer? Or a slice of pizza?" He leaned toward her. "Courtesy of Pizza Bob. Not half bad, and still hot."

"Thanks, but we'd better do something to earn our supper first."

Mr. Horgan nodded, but she saw him slip Elvis a breadstick anyway.

The dog chomped it down in two bites and then took the lead, trotting around to the back of the restaurant. She followed him, passing up half a dozen teenagers painting the fence a shiny white to match the new roof under the watchful eye of Yolanda and Ethan. She waved at them, and they waved back, brushes in hand. They both looked relaxed and happy and very comfortable with one another. She remembered their spooning to stay warm in the teahouse during the blizzard, just as she and Troy had done. The beginning of something good for them—and for Henry. She was happy for them all.

She and Elvis slipped through the fence gate and up the temporary ramp protecting the newly stained deck to the back door. Inside there were even more people at work. The sooty walls had been stripped to the studs and the whole place fogged to counteract the telltale smell of smoke. The new drywall and trim were in place. Volunteers were painting the walls a deep golden yellow and the trim a bright white. As cheerful as Lillian herself.

"About time." Patience stood before her wearing painter's overalls and a big smile. She handed Mercy a gallon of yellow paint, a brush and a roller, a paint pan, and a pair of color-splashed overalls that looked like they'd been worn to a paintball party. She pointed to a gray-primed wall. "I've been saving that one for you."

"Roger that." She slipped the overalls on over her yoga pants and T-shirt. "You can stay here and risk yellow splotches soiling your pretty tawny coat," she told Elvis, "or you can go hang out with Mr. Horgan and beg for breadsticks. Your choice."

"Some choice."

She heard Troy's voice behind her as Susie Bear barreled toward her, black plumed tail swishing ominously close to the still-wet yellow walls.

"Get that beast out of here before she ruins my new paint job," said Lillian cheerfully, stepping into the kitchen from the pantry where she'd nearly lost her life. Henry was right behind her, new clipboard in hand.

"Hi, Henry," said Mercy.

Henry smiled at her. Right at her.

"Why don't we get some root beer from Mr. Horgan," said Troy to the boy.

"Breadsticks."

"Fine," said Troy. "And then we'll find something useful to do that doesn't involve paint." He winked at Mercy. "See you later." He ushered the boy and the dogs outside.

She watched him go, and blushed when she realized Patience and Lillian were watching her watching him.

"Time to paint." She poured some yellow paint into the pan and dipped her roller into it.

Lillian and Patience howled with laughter, causing many of the volunteers to look up from their posts.

"Pay no attention to the ladies behind the curtain," she announced as she rolled swaths of yellow onto her designated wall.

The two old friends settled down and joined Mercy in the painting effort.

"Lillian has a problem," her grandmother said, roller in hand.

"You mean besides all this?"

"Yes."

"We need a new venue for Northshire Annual Wild Game Supper," said Lillian.

The whole town typically turned out for this gala, a Vermont-style wild-game potluck where Northshire's finest donated harvested meat for the hungry and the homeless and prepared a feast large enough to feed all its citizens and then some. It drew a big crowd every year.

"I heard about the church." The supper's traditional venue, the Northshire First Congregational Church, had lost part of its roof in the big storm.

"And Lillian here volunteered to find a new place." Patience rolled her eyes at Mercy. "Like she doesn't have enough on her plate."

"Somebody's got to do it." Lillian dipped her brush into the can of white trim paint.

"It doesn't always have to be you," said Patience.

"If we have to cancel, it will be the first time since World War Two." Lillian held up her dripping-white brush and pointed it at her.

"That would be terrible," said Mercy.

"It would," said Lillian in her best fund-raising voice. "Any ideas?"

"What about Nemeton? I could ask Daniel."

"That was our hope," said Lillian. "If you think he'd let all the riffraff of Northshire into his mansion."

Patience grinned. "I wouldn't call us riffraff exactly."

"I don't know about that," said Mercy with a smile.

For her own part, Mercy loved the gala, if only for the fabulous spread of Vermont delicacies. The best dishes were awarded prizes. For Patience, that meant bringing her venison stew. For Lillian, that meant bringing her moose meatballs. For Mercy, that meant bringing her fork.

"And you know Daniel would do anything for you," said Patience.

That was probably true. The billionaire had approached her after his hunting party had dispersed once and for all and asked what he could do for her in appreciation. Mercy didn't say anything at the time, but she'd thought about it and had come up with a couple of things. One, give Yolanda a job. Two, move Ethan Jenkins from the New York office back home to Northshire. Maybe she could add one more thing to the list.

"Just call Daniel and tell him what you need. Tell him I sent you."

"Perfect." Lillian held out her paintbrush to Patience. "You can finish the trim. My work is here is done. I've got to check on my grandson."

"You worry too much," said Patience, putting down her roller and taking up Lillian's brush. "He's fine with Troy."

"I know. But after all that's happened, I just can't seem to let him out of my sight."

"How *is* Henry?" asked Mercy.

"Better." Lillian smiled. "He's been playing cards with Cal Jacobs. I'm not sure how much good it's doing, but at least he's not wandering around the woods alone."

Lillian left them, and Mercy and her grandmother kept on painting. Gradually the gray-primed walls brightened into a golden bower much like the maples glowing outside. The autumnal colors would be gone soon, but this sunny kitchen would survive the winter to come, and beyond.

There was something very satisfying about this kind of work, she thought, watching the damaged restaurant transform all around her. Instant gratification.

Troy returned just as she was finishing up her wall.

"The dogs are with Mr. Horgan. Did you talk to her yet?"

"I assume you're talking about me," said Patience. "What are you two up to?"

"Henry needs a dog." Mercy filled in the white edges of the wall near the ceiling with yellow paint.

"Lillian does not like dogs."

"She likes Elvis."

"And Susie Bear," said Troy.

Patience smiled, but she kept her eyes on the trim as she painted. "True."

"And what Lillian wants more than anything is for Henry to be safe." She told her grandmother how she'd taken Henry for a walk to the general store, using Elvis to course-correct the young wanderer.

"Very clever of you *and* Elvis."

"You're the vet," said Mercy. "What kind of dog do you suggest?"

"A herding breed would be good. But one big enough and strong enough to keep Henry from going where he's not supposed to go."

"And smart," said Mercy. "Although no dog is as smart as Elvis."

"Or Susie Bear," said Troy.

"Or Susie Bear," granted Mercy.

"I know a dog trainer who's been working with service dogs to help children like Henry," said Patience. "The dogs accompany the kids at home, at school, and everywhere in between. They keep the kids calm and on track."

"Sounds good," said Troy.

"Let me make a call."

"*Let me make a call,*" repeated Mercy. "One of the most beautiful lines in the English language."

"Shakespeare aside," teased Troy.

HENRY WAS NOT lost. Paladin was right, he always knew where he was. The problem was that the grown-ups didn't know where he was. They were lost without him.

It was the perfect day for a walk with a dog. That's what Nana Lillian said.

And now he had his own dog. She was a Great Pyrenees and Australian shepherd mix, with brown eyes, a long nose, and pretty fur that was all different colors depending where you looked. She had a brown face and brown ears, a white belly, and a brown-and-gold back—*brindle,* Patience called it—and white-and-brown spotted legs.

She had a big fuzzy curly feather of a tail like Susie Bear, and was nearly as big, which was way bigger than he was. And his dad said she was just as smart as Elvis.

"Come on, Robin."

This was their first walk to the Northshire General Store alone. Robin was his sidekick, and they were tied together. They were a team. Just like Mercy and Elvis. Troy and Susie Bear. Batman and Robin.

Henry was wearing his new Batman boots, so his feet were warm. Robin had fur on her feet. She didn't need boots. Even though they did make boots for dogs, he'd seen it on Animal Planet.

He saw a peregrine falcon soar over the meadow toward the woods. Migrating south for the winter. Maybe the West Indies. Maybe Panama. Maybe Mexico. Peregrine falcons liked to wander, that's what peregrine meant. *Wanderer.*

Henry plowed after the falcon. But he didn't get far.

Robin stood on the sidewalk and wouldn't move. Solid as a rock. Henry tugged and tugged, but she wouldn't budge. She didn't like it when he tried to go into the woods. She liked to stay on the sidewalk.

"Falcon." He gazed up at the sky and watched the bird of prey as it dove for dinner. Maybe a red-wing blackbird. Falcons liked red-wing blackbirds. He liked peanut butter and crullers. So did Robin.

His dog was waiting for him to get back on the sidewalk that led to the crullers. No chasing after falcons. No counting trees in the woods.

He'd have to count mailboxes instead. *One, two, three . . .* They kept walking, and Henry kept counting. *Four, five, six . . .*

Not all those who wander are lost, that's what Paladin said.

THE NIGHT OF the Northshire Annual Wild Game Supper was as crisp and clean and star-filled as a night in October in Vermont should be. Autumn's last hurrah before winter truly set in. Which could happen as soon as midnight.

Mercy and Elvis arrived fashionably late. *Lillian and Patience must be pleased,* she thought. Their annual supper was always popular, but this year the prospect of going to the billionaire's estate was too good for anyone to pass up. Everyone in the county was there. And in the wake of the storms and the murders and the fire at the Vermonter, they were ready to celebrate.

Feinberg had a special structure erected on the wide expanse of lawn across from the pool. The makeshift hunting lodge was in fact an elaborate tent, big enough to house the entire population of the county, and swank enough to attract photographers from *Town & Country* magazine. Mercy had never seen anything like it, and she was pretty sure no one else in Northshire had, either. Except maybe Feinberg himself.

There was a band, a silent auction, great food, and hard apple cider. Crystal chandeliers hung from the ceiling, exotic orchids graced linen-covered tables, and burgundy, silver, and gold balloons floated everywhere. A disco ball glittered over the dance floor.

The place was hopping. Her grandmother Patience and Lillian were working the crowd in their color-coordinated teal-and-yellow silk dresses, enjoying their roles as organizers of the most glamorous wild-game supper in Northshire history. Brodie and Amy and little Helena were there too, all dressed in steampunk chic. Brodie's idea, no doubt.

Mercy was glad she'd made an effort, swapping her usual pants and T-shirt for an emerald-green velvet wrap dress and black suede heels. A good thing since even her parents were there. They'd come up from Boston just for this event. Not because Mercy had invited them, but because Feinberg had.

The billionaire pulled her aside as she made her way over toward the buffet table to say hello to her parents. "I wanted you to know that George Wilcox will be taking his nephew's remains back to England. He asked me to thank you for finding him."

"How is George?"

He smiled. "I'm afraid his butlering days are over. But he's free to leave the country."

"Thank you, Daniel."

"What for?"

"Playing coy doesn't suit you," she said, and he had the good grace to laugh with her.

"You know, for all this. A glorious finish to a hunting season that started out not so glorious."

He patted her on the shoulder and disappeared into a throng of admirers. Cara Farrow would be jealous—if she hadn't signed that seven-figure book deal and agreed to star in the film adaptation.

Mercy moved to the hors d'oeuvre table, wondering how many of Lillian's moose meatballs she could eat before her mother slapped her hand away.

"You look wonderful," said the perfectly chic, perfectly blond woman who gave birth to her and loved her even if she didn't quite understand her. "What a fabulous dress."

"You bought it for me," Mercy reminded her.

"As always."

Her father kissed her on the cheek. "Looking good, kid."

Mercy was feeling more amenable toward her parents these days. The tangled history of mothers and sons and fathers and daughters that ruined so many lives at Nemeton reminded her that however imperfect her parents may be, they did love her. As Ethan loved Henry. As Amy loved Helena.

Henry bounced up to them, happily outfitted in a full-out Batman costume, his stalwart pal Robin trotting next to him, her lead tied to his Batman waist. The poor dog was wearing a full-out Robin costume.

"Is that Batman and Robin I see there?" asked Mercy. "For real?"

Henry nodded, then looked at Elvis.

"Don't even think about it," Mercy said. "Elvis doesn't do costumes."

Henry nodded again.

"Where's your dad?"

Henry pointed to the left of the bandstand. Ethan stood there with Yolanda, he quite handsome in a slim dark-teal suit, and she devastatingly pretty in a stylish amber-colored dress that George surely must have chosen for her. If not her mother.

Yolanda was laughing. She looked so happy and at home here at this opulent party that she was barely recognizable as the woman who'd been living in a dilapidated teahouse. She deserved all this and more. As Ethan and Henry deserved her. Mercy hoped it all worked out.

Henry scampered back to his father and Yolanda, his dog in tow.

Captain Thrasher, dashing as ever, strolled over to greet her and her parents. First, he said to Mercy, "Congratulations on another job well done." Then to her parents, "Your daughter is quite the hero."

Both regarded him with consternation.

"We're always proud of Mercy," said her mother. "Although we do wish she would try to stay out of trouble."

Thrasher met her mother's serious face with a hearty laugh. "I don't think that's possible. Trouble finds her."

He leaned toward Mercy. "Speaking of trouble, the Buskey boys are in a mess of it. Daryl was the weak link, just as Troy predicted he would be. Daryl's admitted to helping his cousin Johnny poach wild game and trap marten. And to setting the fire and trying to take Henry. But he says he had nothing to do with the guns or the murders."

"I believe him."

"We'll see."

An attractive couple approached the captain, and Thrasher waved them over. "This is Gil Guerrette and his lovely wife, Françoise." Gil wore a dark-gray pinstripe suit and Françoise wore a shimmering gray silk dress, with high-heeled black boots and a festive black velvet fascinator.

"Of course," she said with a grin. "Tyrolean."

Gil shrugged. "It is my duty to educate my clueless *bon ami* about hats. And other of life's refinements."

Françoise rolled her eyes. "Pay no attention to him."

"I do love your hat," Mercy told her. "You look amazing."

Gil beamed. "What do you collect?"

"Is this a trick question?" She looked to Françoise for clarification, but she just smiled enigmatically at her.

"Every woman collects something. For *ma cherie,* it is hats. And you?"

Thrasher answered for her. "That's easy. She collects mysteries."

Mercy shook her head. "I was going to say Shakespeare."

"Same difference," said the captain.

Thrasher and the Guerrettes wandered off to greet other guests. The event had attracted an unusual mix of people. Northshire's leading lights mingled with regular townsfolk, hunters, and Feinberg's fancy friends from New York City.

Blake Montgomery was present, looking thin and worn-out if still stylish. Lillian was talking to him, no doubt trying to cheer the poor man up. Not easy given the fact that his wife, Katharine, was in jail for murder and his son, William, was facing accessory charges. Feinberg was not convinced those charges would stick, and Mercy knew he was doing all he could to make that happen. Just as he was helping Lea fight her indictment.

She wondered if Blake would keep the inn or sell it. For Alice de Clare's sake, she hoped he'd keep the place and remodel it in line with her vision. Her legacy.

Dr. Wright suddenly emerged from the crowd. "I came to pay my respects to your dog."

Mercy laughed and pointed toward the buffet table, where Elvis had assumed his Sphinx position, an elegant beggar if ever there was one. She snapped her fingers, and he picked his way through the crowd to join them.

"Dr. Wright, you remember Elvis."

The professor gave the handsome shepherd a good long scratch between his ears. He tilted his head at her.

"He likes you."

"Smart dog."

"That he is."

Together they watched as Lillian made her way to the stage. After the band played a short musical introduction, Lillian took the microphone.

"Welcome to Northshire's Annual Wild Game Supper. Thank you for coming. First let us thank our generous host, Mr. Daniel Feinberg, for this splendid venue."

Everyone cheered at this, Mercy included.

Lillian went on. "Now, eat, drink and spend a lot of money bidding on the silent auction. Remember, all proceeds go to the hungry and the homeless. Because here in Northshire, we take care of our own. Have a great time."

Everyone clapped and the band started up again. Feinberg led Lillian to the dance floor for the first dance, a lively number that drew other couples to join them on the dance floor.

The next song was a slow dance, "Moonlight in Vermont," obligatory dancing even for nondancers.

Mercy's parents were quick to dance to this one. Patience, too, thanks to her longtime beau Claude, an animal surgeon from Quebec and an excellent dancer. Elliott Academy headmaster Mike Robbins pulled a blushing Dr. Wright onto the dance floor. And Ethan and Yolanda made a very pretty pair out there, her amber-colored skirt flying as he dipped her nearly to the ground.

Cal Jacobs walked over to Mercy. "May I have this dance?"

"Sure." She'd hoped Troy would be here, but he was probably out on patrol. Anyway, she'd worn a dress; no point in wasting it. Cal led her to the dance floor. He smelled good. He looked good. He held her close.

She liked him, but he wasn't Troy.

It turned out he was a good dancer, she had to give him that. She suspected the doctor was good at practically everything. She wondered why she was thinking of Troy Warner when she was dancing with this attractive, intelligent, compassionate man.

She closed her eyes and danced with the man who asked her.

"Excuse me." She opened her eyes and there was Troy, tapping Cal on the shoulder.

"May I?"

Cal bowed his head and let go of her. The next thing she knew, she was in the game warden's arms. "Where's Susie Bear?"

"Over there with Elvis." He lifted his head toward the south end of the barn, and she saw the two dogs in the corner. Both sat quietly, watching the buffet table with great interest, but not moving.

"How long do you think before they go for Patience's venison stew?"

"Not my dog. Maybe yours."

Troy laughed, and he whirled her around. He could dance, too. Who knew? She laughed with him.

"Do you think maybe we could go on some kind of real date sometime? You know, no kids, no cops, no suspects, no dogs."

"No dogs?"

"Well, maybe dogs." He tightened his arms around her waist. Mercy closed her eyes and laid her head against his chest. Dancing with the man she hoped would ask her.

"Excuse me," a woman's voice cut in.

She opened her eyes and there stood a strikingly attractive woman. Madeline Warner. Mercy hadn't seen her since high school, but she was as beautiful now as she'd been back then. Madeline looked at Troy with an unmistakable possessiveness. A gauntlet thrown at Mercy's feet.

"I'd like to dance with my husband."

"What?" Mercy fell back, teetering on her high heels. Surely she'd heard that wrong.

"I can explain," said Troy, putting his arms out to steady Mercy.

She shook him off, twisting herself out of his long-armed reach. Elvis appeared at her side, ears cocked, standing at alert.

"You don't belong here," Troy said to Madeline.

His wife laughed. "You can't get rid of me so easily."

"I can, and I will."

She hadn't seen this coming. "You're still married."

"Of course he is," said Madeline.

Mercy stared at Troy. Suddenly, she had no idea who he was. Elvis barked, one of his signal barks, a warning. A warning she should heed.

"Not for long," Troy told her. "I've filed for divorce."

Time to leave, she thought. But she was rooted to the ground. Elvis nuzzled her hand with his cold, wet nose, bringing her back to her senses. *Come, shepherd, let us make an honourable retreat. . . .*

She executed a clean about-face despite the high heels and did a double-time march off the dance floor to the last chords of "Moonlight in Vermont." Troy ran after her. But Elvis was faster.

"Mercy, wait."

She didn't look back. She threw aside the curtains that were drawn across the opening of the hunting-lodge tent and Elvis rushed past her, leading the way out into the perfect autumn night. She stopped and stared up at the stars, reminding herself to breathe. Elvis circled back to her, tilting his handsome head at her as if to say, *Let's blow this joint.*

"Thanks for getting me out of there," she told him. "Give me a minute, and we'll go home. Promise." The shepherd leaned against her, letting her know that he wasn't going anywhere without her.

That's what I get for wearing a dress, she thought. *That's what I get for dancing to* "Moonlight in Vermont."*That's what I get for thinking I could ever love anyone else but Martinez.*

"Mercy." Troy stood behind her. She could feel his eyes on her, hear Susie Bear panting at his side.

She started down the winding road that led to the iron gate, and Elvis came with her.

"I'm sorry." Troy followed her.

She swirled around, skirt flying, to face him. He looked miserable, but she didn't care. "You lied to me."

"I didn't mean to." He reached out to her, but she brushed him off.

"When were you going to tell me?"

He started to speak, but she ran right over him.

"That's just it. You weren't going to tell me."

"I know I should have told you sooner."

"You were just going to let me believe that you were a free man."

"But I will be a free man. My lawyer has filed the papers."

"It doesn't matter." *It doesn't matter because you're not the man I thought you were. It doesn't matter because even if you were, you're not Martinez.*

"I don't love Madeline."

"Don't start."

"I love you." He looked at her with those warm brown eyes.

"That's enough." She couldn't listen to him anymore. She couldn't look at him anymore. "Come on, Elvis." She pivoted sharply and strode away as fast as her three-inch heels could carry her. Another stupid thing, wearing heels. She never wore heels for this very reason. When you wanted to make a quick getaway, you couldn't.

"At least let me walk you to the Jeep." He hurried after her, and Susie Bear bounded ahead of them both.

Elvis stayed close to Mercy, as if she were a perimeter to be guarded.

"I can take care of myself."

"I know you can." He pulled ahead of her, and turned to face her, jogging backward to keep up.

If she weren't so angry, she would have laughed. "You're going to hurt yourself."

"It would be worth it."

He sounded so sincere she almost forgave him right then and there. But even a lie of omission was a lie. There was no forgiving a lie.

"Leave me alone, or I'll cut through the woods."

"You can't do that."

"Then go."

He stopped short, and he let her pass him by. She heard him call for Susie Bear, and the dog lumbered back to him. She could feel them standing there together, man and dog, watching her and Elvis as they continued along the first of the road's hairpin curves. She didn't look back until she knew they were out of view.

It started to snow.

She stumbled down toward the gate, Elvis close to her side. He kept nudging her knees as she walked, his way of saying he was sorry, too.

"It's okay, Elvis. I'm fine." She saw her Jeep through the trees. "Nearly there."

She skittered along, her feet chilled to the bone. Snow was falling. It was a beautiful night, even if she wasn't dancing with Troy Warner. Even if he had lied to her. Even if . . .

She didn't know what to think. "We're not going to think anymore, Elvis." She kept walking, Elvis trotting alongside.

The Belgian shepherd stopped short, cocking his triangular ears. Alerting. His fur rippled with anticipation. She knew that look. He barked, just once. Signal bark. She stopped.

There he was.

The big bear.

Stomp-walking toward them.

The beast stood, rising on his hind legs to his full height.

A very big bear, she thought. Troy's monster black bear. The bear that had survived the hunting party and the poachers and the twin storms of the century.

His blue-black furry breast was marked by battle scars. A warrior among bears.

She stood very still. He was probably bluffing, but you could never be sure with a bear.

Elvis barked noisily and fiercely and continuously. Doing Gunnar's elkhounds proud.

The bear ignored the shepherd.

He roared at her, a deep and thunderous rolling bellow.

She roared back.

A long wail of rage and regret escaped her. A sound as dark and desperate as his.

Startled by her response, the bear stopped midroar.

"Steady, Elvis," she said, silencing the well-disciplined dog into a reluctant *stay*. She waited.

The bear moved his head back and forth several times, chomping at the air, and finally turned and dropped down to all fours. He lumbered away.

All bluster, no charge, she thought.

The bluffing bear.

Together Mercy and Elvis watched the grand beast disappear into the forest.

Back where he belonged.

She turned to Elvis.

"Exit," she said, *"pursued by a bear."*

ACKNOWLEDGMENTS

As always, the writing of a book requires me to call upon the wisdom, generosity, and grace of a number of compassionate beings, human and otherwise.

Most importantly, I thank my agent, Gina Panettieri, and my editor, "Pit Bull Pete" Wolverton, for holding my hand as I made my way through the perilous journey that can be the second book of a series. My family, too, most notably Mom and Dad and Michael, for their extraordinary patience as I wrote and rewrote this novel. And Bear and Bliss, our two rescue dogs, and Ursula, our rescue cat, who invariably provide inspiration and comic relief throughout my writing process.

The best part of writing about the wilderness in New England is what I learn about our flora and fauna—and from whom I learn it. For all things bear, I thank Andrew Timmins, the New Hampshire Fish and Game Bear Project Leader. Thanks also to Susan Warner, Director of Public Affairs for the Vermont Fish & Wildlife Department, Vermont State Game Warden Rob Sterling, and K9 Crockett, Donna Larson, founding member and VP of the New England K9 Search and Rescue (nek9sar.org), and Gardner "Bud" Browning and Scott Wood of the TSA. All shared their expertise freely and graciously, and any mistakes are solely my own.

A special shout-out to my dear son Mikey and the Nerd Council, for allowing me to sit in on their D&D game and interrupt with questions all night. *Grazie,* my darling daughter, Alexis, who took us to see Sacra di San Michele while we were in Italy, thereby planting the seeds of this story in my subconscious. And to my sweet son, Greg, one of my most perceptive beta readers, along with sister agent, Terrie Wolf, and editor extraordinaire, Dana Isaacson.

A special shout-out to my Scribe Tribe: Susan Reynolds, Meera Lester, John K. Waters, Indi Zeleny, and Mardeene Mitchell. And to my fellow Career Authors: Hank Phillippi Ryan, Dana Isaacson, Brian Andrews, Laura DiSilverio, and Glenn Miller. My pals Michael Neff and Amy Collins provided love, support, and gin when needed (more often than I'd like to admit). And to the magnanimous and magnificent mystery writers who inspired me even as they encouraged and supported me: Lee Child, Ann Cleeves, Jane Cleland, Hallie Ephron, Joe Finder, Lisa Gardner, Kellye Garrett, Elly Griffiths, Kimberly Howe, Larry Kay, Jon Land, William Martin, Spencer Quinn/Peter Abrahams, and Julia Spencer-Fleming.

I'm lucky enough to be published by Minotaur Books, where Pit Bull Pete and a team of amazing publishing professionals have my back: Andy Martin, George Witte, Kelley Ragland, Allison Ziegler, Kayla Jones, Jonathan Bennett, Rowen Davis, David Baldeosingh Rotstein, Hannah O'Grady, Elizabeth R. Curione, and MaryAnn Johanson.

And a final grateful salute to the readers, writers, book bloggers, reviewers, and other book people who have embraced this series. I am forever in your debt.